45 THINGS TO DO BEFORE YOU'RE 45

HAVE YOU EVER WONDERED HOW BOOKS ARE MADE?

Fox & Ink Books (formerly UCLan Publishing) is an award-winning independent publisher. Based at the University of Lancashire, this Preston-based publisher teaches MA Publishing students how to become industry professionals using the content and resources from its business; students are included at every stage of the publishing process and credited for the work that they contribute.

The business doesn't just help publishing students though. Fox & Ink Books has supported the employability and real-life work skills for the University's Illustration, Acting, Translation, Animation, Photography, Film & TV students and many more. This is the beauty of books and stories; they fuel many other creative industries! The MA Publishing students are able to get involved from day one with the business and they acquire a behind-the-scenes experience of what it is like to work for a such a reputable independent.

The MA course was awarded a Times Higher Award (2018) for Innovation in the Arts, and the business was awarded Best Newcomer at the Independent Publishing Guild (2019) for the ethos of teaching publishing using a commercial publishing house. As the business continues to grow, so too does the student experience upon entering this dynamic Master's course.

www.foxandinkbooks.com
www.foxandinkbooks.com/courses/
foxandink@lancashire.ac.uk

45 THINGS TO DO BEFORE YOU'RE 45

Julia Tuffs

Fox & Ink Books

45 Things To Do Before You're 45 is a Fox & Ink Books book

First published as an original audiobook by Audible.

This edition published in Great Britain in 2026 by
Fox & Ink Books
University of Lancashire
Preston, PR1 2HE, UK

Text copyright © Julia Tuffs, 2026
Cover illustrations copyright © istock.com
Cover design by Ami Smithson

978-1-917894-03-6

1 3 5 7 9 10 8 6 4 2

The right of Julia Tuffs to be identified as the author
of this work has been asserted in accordance with the
Copyright, Designs and Patents Act, 1988.

All rights reserved. No part of this publication may be reproduced,
stored in a retrieval system, or transmitted in any form or by any means,
electronic, mechanical, photocopying, recording or otherwise;
or be used to train any AI technologies without the prior permission
of the publishers. Fox & Ink Books expressly reserves this work from
the text and data mining exception subject to EU law.

Set in Kingfisher by Becky Chilcott.

A CIP catalogue record for this book is available from the British Library.

Printed and bound in Great Britain by Clays Ltd, Elcograf S.p.A.

For Danielle – my Cath, Emily and a sprinkling of Dorit all rolled into one.

March

1

HE KISSES my neck.

Soft, gentle brushes of his lips that send me wild. I moan. I can't help myself.

"You like that, hey?" he pauses, lifts his head up to smile at me.

It's Jamie Dornan. Which is a surprise. It's usually George Clooney. And what's more surprising is it's *The Fall*, serial killer Jamie Dornan. Not normally my vibe, but I roll with it, entranced by those ocean-blue eyes and the make-me-go-weak-at-the-knees accent.

He gets back to business, working his kisses down from my neck until he's sucking my nipple. The good, gentle sucking, not the manic, 'can I get any milk out of here?' sucking. I moan again, he looks up to smile again, his perfect-length stubble framing his perfect lips. This time, he's *Fifty Shades* Jamie, which makes more sense. I push his head back down, not wanting to lose the momentum. Finally, he makes it between my legs and I lose my shit. He knows what he's doing.

It feels good.

Amazing.

I'm about to explode fireworks.

Then, all of a sudden, there's a bang – but not the fireworks

kind. And another one. I try to ignore it, to cling on to the about-to-explode feeling.

Under the bed sheets, Jamie has disappeared.

I try to conjure him back.

More bangs, rhythmic bangs, one after the other.

I start to feel them – sharp pinches on my head, angry bees dive-bombing my face. I search for Jamie but he's well and truly gone, as has my momentum, the fireworks not even damp squibs any more. Brightness seeps through my eyelids, my head throbs – and not just from the dive-bombing bees. I go to speak but realise my tongue is a beached whale inside my mouth; my mouth which appears to be full of sand. I move my hand to cover my face, and the effort brings reality crashing in.

"What the f—?" I manage to mumble.

"MUM SWORE!" a voice shouts.

I force an eye open. Jack is standing over me; dishevelled blonde curls, mischievous blue eyes, a smear of jam on his cheek and a Nerf gun aimed at my head.

"MUM SWORE!" Felix parrots from the hallway.

"Did she now?" James walks in, annoyingly fresh-faced and sporty, his salt-and-pepper curls untamed, wearing full nausea-inducing Lycra, bulging pants and all. This is not a good sign.

"I didn't, actually!"

He places a cup of tea, a pint of water and a pack of paracetamol on the bedside table next to me. "Come on boys, take it downstairs."

The boys disappear in a flurry of Nerf bullets, shoves and stomps, my blonde-haired, feral cherubs. I try to open both eyes and sit up but decide against it when a wave of nausea hits.

"Good morning, gorgeous wife of mine," James says. "How does forty-four feel?"

"Like the best years of my life are over and I'm drowning in the shit sand of imminent death."

"MUM SWORE AGAIN," Jack shouts from the landing.

James laughs. "Can you maybe control that potty mouth of yours, Grandma?"

"Can you maybe keep the little sh— children, and their testosterone battle, away from me? And don't with the Grandma, it's not funny."

He strokes the hair off my face. "Sorry, no more old gags."

"Thank you," I mutter, the waft of my stale booze breath nearly knocking me out. "Hey, you're supposed to be letting me lie in."

"I have," James says.

I glance at the clock – 8.21 a.m.

"Dude! Really?"

"I've got a training ride with Jim. And I figured I should leave the kids with a responsible adult – or a conscious one, at least."

I prop myself up – with effort – and grab the water, downing half of it in big gulps, before realising little sips would've been the better way to go.

"Today? Really? You couldn't have one day off being middle-aged sportsman-of-the-year and give your poor wife a lie-in?"

"Afraid not. It's a tight schedule and actually the Ironman isn't that far away."

He's taken the whole Ironman thing way more seriously than I had anticipated when he first announced it was going to be A Thing. And by seriously, I mean hundreds of hours and thousands

of pounds' worth of seriously. I also hadn't anticipated just how much he would feel the need to talk about it. All the time.

"Sorry, I did tell you," he says, patting my leg.

"Didn't."

"I did. You just don't—"

"Whatever. Fine. Go. Go and get some PBs and kudos and stupid motivational medals on your stupid app thing and leave me, in my diminished state, to fend for myself with your feral children who I pushed through my now-ruined vagina."

"I won't be long – I'll be home after lunch. And Chloe said she'll be back from Hannah's before then so she can help out."

He kisses my forehead, making a face at my aroma. "And for the record," he says, "I think your vagina is perfectly lovely and not at all ruined."

"Not that you'd bloody know," I grunt, giving him the middle finger as he leaves.

"Love you, Grandma," he shouts from the hall.

"What's with all the fucking shouting," Cath moans from under the cover next to me.

I'd forgotten she was there. James must've slept on the sofa-bed downstairs.

"MUM SWORE AGAIN." Jack pops into the doorway and shoots a Nerf bullet that hits me right in the eye.

"That wasn't me! And seriously, Jack! Enough. Downstairs now or you'll have no screen time later."

The shouting is not good for my head. In a being-hit-repeatedly-with-a-frying-pan type way. The dull ache morphs into an angry throb. I reach for the paracetamol and try to swallow them without

retching. Sipping my water, I survey the room – my sparkly dress and two pairs of Spanx discarded in the corner, the remnants of wrapping paper from the kids' presents: an anti-ageing hand cream from Jack ('because your hands look crinkly'); a pair of the naffest, blingiest, would-blind-someone-on-a-sunny-day earrings I've ever seen from Felix ('because you always tell Dad you like sparkly things'); and a tight-fitting crop top from Chloe, which we both know I will never wear, or fit into, and is purely for her to 'borrow'. James had given me a USB lead and multi-plug charger, because 'you can never find one, and this one's bright pink so we'll all know it's yours' – with the same Molton Brown bath foam he's been giving me for the past twelve years, ever since I mentioned I like it, thrown in for good measure.

Birthday cards, not that many, are propped up on various surfaces – all of them making reference to either being old or drinking, some making reference to both. In the strips of grey light coming through the curtains, it almost looks like a crime scene – it definitely feels and smells like one. My heart sinks with the depressingness of the whole thing.

I nudge Cath, who responds with a leave-me-alone grunt.

I text Emily, who's in the spare room:

Me: *You awake?*

Emily: *Of course.*

Me: *Bed chat?*

Thirty seconds later, she comes barrelling into the room in her Taylor Swift pyjamas, full of beans.

"Wassssup bitches!" She bounces on to the bed. Small lady, massive energy.

"What is wrong with you people?" Cath mutters, still nestled under the duvet.

"Don't be a Grumpy Grumperson! It's Charlie's birthday." Emily reminds her.

"Yesterday. It was her birthday *yesterday*."

"So I only get an evening?" I ask. "That's my birthday celebration allowance?"

"Yes. So shut up and go back to sleep."

"If I have to be a conscious adult, you have to be a conscious adult with me," I say, nudging her.

Emily joins in, poking Cath's legs and feet. We don't give in until Cath reluctantly emerges and props herself up. Her short hair has gone so bedhead it looks like she's been electrocuted. Combined with the *Beetlejuice* crusty eye make-up and the scowl, she's got proper villain vibes going on.

We laugh.

"Arseholes," she says.

"Shhh! I can't have the kids telling me off again." I pass her the remnants of the water. "Here, drink this."

"It'd better be after ten." She takes the pint glass and sneers at its pathetic contents.

"Of course." I discreetly turn the clock to the wall.

"Totally," Emily says.

Cath downs the last of the water and grunts.

"Guys, forty-four. Forty-*sodding*-four." I whisper the 'sodding', not risking it, even though in my rulebook, sodding is very much not a swear word. "It's so depressing. It's all downhill from here. And by the way, that's literally what my optician said the other day, just a passing, matter-of-fact comment; 'It's all downhill from here'. I need reading glasses. Sodding reading glasses. I'm properly old. My knees and my hips will start going soon. This is how it starts – bad hangovers and reading glasses."

"And bad periods," Emily states. "Aren't you having the coil fitted soon?"

"Yeah, but that's not an age thing, that's just a being-a-woman-sucks-thing," I say.

"She's still in denial," Cath says.

I hate it when they start having these conversations about me like I'm not there.

"She doesn't want to accept she's PERIMENOPAUSAL," Emily says, dragging out the word they know I despise.

"Shut up," I say. "I told you, my sister is four years older than me and she doesn't have any symptoms, my mum said she had periods until she was well into her fifties. It's genetics, I'm fine."

"You're fine because you're burying your head in the sand about it and refusing to engage," Emily says. "Heavier periods – perimenopause. Mood swings – perimenopause. Feeling low – perimenopause."

"You did cry at that nappy advert the other day," Cath says.

"The baby was premature! What kind of heartless bitch wouldn't cry at that!" I protest.

"Feeling overwhelmed by everyday tasks—" Emily continues.

"We get the idea," I say.

"You said it was all downhill when you turned forty," Cath says.

"Yeah, but that was just in the run-up to it. Actually turning forty was quite fun – I got a big party, decent presents, a night away."

"You got to be the centre of attention," Cath says.

She exchanges a look with Emily, a little in-joke they wheel out about how I have main character syndrome.

"Exactly," I say, ignoring them. "For once. But forty-four? Forty-four sucks. No one cares."

"Um, hello?" Emily says.

"Sorry, except for you two."

"And James," Emily adds.

"Only vaguely," I huff.

I pass Emily a pillow so she can prop herself against the back of the bed. She burrows under the duvet, her feet cold against my bare legs.

"He bought me a USB lead and a multi-plug charger," I say, deadpan.

"Very practical," Cath says.

"Well, that's still better than Rick," Emily says. "For my last birthday, he went to the corner shop, got me some grandma-level rubbish card, and told me to go and buy myself something nice. But not too nice – fifty-pound limit."

She attempts a laugh, trying to be light-hearted, but her eyes give her away. The sad eyes she gets every time she talks about Rick. Cath shoots me The Look. It's a look we share often when Rick the Dick gets mentioned.

"Well, you both did better than me and my non-existent present from my non-existent husband, so consider yourselves lucky," Cath says.

There's never anything you can say in response to that.

"MUM!" Felix shouts up. "Eddie Vedder peed on the carpet!"

Emily chuckles, Cath looks horrified, I roll my eyes.

"I will never not find that funny," Emily says.

"I will never find that funny," I groan. "The toileting, I mean. The name I still like."

Eddie Vedder is our eighteen-year-old female cat (my name choice, I was an indie kid), bought in that space between moving in together and having kids, along with her now-deceased brother, Jeff Buckley (James's name choice). From the day Chloe was born, Eddie has been a pet in absentia, emerging only once the kids have all gone to bed to aggressively meow at me for reasons unknown. And to toilet all over the house. Again, for reasons unknown, but possibly a dirty protest at us having kids in the first place.

"So gross," Cath says, scrunching her nose in disgust. "Aren't you going to—"

I wave my hand, "I'll do it when we go down."

She shakes her head at me.

"I think all my turning-forty-depression was glossed over by the fun," I say, bringing the topic back to me. "But now it's hitting home. A delayed reaction. Like, what have I even done with my life? I have no career, let alone a job, even. I'm slowly withering away, surrounded by Stepford Wives dressed head-to-toe in over-priced athleisure wear."

"That's the price you pay for living in the suburbs," Cath laughs.

"It's not the suburbs!" I say, my refrain every time they joke about Tollingford being on the outskirts, even though I have pointed out many times that technically, it is still London.

"You have driveways and a park and no tube and a florist and three delicatessens – it's the suburbs," Cath says, her usual reply.

"All my friends have moved away or are too busy to do anything," I continue, choosing to ignore her.

"Or have other stuff going on," Cath says, pointedly.

"Or have other stuff going on," I sigh. It seems to be my signature move at the moment. "I just . . . this isn't how I pictured my life, you know? It was going to be fabulous. *I* was going to be fabulous. I was going to live in New York and have a big, exciting career and have fabulous friends."

"Dude!" Cath says.

"You're digging a hole here," Emily adds.

"I was going to be successful and drink cosmos on rooftops in New York."

"With your fabulous friends?" Cath asks.

"Yeah, with those bitches," I say.

"You watched too much *Sex and the City*," Emily says.

"And we were going to go to fabulous launch parties and restaurants and on fabulous exotic holidays—"

"And just walk around saying fabulous a lot?" Emily laughs.

"Well, they sound like a bunch of arseholes," Cath says. "And besides, Ems was pretty fabulous with her slut drops last night."

"Two drinks and she thinks she's Beyoncé," I say.

"Always," Cath laughs. "I love the inner Emily being set free."

"I think I pulled a muscle though," Emily says.

I grab my phone. "Pretty sure I've got footage somewhere."

"No one needs to see that, thank you."

"It was like something from *Girls Gone Wild*," Cath says.

"Or it's lesser-known spin-off, Perimenopausal Woman Goes Wild for Four Hours for the First Time in Six Years?" Emily laughs.

I retrieve my phone and open my camera, momentarily caught off guard by the accidental selfie mode which captures me in all my flat-haired, pale-skinned, dark-eyebagged glory. I quickly open the photos, looking for the video from last night and then see a screenshot I took a few days ago.

"Oh my god, I meant to show you this. Look," I say, opening Facebook on my phone. "Jen Holden. Emily and I went to school with her," I explain to Cath. "I had English with her – we used to write silly poems together while Mrs Matthews wasn't looking. And look at her now!"

I shove the phone in their faces and scroll through her feed – exotic beaches, perfect family, big career announcements.

"She's my age and has just published her fourth bestseller. She goes to the Maldives every year, has a gorgeous husband and angelic children and a perfect smile. There's a photo of her with Reese Witherspoon who is adapting one of her books and guess who's going to be in it?"

"John Major," Cath says.

I ignore her. "George Clooney. GEORGE BLOODY CLOONEY! That's her life! I bet she doesn't have to clean up any cat piss from the floor."

"So, you're saying that could have been you? That you want to

be a bestselling author?" Cath says. "Because if that's the case, you should maybe ... write a book?"

"No, that's not the point," I say. "Or maybe it is the point."

"The point is, you need to stay off Facebook," Cath says, snatching the phone from me. "Facebook is for stalking ex-boyfriends and cringing at status updates you thought were funny at the time. No good can come from Facebook. The millennials have taught us that."

"What is the point?" Emily asks.

"Just that I feel..."

"Unfulfilled?" Emily offers, helpfully.

"Exactly." I make a flailing hand gesture to the room. "Unfulfilled. And like there's something more out there for me. Somehow. I just don't know what it is yet."

"Well then instead of moaning about it to your disappointing, un-fabulous friends, maybe you should get off your arse and actually do something about it, Charlie," Cath says.

"There's nothing I can do." I feel Cath's wrath as soon as the words leave my mouth.

"There's always something you can do," she says.

She pauses and glances down at herself. It's fleeting, but I see it.

"There's nearly always something you can do," she corrects. "And definitely in your case."

"Like what?" I ask. A stale tequila wave hits me, bile rising in my mouth. I swallow it down.

"You could get a job," Emily suggests.

"It's been so long, though. My CV will look practically prehistoric in TV terms. And with James's job, and childcare—"

"You could volunteer, or take up a hobby?" Emily says.

"Again, that would be quite hard with the—"

Cath flinches, looks pained. She stands up suddenly, grabbing her bag from one of the many piles on the floor. "I'm going to the loo." She pauses as she's nearly out of the door and turns back around. "You're bored. You're frustrated. If you were a man, you'd have an affair with a younger woman, stop drinking and take up a solo sport – that's the new midlife crisis, isn't it? None of which I'm suggesting you do, by the way. Or maybe do have an affair, I don't know. But if you're genuinely unhappy in your life and it's not just the hangxiety talking then stop making excuses and do something about it. Get a job, move out of suburbia, run a marathon, write a bestseller, or make one of those stupid lists you started before – forty things to do before you're forty. I guess forty-five things to do before you're forty-five." She takes a breath. "Wow, it does sound old when you say it out loud. I'm going to the loo."

I watch her go, stunned by the outburst. "That seemed a bit harsh."

"That's Cath's attempt at being helpful," Emily says. "She's got a lot going on at the moment, with her mum and everything. And crazy hormones. And patience has never been one of her virtues."

"What do you mean, crazy hormones?"

"She was talking about having another go at egg freezing last time I saw her. I don't know if she went ahead, you know what she can be like about that stuff – keeps it to herself."

"What?" A cloud of guilt settles on me. "She didn't tell me that! And I've been sat here whinging on about my stupid problems.

I thought she seemed a bit quiet last night."

"I tried to gently ask but she always just moves the subject on. Though I did notice she wasn't drinking."

"Jesus, does that mean we got through all those margarita pitchers between just the two of us?"

The thought of it makes my stomach churn all over again.

Cath comes back from the toilet, her face pinched and drawn.

"I've got to go," she says. "I've got a thing to do for Mum which I forgot about."

"Oh no! I thought we were going out for breakfast," I say.

"Sorry, this can't wait."

"How's your mum doing?" I ask. I feel myself doing the side-head tilt and pity eyes and correct it.

"Oh, you know..."

I make to stand up to give her a hug.

"Don't bother with hugs, you guys stink anyway," Cath says.

There's a commotion downstairs. More than the standard commotion. Which means trouble is coming. I consider shouting down in an attempt to parent, but decide I can't be arsed; isn't 'letting them sort things out themselves' a type of parenting? I'm pretty sure it is. Encourages independence or something... as long as no one gets injured.

"MUM!" Felix shouts up. Here we go. "Jack just spat cat food on me and some's gone on the carpet!"

"What the—?" Cath scrunches up her face in disgust.

She does not have children. And I can see that to someone who does not have children, this would, in fact, seem disgusting. Not that it doesn't seem disgusting to me – I'm just used to it. And my

children – the boys, anyway – seem to be the epitome of disgusting. Always.

"He dared me to eat some!" Jack shouts up.

"You see?" I say, gesturing to the beyond. "This is the kind of crap I have to put up with. This is my life. Making packed lunches, grocery shopping, meal planning, cooking, washing up, laundry, more laundry, filling in forms for school – all the forms – nagging, cleaning, finding random PE socks that everyone else is apparently incapable of looking for, putting dirty cereal bowls that have been left fifty centimetres from the dishwasher in the actual sodding dishwasher. Cleaning crap off the toilets that no one else seems to notice or care about. No rooftop bars and cosmos and holidays in the Hamptons for me. I just want—"

"I hate to interrupt your monologue," Cath ventures. "But shouldn't you, like, go and see to that?"

"Guessing I can't pull a godmother card?"

"You guessed right. I'm out of here."

"Thanks so much for coming last night, it was fun," I say. "And sorry about the moaning this morning. Maybe you're right, maybe it's just the hangxiety."

She frowns as she puts her coat on. "That's not exactly what I said."

"I think what you said was, 'have an affair'," Emily laughs. "Come on. Let's deal with this, then get out. We need fresh air, food and coffee."

"But most of all, you need to deal with the crap on the carpet," Cath says. "Good luck."

I bury my head in the duvet and let out a scream.

2

MY HANGOVER lasts the whole weekend, a fact that is made worse by my period deciding to make a fleeting, but painful appearance – two weeks early and with a vengeance that makes me feel like I'm being pummelled by a bulldozer. By Monday evening, I've had enough of the week already and the only way forwards feels like gin. In front of *The Real Housewives*. With a tube of Pringles that I intend to keep entirely to myself. Eddie Vedder glares at me from the other side of the sofa and refuses to engage when I try and coax her into sitting on my lap. Jack is reluctantly doing homework upstairs, Felix is at dodgeball, Chloe is . . . somewhere. I never quite know where Chloe is. She often goes round to Rupert's house after school and conveniently forgets to tell me. Rupert, her extremely posh, extremely handsome boyfriend who lives in a mansion, summers in Cape Cod and parties with minor royals. He has the kind of private-school confidence that makes me feel intimidated – even though I'm the grown-up – and leaves me worried that beyond the dripping charm is a layer of predator frat boy.

I settle in and focus on the housewives, head to toe in Louis Vuitton, make-up so thick they must've used a trowel to get it on, looking dazzling and invincible and generally kick-ass. I sip my Gordons and tonic in a chipped Ikea glass as they sip their

Belvedere and soda, with three lemons, carcass out, served in a crystal glass. They are fabulous. I've never seen them go to a rooftop bar, but I bet they do. And I bet they don't have to scrape spat-out cat food off a carpet and break up wrestling children and pick up three-hundred-and-ninety-one wet towels from the floor.

Checking my phone, I see James hasn't responded to any of my messages about how my day's been or the ones asking when he's likely to be home this evening and if there's any way he can cook.

Jack comes into the room, his blonde curls hanging in front of his eyes like a weeping willow. I really must get him a haircut. Eddie Vedder instantly scarpers – her hatred of the children is strong.

"Hey, buddy," I say. "Have you finished your English?"

He flops on the sofa next to me. I lift my arm for him to snuggle up. He smells of little-boy sweat – the nice kind, before the hormones kick in and they start reeking of fried onions.

"Yeah. Can I have screen time now?"

"In a minute," I say, squeezing him. "I'm enjoying our cuddle."

He holds my hand and I feel a bit tearful. He's my last cuddly one. And I know this is the last of him being my last cuddly one.

"Why is she kissing her dad?" he asks, watching the TV where one of the beautiful and glamorous housewives is kissing her husband, who happens to be very old and not particularly beautiful or glamorous.

"That's her husband," I say.

"He looks about a hundred! And she's so pretty."

"Well, he's rich."

"Gross. Can I have my screen time now?"

I sigh. "OK. Thank you for the cuddle, brief as it was."

He gives me a kiss on the cheek and pushes himself up from the sofa.

"Jack," I say. "Please don't ever stop giving me cuddles. And don't just move away and forget to call me and never see me."

"I'll live with you forever!" he says.

"Well, I mean, not necessarily that but—"

"Love you," he says, bouncing out the door in a haze of pre-gaming excitement.

I check my phone again. No message from James still, but there is one from Chloe:

> Chloe: *Coming home to do a quick change. With Rupert. Can you please not be embarrassing.*

> Me: *What exactly would constitute embarrassing?*

Love you too.

> Chloe: *Idk...*

> Me: *Trying to talk to him.*

I take a breath, wait for my rage to pass, push away the giant slap in my face that is knowing I'm an embarrassment to my daughter by simply opening my mouth. She used to love me. Not only that, she used to be obsessed with me. As in, followed me everywhere, wanted to be me, James-couldn't-get-a-look-in obsessed. I can't pinpoint the exact moment that all changed – I guess when the

hormones kicked in around twelve – but it's definitely full force now. She wants nothing to do with me. She has minimal contact with me, spends the majority of our interactions rolling her eyes and treats me like some kind of manservant with no life of my own, whose only purpose is to service her needs. Emily always tells me it's a stage and that we were like that with our mums (I have no recollection of this – I'm pretty sure I was an ANGEL) – but it makes my heart hurt. I miss my daughter.

The front door opens and slams shut. I hear Chloe laughing and the low gruff voice that indicates Rupert is with her. I sit up, brushing Pringle crumbs off me and put my gin glass out of view. It's six o'clock, I should at least pretend to be a responsible parent.

"Hi!" I shout through.

Chloe walks in, Rupert in tow. He's had a haircut and is giving off serious Prince William, when he was fit, vibes. I shake the thought away, knowing that swooning over your daughter's boyfriend is definitely crossing some kind of parenting line.

"Hey, Mum." Chloe does a double take, scrutinising me – she sees the gin glass and Pringles tube, despite my hiding skills. There is a small eye roll. "I'm just getting changed, then we're heading out."

"Are you not in for dinner?"

"Nope." She gestures for Rupert to follow her upstairs.

"I'll wait here," he says. "Have a little catch-up with Mumma Parsons."

Chloe beams at him, like he's some kind of benevolent angel who's just offered to help an old lady cross the road.

"I won't be long," she calls out as she's halfway up the stairs.

I sit up straighter, like I'm about to be interrogated by MI5

and pause *Housewives*, changing the channel to *Ramsey's Kitchen Nightmares* which feels one level up, but still wrong under such scrutiny.

"How was your day?" Rupert asks, settling himself down and spreading his arms along the back of the armchair like he's the CEO of the house.

"Uh, fine," I say. My mind thinks back to my day – loading the dishwasher, unloading the dishwasher, collecting the laundry, washing the laundry, drying the laundry, folding the laundry, distributing the laundry. "Same old, same old."

My phone beeps, a text from James. Finally.

My day's been rubbish too – so busy and lots of annoyances and now I've got to go out for dinner with a new client which is not what I want to be doing!

I grunt at the phone in frustration. It's such a James text – always dumping last-minute plans on me in a way that's supposed to make me feel sorry for him. POOR JAMES, having to go for dinner at The Ivy or Soho House or some other perfectly wonderful – fabulous, even – location while me and my bleeding womb are left to make dinner and deal with the feral children.

"Bad news?" Rupert asks.

"No, just James saying he's out tonight."

He creases his eyebrows in sympathy, like I'm a child who's just told him my parents forgot to pick me up from school.

"Important advertising business?" he asks, in a tone which may well be mocking, but I can't quite be sure.

Chloe comes bursting through the door in cargo pants and a crop top so small she could've taken it off a teddy bear. Rupert

pulls her onto his lap and she wraps her arm around his neck, going in for a kiss. A kiss which turns into a full-on snog, the kind that you have when you're young and passionate and feel like you'll die without each other. And is totally inappropriate to be doing in front of me.

I think back to when James and I first met – when we were only a few years older than Chloe. We couldn't keep our hands off each other, desperate to be together and make physical contact at all times – holding hands, kissing, cuddling, sitting on laps. I had a permanent face rash from the hours we spent snogging. Snogging. That's a lost art. I can't remember the last time we did anything other than a quick peck. Anything more than that and James goes from zero to a hundred, and takes it as me giving him the go-ahead for sex.

"We'd better go," Rupert says. "Mum's making her special seafood linguine."

"Lovely," I say, wondering what freezer feast I'll feed the boys tonight – goujons and chips or kiev and waffles?

Chloe stands and pulls Rupert up from the chair, getting another kiss and, I notice, a bum squeeze. I really should talk to her about toning it down in front of people – me, specifically. She leans down to me, in what appears to be a lovely little hug goodbye.

"Oh my god, Mum!" she hisses in my ear. "Can you please deal with your bloodied granny knickers that are in the bathroom sink. SO gross! You're lucky Rupert didn't go in there."

She skips out of the room, back to Rupert.

"They're not granny knickers," I say. Quietly, and to myself. "And I think you'll find it's Rupert who's lucky he didn't go in there. I don't give a toss."

3

AFTER OUR nutritious dinner, and the bedtime refereeing, and Chloe coming home and stomping around, and two more episodes of *Real Housewives*, and two more gins, just as I'm starting the fourth – *Housewives* and gin – I stop mid-scroll on Facebook. I'm not really on Facebook any more, ever since Chloe told me it's for old people, but I kind of am, in that I have a profile and spend hours on there every day (FOMO).

I let out a gasp.

There's a photo of Jen Holden, my hugely successful author school friend. It's a professional family photo – the kind with the naff blue background, everyone in smart clothes – with her and her husband and their two small, beautiful children. It's the 'Rest In Peace' at the top of the caption that gets me:

> *Friends, it is with great sadness that we say goodbye to our angel Jen today after she lost her private battle with breast cancer. The most wonderful, loving wife to Kevin and whole-heartedly incredible mumma to Caleb and Wilfred. She's gone too early, and had so much left to give, though we're comforted by the legacy she leaves behind – her family and her books (stay tuned for* Secret Wives *TV updates in the autumn). There is a hole in our*

lives, but we know she's looking down on us from heaven and will always be with us. In Jen's own words, Hakuna Matata. x

I am shocked. And not just because there's something deeply wrong about signing off a death post with Hakuna Matata which, I would argue, are very much not Jen's own words.

Jen Holden – dead! She's my age. She has kids. And a husband. A whole life. Success. Another bestseller to promote. An exciting TV series coming soon. Her life just cut short like that. I wonder if she even got to meet George?

I can't believe it. I swallow down a sob and take a screenshot to send to Emily.

Me: *OMG JEN HOLDEN JUST DIED. WTF!!*

Emily: *Oh no! That's awful.*

Me: *I'm bawling. I just can't believe it. So sad.*

Emily: *When was the last time you spoke to her?*

Me: *About twenty-five years ago.*

Emily: *But it's still sad! She used to borrow my Tipp-Ex. And she was really good at rhyming.*

Me: *Her poor family.*

Emily: *Is this it now? Do we need to start reading the obituaries and looking out for friends?!*

Me: *No.*

Emily: *I can't believe it.*

Me: *So sad.*

Emily: *How many gins have you had?*

Me: *One! That's not why I'm sad.*

Emily: *It's late. I've gotta go to bed. Don't have any more gin. Love you!*

Me: *In case anything happens, I want you to know, because we don't say it enough, I really do love you, Ems.*

Emily: *Love you too. Go to bed.*

I ignore Emily and have another gin. It feels necessary. The housewives are a bit blurred now and I've done this enough times to know that I won't remember what happens from this point and will have to rewatch tomorrow anyway. So, I do the sensible thing and turn the TV off – after a quick burst of *First Dates*. But my mind is still going – full technicolour throttle. This is the first friend of mine who's died. The first person my age. It hits different.

I cycle through my memories of Jen – other than the Tipp-Ex and the good rhyming and the generally being really good at English (she was always Mrs Matthews' favourite), I remember how her ponytail always looked perfect, and how she always smelt of White Musk, and how she was the first to get Buffalos, and how she went out with Freddie Bates for ages but there was a rumour Justin Horton fingered her at the Leavers' Ball. Probably not one for the obituary. I'm pretty sure I have photos of the Leavers' Ball.

I decide that I absolutely must find those photos and I absolutely must do it immediately. Pushing myself up from the sofa, half-heartedly swiping some of the Pringles crumbs away, I teeter upstairs. The light is still on in Chloe's room, her laughter tinkling out through the door. I check my watch – 10.47 p.m. Technically, she's not supposed to be on her phone after 10.30 p.m., though James and I are normally in bed before her, so who knows what she actually gets up to in there. I consider saying something and decide against it. Something tells me it would not be a fruitful conversation – especially as my period-stained knickers are still, I remember, in the sink.

Eddie Vedder appears on the landing as I tiptoe through to James's office (for the rare days he works at home). She follows me, loudly meowing, but swerving my strokes. This is her game – I think she just enjoys harassing me. If she could leave a dirty cereal bowl on the side like everyone else, I'm pretty sure she would. She just gives me her dirty protests instead. I sigh at her and close the office door.

Buried deep in the big cupboard somewhere are two Really Useful plastic boxes containing my entire former life – the Teenage

Me, the Other Boyfriends Me, the Meeting James Me, University Me, Career Me and Before Kids Me. On hands and knees, I set about finding them – discarding bags of hand-me-down clothes we've yet to open, sleeping bags, boxes of Duplo that James can't bring himself to throw away and emergency extra duvets – too knackered to use, but passable for if we ever (we have never) have a house full of guests. Eventually I see them, right at the back, dusty and cracked. They're surprisingly heavy and it takes some manoeuvring – and a lot of grunting – to get them out, but I manage, clearing a space on the now covered-in-crap floor.

Opening the lid feels like coming home. My things – my precious, precious, familiar things – the photo albums, the framed photos, the teddies, the jewellery box with a hidden compartment where I stored my Marlboro Reds (they were always way too strong, but I felt hardcore and cooler than everyone else who smoked Silk Cut), my school yearbooks, my signed school shirt from the last day, my gig ticket stubs, a couple of now very scrunched posters (Stone Temple Pilots and Pearl Jam).

Me. The essence of me. In a couple of boxes.

I spot my diaries, covered in band stickers and random words cut out from magazines, which I remember always took days to do. I open one tentatively, remembering the last few times I attempted this, it made me cringe so much I wanted to throw up.

1st January 1994

Dearest Diary,
Hi there, babes! Looks like it's just you and me for the next

corker of a year! Here's to 1994 – may it be an absolute STUNNER!

First, let me introduce myself. I'm Charlie – full name Charlotte – and I haven't got off with anyone. Need I say more! I'm actually being a bit hopeful by getting a whole-page-a-day diary. I'm counting on exciting things happening this year. Well, I can wish, OK. These are my New Year's resolutions:

1. TO GET OFF WITH SOMEONE. Emphasised, underlined and exaggerated!!

2. To not be such a complete bitch and selfish. You know, be kind and considerate etc., et-bloody-cetera!

3. I guess it should really be to work hard, but I think that's too unoriginal and highly unlikely so, to try not to give a shit what people say. Live my life for me and not let anyone get in my way. And be super successful and rich and exciting. But that's probably not for this year.

All my love always,
Charlie

I get lost in the pages, reliving the romance of my first boyfriend, pleased for my fifteen-year-old self that I did, in fact, get off with someone that year – and the rest – which I go on to describe in very explicit detail, despite the fact that this diary was generally just

lying around my room available for my parents to read whenever. I shudder thinking about it.

There's my first time getting pissed (Malibu and red wine at the rec), many Saturday nights out at Jangles (the only club in the town), many tears over teachers giving me a hard time about how I wasn't really doing any work (how dare they), many ups and downs in my love life and way too much information about who was getting off with and fingering who. I laugh at the word, relieved that as adults, we no longer talk about, refer to, or even vaguely mention fingering.

I flick through the yearbook, looking for photos of Jen. There are a few of her in netball-team shots (not with me), one of her in a production of *Bugsy Malone* (not with me) and one of her grinning and clutching an English award (also not with me). The only one we're both in is the year-group photo at the end of sixth form, our faces small, blurred dots amongst the mass of girls. It takes me a minute to confirm the person I'm looking at is actually me.

There are a few copies of the school magazine, edgy student art on the covers. I'm surprised when I find some of my writing in them. In one, an emo poem I wrote about Adam and Eve that ended with Eve killing Adam, in another, a story about ants which I must've thought was an allegory for something, though reading it back now, I'm not sure what. I'd forgotten about these. I'd forgotten I even wrote back then. I remember the boys and the nights out, and the falling out with girlfriends – including The Great Ignoring of 1995 when all of my friends stopped talking to me but didn't tell me why (turns out it was because I talked about Joel Henderson too much) – but I don't remember the writing. I cringe as I read these poems and stories, but I love that Teenage

Me was that passionate about something, that thoughtful, brave enough to put them out into the world. She was a badass – when she wasn't obsessing about boys.

I realise, with a pinch in my stomach, that I miss her.

Leaning back against the wall, a photo of me and Emily in one hand, a gin and tonic in the other, I study the photo carefully. Judging by the asymmetric bob I'm sporting, I must've been sixteen. We'd just had a food fight in the quad, both covered in shepherd's pie dregs. I remember laughing so hard my stomach hurt. Laughing still when Mrs King, our head of year, told us off. Told *me* off, actually. Everyone seemed to think I was a bad influence and whenever Emily got in trouble, it was somehow all down to me – even though we both explained how Emily started it by accidentally flinging a piece of pie at me while gesticulating enthusiastically about the greatness of Charlotte Brontë. I can't remember the last time I laughed like that. Carefree, full-on, stomach-hurting laughter.

I look lovingly at Teenage Me, feeling the impulse to apologise to her for letting her down, for not realising all those dreams and ambitions and hopes she had. For not belly-laughing enough. My mind turns to Jen – the shock, the tragedy of a life lost, a life with things still to achieve.

Cath is right, if I'm not happy – and, I realise, I definitely am not – then it's up to me to do something to change that. Who knows what, exactly, and god knows what the sole cause of the unhappiness is, but I have to do something. I can't go on like this, letting Teenage Me down. Jen is my age. *Was* my age. And now she's gone. I could die any day. Any minute. And what would I

have to show for it other than these two Really Useful boxes and a handful of sub-par, overly-dramatic emo poems? (And my kids, obviously, but this is separate.) I don't want to spend the rest of my life, however long is left, cleaning up other people's crap, and eating Pringles and drinking gin on my own while watching other people be fabulous.

I wonder, for a second, where to start, and then I remember the list. Pushing myself up, swaying slightly, I make my way through the cupboard detritus on the office floor and into our bedroom. I rummage through my bedside drawer and find it: my 40 Things To Do Before I'm 40 list.

I hadn't got very far – there are currently only seven things on the list, and I remember the girls taking the piss out of me for pretty much all of them.

1. *Have sex with George Clooney.*
2. *Take up parkour.*
3. *Swim with dolphins.*
4. *Climb Mount Everest.*
5. *Have a threesome.*
6. *Go to Thailand.*
7. *Eat caviar.*

I stand by them. That's a good start. I have not achieved any of them in the time since I wrote this list. Thirty-nine was a lifetime ago, a whole other version of me – except, if I stop to think about it, not that much has changed – I've gained half a stone, a lot more wrinkles and a teenage daughter who can't stand me, but other

than that, the boys are still wrestling, James is still super busy and hardly home, and I've still achieved sod all, apart from the occasional week I manage to meal plan and stick to it.

A rising fire lights in my belly, a new determination. I need this. I will do this. This list will change my life. I message the girls in my excitement, sending a selfie of me holding the list and grinning.

🍸 *COCKTAIL COVEN* 🍸

Me: *GUYS! I know how I'm going to sort my life out – I'm bringing out the list! (And adding to it, obvs.)*

Cath: *Please record your parkour efforts. I could do with a laugh.*

Me: *I'm being serious. This is it. I could die any day. We all could. We have to live for now. We only have one life.*

Cath: *Have you been on the gin?*

Me: *NO!*

Cath: *You look like you've been on the gin.*

Me: *A small one.*

Me: *BUT THAT'S NOT WHAT THIS IS.*

Cath: *Good for you, mate. Get on it.*

Me: *I'm going to! It feels good!*

Cath: *Let me know how George is in bed.*

* * *

"Hey." James comes into the bedroom, carrying his standard bedtime warm milk. "I didn't expect you to still be up."

"I was waiting up for you," I lie. "How was your night?"

He launches into complaining about The Ivy and having to talk to people and eat nice food and how tired he is. I nod, wishing that I'd been able to have lush cocktails and a dinner more sophisticated than Pringles. I know better than to say anything though, because all I'd get in response is a mini-lecture about how going to nice places is actually a major chore and he'd much rather be at home.

"Well, I'm working on something," I say, changing the subject. Partly because I'm bored of his moaning, partly because I know he'd never ask about my day or what I was up to.

"Does it have anything to do with the carnage in my office, by any chance?"

"Sorry. I had to dig some stuff out."

He frowns, propping up a pillow and sitting next to me on the bed. He looks handsome. Tired, and older, but handsome. "What now?" he asks, sighing wearily.

"Excuse me! There's no 'what now' about it."

"But..."

I fold my list over, realising that No. 1 is not something James needs to see.

"But I have decided what I'm going to do to get myself out of my funk."

He raises his eyebrows at me in expectation.

"I'm doing a forty-five things to do before you're forty-five list!"

He groans. I elbow him, hard, causing his warm, old-man milk to spill.

"Really?" he asks. "Another one of your lists you're not going to finish and then feel bad about not finishing? We're doing that again?"

I've had enough gin that we could quite easily fall into an argument, but I refuse to let his lack of belief and his disinterest in me sap my enthusiasm.

"*We're* not doing it," I say. "*I* am. And I'm going to finish it this time."

"I won't hold my breath," he says, slurping at his milk in a way that makes me feel nauseous. "So, what have you got on there so far?"

"I'm not ready to share it yet," I say, knowing I don't have it in me to deal with the ridicule tonight and that it's probably not the best time to discuss if I can get a hall pass for George. "But I'm really serious about it, James. I found out today my friend from school died and it just . . . it threw me and it made me th—"

"Oh my god, what friend?" he asks.

"Uh, Jen Holden, you didn't know her. We were really close for a while and in English she always . . . but anyway, my point was," I say, trying to stay on course, "every day counts. We could die any

minute. And what would I have to show for it? What's my legacy?"

"Me and the kids? Our gorgeous house?"

"I don't think I can claim you as an achievement, and I'm not counting the kids." He goes to object but I steamroll on. "You've had your midlife crisis with the Ironman, and the not drinking, and the philosophy. This is mine."

"Then I fully support you, darling," he says with the least supportive tone humanly possible. He pats my leg. "Can you maybe add to the list: learn how to not shrink my sports stuff in the wash?"

"Oh, piss off."

"Love you too," he says, leaning over to give me a kiss. "Ahhh, have you been on the gin?"

4

"**AH YES,** a tilted cervix," the nurse says, fiddling with the giant spotlight shining between my legs. "That's what's making it trickier. Can you sit on your hands for me, love?"

She's been at it for ten minutes already. A procedure which I was assured takes five minutes, if that. I do as I'm told, make my hands into knuckles and use them to prop up my arse so the nurse can get a better look up my foof. I've kept my socks on, I always keep my socks on for these things in the hope that it may bring a sense of dignity to the proceedings. It does not. There is no dignity to froggy-ing your legs and having a stranger rummage around in your vagina.

"Just relax for me," she says.

Because of course, everything about this is relaxing; the strip lights blinking in my face, the spotlight illuminating my insides, the tiny scrap of paper towel placed over me, the rummaging.

The nurse makes a puzzled noise from somewhere between my legs, then goes to get a magnifying screen. Wonderful – my vagina getting a close up. She goes in again, makes more puzzled noises, emerges. "We're going to need an extra-long speculum."

The student nurse – because, yes, there has been another person in the room this whole time – goes to the cupboard and clanks around a bit. Her being in the room is giving me flashbacks

to Jack's birth; it was a vaginal breech birth, which apparently are fairly rare these days and therefore required so many students to observe, it was like having a Greek chorus in the room.

"Periods have been getting heavier, have they?" Nurse One says, scrunching her eyebrows at me in sympathy. From between my legs.

"Yeah, much heavier," I mutter, not enjoying carrying out a conversation with my legs akimbo.

"That's the perimenopause for you," Nurse One says. "Periods and pregnancy and childbirth, and then just when you're starting to feel back to normal, we get thrown the menopause. God's definitely a man, that's for sure."

I resist the urge to argue, to explain that my mum didn't go through the menopause until she was well into her fifties and had basically no symptoms so I will be the same. I figure the less conversation in this compromised position, the better.

I think back to some of my heavier periods' greatest hits: the one where we'd gone round to the immaculate house of James's boss for dinner and I very nearly bled all over their white chair covers; the one where I soaked through sheets at the in-laws and had to try and sneak them into the laundry before anyone saw, which of course I didn't manage to do because my mother-in-law is never more than a metre from her laundry room and is a domestic war-horse who will never let anyone do anything to help around the house; and, my personal favourite, the one where I bled all over a rock coming out of the sea on a girls' trip to Spain and had to explain to a concerned Cath and Emily that no, the blood running down my leg wasn't due to an injury, and then had to

painstakingly, on hands and knees, clean up the blood spatters that had left a trail from the rocks to our villa. Yes, my periods have got heavier.

The student nurse comes back over with what can only be described as a medieval torture device. I want to object. There is no way I want that thing anywhere near my vagina. There is no way it would fit, surely?

"Right then," Nurse One says, slathering the torture device in lube. Or whatever medical lube is. "Let's give this another go."

Minutes go by, and my legs start to cramp. I'm basically a giant trash can a racoon is foraging around in. I stare at the flickering strip light and force myself to focus on something other than the stranger in my cervix, something positive – the list. I feel excited at the prospect of it already, and I haven't even started ticking things off yet. Just forcing myself to think about what I want to try, what I want to achieve, and what I feel I need – it's the most revved up I've felt since my first TV work-experience placement. I could barely sleep last week for all the ideas whirling around my head. I'm going to put some easily achievable ones on there, silly things I've been meaning to do forever – drink a martini, eat an oyster, go to a spin class. And some bigger dream ones, including swimming with dolphins and sex with George Clooney – because you never know. Hope tingles from my head to my toes, circumventing my currently-being-violated vagina.

The nurse retreats, eventually. "Still no joy."

Definitely no joy, I can confirm.

"I have an idea, though." She heaves herself to her feet, looking inspired. "I'm going to ask you to stand up and have a few little

jumps for me. I know that sounds strange, but I'm hoping it will coax your cervix down a bit."

She wiggles her finger as she says that last bit, like my cervix is a mischievous child who needs to sit on the naughty step and learn a lesson. The nurse demonstrates what she wants me to do – cupping each of her enormous boobs as she jumps, going bright red after only two. Student nurse is clearly trying not to laugh. I am trying not to cry.

"Just a few should do the job," she says, drawing the curtain around me but still staying in the room.

I push myself up, easing my legs into action, pins and needles electrifying me as I place my weight on my feet.

I am naked from the waist down, exposed, cold and grateful for my dignity socks. Holding a boob in each hand, I copy the nurse and take a tentative jump, wondering how the hell my life has come to this. For a split second, I consider the possibility I'm being pranked – some elaborate practical joke for a TV show. And then I realise it's hardly prime-time viewing – an ageing, half-naked, on-the-brink-of-tears woman holding her saggy tits and pathetically bouncing around in a doctor's surgery. As I jump, to my horror, some drops of blood appear on the floor below me. As if this could get any worse.

"Um." My voice is little. "I'm . . . there are some spots of blood . . . coming out. Is that normal?"

The nurse peers around the curtain, where I am standing, still naked from the waist down. I don't even flinch at this point, my dignity socks now splattered with little blood spots.

"Ah yes, that'll be because all that prodding aggravated your womb. Nothing to worry about."

She disappears behind the curtain, then comes back and hands me some cotton wool. "Here you go. Use this to mop yourself up, love."

Mop myself up?! Like I'm some leaky tap. I pat my vagina with it, bits of cotton wool getting stuck to my pubes. The nurse sets to cleaning the floor up with some blue paper, gesturing for me to get back on the bed. I wonder, not for the first time, if I could just put my clothes back on and run.

"OK then," she says, rubbing her hands together. "Let's have another go."

The spotlight, the magnifying glass, the puzzled noises – now sounding more annoyed than confused. Me and my naughty cervix. I stare at the ceiling, pick out a spider's web to focus on.

"Did you do anything nice at the weekend?" Student Nurse asks.

Really? We're doing small talk?

"Uh, it was my birthday," I say. "I went out for drinks with some friends."

"Ah, how lovely!" She grins at me like I've told her I won an Oscar.

Nurse One sighs and puts her head between her hands in frustration. While still in between my legs. I have a despairing nurse nestled in between my legs. Closer to my vagina than my husband's head has been in three years.

"I've never not been able to do this," she says, finally looking up and sitting back slightly. "But I'm all out of options."

Part of me breathes a sigh of relief. My cervix, probably.

"We shall not be defeated though!"

Balls.

She goes back in, with a steely glint in her eye. "This is going to pinch a bit."

I can feel my cervix shrivel up and retreat even further in fear. *Think of the list, think of the list.* I repeat it like a mantra. The list will sort my life out. The list will make me happy. The list will help me rediscover myself, get me back to me. Whoever 'me' is these days. I imagine myself this time next year – shiny, happy, healthy, wealthy, successful (in something), validated and valued. And with normal, not-heavy periods.

"So where did you go for your birthday?" Student Nurse asks, like we're just shooting the shit. I ignore her, and focus on a rogue cobweb in the corner.

The 'pinching' takes my breath away. It is not pinching, it is viciously lacerating. And it is deeply unpleasant. I glance at the clock; it's been over twenty-five minutes now. Over twenty minutes of my legs being spread to a stranger, of my foof being out, of my insides being rummaged and poked and prodded and pinched.

Finally, finally, she stops the mining and pops her head out. Smiling.

"Success," she says, like she found the gold, so delighted I wonder if she's expecting me to give her a high five or something. "Well, that was certainly a challenge! We got there in the end. I'm afraid I've angered your womb a bit – not as much as it angered me, mind! I'll go and type up your notes, Helen will give you some more cotton wool to mop yourself up."

Please stop saying 'mop' when referring to my uterus. Cervix. Womb. Whatever the hell.

"Get yourself sorted and we'll have a chat."

That definitely sounds like my womb and I are in trouble. I ease up from the bed, cotton wool between my legs, my whole lower half feeling like it's just got back from war. It's good to put clothes back on and join the human race again. I take some deep breaths, readying myself for the chat, whatever it may entail. *A few more minutes,* I tell myself, *then I'll be free and will never have to see these people again.* Which is probably what they're thinking about me and my tilted cervix.

"Right then," Nurse One says as I sit down. I notice that Student Nurse has left – probably gone to de-stress. "So here's a pamphlet with a bit more information about your coil. It's everything we talked about before really – hopefully it will help with your heavy bleeds, though they often take a while to settle in, so you may experience spotting and bleeding or, in rare cases, heavier bleeding for a while – they say up to six months, though I've had some ladies take a bit longer. You may get some cramps too, and I'm slightly worried that after all that effort, that tricky cervix of yours is at a higher risk of expelling it. But like I say, that's the worst-case scenario. So, fingers crossed it all works out – that certainly was an adventure!"

Tears prick at my eyes, as cramps wrack my abdomen. She's basically saying all this – all that – could be for nothing.

She sees I'm upset. Gives me what's supposed to be a reassuring arm rub. "Don't worry love, you're on the home straight now – less than ten years and you'll never have to think about periods again!"

As I leave, I notice spots of my blood on her clogs.

5

I'M RUNNING late for pickup, so me and my bloodied, cotton-wooled downstairs stagger through the high street, John Wayne style, as fast as humanly possible without leaving a trail of blood spots.

Jack's class is already out – I see Clara, one of the mums from the school group chat, head to toe in Lululemon with a full face of no-make-up make-up, fawning over her can-do-no-wrong daughter, Mitzy. Clara is one of the Worthy Mums – she works part-time at a charity of some kind and is a big cheese in the PTA, constantly pushing fundraisers down our throats on the class WhatsApp – cheese and wine evenings, quizzes, eighties nights. The kind of low-rent, enforced mum 'fun' things that make me shrivel up and die inside as soon as they're mentioned. She was class rep last year and gives me evils because I didn't chip into the collection for Miss Fletcher's present. The reason being that Miss Fletcher was a self-important tosspot who once called me in for a full-blown lecture about the necessity of reading with children because Jack had told her I'm too busy watching *The Real Housewives* to read with him. Which is only partially true. But fully humiliating.

I pick up the pace, waving frantically at Jack as I round the corner. My cramping is worse and the cotton wool has been nudged out of place, slipping further out of my knicker gusset with each step.

"Hey, buddy," I say, ruffling Jack's hair. "How was your day?"

"Can I play FIFA when we get home? I know it's not a screen-time day but Finn is playing and wants me to play with him."

"Hey, Mum, my day was great, how was yours?" I reply.

"Mum!" He rolls his eyes. "Can I play FIFA? Please!"

I spy Cool Mum nearby handing out some flyers and speed up. Speeding up is my general tactic on the school run – Worthy Mums, Working Mums, Harassed Mums, Dowdy Mums – I like to avoid them all. Get in late, get out quick – minimal eye contact, avoid as much small talk and awkwardness as possible. School mums are not my people. Or these ones aren't, anyway. Emily tells me there's no way I can possibly know that as I've barely spoken to any of them, but trust me, I know. And the group chats I'm subjected to prove my point. They take pushy parenting to a whole new level, questioning everything ('I just feel giving them different work doesn't give them all the same opportunity to prove themselves'), commenting on everything ('don't they all look so grown-up now?'), even asking for the kids to be given more homework ('they really need to be developing their independent learning skills').

Not. My. People.

I hate how we're expected to bond with each other by virtue of the fact we happened to get knocked up at the same time. I met Emily at school – our shared love of George Clooney, pickled onion Monster Munch and grunge music bringing us together, and Cath and I connected over our hatred of Old English, Professor Derby and our flatmates in our first year of uni. Solid friendship foundations that stand the test of time.

"Um, Jack's mum," I hear a voice behind me say. Balls.

I know exactly who it is and consider just carrying on walking, but she catches up to me and it would be full-on rudeness to ignore her.

"Clara, hi," I say, turning around.

"I was worried you couldn't hear me for a second." She does a fake tinkly laugh that's like fingernails on a blackboard. "I just wanted to remind you to sign Jack up for the sponsored silence. Miss Steele gave me the list of the few children who haven't signed up yet and asked me to chase. Badger Class is going for the record this year so it's all hands on deck!"

I sense Jack tense next to me. "Sure," I say, trying for a placatory smile, or whatever is most likely to get her away from me.

"Great!" she says, before striding her perfectly-formed Lululemon backside away.

I give her the tiniest, most imperceptible middle finger as she goes, which I soon realise, from the snort laugh that comes from next to me, was not as tiny and imperceptible as I was going for.

"She's one of those, hey?" Cool Mum asks, through the snorts. "Class rep?"

I am mortified.

"I . . . I didn't mean—" I try to conjure some explanation. "She's not even the class rep any more," I manage. "She just can't give it up. But that was mean, I shouldn't have—"

"God, no worries!" she says, her eyes sparkling. She lowers her voice, steps in closer. I get a waft of sandalwood and expensive clothes. "This place is littered with them."

She takes a breath. "Charlie, isn't it?"

I'm taken aback by the use of my name. That she even knows it.

Cool Mum has always seemed a cut above the other mums. She's not on the conveyor belt – leisurewear, Veja trainers and leopard-print statement piece, a carbon copy like so many of the other mums – more of a vintage, bright colours and not giving a damn one-of-a-kind, topped off with wild curly hair and about five-hundred-and-three pieces of chunky jewellery on any given day.

"Uh, yeah, hi," I say.

"I'm Dorit, Bodie's mum." My face must react in some kind of way because she laughs at me. "A fellow *Housewives* fan, I take it! I wasn't named after her, clearly. I like to think I'm the original Dorit."

I smile, genuinely pleased to meet someone who watches *Housewives* – it's usually a dirty little secret I keep to myself for fear of being judged.

"Are you coming to the Easter Fayre?" she says, thrusting a flyer into my hand.

"I... uh, I think we're—"

She surveys the playground and leans in. "I know it's normally really dull but I'm running a rum bar this year and there's a silent disco for the kids, and did I mention a rum bar?" She nudges me, like we're old friends sharing an in-joke. I have to admit, I don't hate it. There's something about her energy I like. "You must come! I have a good eye for fun people and I can just tell you and I are going to get on famously. We can moan about all the class reps. And drink lots of rum."

"Well then, I might think about it." I smile.

"I solemnly promise it will be more fun than any other year," she says. Which doesn't mean that much to me as we've never

gone. And by that I mean, *I've* never gone. James never goes to any school events, of course.

She goes to say something else, then glances down at me, her face morphing from warm enthusiasm to shock. She leans even closer.

"Babe, you have a situation." She widens her eyes and flicks them down to my crotch.

Shit.

I don't even look, I know what it will be.

"Thanks," I say, turning beetroot red and pulling my coat around me. Thank god I decided to wear a long one today. "I've just had . . . I . . . coil."

"Oh, you poor thing. It's a 'mare, right?"

I nod, mortified, praying to the school gate gods that no one else saw it and that somehow I never have to see Dorit again.

"Jack! We have to go!" I shout across the playground. He vaguely looks up then goes back to comparing Pokémon cards with his friend. "NOW!" I screech.

"Don't worry," Dorit says, as I'm already walking. "No one else saw, my big arse had you covered. Get yourself a hot water bottle and half a bottle of gin – you'll be grand."

I mutter thanks and speed up, Jack trailing behind me.

"And come and drink some rum with me!" Dorit shouts. "I promise it'll be fun!"

April

6

THE RESTAURANT is all sleek lines, white tables and fancy wood. Mirrored walls and high ceilings bestow it with an air of out-of-my-price-range grandeur. I pull my shoulders back and puff out my chest in an attempt to prove to the three other sets of diners in their very expensive cashmere that I am allowed in, despite my scuffed boots and cat-fur-covered jumper. Thank god I pulled out the Gap trench coat for the occasion.

"Hi," I say to the front-of-house dude who totally gives me an up and down before plastering a fake smile on his face. "I've got a reservation under the name Parsons. For three people at two o'clock."

He looks at his screen. "Ah yes, one of your party is already here. Right this way, please."

I follow him through the restaurant, being careful not to knock any wine glasses with my shopping bags.

"Here we are," he says as we approach the corner table where Emily is sat studying the menu, looking totally at home in that way she has, regardless of where we are. I grin, we hug, knocking over various bits of the table setting. The waiter stands by, awkwardly trying to pour my wine and pull out my seat and take my coat and bags, which I refuse to hand over.

"Cheers!" Emily raises her glass, once the waiter has finally buggered off.

"Cheers! This is fancy, isn't it?"

"Well, you said you wanted oysters and this is one of the best places for them."

"I like it, I like it. I just haven't been anywhere posher than Nando's in a while – it's a shock to the system."

"Oh god, we haven't caught up properly on the glamping yet?" she asks.

"Talking of not-posh places?"

"It can't have been as bad as your messages were making out, surely."

James and I decided, for some reason I have yet to work out, to go glamping over the Easter holidays. I think it came about because we couldn't afford a proper holiday and James didn't have much time off and I'd been influenced by too many Instagram posts showing glasses of fizz shot from a hot tub on a terrace, looking out over undulating, sunset-drenched hills while happy children frolicked in the background. What we'd ended up booking was an oversized tent with a charity-shop sofa that smelt of damp and dead people, complete with the world's smallest wood-burning stove that was as useful as farting on someone to warm them up, and a hot tub with an algae problem that looked out over the A3. All for the princely cost of a week in Tenerife. But with rain. Lots of rain. And unhappy children who did absolutely no frolicking.

"God, it was awful," I say, sipping my wine at the memory of it. "The place was horrible, Chloe was moping around like a heartbroken Victorian because we'd taken her away from her One True Love for three nights, the boys were about as dramatic, but

because there was no WiFi, and James had loads of work to do. I just drank a lot."

"Why Victorian?" Emily asks, mid surface wiping. "Out of interest."

"I feel like they were the most mopey and heartbroken of all the eras?"

"Sure," she laughs.

"How was your Easter?"

"Pretty rubbish too. I threw the kids into activity camps for most of it, then did a bit of a long weekend at my parents' so they could keep an eye on them. Basically just trying to entertain the kids and work, as always. All a bit meh."

"God, I wish my parents were ever around for me to be able to dump the kids on them once in a while," I say. "Did Rick go with you?"

"No, he's really busy. He had a work trip for a few nights, somewhere up north."

"How are you guys doing?" I ask, knowing as soon as the words leave my mouth I probably shouldn't have bothered.

"Fine." She shrugs me off. "Same as always. He's really busy, out a lot."

"Why the hell did you bring us here?" Cath's voice demands, way too loudly, as she approaches the table.

She's a bustle of bags and layers, a hurricane heading our way with force. A barely-adult waiter walks behind her, trying to control the trail of chaos.

"Could I get you something to drink?" he asks, when she's finally settled.

"A negroni please. As quickly as possible."

The waiter nods and scurries away. Cath grabs my wine glass and takes a long sip.

Emily and I exchange a look at the fact Cath is very definitely drinking again and what this might mean, but we don't ask. If Cath wants to tell you something, she will.

"So, this is for the oysters?" she asks. "This place?"

"Yep!" I say. "I'm scared."

"They're oysters, not kangaroo bollocks. Though, to be honest, they probably taste similar."

"Don't!" I say, taking another sip of my wine. I figure the more intoxicated I am, the easier it will be.

"I love them," Emily says.

"Of course you do," Cath says. "You're the fancy one."

"Fancy because I don't eat crisps for dinner like Charlie or smother everything in brown sauce like you?"

"Exactly."

The waiter brings Cath's negroni, which she grabs like it's the last glass of water in the desert.

"Are you ladies ready to order or do you need more time?" the waiter asks.

"Let's order," Cath says. "We want some oysters, please."

"We could have more time," I say. "Chat a bit. I haven't really read the menu."

"We came here for oysters. Let's order oysters. I can't be late home anyway, I've been at Mum's and have loads of work to catch up on. This is an oyster pit stop for me, so let's get on with it."

The waiter looks between me and Cath, deciding Cath is the

more forceful and therefore the one who must be obeyed. "Which oysters would you like?" he asks. "We have the Carlingford Lough from Ireland or the Jersey Rocks from Jersey."

"There are different types of oysters?" I ask, panicking at how complicated the whole endeavour suddenly seems.

"We'll have the Jersey Rocks please," Emily says. "And can we get some Tabasco sauce on the side please?"

"And two portions of chips," Cath adds.

"Any main courses?" the waiter asks.

"No," Cath replies.

"Not for now, thanks," Emily says. The waiter nods and walks away.

"Ooh, I got this for you," I say, rummaging around in my bag, retrieving a hastily wrapped package and handing it to Cath.

"What's this?" she asks.

"Just something little. The box is for your mum – a peppermint candle, which is supposed to be good for nausea, some hand cream, which is supposed to be good for the dry skin and some Debbie Harry fluffy socks. I know how much she loves Debbie – though who knew you could get her face on a sock? And the book is for you, something I heard about on a podcast that I thought might be helpful."

Cath unwraps the book and examines it. *Take Care: looking after yourself while you look after others.* For a fraction of a second, it looks like she might cry, before she wipes it away and resets. "That's really kind, thanks, dude."

"You're so welcome. How is your mum?" I ask.

Cath takes another gulp of her negroni. "In denial, I think. She's

got a few sessions of chemo left and she seems to think this is the one that's going to cure her, even though the doctor was very clear on how that is very much not the case. She's talking about booking a holiday together next year – even got some brochures sent to her. It's mad. And what can you say to that? I just nod and pretend to play along and hope she doesn't actually book anything."

"Maybe she needs to tell herself that to get through this," Emily suggests, her tone gentle and soft. "Maybe the reality is too hard for her to comprehend."

"Of course, but at a certain point, she has to be realistic. *We* have to be realistic." Another gulp. "And Dan's being a total self-centred, selfish prick. He keeps bailing on appointments he's supposed to take her to, and bailing on just going round and checking in on her, getting some shopping in. He acts like because I don't have kids and I can work remotely, it's all on me."

"That's so tough for you," I say. "Have you tried talking to him about it?"

"It just ends up in a fight and I don't have the energy for it right now. I'll say something to him again if it carries on."

"Let us know if there's anything we can do," Emily says.

"Will do," Cath says.

There's a brief silence round the table, a shared acknowledgement that it's highly likely she won't and even if she did, it's highly unlikely we'd be able to contribute anything of any use, seeing as even getting away from the house for an evening takes military-level childcare planning.

"And how's the love life?" I ask, going for an upbeat change of subject and realising too late, from the sinking shoulders and dark-

cloud expression that descends on Cath, that this was a wrong move.

"Don't. Even," she says. "It's so bad it's funny. Except it's not funny because I'm living it. I honestly don't know why I even bother. The latest guy was a giant man baby who lives with his mum and spends most of his spare time on his PlayStation. I thought we left those guys behind once we got into our forties. And the one before couldn't take his eyes off my tits and asked me if I bleach my arsehole – on our first date."

"Wow." Emily mouths the word rather than saying it out loud.

"Sorry I asked," I say.

"You can make up for it by telling me about your list shenanigans," Cath says. "Come on, cheer me up with tales of your parkour attempts."

"Well, since you asked." I rub my hands together and pull the folded A3 list out of my bag with glee. "It hasn't got off to the best start as we had Easter and the kids were being idiots, but I've added a few more things, and I thought we could brainstorm this afternoon." I open it out, pushing glasses and cutlery and pristine napkins to the side to make room. "This is what I've got so far."

1. Have sex with George Clooney.
2. Take up parkour.
3. Swim with dolphins.
4. Climb Mount Everest.
5. Have a threesome.
6. Go to Thailand.
7. Eat caviar.

8. Eat an oyster.
9. Eat snails.
10. Have a martini.
11. Make a sex tape.
12. Kiss a girl.
13. Go to a sex club.
14. Use a sex toy.
15. Eat an insect.
16. Go scuba diving.
17. Do a spin class.
18. Learn to street dance.
19. Read War and Peace.
20. Get a tattoo.

Cath starts honking with laughter the minute she looks at the list, and I can tell Emily is struggling to keep it in.

"What?" I ask, not sure how to take this reaction.

"You're such a twat," Cath says. "A loveable twat, but a twat."

"Why? What's wrong with that? There's some good stuff on there."

"Define 'good'."

"There's some interesting, fulfilling, horizon-expanding things. And a real mix – some culinary, some sexy, some intelligent – you know, a real spectrum."

"Let's talk through a few shall we?" Cath grins, topping up our wines. "So, George?"

"Look, I know it's a long shot, but you never know, right? And he's just so gorgeous. Just imagine what that body would feel like."

"You sound pervy," Emily says.

"I don't get the George thing," Cath says. "Never have. He's too cheesy, white-toothed, all-American pin-up for me."

I sigh. "Seriously? Did you watch *ER*?"

"I do love a bit of George, as you know, but for me, he's been overtaken by Hugh Jackman," Emily says. "He's well fit in *The Greatest Showman*. Or Al Pacino?"

"Jesus, Emily!" I say. "Al Pacino is a pensioner."

"And George Clooney is . . . a spring chicken?" Cath says.

"Compared to Al Pacino, he is! Besides, George has got better with age, like a fine, silky-smooth wine. You have bad taste, Emily! You'll be suggesting Joe Biden and Hugh Hefner next."

"Hugh Hefner's dead," Emily says. "Otherwise . . ."

I make a vomit face.

"And climbing Mount Everest?" Cath asks, grinning. "For someone who couldn't make it round the Race for Life and gets out of breath going up stairs, that's quite a stretch."

"Doesn't it cost like sixty grand or something?" Emily adds.

"Sixty grand to climb a mountain?" I say. "That's mad! And for the record, I *did* make it round the Race for Life, I just walked it." I take a sip of my wine, deflated. "This wasn't quite the support I was hoping for, guys."

The waiter brings some fancy bread and fancy butter, we order another bottle of wine, then I remember the oysters will be here soon and start shitting myself all over again.

"Sorry, you're right," Emily says. "How about putting an easier mountain on the list – one that won't cost your life savings and is doable to train for? Scafell Pike? Or Ben Nevis?"

"Great!" I say. "Now you're talking! Solutions, people, I need solutions, not problems."

"And that's something you could do with James," Emily smiles. "Isn't he quite partial to a mountain?"

"Hmm, he'd probably prefer to cycle up one, but yeah, anything outdoorsy and he'd be all over it. Though he'd probably make us do it in January and wild camp or something – the more extreme, the better."

"You could kill two birds with one stone and do the sex toy one while you're at it," Emily laughs.

"Two climaxes for the price of one?" Cath chuckles. "You'll probably find that butt plugs in tents is a niche fetish," she says way too loudly.

"You've got some good, easy ones on there," Emily says. "Eating caviar, and oysters, and snails. And the martini. I mean, we could do that one now and then you'd be able to cross two off the list?"

"I knew I invited you for a reason!"

"Do you not think you should put something . . ." Cath pauses, searching for the word. "Philanthropic on there?"

"What do you mean?" I ask, not entirely sure what the word means.

"You know, like, something that's giving back, something that helps other people, not just yourself. Like selfless Emily, working for a charity, doing good in the world."

Emily raises a glass to herself.

"I read an article about how that's one of the keys to happiness," Cath continues. "Community, connection and giving back – or something like that."

"God, you sound like one of James's philosophy books!" I say. "But OK, I like it. I'm adding volunteering."

"What about something that will make you stronger and feel better about yourself?" Emily says. "Like, I know you've got a spin class on there but what about boxing? Or weightlifting – I keep seeing loads of women our age take up weightlifting."

"Menopause," Cath says, flatly.

"Perimenopause," Emily corrects.

"Shut up," I say.

"Seriously," Emily says. "It's one of the best things you can do to counteract the diminishing bone strength."

"Well, I'm not going through the perimenopause and I don't want to look like Popeye," I say. "But I'm down for the boxing."

"Can we go back to the sex ones please?" Cath asks, smirking. "I have some questions."

"Oh here we go, Debbie Downer."

"No, no. Not being a downer. Just trying to help you with logistics. And maybe interrogate the motivations a bit?"

"Go on."

"My first question would be, are you OK, hun? Cos, by the look of this list, you are one thirsty lady who hasn't been serviced in a while."

Emily chokes on her wine. "Ew! Serviced?"

"It makes me sound like a vending machine," I say.

"Or a car," Emily says.

"A twenty-year-old rusty Ford Fiesta," I say.

"Forty-four-year-old, actually, and I don't think Ford Fiestas make it that long," Cath laughs.

"Very funny."

"Sorry, I couldn't resist. Seriously, though – the sex club, sex tape too? Where did all this come from? And do you have a secret lesbian proclivity you haven't told us about?"

The waiter seats a couple, white-haired and elegant, on a table two feet along from us. The lady smiles at us, her diamond ring catching the light from one of the chandeliers as the waiter takes her coat. I wonder if she's happy – she looks like she is, coming out for a nice romantic lunch, dripping in diamonds. I wonder if she has kids, imagine that they're probably grown up and good-looking and successful now – lawyers, or surgeons, or investment bankers with beautiful houses and maybe their own good-looking kids. I wonder if she ever had to clean spat-out cat food off the carpet. I conclude, from the size of the diamond, the cashmere jumper and the generally unhaggard look that she likely did not – that would've been the nanny's job.

"Oh my god." Cath sees me staring at the woman, leans in closer. "Are you into older women?"

"Shut up," I say, not sure if she's joking or not. "No, I don't have a secret lesbian proclivity – I just think, I dunno, James and I got together when we were so young. Seventeen – we were babies! And apart from a few random inexperienced school boys before him—"

"One of whom's willy was so small Charlie didn't know if he was fingering her or had gone full penetration," Emily adds, laughing.

"Ah, Jason. He was hot though."

"He was."

"Anyway – as I was saying, there's a lot of stuff I haven't done that seems like it might be fun and maybe dying without even trying it is pretty tragic?"

"What does James make of this threesome idea?" Emily asks, serious now.

"I haven't mentioned it yet, obviously."

"What does he think of the list, in general?" Cath asks.

I shrug. "I don't think he's taking it seriously, but he's happy for me to be getting on with it. As long as I also look after the kids and the house and buy the groceries and feed everyone and do all the laundry."

I see two waiters heading towards us with our food and my stomach suddenly sinks.

"Your oysters," one of them says, placing them on the table with a flourish that is nearly a bow. The second waiter distributes the chips and Tabasco sauce. "Can I get you anything else?"

"Can we have a dirty martini please?" Emily says.

I want to ask for a barf bucket, but realise that's probably not the done thing in an establishment like this. The waiters walk off. I gulp my wine and try not to make eye contact with the slimy grossness in front of me.

"Right then," Emily says, rubbing her hands together.

"I can't look at them," I say, glancing at them and then wishing I hadn't.

"They look like vaginas," Cath says. "But that's your new thing now anyway, right?"

Emily nudges her. "Dude, if yours looks like that, may I suggest going to a doctor ASAP."

"Maybe not vaginas – brains. Or snot. Some part of the anatomy. They look very *bodily*," Cath says.

I feel my stomach churning already. "Not helping, Cath!"

"Just do it already," Cath says. "It's fine – they just taste a bit unpleasant. You've swallowed worse."

"Still not helping," I say.

"I'll get one lined up for you," Emily says.

She takes one of the oysters I'm trying not to make eye contact with, spoons some kind of sauce from a little pot in the middle into it and then adds a few drops of Tabasco and hands it to me.

"Don't look at it – just have it in one big swallow."

I take a large glug of wine, keeping my head turned away from the oyster.

"OK, here goes," I say. "One, two . . . I can't do it!"

Emily laughs. "I'm having flashbacks to your first snog."

It's a sad and true fact – I was, for some reason, petrified of kissing with tongues. I was with Mike Dowd for three months before I kissed him, a couple of times doing a big, dramatic countdown and then bailing at the last minute.

"You're such a wuss," Cath says.

"Fine. Here goes. Again." I mean it this time. "One, two, three."

I hold my nose and slurp the oyster down as fast as possible.

The texture is, indeed, like snot. And like something alive. I shake my head and grab my water and then my wine, fighting the urge to retch, trying to get the taste out of my mouth.

Cath claps. "There you go – not that bad."

"I feel like I've swallowed a load of mucus. Or a tonsil – a salty tonsil. Ugh." I can feel it in my windpipe still, threatening to come back up. I sip more wine. "It's like when you're in the sea and get pummelled by a wave and take a mouthful of saltwater. But with a hint of garlic and Tabasco. Why do people eat those for fun?"

"An acquired taste, I guess," Emily says. "Some of us are just more sophisticated than others."

"Jesus, if you freaked out like that before eating an oyster, imagine what you'd be like before a threesome," Cath says.

"Which is eating something different," Emily laughs.

"And yet similar."

They crumple into hysterical laughter, Emily gasping for breath, Cath banging her hand on the table. The waiter delivers my dirty martini with a curious smile. The sophisticated couple are so sophisticated they don't even flinch or shoot us a look. The added vagina permutations threaten to bring my gullet oyster back up. I take a handful of chips, sip more wine, willing it to stay where it is.

"You guys haven't had a threesome, have you?" I ask. "I feel like it's something that would've come up."

"So to speak," Cath says, giggling.

"My god woman, get your mind out of the gutter!"

"Sorry." Still giggling.

"I haven't," Emily says. "And I have no interest in having one. Not at this point in my life. I honestly don't understand why people would."

A brief silence, the darkness in Emily's face and the weight of her words implying that there is Something Else Going On There.

"I have," Cath says, all nonchalant.

"WHAT?" Emily and I shout in unison.

"It was right after uni. In my crazy days. And honestly, like the bloody oysters, it's not all it's cracked up to be. It mostly just felt awkward and fumbling and the logistics are a nightmare."

"What was the ratio?" I ask. "And why didn't you tell us?"

"It was with two guys, who I vaguely recall seemed weirdly homophobic – in that, they kind of danced around each other and made sure not to touch penises. They both came really quickly and weren't that bothered about whether I was having a good time. Which I guess is pretty standard hetero sex, anyway. I can hardly remember it, other than that it was disappointing. I didn't tell you because you're both prudes."

Emily and I look at each other in faux outrage.

"Honestly," Cath says. "Do yourself a favour – forget the threesome and get yourself a vibrator. The fact you have never owned one is, by the way, tragic. As you'll soon see."

"Just imagine, right," Emily says, her words slurring slightly. "Imagine if James was up for having a threesome and you had to watch him having sex with another woman – or another man. Do you really think you'd like that?" She sips her wine, her cheeks suddenly flushed, her eyes doing the blinky thing she does just before she cries.

"Emily?" I reach out to touch her wrist. "Is everything OK with you and Rick?"

She scrunches her napkin tightly, her knuckles turning white.

"Dude, we're here for you. No judgement," Cath says.

"Things are fine," Emily says. "The same. Things are the same. Except maybe a bit worse. I don't know. I don't know how much is me imagining things."

"What do you mean?" I ask. "Imagining what things?"

"Things like Rick not loving me any more."

"What makes you think he doesn't love you any more?" Cath asks.

"He never cuddles me, or shows me any affection, actually. He never wants to go on dates or weekends away. I suggested we get my parents to have the kids one time so we could have a romantic weekend away and he said he'd prefer we went away as a family. He never comes to bed with me, always stays up late, and sometimes sleeps in the spare room which he says is so that he doesn't wake me up. He's out a lot more. Loads of things. So many things."

We listen and consider, knowing what we say next is important and could end up pushing Emily away.

"That sounds really tough," I say. "Marriage is hard, you know. Especially once you have kids. I think some of that sounds really normal stuff – the going to bed separately, the affection easing off. I think a lot of that is just life taking its toll – you both work really hard and must be constantly knackered. Aren't all married couples who have been together and had kids basically just flatmates who very occasionally bang? James and I spend a lot of evenings in separate rooms watching different things – I just want to veg and watch *Housewives* and he wants to watch some superior, pretentious subtitled documentary about Important Things that I don't have the energy for at that point in the night."

"You've never had the energy for subtitled documentaries about Important Things," Cath says.

"Well, OK. My point is that you don't have to do everything together. Space is OK. It's standard at this point, no?"

"Don't look at me," Cath says. "I've never had a relationship last beyond two years. And the way you're describing it, I'm kind of glad."

I glare at her to let her know she's being unhelpful.

"Relationships have rough patches though, don't they? This could just be a rough patch. Maybe you could do something romantic to surprise him – get a babysitter booked in, go for a nice dinner, wear some fancy lingerie. I feel like that's what they'd do in the movies."

"We haven't had sex for eleven months," Emily says.

"Shit," Cath and I say at the same time.

"Every time I try to initiate it, he pushes me away. He's a man. That's not normal. It's always been me pushing him away when he's trying it on five times a day."

"Shit," is all I manage to say, wide-mouthed and wide-eyed at this revelation.

"Shit," Cath echoes.

"Why didn't you tell us all of this?" I ask.

"I've been hoping it would get better," she says. "And I know you guys have never been his biggest fans."

"That's not . . ." I say at the same time as Cath says, "Well, we kind of . . ."

There's a pause. A brief silence where we all seem to glance at the table.

"Do you—" Cath starts, then pauses, teetering on the edge of whether to speak the words or not. "Do you think he's getting it somewhere else?"

"It's crossed my mind," Emily says, swallowing a teetering cry. "And the thought of it makes me feel sick."

There's another pause. A stiff silence. They both take a sip of wine. I have a mouthful of my martini, which tastes like lighter fluid.

"I might take threesomes off the list," I pronounce, once I've stopped coughing. "You're right, it'd probably be gross watching James have sex with someone else at this point in our lives, especially as that person would probably have way less wiggly bits and a tighter vagina than me."

"And a more respectable, less Amazonian bush," Cath says. It makes Emily laugh, which is worth taking the hit for.

"Ooh that's a good one – I'm putting a Brazilian wax on the list," I say.

"Make it a Hollywood or it's not worth putting on the list."

"Oh Jesus, is that the full shebang one?"

"Yup."

I write it down and make myself finish the rest of my martini, wincing at the strength of it.

"I've really got to go, dudes, sorry," Cath says. "Why don't you two take your oyster buzz and go vibrator shopping? A good vibrator and you'll realise we don't need shitty men anyway."

7

I'M BACK in familiar territory, it's *ER* George. I'm lying on a hospital bed in just a thin, papery hospital gown and in he comes – purposeful stride, green scrubs, white lab coat, stethoscope hung round his neck. He flashes me one of his crooked smiles, his mischievous eyes gleaming at me and then takes his stethoscope and presses it gently to my chest – except it's more boob than chest – and it feels electric. We kiss – he's tender, passionate. His arms start roaming, lightly brushing my nipple, then further still, under my gown. His fingers slip expertly inside my knickers.

My body glows, white hot. I press the button, turn it up a notch, ready to ride the wave, except it's the wrong button, or I've pressed it too high because all of a sudden I'm tipped over the edge and there's an explosion of sensation that rolls over every part of my body and I'm coming, when I wasn't quite ready for it.

"Mum?"

My eyes spring open, mid full-body, uncontrollable shudder.

Chloe is stood at my bedroom door, eyes wide in horror. A school-uniformed version of *The Scream*.

"I was—" I fumble under the covers, trying to work out how to turn the damn thing off and stop the extremely loud buzzing. "I was just. Nap. I was having a nap."

Eventually I make it stop. My cheeks are burning with a post-

orgasm glow doubled with deep, deep shame. I don't know whether to laugh or cry. Probably cry. Crying seems more appropriate.

Chloe shakes her head at me and turns to leave, horror still etched on her face. "Oh my *god*, Mum!"

I spring into action, pulling my knickers and lounge pants up, running my Rampant Rabbit under the tap but not making eye contact with it because I now feel dirty and ashamed. I wrap it in a hand towel and shove it to the very back of my knicker drawer, ensuring there is a mountain of underwear on top of it. I splash cold water on my face, put myself back in mum mode and head downstairs.

Chloe is making herself a sandwich, buttering bread with a vigour that could either be anger or a desperate need to get the job done quickly and escape.

"I wasn't expecting you home," I say, aiming for casual.

"Clearly." She slaps a piece of ham on the bread. "I have a free period. I'd forgotten my history coursework."

She rams the pieces of bread together, shoves the ham and butter back in the fridge and storms past me. I make myself a cup of tea as nonchalantly as I can manage, while dealing with the inner turmoil of wondering if I need to have a conversation with my teenage daughter about masturbation. I could let it go, pretend nothing happened, and I was, indeed, having a nap. But Chloe's not stupid. She knows. And I know she knows. So I think that means I have to confront the situation. Every cell in my body shrivels at the thought of it.

I take my tea through to the living room where Chloe is on the sofa eating her sandwich. The TV is still on from when I was

watching before – the presenters now interviewing a lady who has sex with a ghost. I turn it off.

"Chloe, can we—"

"I don't want to talk about it, Mum," she says. "It's gross. I can't unsee that."

I scour the depths of my memory for the segment I'd seen on *This Morning* a while ago about how to talk to your children about 'these things'.

"Darling, it's not gross," I say. "Masturbation is perfectly natural." I say 'masturbation' in a stunted whisper, my mouth forming the word wide and dramatically like I'm performing for a lip reader.

"It's natural for teenagers, not middle-aged bored housewives with a husband. In the middle of the day. Honestly, Mum. Get a job." Disdain drips from every word.

I go to open my mouth – something about how I did have a job before I gave up my whole career for my children, or something about how having a husband counts for nothing when you hardly have sex, or even something about how my husband has never made me come like that rabbit does, but I decide against it.

"I've lost my appetite." She slams her plate on the coffee table, grabs her bag and storms out of the door.

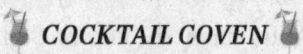

COCKTAIL COVEN

Me: *So, my daughter just walked in on me masturbating.*

Cath: *PAHAHAHAHAHAHAHA*

Cath: *This shit could only happen to you.*

Me: *I'm mortified.*

Cath: *I bet not as mortified as she is.*

Me: *She hates me.*

Cath: *Tell her to get a sense of humour.*

Me: *I mean, it's not that funny for her.*

Cath: *It'll make a good anecdote for your 70th birthday speech.*

Me: *I told her it was natural. She told me to get a job.*

Cath: *HAHAHAHAHAHAHA*

Cath: *Did you explain it's your first vibrator and you're just a bit overexcited?*

Me: *My vagina is red raw. Can you masturbate too much?*

Cath: *LOL*

Me: *Seriously. It's hurting to walk. Oh Christ, I'm totally going to have to go to a doctor and explain I've broken*

my vagina because I've been masturbating too much aren't I?

Cath: *Please do.*

Me: *I'm supposed to be going to a bloody spin class later!!*

Cath: *Sorry, what?!*

Me: *It's on my list. And Cool Mum (Dorit) who got me drunk at the Easter Fayre persuaded me to go.*

Cath: *You really do extremes don't you – sex with George Clooney, spin class.*

Me: *Both give you an adrenaline high and make you sweaty.*

Me: *You OK, Ems?*

Me: *Feel free to take the piss out of my vagina, should you wish.*

It feels strange wearing my activewear to actually do something active. Strange in a good way though, like this new, sporty version of me is a step up. It would probably have felt even better if my vagina wasn't burning with every step, the leopard-print leggings hugging that bit too snuggly. It's a gorgeous day – blue skies, fluffy clouds, bright sunshine. I have a spring in my step as I walk down

our road to the high street. I pop in to Vera's next door to bring her bins in – she's ninety-two and can hardly see or hear and I don't really know how to talk to old people because we all die young in my family, but she lives alone and has no kids, and I like how she sings along to show tunes really loudly (probably because she can't hear), so I make an exception for her. I smile at Bev from eighty-three, the pensioner who makes her own kefir and offers it up for free on the street WhatsApp and likes to mention, at every opportunity, the Ukrainian family she took in. I say hi to the postman. I don't know his name and I always try to avoid letting him know I'm in because he's prone to long, slightly sexist doorstep chats if given half a chance, but I also try and keep vaguely on his good side as he has the power to take packages back to the sorting office which is a giant pain in the arse.

The high street emits its usual buzz of middle-class, middle-of-the-day action: couples stepping out of the over-priced deli with over-priced flat whites; sophisticated silver-haired ladies in designer trench coats holding bundles of fancy fresh flowers, on their way to get their nails done at the posh salon that serves you Prosecco with your over-priced mani-pedi. As I walk past the many cafes and estate agents, I keep my head down, hoping not to bump into any other mums. Tollingford is a nice place – a lovely place, even – and I do know that, but there's something about it that makes me feel claustrophobic, like if I don't venture into Zone One at least once a week, I'll use up all my air and shrivel and die. Probably with an over-priced flat white in my well-manicured hand.

Dorit is waiting in the foyer of the leisure centre, looking all kinds of sporting awesome in her perfectly matched leggings and

sports bra/crop top combo. She's not the typical Tollingford tiny and toned sports type – she's got an almost Kim K arse, big boobs and rolls of fat between her leggings and crop top – and she wears it with a confidence that is inspiring. I pull at the oversized Ironman T-shirt I borrowed from James, feeling suddenly ridiculous.

"Yes, girl!" She grins when she sees me, going in for a big hug. Which, frankly, feels a bit much for a mid-week afternoon spin session. "Are you ready for this?"

I nod yes, my vagina screams no.

"Can I get a HELL YES!" she shouts.

"Hell yes," I murmur back.

"Girl, you're going to have to do better than that in there. Zavvy is a loud and proud ball-breaker. You have to give it good."

A nugget of dread blooms in my stomach, pre-oyster vibes taking over my body. At least this time there's no chance I'll retch and cause a scene in a fancy restaurant. Although, there's a strong chance I'll throw up and cause a scene in the spin class instead. It's only forty-five minutes. I can survive forty-five minutes of pedalling. Surely.

"Do you come here a lot?" I ask. Dorit's taken a pair of the fancy clip-on shoes offered. I declined, scared at the thought of being chained to my bike and not able to escape if needed. And because I could totally see myself, with alarming clarity, fall off my bike, crumple to the floor, and have my legs (broken by that point) sticking out at crazy angles, still attached to the bike.

"Not loads, but most weeks," she says. "Don't look so worried – it's fun."

"Exercise? Fun? I don't think so."

She loops her arm through mine, grabs us a towel each. "You'll see – I bet you'll love it. You watch, you'll become a spin addict and buy yourself all the fancy gear and take it super seriously." She lowers her voice. "Like those guys."

In the dimly lit studio, two men in full fancy Lycra are by the side of their bikes stretching, their faces set with a determination and intensity more befitting of the London Marathon than a Tollingford spin class. It's competitive stretching, I realise, as one of them deftly leans his torso so far to the side he almost makes a semicircle and the other one looks on with a glint of defeat. I worry they might burst into the splits at any moment.

I look at Dorit, suppressing a laugh. "Wow."

"I know, right? That's men for you. Everything's a competition."

"Well, if we're talking drinking gin and watching *Housewives*, I might win," I say. "Spinning, not so much."

"I spin *so* that I can drink the gin and watch *Housewives* without feeling guilty."

"I like your style."

"OK then, gang!" Thumping music suddenly fills the room as Zavvy skip-jumps in, clapping his hands above his head and making a weird grunting noise, which I believe is intended to hype things up, but which I actually find slightly sexual. Maybe it's all the masturbating.

He's so full-on, stereotypical spin-class instructor, it's hard not to laugh – super tight (extremely revealing) Lycra, bulging calves, curated man bun and a glare that says fun but fierce. I navigate Dorit towards the bikes on the back row, not wanting my shame to be full frontal. I watch as she expertly gets onto her bike, clips

herself in, places her water bottle in the holder and positions her towel around her neck. I copy, before realising I can't actually get on my bike seat as I am the approximate size of a hobbit. I make a failed attempt at adjusting the seat height, on the verge of deciding the universe is confirming this whole thing is a stupid idea, when Zavvy comes jogging over and does it for me.

"First time?" he asks, in a way I think might be intentionally sexy.

"How could you tell?" I reply, not sure if I'm accidentally return flirting.

"You'll love it." He pats the bike seat. "Try it now."

I inelegantly mount the bike, trying not to wince as my vagina makes contact with the seat.

"So, this tells you your RPM – generally you want to be between eighty and one-hundred-and-ten. This is your miles covered," he indicates on the screen, "and this is your resistance – I'll tell you when you need to push that up a notch."

"Uh, OK, great," I say.

"I won't take it easy on you just because it's your first time," he says, winking and jogging away to the front of the class.

For some reason, perhaps all the masturbating, I salute and say, "Roger that."

Dorit laughs at me.

* * *

The spin class passes by in a blur of sweat, shouting, bike sprints, banging techno and a throbbing vagina. Dorit starts the class

trying to carry out a conversation with me but soon realises I can barely breathe, let alone chat about whether Kelsey's mum is an alcoholic. I think I'm going to pass out at least three times, believe I'm going to just get up and leave five times over and imagine what sex with Zavvy would be like every time he stands up to cycle. (I decide probably not as good as you'd initially think and definitely way more energetic than is optimal.) I cheat with my resistance through the whole class, looking at the stretch brothers taking it way too seriously and feeling the warm glow of being a spin rebel.

Against all the odds, I finish the class. And against even more odds, I feel strangely good afterwards. Not physically good – I can barely move, everything below my waist is on fire, and I'm so drenched in sweat I look like I've come straight from the shower – but mentally good. I survived and I achieved something that's better for you than my usual achievement of four back-to-back *Housewives*. I'm smashing it.

"Yessssssss, babe!" Dorit screeches, elegantly tapping her towel at the few dewy drops of sweat on her neck. "You did it! What did you think?"

I smile, nearly collapsing as I prise my legs, now useless blobs of undefined flesh, off the bike. "It was OK, you know."

"OK? It was great. I saw you digging it."

"'Digging it' is probably a step too far, but yeah, it wasn't all hideous and I feel good now I've done it."

"Great. And now we drink."

I laugh, thinking she's joking, then realise, with excitement, that she isn't. "Now?"

"Why not. I haven't got anything else on today, the kids are

busy after school. How about you? Can you shake them off?"

I do some calculations, working out that James is away and Jack has photography club and Felix normally goes to Harrison's on a Tuesday and Chloe, well, it's probably best we give each other some space at this point anyway.

"Sure. I can go for one." My stomach flutters at the total spontaneity of it. "I mean, we deserve it."

"Exactly."

We go to the bar of the Italian on the high street. At its core, it's a naff eighties eatery with orange pine tables, breadsticks and serving staff who put on fake accents, but for some reason, it's become a beloved Tollingford institution, as if its naffness is somehow ironic. It's open all day and doesn't feel as brash as going to a pub in the middle of the afternoon.

Dorit places a bottle of wine on the table. "It was only, like, fifty pence more than two glasses," she says, registering my surprise. "We don't have to drink it all. Though, let's face it, we probably will. I remember you giving it large at the rum bar."

She gives me a friendly nudge, like we're old friends. And it does kind of feel like we are. She has something about her that makes me relax, like I've met my mum-friend soulmate. She's not uptight like most of the other mums – she's got serious free-spirited, live-for-the-moment vibes; the embodiment of one of those god-awful 'Live, Laugh, Love' cushions. She pours us enormous glasses and raises hers. "Cheers. To popping your spin cherry!"

"Cheers!"

"So, come on then, why suddenly decide to try a spin class? Not that there's anything wrong with the spontaneous wish to exercise,

obviously, it's just you don't strike me as—"

"As the exercising type?" I laugh. "What gave it away – my husband's oversized T-shirt, my threadbare leggings or the fact I nearly passed out after cycling for more than ten minutes?"

"All of the above?"

"This is going to sound silly." I pause, wondering if I'm ready to unleash my inner middle-aged turmoil on this very kind and cool and put-together woman who will probably run a mile when she realises how boring and yet also unhinged I am.

"Go on. I'm here for silly."

I take a gulp of my wine. "OK, so. I turned forty-four last month and, I dunno, for some reason I suddenly felt old. Like, proper old."

"Oh my god!" she shrieks. "Let me guess – your eyesight's going? Your joints are starting to feel stiff when you get up in the morning? No one – not even the lechiest of lechy men try to feel you up, or catcall you or even acknowledge you exist? And then of course all the perimenopause shite – the heavy periods, the not sleeping, the being so irritable you want to punch your husband's face in."

"YES! That. All of that," I say, excited at the recognition. "Except I'm not there with the perimenopause stuff yet. I just generally want to punch my husband's face in."

"I hear you." She bangs the table with her hand in enthusiasm. "I've been there, done that, got the well-worn, stained T-shirt and come out the other side triumphant. There's nothing silly about that – it's actually super sensible to decide you want to do something about feeling old."

"Well," I say. I realise I could leave it there, but something in me – perhaps the afternoon wine, which totally hits differently to

evening wine – makes me forge on. "That's not the silly bit. The silly bit is that I'm doing one of those lists – I've written a few of them in the past but never finished them – twenty-five things to do before you're twenty-five, thirty things to do before you're thirty – those lists. But this time, I'm going to do it. I had a friend who died recently and it just made me realise that you can't put stuff off, we have to do it while we can."

"Oh god, I'm so sorry." Dorit puts her hand on my arm, scrunches her face in sympathy. "That must be tough."

I realise I should probably explain I hadn't spoken to said dead friend for twenty-five years, but the moment passes and now it's too late and I have to sit in my shame and lean into the exaggeration which, to be fair to me, wasn't really an intended exaggeration so therefore technically not my fault.

"So, yeah." I try and move the conversation away from dead friends. "I realised I'm not super happy and my life isn't what I thought it would be—"

"AMEN to that!"

"And I don't want to look back and have regrets and wish I did things while I could still, ya know, walk or see or whatever."

"That's dark, but I get it."

"So I've written a list – started one, at least. And I'm determined to finish it this time."

"And you put going to a spin class on that list?" She laughs. A big, honking laugh. "I love you for that."

"I've always been a bit scared of spin classes. Organised exercise in general, actually. And spin seems to be a thing so I figured it would be a good starting point."

"And now you can tick it off!"

"Indeed."

"So, what else is on the list?" She rubs her hands together and it makes me feel, for the first time, like my endeavour is not a completely ridiculous middle-aged crisis in written form. "Let me help you!"

"Lots of different things," I say, conscious that even though it is in my bag, we are definitely too early on in our friendship for me to let her see it in all its sex with George Clooney and anal glory. "I had my first oyster and first martini the other day – they were on there. And I know, forty-four is a ludicrous age to be having either of those things for the first time." I don't mention the vibrator. She pours us each another glass of wine and looks at me expectantly. "OK, let's see – climbing a mountain, surfing, swimming with dolphins – standard stuff. I was going to put things like go to the Grand Canyon and the Pyramids but realistically only one trip might happen, and they both seemed like a bit of a waste, so I put Thailand. I've always wanted to go to Thailand. That was on my twenty-five list. And thirty and forty lists."

"Oh my god, I love Thailand! You have to go. It's incredible. And then you could put things like having a drink with a ladyboy and seeing a woman shoot a ping-pong ball out of her vagina!"

I nearly spit my drink out, as does the bartender who, I notice, has been quietly hovering nearby, sipping his coffee and pretending to clean glasses for a while.

"I thought the ping-pong ball was just an urban myth?"

"It's not," she says. "I've seen it! I nearly tried it once but got worried my vagina would just suck it up and then I'd have to go to

the hospital and explain I got a ping-pong ball stuck up my vag. Though, they see worse all the time."

The bartender blushes and shuffles off.

"Add them to the list!" she shouts. "Add them to the list!"

I make a note of them on my phone, not sure that I particularly fancy ladyboys or ping-ponging vaginas, aware that neither constitute a Great Wonder of the World, but also not wanting to offend Dorit. Dorit, who, by this point into the wine is by far my biggest list cheerleader with an enthusiasm and delight that is completely infectious.

"I knew we were kindred spirits as soon I saw you," she says.

I want to interrogate this statement – to ask what it was about me that led her to that conclusion – my non-active activewear, my refusal to make eye contact with anyone or the period stain that seeped through my trousers, perhaps. But I let it slide and enjoy the compliment, wondering if the fact that Cool Mum thinks I'm a kindred spirit makes me, by proxy, cool.

"I am SO here for this list! I love it! I love you!" she says, with another hand slam. "Here's to making our lives better and for not taking any more of the crap we're dealt. And the boredom and the lost dreams and ambitions. And for not putting up with stupid bloody men!"

I cheers, revelling in the spirit of her delivery, if not the exact sentiment.

I send Chloe a pleading text asking her to feed the boys and we order another bottle of wine. We talk about the list, about the naïve hopes and dreams we had in our twenties, about what we were like before kids, about motherhood and how it can be intensely, bone-

achingly tough and unrewarding, but we're never allowed to say that out loud, about husbands not pulling their weight, about the point in a marriage when your spouse starts to feel like your lodger, about periods, about the unfairness of research into women's health issues, about the coil and cystitis and if most people wipe from their bums to their vaginas or their vaginas to their bum and what it would be like to have sex with Zavvy (too energetic, we both agree), and what it would be like to have sex with George and whether Kelsey's mum is an alcoholic and I leave with a giant grin on my face and a heart that feels all warm and glowy. Though that might also be the wine. And possibly the masturbating.

8

I STARE AT myself in the mirror and see an old lady staring back at me. My mousy-brown, uninteresting hair hangs limp and dry, the blonde highlights I experimented with having long since disappeared. My eyes seem to have burrowed somewhere into my skull, giving a punched-in-the-face aesthetic and my lips, which I'm sure used to be OK, now seem to be thin and riddled with smoker's lines. I shake my head, wishing I'd listened to Olivia Sweeney who warned us of these very same lines back when we took up smoking in year nine.

Trying not to make eye contact with myself, I slather my face and neck in special microcurrent absorbing, extremely expensive gel before using the extremely expensive derma-sculpt pulsating machine thing I bought that has done sweet sod all to lift and tone, as promised.

I apply the expensive toner followed by the expensive serum followed by the expensive moisturiser followed by the expensive pore minimiser. I've given up on eye creams, after trying approximately three-hundred-and-six and coming to the conclusion that nothing can be done to save me from the giant suitcase-sized bags that have taken up residence under my eyes and are apparently there to stay. I've researched it – drinking less helps reduce puffiness, and less salt and more sleep, but other than that, it's basically tough titties and

largely genetics. I'm adding it to the things to be mad at my parents for, along with my big nose, thin lips, not letting me go to Grant Vaughan's eighteenth, never getting me a Mr Frosty, despite it being on my Christmas list for five years in a row, and living too far away to be of any help with childcare.

I gently pull the skin round my eyes, the bags disappearing, and suddenly look younger and fresher faced and more like myself – or what I remember as myself. Sometimes I feel like crying when I look in the mirror. Often, actually. But tonight, I don't have time to wallow in my former not-particular glory. We're already running late for dinner at Emily's, and as is usual for a night out, after ferrying kids to and from clubs, and grocery shopping and feeding the children, I now smell like sausages and have roughly seven minutes to attempt to make myself vaguely presentable. So I do my general crap make-up routine – a dab of concealer under the eyes (not too much or it settles in the wrinkles), tinted moisturiser (I've never managed to use foundation without it looking comically bad and like my head isn't connected to the rest of my body), eyeliner (I read in *Good Housekeeping* that all women over thirty-five should apply a smudged line of eyeliner to the bottom of their eyelids to look younger), a fingertip of brown eyeshadow and one coat of mascara. I look at the end result, wishing that at some point during my forty-four years on Earth I'd learnt how to properly apply make-up. Maybe I should add that to my list – learn how to do my make-up.

Grabbing my shoes (small heel as I'm not using public transport and won't need to walk more than three minutes), I run down the stairs.

"James?"

No response.

I open the door to the front room and see him sat in his armchair, eyes closed, hands on his legs, palms up. It takes a lot of constraint not to shout "Oh, for Christ's sake", as I close the door quietly behind me. One of his new things, along with Ironmans, local politics, philosophy and listening to The Smiths (on vinyl) on repeat – meditating. I'm genuinely happy he's finding his inner peace, but my god, he chooses the worst times to do it. Twice a day, the worst times.

"It's my turn to sit in the corner," I hear Felix shout from the snug. "I'll smash your face in, idiot!"

I consider going into the front room and meditating myself, thinking how amazing it would be to just switch off the background noise. Which is basically the boys fighting in one way or another. Sadly, I know that if I leave them, it will only escalate until at least one of them cries or has a nosebleed, or both, and then it's a way less salvageable situation.

"Boys!" I say, in the stern way I say it approximately two hundred times a day.

Felix is sat on Jack's head. Jack is grabbing Felix's balls. There is much leg thrashing and general chaos. It is a two out of ten on the rough and tumble scale.

"Felix, get off you brother please. Jack, let go of your brother's balls."

"It's my turn to sit in the corner!" Felix says, very much not getting off Jack's face.

I sigh. "Do I need to start doing a rota for who gets the corner?

Or do I need to ban both of you from sitting in the corner?"

"No," Felix grunts, giving one last bounce before dismounting.

Jack punches him in the leg as he moves to the other side of the sofa, which makes Felix retaliate with a slap. I erect a wall of sofa cushions between them.

"Neither of you are to cross this boundary. Do you understand?"

"Idiot!" Jack says. "Not you, Mum."

"We don't use that word, thank you."

"Neeb!"

"Boys!" I go louder. "If you can't just sit and watch TV in the same room then you'll have to go straight to bed."

I am reluctant to actually see this through and I know, as I say it, that all that happens when I make them go to their rooms is that winding each other up is simply transferred to another location and is often worse because there is no TV to distract them. But I have to threaten them with something.

"Chloe!" I shout up the stairs.

Nothing.

I try again, louder, not caring if my shouting disrupts James's meditation.

Still nothing. I text her.

> Me: *COME DOWN NOW PLEASE. WE'RE ABOUT TO GO.*

Eventually, she stomps down, frowning with such severity it's like I've just asked her to walk over hot coals or donate a kidney.

"You all right?" I ask, with forced cheer. "You look nice."

"It's my old joggers and one of Dad's jumpers, Mum." Eye roll.

"Well, it suits you. You can pull off loungewear which, let me tell you, is a skill." She leans against the banister, tapping at her phone. I'm struck by how grown-up she looks and instantaneously miss the mini-me who used to wear spotty dresses and pigtails and take her knickers off and do forward rolls whenever I took her to a friend's house for coffee.

"Come here a minute," I say. She snaps her head up and scowls. Only a low level one though. "Come onnnnn," I coax. "You've got a thing..."

She slumps down the stairs and when she's close enough I pull her in for a hug.

"Mum!" she says, recoiling.

"I just want to give my lovely daughter a hug, is that too much to ask?"

I squeeze her a little tighter and eventually she relents. She doesn't hug me back, but she gives in to me hugging her – which I'll take.

"Isn't this nice?" I say, relishing the moment. It's been a while.

"Just so I can plan, how long is this likely to last?" she says, with something like a laugh.

"Not long. We're going in a minute." I release her, buoyed by the physical contact. "Can you make sure they don't sneak on to devices please. And get them upstairs at half eight for teeth and reading time, lights out by nine-fifteen. And you'll probably need to be down here cos they're in wrestling mode.'

"I'm sure they're fine watching TV." She's back to huff mode. "I've got stuff to do upstairs."

"Kissy kissy with Rupey!" Jack shouts through.

"Shut up, butt munch," Chloe says. "He's not even here."

"Yeah, shut up, butt munch," Felix parrots.

"Idiot!"

And just like that, the cushion wall becomes weaponised and a pillow fight breaks out.

"Right then, are we ready?" James asks, stepping serenely out of the front room. I resist the urge to call him a butt munch and ram a cushion in his face.

9

I BRIEF JAMES in the car on the way over to Emily's, as we make our way through the bright lights of the London circular at a snail's pace.

"They're just having a bit of a bad patch," I say.

"Aren't they always bad now?"

"James! No, they're not always." As I say it, I realise it's a lie. "They used to get on really well. Before he turned into an arsehole. But anyway, just avoid the contentious topics – Emily's job, holidays, him going out all the time, Mattie's behaviour stuff."

"How can that be contentious?"

"Long story, but basically the school thinks it might be autism and Rick is saying it's just that Emily has been too soft on her and lets her get away with too much. Or something like that. Something dickish. Sorry."

"Don't apologise to me – you and Emily are the best friends, me and Rick are just the hangers on – acquaintances through association."

"You've never thought of it as we're all friends?" I say. "We've had some good times together. Remember that birthday of yours when we went to that Mexican place and he bought pitchers of margaritas and made us all wear sticky-on-moustaches? That was fun. You guys were up into the early hours drinking whisky and bonding back at ours."

He shrugs. "That was a long time ago."

He always says this, all wistful, like he's a wizened old man looking back on the past with milky old eyes, as if the man he used to be is completely removed from who he is now.

I normally respond by making some dig about how that was when he was Fun James, but that's mostly when I'm feeling mean and I'd really like to keep him onside tonight so I ignore it and push on. "So you don't class Rick as your friend?"

"I mean, not really. You and Emily – and Cath – have your thing and Rick and I and various boyfriends of Cath's have been on the sidelines for some if it."

"That makes me feel sad," I say, my heart sinking.

"Why?"

"Because they're people who are really close to me and I guess I thought by this point, twenty-plus years on, you'd at least consider them friends, too."

"You're overthinking it. It's just friend logistics. Maybe if I liked Rick more and maybe if Cath had a partner I liked, I would feel like we're all friends."

"Ahhh, so you don't like Rick?"

For some reason this makes me feel better, like maybe my husband hasn't just said he's indifferent to my beloved friends, who he's known basically the whole time we've been together and are essentially my beating heart, and actually he just hates Rick. And that, I can get behind.

"I don't *not* like him," he says. "We just don't have a lot in common. He's too alpha male for me."

"Because he likes football?" I ask.

"He's just got that big dick energy thing going on."

"Though interestingly, it's not that big, apparently. So he's probably compensating."

He grimaces. "Why would you tell me that? We're men – we don't discuss each other's penis size. Now that's all I'll be able to think about all night."

"Oh, come on, you must have sneaky looks at the urinals?"

"Absolutely not. Man code."

"Well, sorry. Now you know."

We drive a couple more minutes.

"I hope Emily isn't serving us chipolatas," he says, breaking into one of his lesser-heard snort laughs.

"It's nice to see you," I say, giving his thigh an affectionate rub. "I've missed you this week. How was Amsterdam? Did you survey the red-light district and smoke lots of pot?"

He tenses. Without meaning to, I've led us into possible-argument-territory by mentioning his absence, even though this time I was genuinely being interested and nice.

"I was working," he says, through gritted teeth. "So, no."

"I know, I just thought—" I don't bother finishing the sentence, I know it's no use.

He turns the music up and we drive in silence the rest of the way.

Eventually, we make it to Herne Hill. I look out the window, as we pass hipsters and young families, in awe at the latest over-priced shop to open on the road – this time a wool and craft shop. It probably offers knitting and crochet lessons, but in a cool way. Not ironic, just cool – old lady crafts are the new retro pub sports.

I remember when Emily first moved here, before Rick, when we were all young and child-free and interesting. It felt cool by virtue of its proximity to Brixton, even though Brixton was already teeming with private school, post-uni house-shares and high street chains by then. It's warmer than it should be for this time of year – the evening lighter, the smokers outside the pubs cheerier. We find a parking spot, with difficulty, squeezing in between the Audis and BMWs. I take a deep breath and reset, knowing I need to get James back onside before we go in.

"You look handsome," I say, as we get out of the car.

He smiles, softening. "Thanks."

I readjust my top. I'm experimenting with tucking tops into high-waisted jeans, having read it makes short legs look longer. I mainly just feel like my mum in the eighties, but I've been pushing through the discomfort.

"Do I look all right?" I ask.

James takes half a glance at me as he retrieves the wine and non-alcoholic beers from the back. "Lovely."

I wish sometimes he'd just give me a compliment without me having to wheedle it out of him. We link arms and walk to the front door, him towering over me, as always. It feels nice to be together, out of the house and doing something sociable.

"So, what aren't we allowed to talk about again?" he asks, grinning. I elbow him.

"Brush them properly!" Emily shouts up the stairs and she opens the door. "Use the timer!"

"Well hello to you, too."

"Sorry! Hi. Come in. They're being arseholes, for a change," she

says, giving us both kisses before storming back to the kitchen. "I'm just finishing the chilli."

Rick comes sauntering through the hallway carrying a beer, dressed head to toe in impeccably ironed designer wear, his dark hair scarily neat and precise, as always.

"Welcome," he says, oozing charm. He is, for sure, a charming man when he wants to be. And a good-looking one, though that shine rubs off once you get to know him better.

He kisses me on the cheek. "Looking lovely, Charlie, as always. Love the jeans."

It's a perfectly innocent compliment, delivered in style, but the way I feel about this man makes me wonder if he's actually throwing some veiled shade and it causes me to doubt the high waist.

He does some manly greeting with James, saying something about leaving the ladies to get on with it and whisks him down to the basement where there is a pool table and the biggest, highest spec screen and all the gadgets to accompany it. Small dick syndrome in play if ever I saw it.

The look James gives me as he heads down the stairs indicates he very much does not want to go through, but he knows it's couples' protocol in this situation so does as society tells him he should and follows Rick. I put the wine we brought in the fridge, get myself a glass of the one that's open and perch on a bar stool at the island.

"Cheers," I say. "Nice to see you."

"You too, dude." Emily opens an avocado, scoops its insides into a bowl and sets about mashing it with a fork.

I pick up a lump of cheese from the side, take the grater from the cupboard and set to work, without her needing to ask me. It's that best friend kind of language that comes from knowing each other, and each other's houses, for forever.

"So check me out with my spin class, hey? Like, who is this new and improved exercise machine Charlie?"

"Ah, yes. The spin class. And you said you enjoyed it, right?"

"Enjoyed may be a bit of an exaggeration," I say, remembering how I could hardly walk the next day. And how I vomited. Though I think that was the two bottles of wine and three cocktails that Dorit and I ended up having. "More, I survived it. I really enjoyed the after-party though. And oh my god, I love Dorit. She's amazing – so positive and outgoing and totally up for anything fun. She loves my list – we've been texting ideas back and forth. The spin class afternoon was really bonding."

"So, you basically love her because she took you to the pub on a weekday afternoon and got you drunk and made you forget your responsibilities?" Emily laughs. "Oh my god! Is she *fabulous*? Have you finally got a fabulous friend like you've dreamt of for all these years?"

I flick a bit of cheese at her across the island. "Do you know, I think I might. And thank god someone fabulous turned up."

"Have you crossed anything else off the list?" she asks. "Anything exciting – apart from masturbating to within an inch of your vagina's life?"

"Shhh!"

"Oh my god, have you not told James? Have you even told him you got a vibrator?"

"Of course I told him. He's delighted now he's realised it's basically a lazy sex pass for him – he finishes, then hands me the vibrator and falls asleep next to me."

"You're kidding!" she says, a spec of avocado landing in her wine.

"Only partly."

I look into the general direction of the basement, listen out for male voices, make sure the coast is clear and lower my voice. "Have you and Rick still not . . . ?"

Emily shakes her head. "I tried again the other day. Talking to you at that lunch made me think maybe I was overreacting and it was just a rough patch and I needed to put a bit of effort in. But he wasn't having any of it. He just pushed me away and said he was tired."

"Maybe he *was* just tired?" I offer, wanting to make her feel better even though I have a bad feeling in my stomach about it.

"For eleven months?" She raises her eyebrows at me.

We are forty-four years old, which is roughly thirty years' worth of knowing that men want sex all the time, basically. When we're doing the washing-up, first thing in the morning, in the middle of cooking dinner, in the cab on the way home, on your period or off your period – you're never safe to be affectionate or go in for a cuddle as there's always the possibility – likelihood – that there will be an awakening and all of a sudden, one boob squeeze later, they're expecting sex. Unless extremely, bedridden ill or injured. And even then, sometimes. So yeah, I can see it's worrying.

Emily puts the fork down, sips her wine, and comes round the island. "I went through his drawers the other day, and his coat

pockets. I don't even know what I was looking for, I just needed something – some proof that I'm not going crazy, that something is properly wrong."

"Did you find anything?"

She shakes her head.

"Have you gone through his phone?"

"I don't know his passcode and he never lets it out of his sight."

I take a second to feel grateful that James and I are often on each other's phones for whatever reason – putting music on in the car or searching for something online. There are lots of reasons our relationship is not perfect, but not trusting each other is not one of them. I don't really know what to say, or how to play it. I want to give my best friend good advice, but my advice would be that she can do so much better and that she deserves someone who really sees her and who loves and adores her the way that Cath and I do (but with sex) rather than someone who acts like she's a possession or a thing to manage. But I don't say that, because that's not what she needs to hear right now. And I have every faith that sooner or later, she'll work that out for herself.

"Look, I'm sure it's nothing," I say. "Like, not *nothing*, you're obviously having a rough time, but I'm sure he's not cheating on you – it just feels that way because you're second-guessing everything."

She sighs, sniffing back a tear. "You're probably right. God, maybe it's the perimenopause rearing its ugly head again. Anxiety is another symptom, you know."

I roll my eyes. "Shut up."

James and Rick come up from the basement. Rick is beaming in

that easy, sleazy way he has, no matter the situation. James looks slightly traumatised.

"We're starving," Rick says, slapping Emily's bum as he walks past to put his empty beer can in the recycling.

He does a dramatic tut and a sigh. "You've done it again," he says to Emily, shaking his head.

She glances over from stirring the chilli and slumps her shoulders.

"Come here." He makes himself taller, like he's readying himself to tell a child off.

The embarrassment radiates from Emily. I busy myself with taking things to the table so she doesn't feel we're watching this interaction take place. James follows suit.

"How many times have I told you, these cartons are not recyclable," Rick says. "You have to take them to the supermarket to recycle. And all of this needs to be rinsed out. They don't take contaminated plastic. Do I need to put a sign on the bin?"

"Sorry," Emily says, her voice quiet. "I was in a rush. I'll sort it out later."

"Good," he says. "Maybe then you'll learn. Honestly, that brain of yours. In one ear and out the other." He kisses her on the forehead and I swear my blood runs cold. "James, come and sit," he says, gesturing to the table.

Rick gets the fancy decanter full of red wine from the counter, holding it aloft like it's his prized possession. "I opened a bottle of the 2016 Lafitte before Emily told me you're still not drinking." He rolls his eyes.

"Charlie loves her red," James says, very much not going over to

sit at the table, which I'm pleased about. "I'm sure she'll appreciate it on my behalf."

"And Emily," I add.

Rick pours me and Emily some, reluctantly, and, I notice, pours himself a bigger glass before sitting down at the head of the table, manspreading like he's Henry the Eighth.

"What can we take through, Emily?" I ask, trying to make a point.

"Ah, thanks," she says. "All of that stuff can go – the sour cream, guac, salad."

Rick stays sitting while James and I ferry things to the table and Emily runs around, putting more things into serving bowls, lighting candles, putting music on and getting everyone water, until eventually, we're all seated. I'm already inwardly raging, but try to push it to one side.

"This looks delicious, Ems, thank you," I say.

"Sorry it's just chilli. I was going to do something fancier but I ran out of time."

"She's been working most of the day," Rick says, serving himself then passing the bowl to me.

"Well, not all day," Emily says. "I took the kids to their swimming lessons this morning, and took Kian to tennis and went to the supermarket."

"They don't pay you enough to work at weekends," Rick says. "They barely pay you at all. You'd be better off not working; I make more than enough for all of us. Then maybe we could dial it up a notch from chilli when we have guests round."

"She does it for the love though, Rick," I say, keeping my tone upbeat. "And to be a good person and give back to the world. No

one works in the charity sector for the money. It's a vocation, not a job. I'm jealous she has one. And she's amazing at it."

This is true – Emily is amazing at her job and she does love it, mostly. And I'm jealous of how committed she's always been. Emily's the kind of person who has never been able to tolerate injustice. She was constantly rescuing animals and starting up petitions and kicking ass in the student council. She even used to volunteer for litter pickup. That's what a good person she is. It's just a shame arsehole, banking people get paid so much more than genuinely good people who make the world a better place.

Emily blushes. "Thanks, dude."

"Ooh, did I tell you," I say, "Chloe's looking at doing English at uni. Nothing definite yet – she's also thinking of history or sociology so, you know, a wide spectrum, but it's nice she's considering it. I'm even trying to get her to look at going to Leeds – that would be weird, wouldn't it? We could go and visit her and go to some of our old haunts. I could pass on my ginormous Norton anthologies."

"Your old haunts," Emily says. "I was just the occasional tag along."

"Oh, I don't know – you were there for a lot of it. We had some good times!"

Rick shuffles in his seat. He doesn't like it when we talk about Emily before he was on the scene. Especially not in the context of her having fun.

"What brought that on?" Emily asks, moving the reminiscing on and shovelling a tortilla chip into some guacamole.

"I think it was studying *Macbeth*, you know," James says. "Ah, I loved *Macbeth*. 'Tomorrow and tomorrow and tomorrow—'"

"Thank you," I interrupt his party trick. "We don't need a rendition of all your memorised quotes."

"I've always thought of you lot as a bit like the three witches." He laughs. "But less powerful."

"Hey. Cheeky!" I say, nudging him. "We're very powerful, I'll have you know. We have the power to drink pitchers of margaritas and to cry a lot on nights out."

Emily stiffens slightly as I say it, and I see Rick's expression tighten. It's like walking a tightrope with him – it has to be very small, light steps, testing the way as you go. Hoping you don't fall off into the dark beyond. Something like that. I hope I haven't accidentally landed Emily in it for some reason.

"I thought *Hamlet* was better though, for the record," I say, trying to ease us back to safer waters.

"I think it's all a load of bollocks," Rick says, leaning back in his chair and spreading his legs a bit wider. "What actual use is reading and studying all those texts and books for three years, anyway? Reading is a waste of time in my book – I want my kids to be out doing things, learning life lessons. Not have their head stuck in a book. And what's the point? You spend three years partying and drinking and leave with a qualification that's of no use and a mountain of debt. University of life, I say. It served me well."

Emily gently puts her hand on his arm, the historic spousal code for 'bring it down a notch' or 'be careful' or 'stop being a dick'. He shakes it off and she sits back, scorned.

I don't know if he genuinely believes the crap he's spouting or if he's trying to get a reaction from us, though I truly worry it's the former. I could bombard him with statistics on literacy

and childhood development and the very conclusive and very important benefits of children reading – not that I have those to hand, but I definitely know they exist and I could definitely google them – but I also know that would be pointless and make the evening even more uncomfortable. Another thing to know about Rick is that he's not one for informed debate – more a spouting of total rubbish with pretend facts and anecdotes about his mates to seemingly back up his total rubbish.

"How are the markets at the moment?" James asks, making me feel grateful for him all over again.

Rick smiles at this one, a *Wolf of Wall Street* smile. I half expect him to rub his hands together in glee and reveal a gold tooth that catches the light. The question sets him off, like one of those clockwork cars, and all of a sudden, we're sitting through a TED Talk on hedge funds and lots of other things I don't understand and have no wish to.

* * *

The evening goes on and we manage to avoid too much beyond the odd dig at Emily that she shrugs off. I'm helping Emily in the kitchen with the coffees, Rick is waxing lyrical at James about something he clearly knows very little about – some space conspiracy theory, I guess from the snippets I pick up.

"What's next to be ticked off on the list?" Emily asks, pouring water into the fancy coffee machine; coffee being one of the many things Rick is very particular and stuck up about.

"I've got my Hollywood booked in for Monday," I whisper.

"Already feeling the fear. Dorit's going to come with me – but just for after – not in the room. Jesus, that would be a very bonding experience."

"Or a traumatic one."

I take one of the cups of espresso and add the foamed milk. "And after that, before it goes stubbly, I'm going to try for the make a sex tape one – I haven't told James yet, though."

"Jesus, don't do it too soon after – you'll look like a plucked chicken down there. With blood spots."

"Really? Well lucky old James then," I say. "Chicken's his favourite."

We laugh, which causes Rick to pay attention.

"Ooh and Dorit's found a street dance class we've booked in to – that's this week too, I think. Oh, and I told you I've booked myself in for an open-mic night in a few weeks – I sent you a save the date. Dorit's idea. Just need to write the bloody thing now."

We take the coffees over and Emily opens a fresh box of mint Matchsticks – our standard fancy post-dinner chocolate of choice since uni.

"What were you guys giggling about?" Rick asks.

"I was just filling Emily in on my forty-five things to do before you're forty-five list progress," I say.

Rick rolls his eyes. "I've heard about this. And you're all right with her doing it?" he asks James.

"She can do what she wants," James says. I smile and give him a congratulatory thigh rub for saying exactly the right thing. "As long as she's home to pick up the kids and feed them, I'm good with whatever." Less the right thing. "I mean, you know, because

I'm not there, but—" He has the decency to realise his mistake and try and back-pedal a bit.

"You need to get out more," Rick says to me. Then to James, "Sounds like a midlife crisis to me. I'd be careful, mate."

Emily does the arm squeeze again but this time Rick is too drunk to honour the silent spousal code. He shakes her off, more violently this time. "God, woman, you're irritating."

"You've had too much to drink," she says, quietly.

"I've had just the right amount to drink, thanks, and for your reference, I'm quite capable of deciding how much is too much." He fills his glass of wine again, making a point. "Sorry," he says to us, making us complicit. "She always does this, nags me. I'm not your dad, Emily, I know when to stop."

Emily recoils.

"Rick." I say, more feebly than intended.

"We should probably get going," James says, standing up. "It's late and I'm up early for a ride tomorrow."

Rick rolls his eyes at this too and part of me wills James into tackling him on it, but he doesn't. Emily tries to put a smile back on her face, but I can see she's mortified by the whole thing and it breaks my heart. There's always an element of treading on eggshells around them as a couple, but it's never felt this bad, this obvious.

We say our stilted goodbyes with promises of dinner at ours next time and on the way to the car I give James a hug – I can put up with the working too much and the not cooking and the taking hours at the weekend for Ironman training and the never wanting to go dancing and the blanket hatred of all pop music,

if the alternative is Rick. I smile, thinking how I'll reward him with my sexy, plucked-chicken vagina.

10

🍹 *COCKTAIL COVEN* 🍹

Me: *you were right, Ems – my vagina looks like a bloodied, plucked chicken.*

Cath: *EXCUSE ME? What have I missed?*

Me: *I had the Hollywood. And my vagina feels like it's on fire.*

Me: *There is no way this is sexually attractive. I was supposed to be making the sex tape tonight!*

Cath: *PAHAHAHAHA!!*

Me: *It's not funny. I am traumatised. At one point, the lady had me in the foetal position to do my arse. THE FOETAL POSITION!*

Cath: *What about your piles?*

Me: *I KNOW!*

Cath: *Did she manage to wax them off too?*

Me: *Still there. Just extremely bald. She waxed my lips.*

Cath: *Your fanny lips, right? To be clear?*

Me: *Yup. I don't understand why people do this to themselves.*

Cath: *It's porn, innit.*

Me: *I'm going to google how long it takes a bush to re-grow.*

Cath: *So, what are you going to do this evening now?*

Me: *Sit on my side with a pack of frozen peas on my vag and read* War and Peace. *Which, by the way, is BLOODY DULL.*

Emily: *Oh my god you guys – I'm at work pissing myself. I'm sorry you're in pain, Charlie, but I'm enjoying the chat!*

Emily: *How was your date the other night, Cath?*

Cath: *Abysmal. 3/10.*

Me: *Tell us more.*

Cath: *He lives with his wife, who he's separated from, though he said we can still go back to shag in the spare room as long as we didn't wake the children up.*

Me: *Oh maaaaan.*

Cath: *He licked my hand at one point.*

Emily: *Why?*

Cath: *God knows. I think he was trying to be sexual. But he left a bit of bread where he'd licked and I nearly vommed.*

Me: *Oh maaaaan. And ewwwww.*

Cath: *And he wore loafers. LOAFERS.*

Emily: *You should've walked out as soon as you saw them. RED FLAG.*

Me: *You gotta kiss a lot of frogs . . .*

Cath: *Dude, I've kissed the entire frog population at this point. There are no princes to be found. How was your couples' dinner the other night?*

Emily: *It was lovely.*

Text to Cath:

Me: *It was terrible! Rick was a total arsehole.*

Cath: *Worse than usual?*

Me: *Definitely! James even thought so and he never bitches about people. Emily actually opened up a bit though. Which was good. I'm worried about her.*

Cath: *We should try and get her out for something fun.*

Me: *Good idea!*

🍹 COCKTAIL COVEN 🍹

Me: *Do you guys want to come to puppy yoga if I can get us tickets? I've put it on the list!*

Cath: *What the bejesus is puppy yoga?*

Me: *What it says on the tin – yoga with puppies.*

Emily: *Do the puppies do the yoga?*

Cath: *If you hang one upside down does that count as downward dog? LOL.*

Me: *I don't know how it works exactly – I guess you cuddle them while you do yoga? It's supposed to release happy hormones.*

Cath: *Sounds like utter hippy dippy hogwash to me – sign me up.*

Emily: *I'm in. I'd need to check with Rick, but vaguely count me in.*

Me: *Yay!*

Me: *Gotta go and get some more peas.*

* * *

"Charlsberg, come on." James is unable to contain his laughter. "You have to show me, please."

"Trust me, you don't want to see it. It will scar you for life. It's scarred me for life and it's my vagina."

"I've seen your vagina plenty of times."

"Not like this."

"I bet it looks kinda hot," he says, coming up behind me and putting his arms around me. I can feel his cock against my back.

It's kind of nice – not the cock against the back thing, per se

– but seeing him laugh, and be silly and playful. I almost want to reward him for it, but I know it's too soon.

I turn off the main light, dimming my bedside lamp and wait until James has gone to the bathroom to take my clothes off. It's weird how I used to walk round naked the whole time, without a care in the world, and now I time my sneaky undressing like I'm a wart-covered troll who will instantly combust if someone catches sight of one of my droopy boobs or rolls of fat.

I get under the covers and am getting my eye mask and ear plugs ready when James slips into the bed next to me. He brushes his hand against my crotch and I yelp in discomfort.

"God, sorry," he says. "Does it hurt that much?"

"Yes! It's burning like hellfire! It'll be fine, though. Eventually."

"Remind me why you thought this one would be a good one for the list?" he asks, selecting one of the twenty-three philosophy books on his bedside table to read.

"Because I'm a fool?"

"No seriously, why?"

I sigh, thinking. "It's like some of the other kind of silly ones – it's something lots of people do, that I've never been brave enough to do, that I thought would be out of my comfort zone and therefore a challenge, but also might be, ya know, kinda fun."

"Kinda fun, hey?"

"But not tonight. And not until I've processed it properly."

He salutes. "Understood."

"Are you planning our Ben Nevis walk?" I ask, heaving my copy of *War and Peace* over.

"It's planned! We just need to decide a date. I'm excited."

"Me too?" I grimace. "I'm excited that you're excited, at least. It'll be fun to do something together. And without the kids."

"I really think you'll love it. It's so gorgeous there." His eyes light up, as they always do when he talks about The Great Outdoors. "It'll be tough, but so worth it. And I promise I'll find you a celebratory cocktail once you've done it."

"Now you're talking my language," I say, leaning over and kissing him.

I read four lines of *War and Peace* before giving up and turning my light off.

"Just one quick look, please?"

"Piss off."

May

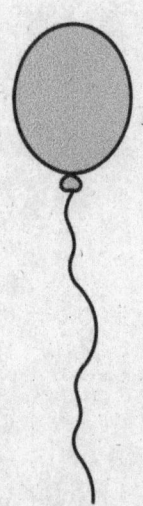

11

🍹 *COCKTAIL COVEN* 🍹

Me: *I miss being young and flexible and agile.*

Cath: *In the many years I have known you, you have never been young and flexible and agile.*

Emily: *Where has this come from?*

Me: *From me attempting to rock climb. And do parkour. I was astoundingly bad, unsurprisingly.*

Cath: *OMG you did the parkour?! WHERE IS THE FOOTAGE?*

Emily: *You were rubbish when we did the climbing wall on the school trip in year six.*

Cath: *See! Never young and flexible and agile!*

Me: *My finger is swollen. I think it's arthritis.*

Emily: *Perimenopause...*

Me: *Shut up.*

Cath: *Suburbs...*

Me: *Shut up. I also think I'm growing a moustache.*

Cath: *Intentionally?*

Me: *No!*

Emily: *Perimenopause.*

Me: *Shut up.* War and Peace *is still boring. Do I have to finish it for it to count as me having read it?*

Cath: *Yes.*

Me: *Balls. In other news, I volunteered at the drop-in cafe the other day and actually really loved it. Very cool people running it. And not like, people in their forties who can carry off Air Jordans cool – like, decent cool.*

Cath: *Baby's grown a conscience.*

Me: *??*

Cath: *Good for you. You should keep going with it.*

Me: *FYI I long to be one of those people in their forties who can carry off Air Jordans.*

Cath: *Promise me you will not wear Air Jordans.*

Emily: *They wouldn't go with her high-waisted jeans.*

Cath: *LOL.*

Me: *I long to be one of those women in their sixties who don't give a shit – wear what they want, say what they want.*

Emily: *Legend has it that happens after the menopause.*

Me: *SHUT UP!*

June

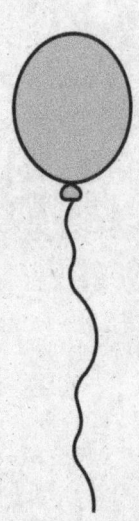

12

MY ALARM goes off at 6 a.m.

I have decided if I want to write my book, I need to take it seriously and serious writers get up at 6 a.m. and start writing. Or work into the early hours of the morning, but that is not an option for me because by the time I have wrangled the children into bed, my brain is mush and I am so exhausted my eyes don't focus properly and are only good for watching *The Real Housewives*.

I tried to be all Ernest Hemingway about it the other day, going up to my desk (James's desk) with a bottle of wine and a notebook, but I basically just got drunk and ended up writing incomplete rude limericks – which is not the literary direction I am aiming for, fun though they are.

> *There once was a housewife from Hull,*
> *Whose life was incredibly dull,*
> *So she got her muff stripped,*
> *And tried getting whipped,*
> *And got*

I creep down the stairs, trying not to wake the children, make myself a coffee and stare out of the kitchen window a bit. By the

time I make it to the office, it's 6.30 a.m. already. I don't know how that's happened. I sip my coffee and stare out of the office window. My notebook is open. I write 'Book Idea' on the first bright white page. Then stare out the window some more. They say your first book should be about what you know. I write 'bored housewife' on the page. Then brainstorm:

Has kids who constantly wrestle.
Has a husband who works all the time and is boring.
Leaves her family.
Goes to Greece, meets foxy man, has an affair.

I look back at what I've written and it occurs to me it sounds remarkably similar to the plot of *Shirley Valentine*, from what I can remember. Without the wrestling kids, possibly. I cross out Greece and change it for Thailand. Bit more exotic. I'm liking this – the inspiration is flooding over me, ideas spilling out like rolling waves – I'm even thinking in similes now! I write some more.

Does she run off with the foxy man for good?
Does that mean she never sees her children again?
Is this too mean?
CAN'T HAVE AN UNLIKEABLE WOMAN –
NO ONE WILL READ THE BOOK.

I hear Felix emerging from his room and realise, with a heavy heart, it's officially the getting ready for school madness time. Pram in the hall being the enemy of art and all that. I've made a

good start though. I text Dorit:

> *I've started writing my book! Do you fancy a coffee after drop-off?*

* * *

"So, what's it about? Your masterpiece?" Dorit asks, bringing our lattes and two massive pieces of carrot cake over to the table. "Your *War and Peace*?"

"Jesus, I hope it will be more interesting than *War and Peace*. That beast is duuuuulllll."

"It will be a bestseller – I can feel it in my bones!"

She grins, her huge hoops swaying with her enthusiasm. She's looking peak Dorit – luscious, wild, curly hair that falls perfectly, bold, bright jumper, big chunky jewellery and some trousers that look like they came straight from a dead old man but somehow manage to look the height of fashion on Dorit. And sparkly eyes – always the sparkly, enthusiastic eyes.

"Well, thanks for the vote of confidence, but it's very early days. I did really enjoy it, though – the thinking about it, using my brain for once."

"Of course you did! Snatched minutes away from the family and the chaos and the responsibility. Time to try and remember yourself."

"Exactly!" I dig into the carrot cake. "I'd forgotten how much I used to love writing until I found some old yearbooks that had some of my poems in them. I used to think I was some kind of Oscar Wilde – but a straight, feminist version. Not that any of us really

knew what feminism was in the nineties, obviously, otherwise we wouldn't have structured our whole lives around wanting to be groped by boys at parties."

I think back to nineties me – how I used to cut shapes into my school shirt and not brush my hair, thinking that stupidity and lack of hygiene were somehow cool. How I obsessed over boys with every waking thought I had. How I borrowed Sam Olsen's Levellers top and Dr. Martens that were four sizes too big for me because it felt like it solidified our relationship somehow. I must've looked like a clown. Or a golf club.

"I always wanted to be a music journalist, you know," I say. "I thought it was the perfect mix of writing and music and cool."

"Why didn't you then?"

"I accidentally fell into TV."

"How do you 'accidentally' fall into TV?"

"I applied for a television and young people training scheme thing when I was in my second year at uni – lots of workshops and talks and stuff from different production companies and I ended up getting some work experience through that and I was really good at it, so they gave me a job and it all kind of went from there."

"Did you enjoy it?"

I so clearly remember the excitement of those first jobs – the first time being in a proper production office, the pinch-me thrill of being on a shoot for the very first time, and working on a live show. How frenetic and fast-paced it was, having just hours to find a guest and write the interview, running through the studio to drop off a tape for editing, dealing with last-minute emergencies, speaking to all kinds of interesting people every day. And those

were just the contributors – the people I worked with were even better. We were all young and fun and hungry for it. We'd go out nearly every night, up until the early hours, working our way round the bars and clubs of Soho.

"I loved it," I say, just now remembering how much I really did.

"Why did you leave?" Dorit asks. "Or hang on – let me guess. You got pregnant, thought you could go back to work afterwards and continue as you were and you tried that, with the best intentions, but actually it was completely bloody impossible and you were being pulled in a million different directions, and not able to be a mother or do your job properly, and you weren't even making any money for the privilege as childcare is so ludicrously expensive? Is that about right?"

"Scarily right."

"Same old story." She elegantly puts a massive piece of cake in her mouth and I make a mental note of her tactic.

"Same for you?" I ask.

"Something like that," she says, through the mouthful of cake. "Acting is definitely not a mother-friendly profession."

"You're an actor?" I asked, gobsmacked. "What have you been in?"

"*Was* an actor. And for the record, that is *the* most annoying question you can ask an actor. But, to answer it, probably nothing you've seen – or not a speaking part in anything you would've seen. I was a struggling actor – not doing it successfully enough to make it worth me going back. But for you – why haven't you gone back to TV? Your kids are old enough now to be more independent, they'll all be in secondary school by next year. This is your moment."

"I have thought about it, you know."

"What's stopping you?" She stares at me with those sparkly eyes and makes me believe it could actually be a possibility.

I take another forkful of cake, sip my latte, think. "I guess it's always been logistics – nursery drop-offs and pickups to begin with, then school. The school day is basically a half day in media. And it's all freelance contracts with shoots away. It's not a particularly child-friendly industry. Honestly, the only older women who worked at the production company I was at either didn't have kids or were nannied up to the eyeballs and never saw their children. And we weren't rich enough to nanny up to the eyeballs. Plus, it was always me that had to stay at home when the kids were ill or there were staff training days or any of that crap, because I earnt about a tenth of what James earnt – and they were always ill and there were a lot of staff training days."

I go from revelling in the nostalgia of the excitement of those days to remembering, viscerally, the constant, tight-stomach chaos of them, building up to a thick, bubbling rage at the injustice of it all.

"It's not fair, is it?" Dorit says. "The bloody patriarchy, man. They've stitched us right up. How are we supposed to have a career when childcare is at such a premium, when the whole world is rigged for men? Balls to that – pun intended. Sod them!" Her hoops go mad as she shakes her head in anger. "You need to get back out there. You're a valuable member of the workforce. You've been limiting yourself for too long – hiding yourself away beneath laundry and chicken nuggets. Now is your time to shine!"

"Chicken goujons, if you please. I am a classy lady."

The sparkle in her eye suddenly turns more intense – more

purposeful. She pulls out her mobile and starts looking something up. "And, oh my god, I have the perfect idea! A friend of mine, a mum friend from years ago when Gael was at Park Road, she works in TV! I'm going to hit her up on your behalf. It's perfect!"

A glimmer of hope flutters in my chest. Quickly replaced by fear.

"But it's been so long," I say, feebly. "I don't know if . . . I might not . . ."

Dorit puts the phone down and takes my hands in hers. "Look at me." I do as I'm told. "I know it feels big and scary, and I know it's easier to say no and to carry on as you are – with the laundry and the chicken nuggets—"

"Goujons," I mutter.

"But you can do this. You used to do this, it's in your blood."

"I'm not sure if TV is something that's necessarily in your blood, so to speak," I say.

"You have these skills – they don't suddenly disappear when you pop a baby out. They might be rusty, and sure, there'll be loads of tech stuff to brush up on, but the essential stuff – the ideas, the people skills – you've still got that. This is your chance, babe. This is your chance!"

I have the last sip of my now-cold coffee, my hand shaking as I put it back down. I consider whether this is something I could actually do. Logistically, I probably could. Mentally, though?

Dorit isn't giving up. "Isn't your list all about finding yourself again? Going back to those passions, the things that brought you joy, that made you *you* – before marriage and kids and suburbia sucked it all out of you?" I consider protesting at the use of

suburbia but decide against it and nod instead. "Well, this is perfect then. And look, it'll just be work experience or an internship or something and if you don't like it any more, at least you've given it a try. Nothing to lose."

She's right. Totally right. Eating an oyster and drinking a martini may be fun, but in the grand scheme of things, are they really going to change my life? Possibly not. But this? Going back to work, to a job I loved? This might. And what have I got to lose? Time in the afternoons to watch *The Real Housewives*, the luxury of grocery shopping in the middle of the day, but that's about it.

"You're right," I say, emboldened. "I'm up for it. Let's find me a job."

"That's my girl!" she says, typing up an email.

"But what about my book?" I say, a sudden panic that my far more interesting than *War and Peace* masterpiece will never get written.

"You can do both, bitch. Nothing will stop you now!"

* * *

I spend the rest of the day letting myself get lost in the excitement. I look for jobs, sign myself back up to the online TV jobs recruitment page (amazed it's still going), and order some trendy looking clothes, pleased that I've persisted with the high-waisted jeans, though slightly worried they're only trendy close to the Surrey border. I make the kids sit at the table for dinner, which causes much protesting, but makes me feel like a good parent. Until Felix starts throwing spaghetti at Jack and I have to tell Chloe seven

times to put her phone away at the table. I don't let it get me down though, my hope is too gloriously big for that.

"You all right, Chloe?" I ask.

"Yes," she snaps. "But I have important stuff going on I need to sort."

"Like what, darling?"

"You wouldn't understand."

"You'd be surprised," I say. "I know it's hard to believe, but I was a teenager once."

"Yeah, in the 1930s," Jack says, which causes Felix to burst into hysterical laughter. "Bet they didn't even have phones then!"

I mean, he's wrong and he's right.

"It's fine, Mum," Chloe says, like I'm a petulant toddler who won't let go of her leg. "Just leave it."

"Well, I'm here if you need me," I say. "And even though we didn't have phones, I still understand a lot more than you might think."

"Whatever you say, Grandma," Felix says.

He's at that annoying age where he's experimenting with sarcasm, and humour in general, and some of his one liners either completely cross a boundary or are just not funny. Or both. I shrug it off.

"So, I have some news," I say, unable to contain my smile.

I wait for some response – enquiries, excitement, eye contact – but Felix decides to flick some more spaghetti and the moment is lost.

"Guys!" I say. "Stop with the food throwing or you won't have any device time later."

They down forks and hiss at each other. Sensing distraction,

Chloe grabs her phone again.

"So, my news," I say, persisting. "Is that I might be going back to work!"

"You used to work?" Jack asks.

"I did, yes. A long time ago. I took a break to have Chloe and went back until I had you."

"And then just gave it up to stay at home?" Chloe says. "That's not very feminist of you."

I take a breath, feeling my smile falter. "I gave it up so that I could be at home to raise you all and give you a secure home life. And because we couldn't afford the extortionate childcare and yes, it probably isn't that feminist of me, but that's how the world is organised – it makes it almost impossible to have children and a successful career and not feel like you're split into a million pieces. So if you're feeling like being a good feminist, go ahead and do something about that. And for the record, at least I kept my surname."

"Rupert's mum works. She's got her own PR company," Chloe says.

"What did you used to do?" Felix asks, like he can't possibly imagine what I'd be fit for.

"It was quite exciting, actually," I say. "I used to work in TV. On really fun shows."

"You went to the pub with Ant and Dec," Chloe groans. "We know. Well done for having a pint with a couple of TV presenters once upon a long time ago."

"Did you work on *The Masked Singer*?" Jack asks.

"Uh, no but—"

And just like that, they lose the small scrap of interest they had and return to flicking food at each other and pinging text messages.

James comes home when we're at the end of pudding, the first family dinner he's managed to attend even a bit of for weeks.

"Viennetta?" he says, kissing the kids on the head. "Were you having Viennetta behind my back? And on a Wednesday too!"

"Do you want some?" I ask.

"Sadly not," he says. "I've got to carb load for my brick session tomorrow. Not long now!"

I roll my eyes and cut myself another slice, hoping he doesn't launch into his intricate and extremely boring training session specifics.

"Mum's got a job!" Jack says.

"Has she?" James looks shocked, which is probably fair enough as getting a job and not telling your spouse would be weird.

"That's not exactly what I said," I clarify. "I haven't got a job, I'm just thinking of going back to work. Dorit has a friend who works in TV and she's going to try and hook me up with some work experience or an internship or something."

"Can we watch YouTube now?" Felix asks, already getting down from the table.

"Put your bowls in the dishwasher!" I shout after them, too late.

Chloe slopes off upstairs, eyes still glued to her phone, her expression tense.

I go to the kitchen and reheat a bowl of spaghetti for James, grabbing a non-alcoholic beer from the fridge for him.

"So, go on then, tell me more about the work thing," James says, as I sit back down, his voice thick with suspicion.

"There's not much more to tell until Dorit's heard back from her friend."

"Do you think now's the best time to be doing that? Chloe's got exams coming up next year and Jack's going up to secondary. It just feels like maybe it could wait?"

I take a breath, attempt to keep a smile on my face. "The kids are that bit older, and more independent – Jack going up to secondary means no more school runs and all of that, so I'm needed here less and I just thought maybe now's the time to do it. I miss working – I think. I do – I miss using my brain and feeling like I'm achieving things and feeling validated and challenged. I think it might be great for me."

"But you said work experience or an internship, right? So we're talking either no money, or basically no money? And won't we need to get childcare of some kind? Because you won't be home in the evenings before about 7.30 or 8 p.m. And then, add your travel on to that too. That adds up." He sips his beer, frowning. "And I'm away a lot with work and can't cut down on any of that, especially with this big client we're pitching for – now's the time I need to be pushing."

I deflate like a popped balloon, all the hope and excitement that had built up in me released in one fell swoop. When's the time for me to be pushing, I wonder? Though I don't say it out loud, of course.

"I'm not saying don't do it, obviously," James says, reading the room. "I just think maybe it's something we need to look into properly before you commit to anything. And it's not a 'fuck the patriarchy' type thing, before you get on that, it's about thinking of

us as a family unit and what works best for us, at this moment in time. I'm just not sure it makes sense."

What works best for *you*, I want to scream. Because I'm sure as hell not being considered in this scenario at all.

"You do get that, right?" He softens his tone. It's too late though, the damage has been done.

"Yep. Sure," I say.

I get up and clear the rest of the table, put the children's bowls in the dishwasher, put the leftovers in the freezer, wipe the table and pick damp, trodden-on spaghetti strands off the floor with my nails.

James goes through to the living room, putting his bowl on the surface next to the dishwasher. Next to. Not in.

* * *

🍸 *COCKTAIL COVEN* 🍸

Me: *Guys! I'm thinking of going back to work. Or trying to.*

Emily: *OMG! That's amazing news! What a great idea!*

Cath: *Good for you!*

Emily: *How are you going to go about it? Have you got many friends in TV still?*

Me: *Dorit knows a mum from round here who has a*

production company – she's going to ask her. It would just be work experience or something to begin with. I'm excited though. And nervous.

Emily: *Of course – it's a big step. But try not to be intimidated. You can totally do the job – you kicked arse before.*

Cath: *You'll kick arse again. You're a born arse licker. Sorry, autocorrect. You're a born arse KICKER.*

Emily: *You never know, she might be into arse licking now she's got her bald bum.*

Cath: *Thanks for that visual.*

Me: *Can we not talk about my bare arse, please. Talking of kicking arses. If James is ever found dead, it's likely I murdered him for never, ever, ever, no matter what the circumstances or how clearly I can indicate the dishwasher is empty, put his dirty dishes in the dishwasher.*

Cath: *Just leave them on the side until you run out of bowls.*

Me: *I've tried that before but the cleaner comes on a Friday and just tidies them away and looks at me like I'm a slob.*

Cath: *Please don't tell me you clean before the cleaner comes?*

Me: *Dude, you've seen my house and met my children and witnessed our toilets. I have to. Otherwise she'd quit.*

Cath: *Yeah, true. I won't be able to visit you in prison, I have enough on working and looking after Mum and dating diabolical morons.*

Emily: *Hey, prison might be a good place to cross 'kissing a girl' off your list.*

13

"**WHAT IF** they crap on us?" Cath asks.

We're on our way to puppy yoga, winding through the merry streets of Saturday morning Islington. I love it. I always love coming into town, any part of town, remembering there's a whole exciting world on my doorstep, with all different types of people – drunks and crazies and all. It reminds me of when we first moved to London. James and I had a tiny attic flat in a big townhouse in Vauxhall. There was no central heating and we shared a bathroom with two other flats and paid cash in hand. And could hear everyone's every move – including the lay priest who lived below us and had an indecent amount of sex for someone so into God.

James says I'm looking back with rose-tinted glasses, that actually it was pretty hideous, we never had money and were always cold. And there were infestations of ants. But I remember loving it at the time, too – it was our first place together and I loved making a home, the merging of our two lives – my multi-coloured polka-dot duvet cover and his threadbare ethnic wall hangings that smelt of death, my grunge CDs and posters and his extensive DVD collection of niche documentaries I hadn't seen and had no inclination to. Though back in those days, I'd at least cuddle up with him while he watched them.

"Seriously, guys," Cath says. "What if they crap on us? Like, puppies crap a lot, what's to stop them?"

"Maybe they take them all to the toilet beforehand?" I say.

"I'm wearing my best Sweaty Betty," Cath says. "If I get puppy crap all over it, I'll be raging."

"They could pee too," Emily unhelpfully suggests.

"Guys," I say. "Come on. This is supposed to make us zen and happy – not anxious. I'm one hundred per cent sure the puppies toileting on people is something they've considered and addressed, in some way. Happy vibes, people, happy vibes."

James is off somewhere Up North – finally, after all the months of wanging on about it – Ironmanning, and it took much persuading and outright bribery to get Chloe to agree to watch the boys, so I need to milk every last minute of freedom and puppy endorphins.

We're welcomed into a warehouse room with two long lines of yoga mats placed closely together, a teacher's mat in the middle, and an overwhelming smell of dog piss. Cath wrinkles her nose in disgust. Cath is not a dog person. We settle ourselves on our mats, and wait as other groups of excitable friends turn up. The class is introduced by Cassie, a super smiley twenty-something who gives us instructions on how to hold the puppies correctly, why the session is beneficial for us and how to tag the puppies on Instagram.

While the puppies we have yet to see squeal and snuffle in a back room, we do a short yoga sequence, which involves simple moves I cannot do (the reason I do not go to yoga classes) and occasional easy stretches I can – and finally, it's puppy time.

"Use these to entice them over to you," Cassie says, walking through the class handing out random toys and blankets. "And do let one of us know if there are any accidents."

"See!" Cath whispers. "I told you they're going to crap and piss everywhere."

"You don't know that – they just said *if*."

One by one, Cassie and her equally smiley twenty-something helpers bring the puppies out. They change them each week, we're told. This week we seem to have landed the world's ugliest, least cuddly puppies – bug-eyed shih tzus.

"What in god's name are these?" Cath whispers.

"I think they're called puppies," Emily says.

"Well, they're dog ugly," Cath says. Then laughs. "Get it? Dog ugly."

Just as she says it, one of them comes up and pisses right next to her mat, as if making a statement. Emily and I burst into hysterics. Cath, not so much.

We play with the puppies, attempting to cuddle some of them, we tug of war with them, we take photos for Instagram and bit by bit, Cath softens to the point that one of the puppies actually comes and falls asleep on her. The puppies have accidents everywhere, despite the careful placement of toilet mats all over the room. The teacher tries to do another yoga sequence which no one pays any attention to, and then at the end, we lie down for the relaxation bit. The lights are dimmed, soft music is put on, the twenty-somethings use treats to try and coax the puppies to lie on us. And halfway through the relaxation, I open my eyes, look to the girls' mats either side of me, and see that they are both crying.

* * *

We decamp to the nearest cafe and I get the coffees in. And double-chocolate-chip cookies. They seem essential. The cafe is one up from a greasy spoon – windows dense with condensation, a table of builders in the corner shovelling full breakfasts down, a lone octogenarian nursing a pot of tea, Radio 2 playing in the background.

"So." I distribute the coffees and cookies. "Who would like to start?"

They stir their coffees, and I see Emily welling up again. And then it suddenly breaks into a cry laugh and then Cath joins in and I can't help myself and we're all stirring our coffees snort laughing, and the builders and the old man are staring at us like we've gone mad. Which, for all I know, we have.

"Sorry," Emily says, eventually catching her breath. "Those poor instructors, they looked terrified. Bursting into tears probably isn't the reaction they're used to."

"Poor bloody puppies!" Cath says, wiping her nose with a napkin.

"I honestly don't know what it was," Emily says. "I was totally fine one minute and then, bam, totally not fine. I think it's the hormones. I could cry at the drop of a hat at the moment."

"I think it was the puppies' eyes for me," Cath said. "They look so . . . innocent and pure and helpless."

"But what were you crying *about*?" I ask.

"Everything, Charlie," Cath says.

I stay quiet. I read an interviewer talking once about how the

best way to get someone to open up is to give them the space to fill. It works.

"Mum is deteriorating, massively. She's walking the hallways in the night, not knowing where she is or what she's doing. She's not eating unless I force her to. She's started saying crazy things, talking like Dad is still alive. And I'm on the phone for literally hours nearly every day trying to sort some kind of proper care for her, but it's like chipping away at the Great Wall of China or some shit, so much endless bureaucracy. And I'm behind with my work but I can't afford to take any time off. And I'm tired. So tired. Sometimes I feel like my bones are about to collapse, I'm so tired. But most of all, it is just so hideously grim and painful to see Mum like this – she was always so strong and forceful and ball-breaking and full of life and now she's . . ." She gulps down a sob. "She's just not her any more."

"Jesus, that sounds horrendous, Cath," I say.

My chest tightens with pain for my friend. Cath has always been the feisty one, the tough one, the one who deals with whatever comes her way and let's stuff roll off her back. It's hard to see her like this. I want to help, so badly, but this feels like grown-up stuff that I am not equipped to deal with.

"Is Dan helping at all?" Emily says. "You said you were going to have a word with him if he didn't start helping more."

"He's been up a couple of times when I'm there, but I wouldn't say he helps exactly. Just barks questions at me about what I haven't sorted and then regresses into a sulky teenager and expects me to bring him tea. He's finding seeing Mum like this hard to deal with."

"But so are you," I say, stating the obvious.

"Yep." She sighs. "But we're women, aren't we. We find shit hard but we know ultimately we have to deal with it – it's not going away."

"I guess he knows that ultimately you'll pick up his slack because you don't want your mum to suffer because of his crapness?" Emily says.

"Oh my god, that's so the same for me with the kids and the house!" I say. "Like, I know we should read to the kids at bedtime and if James is ever around for it and I ask him to do it for once, he'll say he's too tired, but then I feel guilty and end up doing it because I don't want them to suffer. And the laundry – like, I've tried going on strike and leaving it, but then I feel bad the kids won't have clean clothes and I ended up doing it anyway!"

Emily stares at me. I realise that this was perhaps not the most helpful comparison.

"Sorry, that was a really inappropriate comparison," I mutter.

"You've got to get some help, Cath," Emily says. "You can't take all of this on by yourself."

"Who's going to help me?" Cath says. "I haven't got anyone. Literally, no one except for Dan and he's as useful as a chocolate teapot."

She bursts into tears again. Emily and I scooch closer and rub her back.

"God, sorry," Cath says. "That was a Mum saying."

She wipes her face, has a bite of cookie. "I guess at least this one time, I should be grateful for not having kids?" she says. "You hear of those women who are dealing with crappy teenagers and

exams and a dying parent at the same time. I guess at least I don't have that?"

Her voice wobbles at the end, we all know she doesn't really mean that.

"The sandwich generation," I say. They look at me, puzzled. "That's what it's called, isn't it – the sandwich generation. Caught between ill parents and difficult teenagers. Women. It's always on us, isn't it?"

"Sorry, guys," Cath says. "I normally hold it together, but those damn puppies broke me. I think I just need some sleep. Anyway, spotlight on you, Ems."

She holds a fork towards Emily, like a microphone.

"Oh god, no," Emily says. "You have just put my problems thoroughly into perspective. I'm fine."

"Clearly, you're not," Cath says. "This is a sharing circle now. A shitness sharing circle."

"A circle of shit," I say.

"A shircle?" Cath says.

"Oh, that is shit," Emily laughs.

"Come on then," Cath says. "Share your shit."

"Honestly, I feel silly even being upset about it," Emily says. "It's just boring old marriage stuff."

"Spill," Cath says. "Your shit is our shit. Or something like that."

"There's actually not even anything specific to spill." Emily sighs, a loose strand of her blonde hair rising up with her breath. "I just feel so rubbish about it all. Like, there's a proper stone in my stomach that grows bigger every day, with every interaction

Rick and I have. Things are not good. And they've been not good before, plenty of times, but it feels different this time. Like there's no coming back from it."

"Have you tried talking to him about it?" I ask.

"Yep, he won't talk about it properly – just says he's busy at work and I'm working too much. I even suggested marriage counselling but he outright refused. Looked at me like I was mad and said I'm obviously the one with problems and maybe I should see a therapist before we think about going to see one together and even then, he's not sure he wants to air our dirty laundry to a stranger."

"And do you think he's seeing someone else?" Cath asks gently, tentatively.

"Honestly, I have no clue," Emily says. "Logistically, he could be – he's away a lot with work and home late, but he's always been like that and I haven't found any other evidence of an affair – no receipts for fancy dinners or presents, no lingering perfume smell. That's what they look for in the movies, isn't it?"

We both nod, agreeing that they do seem to be the traditional affair giveaways.

"So, what are you going to do?" I ask.

"Well, nothing for now. I've got a mental few months with trying to get a funding application together. So it's terrible timing. I guess I'll keep going, as I have been, and see what happens. And if it's still like this by the end of the summer, I'll have a rethink." She exhales. Big and deep. Her shoulders slumping with the weight of it all. "I'm sick of thinking about it, to be honest. It's doing my head in."

"We need a trip away, girls!" The thought comes to me suddenly, with a wave of excitement at being able to offer something helpful.

"You both need to get away – we all do. It's been ages since we've had a girls' trip. Dorit has a friend who has an Airbnb in Cornwall and she said we could use it. It would be perfect – good food, good wine, sea air, bonding time!"

Cath frowns. "I really don't think I could be that far away from Mum."

"I don't think I'd get a pass from Rick for a whole weekend," Emily says. "Do you know the lengths I had to go to to escape this morning?"

"Guys, come on!" I persist. "I know it'll be tricky, but we can make it work – Cath, you can insist that Dan covers your mum that weekend – he owes you, hugely, it's the least he could do. And he's got his wife to help out if needed. And Emily, you deserve it too – Rick can step up for once – you've had the kids so much while he's been away, and all the other bloody times. Just say I'm having a mental breakdown or something."

"I mean, you kind of are," Cath laughs. "That's what the list is, right?"

I throw a cookie crumb at her. "Seriously, I think it would be perfect for us. Just what we need."

"I'm really sorry," Emily says. "It's just terrible timing for me at the moment. It's so far away, and I have so much work to do, I wouldn't be any fun. Can we do it another time – in the autumn, maybe?"

I concede. With a huff and an arm cross.

"It's a lovely thought," Cath says. "And we'll definitely do it. Just not right now."

"Hmm," I grunt.

I am a sulker. I can't help it, I think it's a hangover from my

teenage years. The only way I deal with disappointment or difficulties or arguments is to regress to my fifteen-year-old self.

"So, this Dorit," Cath says. "She's your new fabulous friend, yes?"

"Yes," I say. "And she's a lot more fun than you arseholes."

"Well, if she's so footloose and fancy free, why don't you lovebirds go on your own?" Cath says. "You could tick kissing a girl off your list."

"I want to go with you guys too," I say, with a hint more toddler than intended.

"Come on then," Emily says. "Tell us what the list's latest is. Where are you at with the parkour?"

This perks me up. The attention being on me and the fact I have news to report. "So, I told you Dorit—"

"Fabulous Dorit," Cath says. "Let's give her her full title."

I roll my eyes. "So, I told you Fabulous Dorit had a friend who runs a production company?" They nod. "I met with her the other day and she is amazing. Full on boss-bitch but also lovely and kind, amazing. She was so understanding about my situation."

"What's your situation?" Cath asks.

"That I've been out of work and mired in childcare and dishwasher loading and laundry for sixteen years," I say.

"Ah, that one. Sorry, continue."

"So yeah, I met her – Jodie – she's amazing, and she was more than happy to give me some work experience. There's a special scheme they've used before exactly for people like me who have been out of work for a while, so she's going to do it through that. She did say I'd have to start as a runner again, but I expected that." I can feel myself glowing as I announce the news. "So, you're

looking at a future employee – kind of – at Red Raw Productions."

Cath nearly spits her tea out, then starts bellowing with laughter. "Sorry, sorry – just to confirm – you're going to be working at production company named after your vagina?"

Emily starts giggling.

"Oh yeah, I hadn't thought of that." I laugh. "Probably something I shouldn't mention though, I reckon. And for the record, mine is now spiky like a hedgehog."

Cath wipes tears from her face – at least they're happy ones this time.

"Charlie, this is so brilliant!" Emily squeals, once we've all calmed down. "I am so excited for you! When do you start? What show will you be working on?"

"I start in two weeks – I said I needed time to sort out childcare and all that. And James and I have had massive arguments about it, mostly over text as he's barely been here, so I need to get all my ducks in a row before I start."

"What's his problem with it?" Emily asks. "Surely he should be happy you're going back to work?"

"He's going to miss his 1950s housewife who runs the house so he can work as much as he wants and not think about anything else, right?" Cath says. "God, what I'd do for a 1950s housewife. We all need one of those."

"It's not exactly that," I say, feeling a strange urge to defend James, which is ridiculous as he's really pissed me off about the whole thing. "Logistics are a bit tricky, which I understand. And I won't be earning any money, so I understand that too." Cath scowls, I decide to move on quickly. "It will just be office running

to begin with, but they have loads of other shows they make, including a couple of live ones so I might get put on one of those. Jodie said they try to move the work experience around to different departments and on to different shows. I'm absolutely shitting it. But also piss-my-pants excited!"

"Wear some TENA Lady," Cath says. "Not for the excitement, but, you know, we're older ladies now – and you've pushed three kids out your vagina, your bladder won't be what it used to be. You don't want to lose any opportunities to the box-fresh twenty-somethings because you're having to go and piss every three minutes."

"Good point," I say.

July

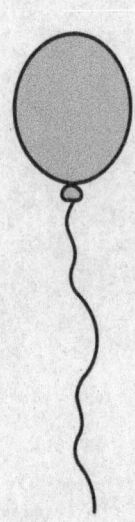

14

THE RED Raw offices are very TV, in a good way, and everything you would want from a working environment – exposed brick walls, glass meeting rooms, posters of all their shows on display and brightly coloured beanbags. Jodie told me to come in a bit later on my first day, so when I walk in at 11 a.m. it's already buzzing with brilliance and creativity. Someone is discussing last night's TV, another is talking about a play they saw and someone else is asking where the gold lamé underpants for a shoot are. No one is talking about lost PE kits or homework or PTA quiz nights. I almost want to cry at the wonder of it, that this is my workplace now.

The young receptionist with the slightly weird nose piercing that looks like something you'd attribute to a pig but, I understand, is the height of coolness, greets me with a big friendly smile and delivers me to someone called Zac who is Head Runner, and therefore my line manager. He looks twelve.

"Zac," the receptionist says (I did not get her name, it was something unusual). "This is Charlie, the new Back to Work intern. Charlie, this is Zac. I'll get on with sorting your pass, but if you need anything else, hit me up. Enjoy!"

"Hey." Zac looks me up and down, in a way that is far more obvious than it should be.

I suddenly feel extremely self-conscious in my Gap petite black suit trousers and very expensive pinstripe shirt I bought especially for the occasion from a fancy label that's all over Instagram and I thought was the height of fashion, but actually looks borrowed from a businessman. I realise now that my Instagram algorithm is perhaps not the coolest. I decided against the high-waisted jeans, or jeans in general – that's what we all used to wear in TV, but I didn't want to assume. Looking around, I needn't have worried – there are people here wearing jeans so holey it's hard to see any actual jean. Getting ready this morning was the most stressful thing I've done since childbirth. Apart from the Hollywood, maybe.

"Do you want a coffee or anything?" he asks.

I'm desperate for a coffee, but also terrified of needing to pee. So terrified I did, as Cath suggested, bring some TENA Lady with me. TENA Lady or TENA Ladies? TENA Ladies sounds like a gung-ho group of women in their sixties making a nudie calendar.

"I'm fine, thanks," I say. "I just had one."

This is a lie. I have not had even a sip of water since taking my Omega 3 supplement at 7.30 a.m. this morning.

"Right then," he says. "I guess I'll show you around and we can get cracking on the list."

He stands up, and even though he turns out to be about six feet tall, I can't help thinking he still looks twelve. Maybe it's the beanie hat, or the too-big jeans scrunched up with a too-tight belt at his waist, or the patches of pimples.

"So, here's the kitchen, obviously."

It's less of a kitchen, more of an open-plan breakfast bar. There are fancy coffee machines, and clear Tupperware containers filled

with different cereals, all neatly labelled, and a big red Smeg fridge with Polaroids of who I assume are members of the team with their coffee preferences written underneath. Gavin 'cortado one sugar' looks particularly hot, I notice.

"Help yourself to any of these," Zac says, waving his hand at the big glass jars filled with neatly stacked Oreos and Lotus biscuits, the likes of which I've only ever seen in the Kardashians' kitchens. I also spot a Free Drink Friday sign-up sheet on the wall – Zac sees me looking.

"We have drinks in the office on a Friday evening for anyone whose around, a cocktail dude comes in. Or you can just have wine, or beer, or kombucha or whatever. So yeah, when you know if you're going to be here, write down what you want, there's a list on the side."

Kardashian cookie jars? Free cocktails? I'm in heaven.

He slopes off from the kitchen area towards a group of desks at the side. "This is development – Katy, Connor and Sally." They all look up from their screens, mutter hellos and wave at me. "Guys, this is Charlie, the Back to Work intern."

I'm not sure how much I love the 'Back to Work intern' label, but I suppose at least it recognises I was at least once at work in the first place. Which is better than 'the bored, middle-aged housewife who's been cleaning piss off toilets and doing the school run for sixteen years' label.

We walk to another group of desks. "This is the *After Hours* team – Betty, researcher, Kate, AP and Gavin, producer."

Gavin Cortado is even foxier up close than in a Polaroid. So foxy, I feel a blush coming and have to look away.

"Guys, this is Charlie, the Back to Work intern."

"Nice to meet you, Charlie," Gavin says. "Jodie mentioned she might put you on the team at some point?"

"Uh, yeah . . . I think . . . yeah, she said . . ." I say, eloquently, making a mental note to work on my people skills. Or, like, just talking in general.

"Great, looking forward to it."

Zac shows me the rest of the office, introduces me to the other teams. I read something once about remembering people's names by memorising discernible features they might have, so I try that – Hector Man Bun, Betty Big Eyebrows (though, to be fair, most of them have big eyebrows), Karen Green Eyes (less helpful when I saw someone at the next group of desks also had green eyes), Josh Buffy Tattoo, Lulu Pig Piercing and, of course, Gavin Cortado. I hate myself for swooning, but also, I'm kind of relishing in the swooning. It's been a long time since I've really swooned at anyone – with their receding hairlines and sensible Merrells, the dads at the school gate are not exactly cream of the hot crop.

"So that's the office," Zac says, back in our corner. "Any questions?"

I have lots of questions – like, when is lunch, how often do people go for drinks after work, who is the scariest, how old are you actually and is Gavin married?

"Think I'm OK for now," I say. "I'm sure they'll come up, though."

"Right, so, first thing we have to do is source some gold lamé pants, red feathers and whipped cream."

"What's that for?" I ask.

"A new segment on *After Hours* – it's a truth or dare thing with celebrities. One of the dares is how quickly you can cover yourself in feathers and whipped cream."

"While wearing gold lamé pants?"

"You got it!"

"That totally sounds like the kind of stuff I used to work on," I say.

"Yeah?" He looks interested now, like maybe I'm not quite the washed-up housewife he assumed. "What did you work on?"

"I worked on a show called *Date Fish* that was a cross between a dating show and a prank show – a minor celebrity who essentially just catfished people and we recorded their responses. Another one called *WATCH OUT!* had presenters doing crazy dangerous things – a bit like *Jackass* but less funny. A short-lived breakfast show called *AWAKE!* Ooh and I did work experience on *SMTV Live* – the one Ant and Dec used to present."

I smile at the memory. That show was fun! As was everyone going to the pub after the show. Every time we watch *Saturday Night Takeaway*, I tell the kids I've been to the pub with Ant and Dec, and they don't seem impressed.

"I've never heard of any of those, sorry," Zac says.

"They were probably before you were born, to be fair."

"I know I look fifteen, but I'm actually twenty-three," Zac says.

"Truth be told, they were pretty bad shows," I say. "But fun to work on. It was the noughties, TV was like the Wild West, you could do whatever you wanted. We used to smoke in the office," I say, relishing in his disbelief.

We spend the morning on the hunt for the gold lamé shorts,

which, I have to say, I do very well at thanks to old-fashioned phone skills Zac doesn't seem to possess. We rush out to pick up Jodie's dry cleaning and get a super-food salad from Leon. The only thing she eats at work, Zac tells me. And then we pick her up a flat white from the cart round the corner, the only coffee she'll have, Zac tells me.

When we get back to the office, another runner, Hattie, has appeared, having spent the morning on a shoot. She looks like a slightly older version of Chloe and I know already I'm going to have a hard time remembering not to mother her. It takes all my energy when I first see her not to suggest she put another layer on because it's far too cold to be running around in shorts, even if they are paired with platformed boots. She seems a bit more suspicious of me, like maybe she's concerned I'm going to try and mother her, too. She can't be worried I'm going to take any potential jobs from under her, surely?

Eventually, Jodie returns to the office and summons me in. I scuttle along behind her and take a seat on the teal velvet chair in front of the king-sized desk. I love how womanly her office is – bright, deep colours, beautiful artwork, fluffy rugs, warm woods – it's a statement, but also inviting; it says 'I'm welcoming, but don't mess with me'.

And Jodie's vibe is exactly that – warm and scary at the same time. Her silver-stranded dark hair is in a sharp bob, lips painted a bright red and she's dressed head to toe in the kind of expensive older working woman boss-bitch chic I was aiming for with my businessman-from-the-city pinstripe shirt. The kind of stuff you get from Cos or Em & Me or Net-A-Porter – the kind of stuff I have

never, and will never, be able to afford. She puts her black, thick-rimmed reading glasses on and I marvel at how she can make even reading glasses look stylish. The ones I reluctantly bought for myself make me look like I've strapped Coke-bottle bottoms to my eyes.

"Sorry, one minute," she says, typing up an email and aggressively pressing send. "Bloody Netflix. Honestly, why we need five separate sets of notes is beyond me." She takes her glasses off, leans back in her chair and focuses her attention on me. "So, how's your first day going?"

"Great!" I say, way too enthusiastically.

"Zac's showing you the ropes?"

"Yep. He's introduced me to everyone, showed me where everything is. All good. I'm looking forward to getting stuck in."

"Good. We've got a lot of interesting stuff coming up and we're always looking for good people, so do well and there might be a position for you."

My stomach whirls. I try and contain my grin.

My phone pings.

And pings again.

I fumble getting it out of my pocket to put it on silent, see that I've had four messages from Felix, three from Chloe, one from Jack saying 'URGENT'.

"Sorry ... I ... it's my kids," I say, mortified.

"Take it if you need to take it," Jen says, her expression stony.

I have a quick scan of the messages:

Felix: *Mum, can Curtis come back for a play, please?*

Felix: *MUM, please?*

Felix: *Mum, he needs to know now otherwise he'll go to Ethan's house.*

Felix: *MUM?!?*

Chloe: *What's for dinner? I'm going round to Rupert's but let me know what's for dinner and I'll decide whether I'll stay at his for food or not.*

Chloe: *Can you pick up some cotton-wool pads, we're out.*

Chloe: *And tampons.*

Jack: *URGENT I FORGOT MY KEYS WHAT IS THE CODE FOR THE KEY SAFE.*

Frustration blooms in my chest. I can't leave them for one bloody day, even with the strictest of instructions. And it had to be right now, as I'm in with Jodie, that they decide to bombard me. I look at the clock and realise it's the end of the school day. I quickly text Chloe, reminding her she's supposed to be at home with the boys today and heating up the spaghetti bolognese I made last night and left in the fridge for their dinner.

I did everything – I made Jack's packed lunch and left it out, laid out all their uniforms (uniforms I had collected on Friday evening and put through the laundry), made their dinner for tonight, and

for three other nights in the week, knowing I'll be exhausted in this first week. I notice how even though they all knew this was my first day in a new job and it was a big deal to me, they all still contacted me rather than James.

I take a breath, reset.

I text Jack to remind him of the key code and inform Felix that today isn't a day for a play date at our house. Then I silence my phone as I know all of them will come back with various, and numerous, angry texts about all of that. I push the frustration away, readjusting my face and trying for a smile again.

"Sorry about that," I say. "Kids, hey?"

I'm going for maternal understanding, for a shared in-joke, some acknowledgement about how endlessly frustrating it is. I get a sceptical stare in response. I wither into the plush teal chair.

"I'm here to support you," Jodie says. "As a fellow woman, and mother. But – and this is going to sound harsh, but I want you to know it's coming from a good place – this industry is bloody hard – for women, and especially for mothers. There are no allowances – yeah, we have the legal maternity leave we're entitled to, but the more time you take away from the job, the bigger that black mark against your name gets. The times you have to leave early to take them to a hospital appointment, which for some reason they always seem to schedule in the middle of the bloody day. Or the times you don't make it in at all because one of them is ill. And god help you if it's chicken pox and you can't even pay a childminder to have them. Staff training days when they close the bloody school and parents' evenings that aren't actually in the evening, because since when has 4.30 p.m. been the evening? It's a

logistical nightmare at the best of times, and at the worst of times, it seems impossible. Most of the women I started working with have all gone. And you know who floats to the top, no matter how talentless they actually are? The men. And you know why? Because they all have wives at home who raise their children – who drop the kids off and pick them up, who stay at home with them when they're ill, who take them to the appointments, who go to the plays and the parents' evenings, who sort the packed lunches and the World Book Day costumes and the Roman Day costumes and the Victorian Day costumes and all the rest of the endless admin that needs doing."

She pauses, takes a breath. "I have had to fight tooth and nail to get where I am. I've made many sacrifices – including not seeing my children as much as I would've liked to. Everyone is looking for opportunities to drag us down, to make us think we can't do these jobs, so my advice, for what it's worth, is to make sure you can. And that you really *want* to. Make sure you have a partner who is fully supportive and make sure you have enough money to throw at it. Though that won't alleviate the guilt, of course. That, you just have to learn to live with."

A wave of uncertainty washes over me. That wasn't what I was expecting. Or hoping for. I thought we might go more down the solidarity route. She's scared me, and I wonder if that was her intention. Is she trying to scare me away? Did she even want me here in the first place?

"I . . . it's just first day adjustments," I say. "They're not used to me not being there. I need to train them better."

She smiles, and just like that the subject is done. "My thinking

is that we'll keep you in the office for a few weeks, give you a chance to see some development and get to grips with the company and our shows in general, then on *After Hours* for a few weeks to give you some live show experience. You've done live before, haven't you?"

"Yes," I say. "A breakfast show called *AWAKE!* It was fun."

"Nothing quite like the thrill – or stress – of live TV. It goes out on a Friday night, of course – I'm assuming that won't be a problem."

"Not at all," I say with false confidence, aware that James has got a work trip to Dubai coming up at some point in the near future.

"Good. That's that then. If you have any problems, let Zac know. I'll catch up with you in a couple of weeks."

"Great!" I stand up with more enthusiasm than I intended, rocketing out of the teal chair like I'm about to lead a charge somewhere. "Thank you. And thanks again for the opportunity."

She's already looking at her screen and frantically typing again as I go to walk out.

She pauses, looks over her glasses at me. "How's Dorit doing?"

"Great," I say, confused by her concerned scrunchy eyebrows.

"The kids are OK?"

It occurs to me that Dorit hardly mentions her kids when we're together. "I think so? She hasn't really said."

She scrunches up her eyebrows even more. "Are you two . . . close?"

"We see each other quite a lot," I say, aware that I'm being interrogated in a way I can't quite make out.

"Right." She nods and goes back to her screen.

I take that as my cue to leave.

* * *

🍹 COCKTAIL COVEN 🍹

Emily: *How was it?!?!?!?!?!?!*

Cath: *Spill.*

Me: *It was GREAT! A bit daunting, way too many names to remember, a twelve-year-old boss, gold lamé pants, Kardashian-esque cookie jars and Gavin Cortado.*

Cath: *That's a lot to unpack.*

Emily: *Please tell me you had to wear the gold lamé pants.*

Me: *Fortunately not. Jesus, can you imagine?! I'd def be out of a job.*

Cath: *Explain Gavin Cortado. Is he some z-list celebrity I don't know about?*

Me: *He's the producer on* After Hours. *And is foxy. And drinks cortados.*

Cath: *Don't start an affair with your boss. It will not end well. Hang on, is he the 12yo? Def don't start an affair with a 12yo boss!!*

Emily: *OMG do they make* After Hours! *That show is amazing – in a car crash, 'what the hell am I watching' way!*

Me: *I know!! And I'm going to get to go on set!! I'm so happy guys – it felt brilliant to be back. And I was actually pretty good.*

Cath: *If you do say so yourself.*

Me: *I do. Totally knackered now tho. And obvs James was running late. House was carnage when I got back.*

Cath: *Were the kids alive?*

Me: *Yep.*

Cath: *Well, you're fine then.*

Me: *True!*

Emily: *Can you get us in the audience at* After Hours*?!?!*

Cath: *I don't particularly want to see minor celebs pouring baked beans over each other or whatever other low-rent crap they do.*

Emily: *Don't be boring!*

Me: *I'll def see if I can. And you're coming to the open-mic night, right?*

Emily: *Need to check with Rick. Hoping to.*

Cath: *Yep. But know that I will be dying on the inside.*

Me: *ME TOO.*

15

I AM BONE tired. So tired, everything looks blurred through my pinhole eyes. So tired, my tongue hangs limp like a dead slug in my mouth when I go to speak. So tired, I can barely manage to put one foot in front of the other. Or function, in general.

Yet I am cooking a roast. Because it has been deemed (by James) that we are not having enough family time and the kids aren't eating well enough. Which is to say, he thinks I am not here enough and the meals I bust a gut to cook over the weekend are not nutritional enough when combined with the beige freezer food that constitute the other couple of days in the week. So, I feel the need to prove that the family won't suffer by me working, that I can be a reasonable employee and a reasonable mum and a reasonable wife, though to be honest, my spousal duties are truly at the bottom of my list.

This feeling, this unease – the being stretched too thin, like one of those gross sticky toys the boys always get to throw at the walls that if you stretch enough, just go thin and then break – I remember it well. Everything feels like a battle. Like you're walking up a mountain carrying a boulder, except it's three boulders and it's not a mountain, it's a treadmill on an incline because you're never actually getting anywhere. Along with the not making any money, it's the main reason why I stayed at home in the first place. I do not

a good stretchy woman make. I honestly don't know how women do it. Especially women with big, important jobs. I guess, like Jodie said, you either need a super supportive partner or enough money to throw at it. Neither of which I currently have.

As I baste the chicken, I think of what my mum said on the phone the other day, all the way from their Caribbean cruise – the third cruise this year, if you're counting. Which I am. It's the same thing she said all those years ago when I was struggling. "Your generation have made it too hard on yourselves with all this wanting to have it all. You've given yourself double the work. Don't try and have it all, because what you'll end up having is a heart attack – or a divorce. Pick a lane."

Janice Parsons, ever the feminist.

Emily and I often talk about her sister, Pam, and how sometimes we wish we had it in us to be like her. She stayed at home to bring up the kids from as soon as she had the first one and is the perfect 1950s housewife – keeps the house immaculate, goes above and beyond for the children – homework monitoring, extra tutoring, kick-ass World Book Day costumes and general super involvement with the school, she makes sure there's always a home-cooked meal waiting for Rob when he gets home. It wouldn't surprise me if she stands at the door with a smoking jacket, whisky and cigar to greet him. She loves it – all of it. She feels it's a privilege to be able to stay at home, feels grateful to Rob for going out and making the money so that she can.

And I get that, I do. There were some days, particularly those when I took myself out for breakfast, then coffee with a friend, then home to an afternoon on the sofa watching *Housewives*, when I did

feel grateful. But there were other, more frequent, days when I was resentful of James for having a career and being able to focus on it, and the fact we decided to have children having no impact on that. With me at home, he could leave for work as early as he wanted, get back as late as he needed to, go out for any work dinners it was helpful to attend, go on any work trips without needing to frantically piece together any kind of childcare. And frankly, that's a massive privilege too.

But now we're back in this hinterland of us both working and scrambling to fit it around the children. Or rather, I am.

I forget to cook the carrots till the last minute, leave the Yorkshires in too long, and balls up the gravy. Clearly not fit for purpose.

"Dinner!" I shout up.

Silence.

The gravy is not in a safe enough place for me to leave so I just shout louder. And louder. Until eventually James hears me.

"All right, all right," he says. "No need to shout."

"Well, there was, actually," I snap. It comes out too snappy. "Sorry, I couldn't leave the gravy and—"

"It's fine, all chill," he says, getting himself a pint glass out for his non-alcoholic beer and standing right in the middle of the kitchen and in my way in the process.

"Can you go and round up the kids?" I ask, blowing a strand of hair off my face.

"Sure." He slowly pours his beer into the pint glass. Then slowly walks to the bin to throw the can away. Then slowly slip slops in his slippers to the bottom of the stairs and shouts up. No sense of urgency.

I take a deep breath, repeat the mantra: it doesn't matter if the food is cold, it doesn't matter if the food is cold, it doesn't matter if the food is cold. I do this sometimes when I feel my rage boiling over. The rage makes me feel like a nagging housewife. But really, it shouldn't be too much to ask for people to make it to the table on time when I've spent hours cooking. This is especially pertinent with eggs, because, as I remind James every time his lateness to a soft-boiled egg renders it a hard-boiled egg and he looks at me with disappointment – EGGS CARRY ON COOKING.

* * *

"This is lovely, isn't it?" James says, forking the last of his three servings into his mouth and leaning back in his chair. "Us all being together and eating at the table like a proper family. It's nice to have you around, we've missed you."

I grind my teeth, but let the comment go.

"The Yorkshires were a bit flat," Jack says with a scowl.

"Well yeah, but it was still lovely," James says, winking at me.

"Thanks, Mum," they all repeat, in varying levels of muttering.

"You could always cook if it's that much of a problem," I say.

"Don't let Dad cook!" Chloe says.

"He burns everything," Felix adds.

"Guys, come on!" James puts on his *Godfather* accent. "I've got my special pasta."

"Special, as in, disgusting?" I laugh.

He sticks his tongue out at me.

"How's your history revision going, Chloe?" I ask.

She looks different, though I can't place in what way. I haven't really seen her for a few days as she's been out or locked away in her room and there's definitely something about her now that doesn't seem like normal Chloe. Maybe it's just the exam stress.

"OK, I guess." She shrugs, pushing the last scrap of potato around her plate. "As OK as revision ever is."

"Talking of history . . ." James says, grinning.

The boys perk up. "It's a dad joke!" Jack says, delighted.

Chloe and I groan.

"Why was the pharaoh boastful?"

"Why was the pharaoh boastful?" Felix asks.

"Because he sphinx he's the best!"

The boys and James collapse into laughter, and eventually Chloe and I concede and laugh too. Dad jokes are James's thing. That and dad dancing and jumping out at people to scare them, even though that has ended in tears many times. He used to do all of those a lot, less so now that he's always busy or stressed or hardly ever here. His silliness is one of the things that attracted me to him. Being weird together. There's a quote about that from someone famous – Beyoncé or Cherie Blair or Dr Seuss. Well, that was James and I, being weird together. Not so much any more though; the weirdest we get now is synchronised pillow spraying at bedtime.

We clear the table, play cards and have ice cream, rolling out the family in-jokes and mercilessly taking the piss out of each other. I laugh so much at Jack doing an impression of James I almost piss myself. It feels good (the laughing, not the nearly pissing myself). We have an entirely different family dynamic when both James

and I are here, and I relish not being the only one telling the kids to do things (use cutlery to eat), picking them up on bad manners (no nose-picking at the table), nagging at them to get off their phones (I'm sure it's not essential that you take your BeReal right this minute).

As I look around the table, it occurs to me that I've been enjoying them more recently. I'm less bothered by Chloe's constant eye rolls and by Jack pleading for device time every five minutes. I can even manage to handle the wrestling without completely losing my temper at the first instance of one of them sitting on the other one's head. I realise that, despite my bone-aching tiredness, my tolerance seems higher. Which is a great thing. Because my tolerance tank was for sure running on empty before.

"Who's for a film and popcorn?" I say. "I may even have some chocolate I can dig out of the cupboard."

It doesn't even bother me when Felix and Jack run through to the living room, without putting their bowls away, and wrestle for the corner seat on the sofa, or when Chloe calls them both idiots, or when, later, James chews the popcorn so loudly it's like sitting next to a washing machine.

* * *

I snuggle up to James in bed, leaning into the increasingly rare moment of peace and goodwill. He's reading another philosophy book and looks handsome in his concentration. I pretzel myself to put my cold feet on the inside of his thighs to warm them up. It's a move I can only do when he's in a good enough mood.

"No, no, no, no, no!" he shrieks. "Get those ice blocks off me!"

"I need warming up," I plead. "Just thirty seconds. You're so hot."

"Why, thank you."

"As in, your body temperature."

"Why, thank you."

He carries on reading. I lay my head against his chest, he moves the book to accommodate me.

"I had a nice day today," I say. "It was a perfect chilled Sunday."

"Yeah, it was nice," he says. "Apart from the flat Yorkshires, obviously."

I tweak his nipple.

"Oh, I seeeee," he says, a glint in his eye. "You're in a cheeky mood, are you?"

He puts his book to the side and tickles me. I squirm and resist, part of me loving the feel of his hands on me and the closeness. Soon we're kissing and the tickling has turned to touching.

16

🍹 COCKTAIL COVEN 🍹

Me: *Holy fuck, anal hurts.*

Cath: *WTF?!?*

Emily: *Explain yourself!*

Me: *I will not be taking questions at this time.*

17

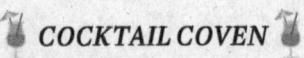

Me: *Is it OK to fancy Damon Albarn even though he suggested Taylor Swift didn't write her own songs?*

Emily: *No.*

Cath: *No, because he's a crusty old man. And a misogynist.*

Me: *But he's kind of hot. In a crusty old man way. And he's got a weird lisp/whistle type thing when he talks that I find quite sexy.*

Cath: *You are so strange.*

Me: *If you were Justine, would you have gone Brett or Damon?*

Cath: *What the hell are you on about?*

Emily: *Justine Frischmann – lead singer of Elastica,*

left Brett Anderson (Suede) for Damon Albarn. Charlie obsessing about nineties drama thirty years after the event.

Me: *Has it been thirty years?!?! God, we're old.*

Emily: *Damon btw.*

Cath: *They're both gross. Arrogant, narcissistic men who are not as talented as they think.*

18

"**WHAT ABOUT** something on how annoying your husband is?" Dorit suggests.

We are in a bar in Soho, a couple of hours before my open-mic slot, trying to brainstorm some material for me. Because, like the chaotic twat I am, I haven't written more than two jokes and I certainly haven't practised anything.

"I think James is coming tonight," I say. "And honestly, he was not keen. I practically had to beg him to come and support me and even then, he gave me a list of reasons why he couldn't and/or didn't want to. So it's now quite a big deal and I probably shouldn't be mean about him in public."

"But it's funny," she says, sipping her margarita. I managed to duck out of work early enough to make happy hour. We currently have six margaritas on our table. Dorit said I need the Dutch courage. "It's like how all the men take the piss out of their mother-in-laws, or wives. People know you're exaggerating. They find it funny. It's poetic licence – he won't mind. Trust me. And drink up, I'm way ahead of you."

"What would I even say about him, though?" I ask. "He's annoying and enraging, but not in a funny way. Oh my god, how did I let you talk me into this?"

The dark walls suddenly feel like they're folding in on me, the

stench of old booze catching in my nostrils. I want to vomit.

"Deep breaths," she says. "Do I have to give you your list pep talk again?"

I look at her questioningly.

She pushes on. "How the point of this list is for you to get out of your comfort zone, to push yourself, challenge yourself? You'll never grow if you're not challenging yourself. You'll stagnate. And you've been doing that for too long. So what if you bomb? You'll never see these people again."

"Except for you. And my husband. And my friends. And some of my colleagues," I say, fear pinching with each one I list.

"Well, clearly you don't have to worry about making a tit out of yourself in front of me – I've been to parkour with you, remember?" She slaps the table and lets out her honk laugh.

It eases me up a bit. She's right – it can't be worse than parkour.

"And your husband and friends would've seen you do worse, too." She takes another sip. "Your work colleagues though . . . are you sure that was wise?"

"Oh god, do you think it's a terrible idea?"

"Lighten up!" she shouts. "I was joking! And can I just add – how great is it that you've got work colleagues now? Cheers to that."

I smile, taking it in. It is pretty cool. I always joke to James that my work Christmas party consists of me getting drunk, shouting at my co-workers (the kids) and eating all the Pringles. This year, I may actually have a proper Christmas party to go to. Probably in a swanky Soho bar. So, it's probably a good idea to not make a fool of myself tonight.

"Is Jodie coming?" Dorit asks.

"No. She thanked me for the invite but said she'd rather not witness a member of staff completely wipe out in public and then have to make eye contact with them again."

Dorit laughs. Big and hearty. "Very Jodie."

Last time I saw Dorit, I mentioned Jodie had asked after her, though I didn't explain that the way she asked had seemed a bit strange. After that interaction with Jodie, it had occurred to me that I actually know very little about Dorit apart from the names of her kids and that she was an actor and likes margaritas and her red wine of choice is a pinot noir. We always meet up at mine or out somewhere and she always seem to deflect or answer in a vague, non-specific way when I ask her questions. I've made a point to ask her more, but she's like a stone wall. One of those Yorkshire Dales ones that are impenetrable and multi-layered. Which, it occurred to me, I should probably find frustrating, but weirdly, I don't. I think I'm enjoying having someone so invested in me and my problems and my list for a change. Emily and Cath would roll their eyes and say that's my main character syndrome.

"Come on, no more chit chat. I don't have long. And so far, all I have is a dad joke about a pharaoh that may or may not be plagiarised."

* * *

Zac, Fliss and Lulu arrive an hour later and Dorit gets another round of cocktails in. Though Zac doesn't drink because he can't afford it ('the money and the hangxiety'), and Lulu doesn't drink because she has to be up early to record the podcast she does with

her cat (*Lulu Loves Lola*). I don't remember anyone not drinking when I worked in TV before. I more remember people drinking way too much, all the time, and making dicks out of themselves (me included). One of the other researchers I used to work with on *AWAKE!*, Tanya, would always, without doubt, get totally wankered and end up flashing her tits at someone, or multiple people, at the end of a night out. We called her Tanya Tits, which, in hindsight, is a decidedly uncreative nickname for a bunch of creative people to have come up with. I had a habit of dancing on tables at any and every opportunity, and our producer Gabe was known for shoving coke up people's noses. Though that was all through the day, not just on nights out. And in hindsight, was clearly a violation at best, a full-on crime at worst.

I've written a lot more of my book. It feels like it's flowing now. And Dorit finds everything I suggest hilarious so I'm feeling more confident. I try some material on Zac and Fliss and Lulu – they don't laugh like Dorit does. In fact, they don't really laugh at all, but they're probably just a bit too young to get some of it. I guess it's hard to laugh about a relationship twenty years in if the longest you've been with someone is six months. They smile and nod though, in a generally amused way, so I'm taking that as a win.

I stay for a quick drink, then leave them with Dorit and head over to the venue to do some prep on my own. I stumble a bit as I stand up. Those cocktails were stronger than I thought. Or I had more of them than I realised. I make a mental note to drink some water. But not so much it'll make me need a wee.

* * *

The venue, the Lotta Laughs Club, is a pokey, dark bar at the back of a pub, nestled between a swanky cocktail bar and a sex shop. I'm met by a burly man in a way too tight Newman and Baddiel tour T-shirt, like that somehow shows his comedy credentials. He tells me his name is Dave and he's the organiser and he looks me up and down in such slow motion I feel like I'm being x-rayed. He gives me a spiel about how he came to set up the night, listing all the famous comedians he's had on (all men, I notice) and ticks off my name.

"This your first time?" he asks, smirking.

"Sure is!" I say. With too much enthusiasm.

"Should be a good crowd tonight, though you always get at least one or two who have been at the pub all afternoon. Expect some heckling."

His smirk is wider, he's enjoying scaring me, like I'm a mouse he's brought in and is toying with. "I'm sure I'll be fine." I say it with a margarita-fuelled confidence.

Groups of people are slowly filtering into the bar and I realise I really must practise, so I thank him, coldly, and ask where the toilet is. I lock myself in a cubicle and perch on the extremely dodgy-looking toilet seat, pleased to be wearing tights. I take in the graffiti as I get the hip flask of tequila Dorit gave me out of my bag, figuring the only way through it is . . . through it with tequila.

Maz sucks good cock.

(Interesting. I wonder what constitutes good cock and if she knows beforehand?)

Call Hazel for good times.

(More straightforward.)

All you need is love.

Then underneath it, someone else has written:

Actually, I need a shit.

Life is beautiful, life is sweet,
Please don't piss on the toilet seat.

Scissoring for the win.

I'm hit by inspiration and rummage around in my bag to find my emergency Sharpie (for last minute name-labelling of sports kit/uniform).

I consider what to write – toying with 'Enjoy life while you can', 'Your 20s are better than your 40s, FACTS' and a basic, old school, 'Charlie woz here', but a last-minute contender sweeps in and I write:

No one tells you this, but you actually shit during childbirth.

And then, inspired by the mention of bum stuff:

Anal hurts.

My phone pings, a text from Emily:

> Emily: *Mate, I'm SO sorry but I'm not going to make your big debut tonight. Couldn't get a sitter and it's all gone a bit pear-shaped my end. I'll take you out for a drink and you can tell me all about it. Sending lots of love.*

> Me: *NOOOOOOO! You've known about it for ages!*

> Emily: *I know. I'm sorry. Really couldn't be helped. Love you! You'll be amazing.*

A nugget of anger flares up in me. This is a big deal for me and she didn't bother to sort childcare or persuade Rick to have his own bloody kids, even though I gave everyone plenty of advance warning. I know babysitters are a faff but they're never impossible, not now we've got those apps. If you don't mind strangers looking after your kids. Which, for something as important as this, would've been not ideal but perfectly fine. I take a deep breath and another swig of the tequila, which reminds me I need to get some water. I'll just have to push thoughts of Emily to one side for now – at least Cath and Dorit and James are still coming. I text James and Cath to double check.

James replies instantly:

> *Sorry, meeting ran over. Will be a tiny bit late. On my way now though.*

The anger nugget flares again, a goujon this time. This is so standard James. With the amount of dates we've had scheduled – dinners, comedy, theatre – that James has turned up late to, I should've seen this coming. I guess I was hoping he might make an extra effort with tonight. Not so, apparently.

Cath replies:

> Cath: *I'm ready and waiting! Where are you?*
>
> Me: *In the toilet – I need to practise! I'll be out in a minute when it starts. We've got reserved seating – has my name on it.*
>
> Cath: *It starts in 10 mins dude.*

Shit.

Shit.

I have not practised.

It's only a five-minute slot – that's nothing. And I have time to at least read it through now. So, I do that. Though the words are a bit blurred. Dorit said most stand-ups don't use notes and just write key words to remind them of the segments on their hands, so I get my Sharpie out and scrawl words all over my hands in the hope that they'll bring me some kind of reminder or inspiration. Divine inspiration at this point would be amazing.

* * *

Everyone is taking their seats as I slide into mine next to Cath.

"Hey!" she says, giving me a massive hug.

"I'm so excited," I say. "I'm so pleased you came. Can't believe Emily didn't, you know, cos I told you guys ages ago and babysitter, I mean, bloody Rick the dick babysitter could've—"

Cath's eyes widen in horror. "Dude, are you wasted?"

"What?" I bat the idea away. "No, I just had some cocktails with Dorit. Dutch courage. Dorit! You must meet Dorit. And my work colleges." I laugh hysterically at my mistake. "Colleagues. My work coll-eeeee-agues."

I see Dorit is sitting an empty chair away from Cath, currently deep in conversation with Fliss. "Dorit!" I shout. I lean over Cath to tap Dorit on the shoulder, which ends up being more a yank than a tap. "DORIT!" She turns around.

"There she is!" She grins, claps her hands together in excitement.

"Dorit, meet my best friend, Cath. One of my best friends, anyway, the other one didn't bother to—"

"Emily's having a really tough time," Cath says, almost under her breath. "Don't be too hard on her."

She must see I'm about to go in for another rant because she turns her attention to Dorit. "Hi, Dorit, so nice to finally meet you – I've heard all good things. Lots of good things!"

"You too, Cath. Isn't our girl doing well? She's a legend – so bloody brave doing shit like this. I love it!"

"Yeah." Cath nods, unconvinced.

It pisses me off, to be honest. And is the clearest, most obvious indication of the divide between Cath and Emily and Dorit – the girls, always doubting me, looking down on my list and my need

for change, and Dorit who has always been one hundred per cent behind me, cheering me on, believing in me.

Fliss, Zac and Lulu wave at me from the seats beyond Dorit and I realise I should introduce Cath to them too, though now I'm feeling reluctant about the whole merging-of-the-worlds thing.

Cath turns to me, all serious. "Charlie, you can't go on this pissed. It'll be a disaster."

I roll my eyes. "Of course you'd say that."

"What's that supposed to mean?"

"You have no faith in me." It comes out sulky. "You don't support me. I don't even know why you bothered coming."

Cath's face contorts into disbelief. Or maybe anger. Or confusion. It's hard to tell when it's also a bit blurry.

"Look at me." She takes my face between her hands and stares right at me. "I'm going to ignore everything you just said because you're clearly drunk. I'm going to get you some water. Have you eaten anything?"

I shake my head, the last thing I ate was a day-old croissant that had been left in the office kitchen. It was a busy day.

"Right, I'm going to get you some water and food of some kind. Do not drink anything else, OK?"

I nod.

Cath squeezes past me to go to the bar and about thirty seconds later, the lights dim.

Dave comes on to the stage, introduces the night, says some random things about what a treat we've got lined up for us this evening and when the bar is open. I'm not really listening because I'm suddenly nervous, my margarita confidence starting to wane,

and I'm just listening out for my name. I worry about how my high-waisted jeans will look on stage. About if I have lipstick on my teeth. About which segment I decided on doing first. About what the words on my hands mean.

And then all of a sudden, he's said my name and is looking directly at me and Dorit is clapping and shrieking and that gives me the burst I need to move my legs and get up onto the stage. And then I'm there, looking out at a sea of strangers, except I can't see much because the lights are quite bright in my face. I realise this is it, I'm doing it. I'm doing the big scary thing.

"Hi, everyone!" I say, as loudly and confidently as I can muster. I've been watching some stand-up in the run up to this. Confidence is key.

The mic stand is way too high for me. I fiddle with the adjusting thing on it but I make it too loose so it suddenly shoots down. I try again, pulling it up and trying to tighten it. The mic makes a loud screech as I accidentally wallop it with the hip flask I realise I have brought on stage with me. I place the flask on the floor, banging my head on the mic as I come back up, swaying a bit with the effort of it all. The energy in the room shifts. People start to shuffle, whisper, snigger. I give up on the mic stand and manage to wrestle the mic out of the holder, just as Dave is about to, belatedly, come and help me.

"Well, that was awkward," I say.

It gets a few laughs. That's the other tip I picked up from my research – if things are going wrong, take the piss out of yourself, acknowledge the thing that's going wrong.

"Let's try again. Hi, everyone!"

A few people mutter a response and I hear Dorit shout a big booming, "HELLO!"

"So as you might have guessed, I'm a middle-aged woman. Can you even . . . can people even see me?"

Dave looks quizzically on from the sidelines, a few people turn their heads, looking around, as if I'm asking a genuine question, like I'm asking for the lights to be adjusted.

"Cos, you know, women all turn invisible as soon as we hit forty – am I right?"

"You know it girl!" Dorit shouts. This gets a small titter.

"You may as well call it muddle-aged though," I continue. "Because let me tell you, it's confusing as fuck. I wanted kids, but now I have them, my god, they're bloody annoying. They should include these in *What to Expect When You're Expecting*: they piss all over toilet seats AND walls, never stop wrestling, don't put dirty dishes in the dishwasher AND rip your vagina to shreds. If I'd have wanted a shredded vagina I would've—"

My mind goes blank. I can't remember what the end of that joke was. I search the Sharpie on my hand but it's all blurry – I can make out 'SEX', 'BORING' and 'ANAL' but I decide they're not relevant.

"Yeah, kids," I conclude. Hoping to go for a general rounding out. "Who'd have 'em?"

There's a pause, more shuffling.

"So, I've been married for a long time." This is a good segment segue. I'm doing well. "Who here is married?"

(Another tip I picked up from my research – get the audience involved.)

There are a few grunts.

"It's a whole job in itself, isn't it?"

A door at the back of the room opens. I squint through the lights and see it's James.

"Ah, and here's my husband now. Late as usual."

The whole room turns round and looks at him. He squirms, makes a quick eye contact with me before staring at the floor, then heads towards Cath who is beckoning him to his seat.

"They should change the vows too, you know, something like: I promise to not get angry with you every time you work at weekends, or go away for work trips or leave the toilet seat up or chew really loudly." I look at my hand. I'm pretty sure it's not the anal bit yet. I see 'VOWS'. I'm not sure where it went next, but I vaguely remember it's in this general bit. It will do.

"Forget this in sickness and in health bollocks, they need to make it in sickness and in middle-age. Because, you know, by the time you've been together twenty years, you're definitely sick of them."

The lights are making my head pound, a pressure like a jackhammer starts up on my temples. I'm losing them. I can feel I'm losing them. Though I'm not sure I ever really had them. My tongue is furry, sticking to my desert-dry mouth like Velcro. I need to turn this around. Sex. Dorit said sex is always a good topic. 'Universal', was I think the word she used.

"And the sex. Well." I pull a face and shake my head. "Twenty-year-old sex is a whole other story, isn't it? I mean sex with the same person for twenty years, not having sex with a twenty-year-old – that probably *would* be fun at this point."

That gets a laugh! And I hadn't even pre-written that one! I'm

genuinely funny. I'm doing The Thing and killing it.

"It all gets a bit boring, doesn't it? Tweak here." I make a nipple tweaking motion. "Finger up here." I make a fingering motion. "And then they expect you to boil over like a kettle."

People look confused. I wonder if it was the mimes.

"Well, you'll need to descale me first, love. You'd think twenty years would be long enough to find my clit, am I right?" Clit talk was one of Dorit's suggestions. She said it's a fail-safe comedy topic. "Typical man though, they have a man look, which really must be basically with their eyes closed, and don't see what's right in front of them. Staring them in the face. Though I guess that would require his face being down there once in a while."

A few groans. I need to get them back, I need to up the stakes.

"We tried anal for the first time the other day."

This gets some titters. Though I notice a lot of people snap their heads round to look at James.

"Anyone else here done anal?"

My audience participation tip is not a success this time. No one puts their hand up. Though there is some snickering. Maybe I can build on that.

I'm about to launch into the next bit, which I can't fully remember but involves something about how much it hurts, when I go to take a step and see the microphone cord has twisted around me. I saw this happen on shows I researched too – you have to elegantly disentangle while still speaking, never dropping a beat.

"Well for those who haven't, let me tell—"

I twirl, trying to unwind the lead, but the motion makes me dizzy and as I go to take a step to steady myself, the lead catches

me. I fall, in a kind of weird action film slow-motion, and land hard on my elbow. A white heat of pain sweeps through my arm, shoulder, side, but I know I have to keep going. Dave is suddenly there, and Cath and a few randoms from the first row. I push them off me and manage to stand back up, feeling like a foal finding its feet for the first time.

"I'm fine!" I proclaim to the crowd.

They cheer.

Dave grabs the mic from me and ushers me off the stage. Which is a shame as I feel like I was just getting into my rhythm.

"And that was Charlie Parsons. Available for weddings and funerals – and divorce parties. Possibly her own."

The crowd laugh hysterically and my whole body glows with warmth and validation.

I walk back over to my seat, taking note of the empty one next to it.

"Girl!" Dorit leans over Cath to give me a high five, then passes me a glass of wine. "You are a bloody legend!"

"Was it OK?" I ask, grinning. I drink the wine gratefully. It's sharp and sour, but it's wine, and I'm in need. I deserve it.

"Legend. Just legend," she says. "I laughed my tits off."

Zac and Fliss and Lulu smile weakly and nod at me.

"Where's James?" I ask Cath.

"He left." She says it pointedly. Sharp.

"Ah, probably had to get back for the babysitter," I say, though I'm pretty sure Chloe was looking after the boys tonight.

"I think he was upset, Charlie." She sighs. "What the hell was that?"

"That was comedy," I say. "And a bit of poetic licence."

Dave introduces the next act, I don't catch the name but a tall gangly guy with ripped jeans and a suit jacket hops on the stage.

"Wow, how to follow that, hey?"

The audience laugh. I glow again.

"Do you want to get out of here?" she asks. "Go and get a coffee somewhere? And lots of water."

I roll my eyes. "No way. The hard bit is done. Now I can relax and have a drink."

"I think you did plenty of that before you went on, didn't you?"

I choose to ignore that comment, though it pinches. I'm on a high and I'm not going to let her bring me down. "Dorit and I might go dancing after this if you fancy coming?"

She looks at me. Like, really stares. It makes me feel like a teenager.

"No, I don't want to go dancing on a Tuesday night in some seedy Soho bar that will be full of rabid twenty-somethings and pervy old men. You have fun. Give me a call when you're normal Charlie again. Or when you start remembering tonight and with some clarity."

She waves a terse goodbye to Dorit and my work friends and then pushes past me to leave and I'm left wondering when my friends all got so boring.

19

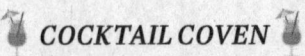

Me: *I am in the bad books.*

Me: *Think I went a bit far with the comedy.*

Me: *Not that I can remember that much.*

Me: *But he didn't like the jokes. Even though it was clearly just for laughs and was poetic licence. But I do feel bad. I guess. But also, he needs to get his sense of humour back and maybe try supporting me once in a while.*

Me: *Two weeks on and he's still giving me the ice-cold shoulder. From Dubai.*

Me: *Ugh, so annoying. Just as things are getting good with work stuff, home stuff is now utterly shite.*

Me: *I don't know what to do. Not sure I have the energy to try and hash it out and make nice.*

Me: *So yeah, I'm ignoring it for now, because work is AWESOME.*

Me: *OMG I forgot to tell you, I'm starting on* After Hours *this week! I'll get you guys tickets!*

Me: *Guys?*

Emily: *Have you thought about couples counselling? I could never get Rick to agree to go but I know some couples it's worked wonders for. Might be helpful. Exciting about* After Hours. *Good luck!*

Cath: *I'm in Margate for a bit, Mum's got worse. Won't be able to make it. Have fun.*

* * *

I get to the office late, missing the first twenty minutes of the production meeting.

Which is not a good look, but I try and style it out with excuses about trains. The truth is, I was out with Dorit at pop choir last night and we decided to stay and have a few drinks after and before I knew it, it was kicking-out time and then she insisted we went to the hotel bar for 'one for the road', and even though I decided to be sensible and stick on the water, I lost track of time and I snoozed my alarm too many times this morning because my head was in no way ready to face the day. But I've put mountains of concealer

on and used the eye drops Dorit gave me ('for the days you need to hide the fun you've had') and eaten approximately a whole pack of Smints, so I'm good to go.

I make my apologies, mumble for too long about trains, and sit in the one remaining chair at the big table.

"Ah great, you're here," Gavin says, with a tone I can't quite decipher but I'm choosing to believe is warm and friendly. He's standing by a whiteboard covered in messy scrawls and arrows and question marks. "For those of you who haven't met, this is Charlie. She's going to be joining us as a runner for the next few weeks."

A few new faces nod at me. Gavin does the introductions – the floor manager, Gus, another runner, Ben, and a couple of other people whose names I don't pick up because I'm focusing on how handsome Gavin is and worrying that I look like shit.

"We're just talking through segment ideas for Friday's show," Gavin says. "So, Betty, can I leave you to do pre-interviews with Zara and Elise about the celeb food fight?"

Betty nods.

"Ben, I see where you're going with that idea of mums having to guess whose genitals are their grown-up son's – a kind of *Naked Attraction* meets . . . I don't know. But I think it's a step too far."

Ben looks despondent, but shrugs it off.

"Anything else people want to throw into the mix?"

"Celebrity mud wrestling?" Ben suggests. "But in tiny bikinis and maybe with baby oil?"

"That's a bit too similar to celebrity food fight," Betty says.

Ben looks deflated.

"We could get Kaya or Rafe to get a colonoscopy and record

that as a VT, not a live segment," Kate says.

Kaya and Rafe are the gorgeous, fresh-faced, naïve presenters who are early enough in their careers that they're still likely to be up for anything, not realising yet the impact it will have down the line. We went through these kind of presenters like teabags when I worked on *AWAKE!*. You get them early, while they're still grateful for the job and prepared to do what you ask. That lasts about six months to a year, if you're lucky, then all of a sudden, they're asking for certain foods in their dressing room, and getting shitty with wardrobe, demanding cars everywhere and refusing to do simple VTs, like going to a sex camp or being covered in leeches.

"We did a colonoscopy on *AWAKE!*," I hear myself saying. Kate glares at me and I wonder if I should've just let that go. "But god, you know, that was years ago. And it was funny, so yeah, let's do it again."

"I'll put it as a possible," Gavin says, writing it on the board with a question mark.

"Lie detector?" Ben suggests. "Take a celebrity couple and rig them up to a lie detector and get them to ask each other questions and when they lie they get a little electric shock?"

"Been done," Gavin says. "Very recently."

I remember this now. The mad spitballing of mad ideas. Frenetic, stupid, far-fetched, gross. Throw anything out there and see if something, or some slither of something, sticks. And it's all fun. No one judges you because, no matter how preposterous you think your idea is, there's always something more preposterous that's already been thought of or shot already. It's silly. And creative. And fun.

"I've been watching that sex programme with the supermodel," Kate says. "She's done all kinds of crazy things like going to a masturbating circle and sex clubs. How about something along those lines – a masturbating race or something. We wouldn't be able to get the talent to do it, but we could one hundred per cent find civilians who would. Get a load of blokes in a line and get them to wank, quickest wins. We wouldn't be able to show the actual... action. But the way they cut it in the supermodel show worked pretty well. We could call it *Race to the finish*; *Wank to the finish*; *Wank Off*?"

"*Great British Wank Off*?" Ben suggests. "We could put a cake in the middle or something, like soggy biscuit but with cake."

People laugh. Gavin nods.

Ben smiles, pleased with himself, at last.

"*Jerk-off Chicken*?" he says. "Instead of cake, make it jerk chicken?"

"Uh, no," Gavin says.

Ben goes back to looking despondent.

"You could make it a woman instead of a man?" I suggest, tentatively.

"That's good," Gavin says. "Bit more interesting."

He looks at me and doesn't break eye contact for what I'm sure is a second longer than is reasonable. I blush and look away. I like the praise. My heart starts beating faster as my mind whirs with ideas of how to make this work. "Or instead of wanking, men getting a woman off. So like, you take some men who think they're amazing in bed – the cocky, full of themselves kind. And each one of them has to make the woman come and whoever does it fastest wins."

"The same woman?" Ben asks. "Surely the later men will have an advantage."

"The poor bloody woman will be burnt out by then," Betty says.

"We could make it a regular segment and we do it every week," I continue, feeling the long-buried buzz of a good idea in my stomach. "With the same woman. But a different man each time. Like that *Top Gear* segment where celebrities do laps in cars and there's a leader board."

Gavin's eyes widen, he's nodding.

"And we make it scientific," I say. "So we have a proper scientist, doctor person in and we attach the woman to machines that monitor her heart rate or whatever and we never actually see the woman, obviously – we just see the machines. And maybe we hear little snippets. And it can be like a thing we check in on during the show – like, 'and now we're going to cross live to our come monitor to see how we're doing'."

"Love that!" Betty says.

Gavin nods, looking thoughtful. He writes it on the board with a question mark. "I'll need to see if we can get it past legal, and I can't see that going through for this week, but can I hand that over to you to start looking into, Charlie? We need a scientist, preferably one who can provide the machines, and contributors, which I can't imagine will be easy."

I'm grinning. Beaming, actually. So much that my cheeks are hurting. I'm being trusted with my first proper segment, which feels like a lot. Maybe Gavin can tell I have experience, even though it was a long time ago, or maybe he can sense my instinct for this kind of thing and just knows I'll do a good job. Either way,

I'm thrilled that he's relying on me to make it happen. I cannot mess this up.

I scribble down notes and spend the rest of the meeting not really listening, just scrolling through ideas of where to start in my head. And trying not to shit myself. I make a mental note to not have any late drunken nights for a while.

As everyone is filing out of the room, the meeting having been declared over, Gavin lingers and asks to have a word. I worry at first I've done something wrong, and then see his smile.

"Great ideas today, Charlie," he says. His perfect green eyes look shiny and intelligent framed in his perfectly cool tortoiseshell glasses. "You're obviously quite experienced, then?"

My heart does a little flutter and I feel the heat rising to my cheeks.

He laughs. And I swear it's a naughty laugh. "In light entertainment, I mean."

Holy crap. I think he's flirting with me. Silver fox Gavin Cortado with the lustrous hair, the clever glasses and the just the right level of skinny-but-not-too-skinny jeans is flirting with me. Maybe the high-waisted jeans are working for me.

I'm blushing so badly, I must look like a radish. "Well . . . you know . . . a while ago . . . Channel 4 . . ." is all I manage.

"Good luck with the segment," he says, cool as a cucumber. "I'm sure you'll smash it. Maybe next week we can do a catch-up in the pub?"

I nod. Stunned. Flattered. Imagining what it would be like to have sex with him, to run my hands over those toned arms and lace my fingers through his hair, to stare into those eyes, to be married to him. Sure that he goes on fancy holidays to the Maldives.

* * *

🍸 COCKTAIL COVEN 🍸

Me: *OMG GUYSSSSSS!!!!!! I've been given my own segment to research and it's one that was MY IDEA. AND I think Gavin Cortado was coming on to me.*

Emily: *That's amazing! I mean the segment, not the sexual harassment from your boss.*

Me: *Not sexual harassment. I just think he might fancy me!*

Emily: *Be careful with that.*

Me: *It's fun. And flattering.*

Emily: *What's the segment?*

Me: *It's a bit crazy but FUN – we have a woman on the live show, in a secret little room and a different man each week has to make her orgasm and whoever does it the fastest wins. It sounds mad but it will be done really tastefully and you won't actually see the woman – just the machines she's hooked up to and occasionally some noise from the room.*

Cath: *WTF?!? That's porn, Charlie. You're making porn.*

Me: *Actually, I'm thinking of it as a bit of a feminist statement – we're exploring women's pleasure, which traditionally hasn't been shown enough on TV.*

Cath: *Whatever you say.*

Emily: *It's great they think you're good enough at the job to give you your own segment.*

Me: *Exactly! I'm really proud of myself. Just waiting to see if it can get through legal. But I've already started looking for contributors – so if you know any men who think they're great at getting women off or any women who would be up for orgasming once a week on live TV – send them my way.*

Cath: *I do not.*

Text to Emily:

Me: *Jesus, Cath's being such a Debbie Downer! It's a really big deal, I wish she'd just be excited for me rather than so judgemental about the whole thing. It's entertainment TV – it's always pushing the boundaries!*

Emily: *It is a bit of a weird one though, I guess. But I'm sure you'll find a way to make it work.*

Me: *THANK YOU for the belief!*

Emily: *You guys probably need to talk anyway.*

Me: *About what?*

Emily: *Uh, the comedy night.*

Me: *Oh gawd. I thought we'd just put it down to another drunken argument and we'd move on.*

Emily: *I think her feelings are quite hurt.*

Me: *Why?! It wasn't that bad.*

Emily: *And you remember this?*

Me: *... Not so much.*

Emily: *I'd talk to Cath if I were you. Take her out for a coffee or something. Sort it out.*

Me: *I'll try, but honestly, I only just have time to piss atm. I'm so busy with this segment.*

Emily: *Maybe when you're done making porn then.*

Me: *Haha.*

August

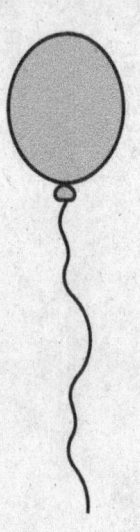

20

I WALK INTO Dr Deb's office late, annoyed at myself that I'm immediately on the back foot and the one in the wrong, especially when it took so much effort to persuade James that counselling was worth a try in the first place. He wasn't Rick levels of not into it, and was at least able to see that we might need some kind of help, but there was much moaning and resistance about how much time it would take up and therefore what impact it would have on his work.

Of course. I wasn't even sure I could be bothered with it myself and had only mentioned it on a whim one night after getting the fear he may never look me in the eye again after the comedy night debacle. But then his resistance to the idea fired up my insistence on it and now here we are, in the basement of a townhouse in Chiswick decorated with naff motivational quotes and exotic wooden carvings.

Dr Deb is welcoming and all smiles, looking every bit the Woody Allen therapist in her loose silk shirt, wide-legged smart trousers and thick-rimmed glasses. I studied her closely in our last session, trying to work out how old she is, but she has the kind of sophisticated ageing thing going on that places her anywhere between Sarah Michelle Gellar and Jane Fonda and I cannot work out which one she's closest to. I'm putting it down to having the

money to afford good tweakments and facials. It's a dream of mine.

"So sorry I'm late." I fluster in, red faced and sweating from the manic walk-run here. "A meeting ran over, trains were buggered."

James eyes me suspiciously from the sofa as Deb takes my coat, gives me water and tells me not to worry. I take my seat, trying to sit as far away from him as possible in case the whole packet of Smints (it's become a thing) I had on the way over have not done their job and he can, indeed, smell the two glasses of wine I've had. One of which, to be fair, was in a meeting – Gavin likes to have occasional production meetings in the pub, 'to get the silly idea juices flowing'. The second one was me not wanting to stop having fun and forgetting how long it takes to get here.

James is still staring at me, which doesn't bode well. I sip my water and give him a weird thigh rub as some kind of reassurance.

"You've been drinking," he says.

Damn. Maybe the weird thigh rub was too obvious.

"I've been at work," I say. Because that is a fact.

"And drinking."

"Well, yes, but we had a production meeting in the pub and everyone else was drinking and what was I supposed to say? No thanks, I've got therapy with my husband coming up and he already thinks I drink too much?"

"For god's sake." He turns all red and angry and scrunches up.

"What about that upsets you so much, James?" Dr Deb asks.

"That she's not taking this seriously," he says. "And I'm not upset, I'm angry. I've given up my time to be here, cancelled meetings, actually, and she turns up drunk and late."

"First of all," I say, angry myself now, "bravo for cancelling

a meeting for once in our married life and second of all, I'm not drunk, I've had one glass of wine."

We both know that's not true, but only I know it for a fact.

"Let's just take a minute to pause," Dr Deb says, "and remember what we discussed in last week's session about thinking really carefully around how we talk to each other. I think it's also important to remember that you both willingly agreed to take part in this process and therefore you both agree that your relationship is important and worth spending time on. This is sacred time to do that."

I can't work out if she's subtly telling me or him or both of us off. Either way, I feel put in my place. But in a friendly way. Dr Deb is like a smiling assassin.

"We're going to put a pin in that for now, because I'd like to go back to where we left off last session."

I take a breath, hoping that means I've got away with it.

"You were telling me about how you met," Dr Deb says. She looks back over her notes, smiling. I feel like we've earnt some kind of brownie points for having a good meet-cute, a worthy origin story. Which it was. It was something like a film. I knew straight away, the minute I met James at the seedy, long-since-closed local club, Jangles, that I was going to love him. It was the potent mix of uninhibited dance moves, knowing all the words to 'Gangsta's Paradise' and the fact we passionately talked about our cats for a full half an hour. And how gorgeous and tall and curly-haired he was, obviously.

I didn't know for sure we'd stay together, especially when I went off to university in Leeds and he went to Exeter, but I knew

I was going to love him. Cath says that's nostalgic bollocks and I'm looking back with rose-tinted hindsight, but that's my story and I'm sticking to it. That's how it's always felt to me, a Great Love Affair.

"We talked a lot about that sense of fun you had in your early relationship," Dr Deb says. "And how you both felt a bond like you'd never experienced before, that you had, in your words, Charlie, 'met your person', and in your words, James, 'become a team, just the two of you'."

James and I glance at each other, there's a hint of a smile on his face, but almost like he's fighting it. I wonder how many hours I've spent looking at his face, in one way or another. I think how crazy it is that it used to bring me such joy and comfort, flood me with a love that felt total and overwhelming and sometimes unbearable, and yet now, more often than not, it spikes a horrible mix of resentment and anger in me.

"Last session, I asked you to think about whether you believe that closeness and intimacy are still there, somewhere underneath all the frustrations and past wounds, and whether they're salvageable. What did you decide about that? I'll come to you first, James."

He jiggles his leg, the way he always does when he's thinking.

"Yes, I think they are there, somewhere," he says. "Those things can't just disappear."

"But do you still know all the words to 'Gangsta's Paradise', though?" I ask.

He starts rapping. I laugh.

And then I want to cry. Because I miss him.

Dr Deb writes something in her notebook and gives James a teacher-ish nod which means, that was amusing but now let's move on.

"And what about you, Charlie? What did you decide?" she asks.

"Yeah, the same. It's got to still be there. We can't have just lost all of that stuff."

"And is that what it feels like? A loss?"

"One hundred per cent," I say.

"Which part in particular feels like a loss?"

I consider this. There's so much – the fun, the adventure, the spontaneity, the laughter. God, we used to make each other laugh. James was always being silly – silly voices, silly names, silly raps and dances, silly games, like potato bowling, pin the tail on the sausage (not as dirty as it sounds), and coming out with random thoughts, like 'how weird it is that we call the end of fingers fingertips, but we don't call the end of our toes toetips, yet we do talk about tip-toeing?'. We used to travel and go on adventures – jazz clubs in Prague till 3 a.m., playing shithead for hours in our tent in Cornwall to distract ourselves from the endless rain, dive bars and dim sum and double bills in the middle of the night in Soho. Being with him made me feel invigorated and excited to try new things because I knew we were in it together, whatever.

"Lots of parts feel like a loss, but probably the one that hurts the most is that we don't feel like a team any more. It feels like we're always against each other. A constant war."

Dr Deb nods. I wonder how many times she's heard this before. "When do you think that shift happened?"

"When we had kids," I say, too quickly. I could pinpoint almost

the exact moment if she asked. "It started with the usual new parent things I guess – I changed the nappy last time, it's your turn, you had two hours more sleep than me – that kind of stuff, but I feel like maybe it's never stopped since then, it's just kind of escalated."

"Would you agree with that James?" she asks.

"Yeah, probably. I guess that's when the work stuff came into it too."

"What do you mean by the work stuff?" she asks.

I brace myself. Here we go.

"My work is very demanding. It takes up a lot of my time, and headspace. It's become a . . . thing in our relationship." Dr Deb does that staring-at-him-waiting-for-more thing. "A problem. An issue. A mistress – Charlie always says there are three of us in this relationship."

"OK, so let's unpick that a bit. I'm going to go back to something you said at the beginning of the session, Charlie, about James cancelling a meeting today being the first time in your married life. Can you elaborate on that?"

"He always puts work first," I say. "I've been in hospital with our child and he's gone to work, I've been in hospital myself and he's called to ask me if I need him to come home, like he was hoping I'd let him off the hook, I've had birthdays when he's had a work event he's had to go to, anniversaries when he's physically been there for dinner but he's spent all of it firing off emails. Weekends, holidays, always work first. And the time he does make, he spends with the children, or focuses on the children, I guess. Which, don't get me wrong, is great – he's an amazing dad, when he's around. But I'm never his priority any more. I come low down the list."

"And how does that make you feel?"

"Upset. Angry." She looks at me expectantly, wanting more. "It makes me feel like I'm not important to him."

I know what James's response will be before he opens his mouth.

"I have to work. How else do you think we're going to pay the bills?" I was right. "And do you know how that makes *me* feel – all of what you just said – it makes me feel pissed off. You never acknowledge how hard I work, how I'm constantly busting a gut to be able to pay for everything that we have. You've made my work become this terrible thing that I have to hide from you and feel guilty about. I'd love to spend more time with you and the kids, I'd love to take the day off on your birthdays, I'd love to not have to work on holiday, clearly, but I can't do that."

"See what he does there," I say, feeling the fight now, pleased that we have a referee, someone to finally see my side. "He makes me feel crap – like I'm some dosser who lounges around all day fanning herself that he has to support." I push away thoughts of my Thursday afternoons which have traditionally been my *Housewives*-athon. I earnt those afternoons. And there was no fanning.

"If you worked less," I continue, "and contributed more around the house, maybe I could've gone back to work and actually had a career, but as it was, I was doing everything to do with the house and the kids and trying to hold down a job. Like your job and your career was the be-all-and-end-all and more important than my job and my career."

James shrugs. "I know you're not going to like this and probably

take it in the wrong way, but in the interest of being honest – it kind of was more important. But only because it was bringing the money in."

And there it is.

I look at him and see he's bracing for my reaction. But I don't have the energy to fight. I just feel sad. And lonely. And like I miss him and our old relationship so much it makes my insides shrivel. I long for silly raps and dances and potato bowling and a world in which he loves me like he used to.

21

IT'S GROSSLY, stickily hot. The kind of heat that even on holiday with a sea breeze and a pool to cool off in would seem intense, and in London feels like you're melting as you walk through hell. I am sweaty. Grossly, stickily sweaty, but I am also already late. Again.

Walk-running up our road, I decide that today is going to be another takeaway day – for me and the girls and the kids. I had good intentions, planning on making my famous Hangover Chicken, Cath's uni favourite, but as it turns out, I'm too tired to cook.

I wasn't supposed to go out again last night, but Fliss wanted to go to this immersive theatre thing in an old hospital and it sounded fun and I'm trying to make the most of being in town and it's the school holidays so it feels less frantic anyway and Dorit was up for meeting us after, so I leant into the spontaneity and went for it. Which was fine, except for the fact I carried on leaning into the spontaneity, until the early, spontaneous hours of the morning, at some dive bar off Tottenham Court Road and then at Soho House. And I thought I was being saintly and sensible because I only had two glasses of wine the whole evening, but it turns out wine hits different at the moment, and it also turns out that only a few hours of sleep makes you feel as bad, if not worse, than a truckload of

alcohol, and I ended up late to work and struggling through the day again. Though I don't think anyone noticed this time.

Working in TV was definitely easier when I was twenty-five and my only other responsibilities were making it to hair appointments and remembering to feed Eddie Vedder and Jeff Buckley (RIP). Remembering to feed children and the thousand other things I have to keep in my brain is a lot more taxing. Working in TV was also a lot easier when I had the endless energy that being twenty-five brings. I am desperate to flop on the sofa and watch *Housewives* or whatever other fun and mindless TV I can find and have a quiet, restorative night ahead of show day tomorrow, but tonight was the only night for practically the whole summer that Cath and Emily could do and I know I'm on shaky ground with Cath as it is. I texted her a heartfelt apology about the comedy night miscommunication – as heartfelt as I could make it when I don't actually think I'm entirely in the wrong – and she replied with a low-key acceptance, but I'm guessing there's still some grovelling to be done.

I work back through the takeaways we've had this week – on Monday I actually fed the kids semi-properly (chicken steaks and oven chips, but the nice chicken steaks from M&S), Tuesday we all had Nando's, and last night I told Chloe to order pizza. Chinese it is. I'm pleased James being away this week means I escape judgement. Though, as I pointed out to him in our last session with Dr Deb, if he's that concerned about what I'm feeding our children, he could feed them himself. I make a mental note to definitely, *definitely*, batch cook this weekend and get some wholesome things in the freezer that I can defrost at the last minute.

I open the front door and a burst of warmth and light hits me. Fleetwood Mac is blasting out of the speakers (Cath's choice, for sure), my special occasion Jo Malone candle has been lit and there's a pleasing hubbub coming from the kitchen where I can see Emily is washing up, Cath is loading the dishwasher and Chloe is lounging on a bar stool at the island chatting to them. She looks out of place there, I can't remember the last time she did that with me.

"Well, hello," Emily says, turning around, one soapy hand on her hip. "Nice of you to join us."

"Sorry, sorry!" I hang my coat up, grab the two bottles of wine out of my bag and walk through.

I give rushed hugs, pretending not to notice the way Chloe's face drops when she sees me.

"Where are the boys?" I ask.

"Felix went to Max's house after hockey camp," Chloe says, a touch of disbelief that I could've possibly forgotten that. "Jack is upstairs. I told him he has to read for a bit before he can have any screen time. I'm going to go and check on him." She delivers it with a touch of the judgement I'm used to from James. "Nice to see you guys," she says to Emily and Cath.

"You too," Cath says. "And remember what I said – don't put up with that shit."

Chloe gives her the thumbs up and leaves. I shout something after her about how we'll be ordering Chinese but she either doesn't hear me or chooses to ignore me. I set about opening the wine.

"What was that about?" I ask.

"Just all the stuff with Rupert," Cath says, chiselling away at the dried cereal in a bowl that I'm pretty sure has been there all week.

She gives up and puts it in the dishwasher as it is.

I want to ask what Rupert stuff, but I'm stung that I don't already know, that I have no idea what is going on with Chloe besides when she's around to babysit the boys. So I shrug it off, making a mental note, along with the one about the batch cooking, and the not going out drinking too much, to find a time to sit down and ask her.

"Guys, please," I say. "You really don't have to do that. I've just had a bit of a mental week."

"You know what I'm like," Emily says. "I can't resist. I love cleaning."

"You can't bear a dirty house," Cath says. "I'm just joining in because otherwise I look like the bitch."

I walk over to Emily and manhandle her away from the sink, taking the sponge from her with the aim of finishing but then deciding I'll do it in the morning.

"Work's been totally mad!" I say, opening the wine. "It's the big show day tomorrow. And you'll be pleased to hear the porn segment got through legal."

"Oh, yay," Cath deadpans. "So pleased."

"I managed to find this awesome woman who's totally up for doing it and the men were easy to find. But yeah, I've basically been talking about orgasms and orgasm science for weeks now. Which is actually pretty cool for a job. And I got to write the script for the VT we're filming, and Gavin Cortado said it was great work. And I put forwards an idea for a new show – I'll pitch it to you – *Seven Brides for One Brother* – working title, I don't think it's catchy enough. But basically, it's about polygamy and we'd go to one

of those Amish places and it would be a cross between a dating show and a documentary on polyamory and there'd be one guy, the brother, and he'd marry seven women and they'd go through a range of tasks and obstacles and each week, one bride would go until he's left with the winning one."

Cath scowls. "Isn't that just a normal dating show but they start off married? Like *Love is Blind* but reversed? Being able to see them?"

"Kind of," I say, annoyed. "But you get the documentary side of it, too – looking at polygamy and how it works, all that stuff."

"Well, good luck," Emily says. "And good luck with the show tomorrow."

"I'm actually nervous," I say. "It's been years since I've done live TV. What if it's all changed?"

"Pretty sure nothing's changed," Cath says.

"Here." I pass them both a glass of wine, feeling the irritation bite but pushing it away.

"Not for me," Emily says. "I can't on a weeknight. Makes the days at work too impossible."

"Since when?" I ask.

We have always drunk on work nights. We have often *been* drunk on work nights.

"I'm not sleeping well at the moment," she says. "And when I have wine, I feel like I barely sleep at all."

"Bloody menopause," Cath grunts.

"Perimenopause, if you please," Emily says. "And you might be right. The supplements felt like they were helping a bit, especially with the sleep, but they seem to have worn off now. Or maybe it's

the stress and anxiety. Who knows? It's like playing Cluedo, trying to work out what's causing what."

"Guys, we're not even forty-five yet," I protest. "Don't start with the perimenopause chat again. I'm going to drink the wine while I still can, make hay and all that. I haven't had anything yet – not a single hot flush."

They glance at each other. "Mate, we keep telling you, it's way more than that," Emily says. "You know that, right? You've watched the Davina? Tell me you've at least watched the Davina?"

"The Davina?" I grab the Chinese menu and a post-it note out of the drawer.

"Davina McCall," Emily says.

"I know who Davina is," I say. "Perma-smiley *Big Brother* presenter who married the Irish fitty. What's she got to do with the menopause?"

Emily looks shocked, Cath laughs. "Sometimes I wonder if you live under a rock, Charlie."

"Davina is the Queen of Menopause!" Emily says, excited at being able to give me shiny new menopause information. "Honestly, she's amazing. She's written a book and she made an incredible documentary. Eye-opening. You have to watch it! I'll send you a copy of the book, but promise me you'll actually read it."

"Ugh," I groan. "I don't need to watch the Davina or read the Davina yet. I want to stay young and innocent while I still can."

"Except for the coil that you needed because the perimenopause was making your periods unbearably heavy?" Cath says.

"Well, yeah, but that's it. And that's not even definitely to do with the perimenopause."

Cath and Emily exchange a glance. It makes me rage.

"I'm sure you said you were having problems sleeping?" Emily asks.

I think back over the past couple of weeks. Quite a few nights I've gotten in so late, all I could do was pass out, sleep like a log for a few hours then drag myself up, so that doesn't count as having problems sleeping. I suppose there have been a few not so great nights. And a new thing where I lie awake in the middle of the night and my brain frantically thinks over every possible thing that could go wrong in every possible area of my life.

"I do sometimes wake up in the middle of the night and struggle to get back to sleep for a bit, but that's because my mind is whirring with work stuff and kids stuff."

"Around 3 a.m.?" Emily asks.

"Yes, actually, but I think that's just when my bladder—"

"Till around 5 a.m.?" Cath asks.

"I guess." I shrug, annoyed at their rightness.

"Menopause, mate," Cath says.

"Perimenopause," Emily corrects.

"Same difference," Cath says.

"I've had that – nearly every night, almost exactly between three and five." Emily is suddenly animated. "I've had the worst mood swings, like, completely sobbing out of the blue at random things – the Macmillan advert, the bloody McDonald's advert where he brings his wife home a McChicken sandwich! I've been getting so irritable with the kids that I sometimes have to walk away. Ooh, and I've had this weird mouth thing that I looked up and could be perimenopause. Though it could also be diabetes.

Or just a yeast infection. Mostly though, I just don't feel myself. I feel like things I normally would've been able to deal with feel completely overwhelming. The other day, I just couldn't get my head around what we were going to have for dinner. Literally stood in front of the fridge and had a headspin and a cry and then a breakdown trying to do the online shop. I've actually made a doctor's appointment for next week."

I drop the pencil on the island. "Whaaaaaat?"

I didn't realise we were there already. I've only just started feeling slightly more like a grown-up and now I'm about to go through the final chrysalis stage of becoming an official Old Woman?

Cath's face is drawn, dark. "Can we not, please," she says. "Can we change the subject?"

"See!" I say, smiling. "Cath isn't on board with this either!"

Cath shakes her head at me. Barely perceptible, but for sure a head shake. I don't understand why. I thought we were having a bonding-against-perimenopause-chat moment.

"Do you not just think some of that is partly because you're going through a rough time with Rick?" I ask, pushing on. "And that's causing stress?"

Emily glances at Cath. Again. And I can't read it. Which is annoying, because normally I can read them both like a book – an *Introduction to Phonics*, easy-to-read, three-word level book at that. But recently, they're feeling more opaque. More like bloody *War and Peace*.

"How are things with you guys, by the way?" I ask. "Oh, but before that, I need to order. Our usuals, right?"

I write down quarter-duck pancakes, sweet-and-sour chicken, chicken in black bean, prawn toast, two fried rice and beansprouts. The same order we've had since uni, with the relatively recent addition of the beansprouts when Emily read some article about gut health and decided we needed to add some form of official vegetable.

They're looking secretive, or something, when I look up from my post-it note and Cath is doing a weird nudging thing to Emily.

"Guys?" I say. "You're being weird. And it's annoying. What's going on?"

Emily sighs. "I've been meaning to tell you, but you were so busy and I didn't want to do it over text and I did try to arrange to meet but . . . this is the first time I've seen you since—"

"What?"

"Rick and I have separated. Kind of."

My skin prickles, a cold whisper on my neck. I open and close my mouth a few times like a goldfish. "What . . . wh . . . what, do you mean split up? What the fuck? Emily! Are you OK? What happened?"

Her eyes go all glassy and she fast-blinks, which she always does before she cries. "It was a few weeks ago, just before your comedy gig, actually."

"I'm not sure we can class that as comedy," Cath mutters.

"We'll get on to that," I say. "But also, ouch."

Emily pauses to check we're not going there yet, then continues. "He'd been getting even weirder with me, more off, more absent. I was miserable. And feeling completely worthless and nothing I tried was working, so, in the end, I gave him an ultimatum – I said

either he agrees to couples counselling or we're done. He didn't agree to couples counselling. So we're done."

Cath puts her arm around Emily, gives her a shoulder squeeze, like they've done this before and now have a routine, a secret language. They've already had this conversation, Cath has already consoled her and I'm shut out, a random on the same level as Brenda at work who she may or may not have told. I know it's not what I should be focusing on, but it burns.

"Jesus," I say. "That's big. What happens now? Where's he living?"

"He's still in the house, just moved into the spare room officially, even though he was basically there already. He said he's going to buy a flat but he doesn't know when it will be and he needs time to work it out. He tried to get me to move out at one point until he realised that would leave him with all the childcare."

"Can't you make him give you a timeline? It sounds like some kind of purgatory, living together once you've broken up?"

"I know," Emily shrugs, defeated. "It's awful seeing him every day. But I also feel like I'm kind of on the back foot as it was me that forced the break-up. Even though he had so obviously checked out of the relationship. I don't even know what will happen with the house – we might need to sell it and I'll have to get somewhere smaller for me and the kids, or I might have to buy him out somehow, which I can't afford. It's all really complicated and I can't get my head round it yet. I'm still just dealing with the fact that it's over."

"Did you talk to that lawyer friend of mine?" Cath asks.

"She's calling tomorrow," Emily says. "And thank you, again."

"Of course. Anything," Cath says. "Let me know if there's anything I can do."

"Me too," I say, too quickly. "I'm here to help!"

I can feel my phone buzzing in my pocket. As it has been doing for the past five minutes. I'm itching to get it, worried it's work, but I know I have to tread really carefully in this moment.

I walk over beside Emily. To put my arm around her, I'd have to shove Cath's arm off, which is a step too far, so I end up doing a particularly awkward arm rub that looks like I'm trying to come on to her.

"I'm so sorry, Ems," I say. "I didn't think . . . I never thought you'd actually . . . I thought it was just a rough patch and you'd find a way through. This sucks. I'm really sorry."

She cries. I carry on awkwardly rubbing her arm. My phone carries on buzzing.

"Do you need to get that?" she asks.

"What?"

"Well either you've got your vibrator in your pocket or someone is really keen to get hold of you."

"Sorry," I say. "I probably should, in case it's work stuff for tomorrow."

I take my phone out and see some missed calls from Betty and a string of texts from Dorit.

> Dorit: *Last night was fun!*
>
> Dorit: *Only just recovered now.*
>
> Dorit: *Yo, yo. Are you home? Let's bust out of suburbia and go somewhere.*

Dorit: *Charls??*

Just then the doorbell goes.

"Is that the food?" Cath asks.

"I didn't get round to ordering," I say. "It's probably Felix."

"Whad up, bitch!" Dorit's voice calls through the letterbox.

It's not the perfect timing, but I think maybe Dorit might be just what we all need to lighten up the mood a bit. That's definitely Dorit – a mood booster.

I let her in with big hugs and squeals, our standard greeting now. In a black shirt and sleek wide-leg trousers, she's looking exceptionally glamorous for a Thursday evening, especially one after a heavy night.

"Heeeeey!" she says, coming through to the kitchen.

She wraps a slightly bemused Cath and Emily in hugs and puts the bottle of pre-mixed old fashioneds down on the island, grabbing glasses and ice while she talks.

"So sorry to interrupt – I didn't realise you were entertaining."

"I'm not, just having a catch-up. Don't worry," I say. "This is Emily and Cath."

"We met at the open-mic night," Dorit says to Cath.

"Ah yes!" I say. "I forgot."

Cath nods, grimly. "We did indeed."

"That was so much fun," Dorit says, clapping her hands together in excitement at the memory.

"It was definitely something," Cath says.

I take a swig of the old fashioned Dorit offers me, girding my loins. I was only going to have one glass of wine tonight in

preparation for show day tomorrow, but Dorit's already poured it and maybe an old fashioned will help take the edge off Cath's barbed comments and bad attitude. Just the one though.

"Come on, then," I say, dread pulling at my stomach. "Let's get into it."

Emily looks to the floor and goes to top up her water, Dorit looks confused.

"Get into what?" Cath asks.

"Let's talk about that night. I know you're pissed off at me still, even though I've already apologised. But again, for the record, I'm really sorry but I was very drunk and didn't know what I was saying."

"Clearly," she huffs.

"Emily said that I suggested you weren't being all that supportive."

"Yeah, that's not exactly what you said." Cath stares at me. "Do you really want to talk about it now? In front of everyone?"

I don't think Cath has given me her stare since approximately 1999 after the famous Suede night where I was reviewing their gig and got us free tickets, but then drank so much, I spent most of the gig in the toilet and she had to miss it to look after me and we couldn't make the after-show party at their hotel. I don't feel like the open-mic night deserves anything like the same level of wrath.

"Why not," I say, suddenly emboldened by Dorit and the old fashioned. "Tell me what I said then, because my memory from that night is hazy," I say.

"I'm sure it is," she says, with something like a sneer. "Your

exact words were that I have no faith in you, I don't support you and you don't know why I bothered coming."

I consider this, and quite honestly, I don't think it sounds *all* that bad. I'm sure I've said worse in our years together. "I'm sorry," I say. "Like I said, I was very drunk. But also, that's how I was feeling at the time. But I am sorry my delivery wasn't great."

"I was looking out for you, Charlie," she says. "You were totally wasted and about to go on and make a fool out of yourself, which, I might add, you did. And not only that, you completely humiliated James."

"It was just a bit of fun," Dorit says.

"Yeah," I add. "It was a bit of fun. And I might have gone a tiny bit too far but, you know, poetic licence."

Cath boils over. She visibly clenches her fists and takes a breath before speaking.

"I'm pretty sure James didn't think that telling the world you're sick of him, that he's rubbish in bed and that you tried anal the other day, was just a bit of fun," Cath says. "And for the record, I do support you. That night, I spent two hours rearranging my mum's care and travelling down to come and support you. What I don't support is you totally wasting good opportunities by being a thoughtless twat."

Emily comes back to her seat with some crisps and nuts from the snack drawer and a glum look on her face.

"He knows he's good in bed." I mutter it, aware I sound like a petulant toddler, but unable to help it. Cath rolls her eyes at me, opens her mouth to launch into another attack.

"Guys, come on," Emily says. "You're supposed to be sorting

this out. You love each other and I need both of you right now."

My heart is beating like a jungle drum, my chest tight with the pressure of injustice. But I know Emily is right, and I know we do both need to be there for her.

"You're right, sorry," I say. "I'm sorry for being a thoughtless twat. Let me offer you some conciliatory beansprouts and we'll have a nice evening."

Cath sighs, defeated, tired. "I should actually go. I can't have a late one tonight anyway and by the time the food gets here—"

"Stay!" Dorit says. "We've got cocktails and crisps and love in our hearts – who needs anything else?"

"I need some sleep, actually," Cath says. "Thanks, though. Do you want a lift, Ems?"

"Not you too!" I say. "Stay! Have some food."

"I should probably go too," Emily says. "I had to get a sitter in as Rick is out and I could do with not being too late, and if Cath's offering a lift—"

"Fine," I say, deflated. Aware that the lovely friend bonding night I planned has been a total disaster. "But let's get something else in the diary, yes?"

They both nod and say their goodbyes – Cath's stiff and stilted, Emily's sad.

"Bloody hell, I need a top up," I say as soon as I close the front door after them.

"Already on it, babe," Dorit says. "Already on it."

* * *

At some point, Felix comes home, after me forgetting that I was supposed to pick him up from his friend's house. At some point, I manage to make them a packed lunch dinner and get them into bed, and at some point, around midnight, in the middle of our kitchen disco, I decide to plug my phone in and see I've had three more missed calls from Betty, all with angry voicemails about different ways in which I've screwed up tomorrow's show.

22

I'M LISTING some, but not all, of the things I think about as I lie awake between 3 a.m. and 5 a.m. Which happens more than I admitted to Cath and Emily. And happens to me tonight, because they are witches who have cursed me.

1. The time I tried, unsuccessfully, to have sex with Dan Price in the bathtub at someone's house party in year eleven.

2. The time I danced on a table at a Lowdown Production party and fell off and banged my head.

3. The time I vomited onto my plate at one of James's colleague's wedding.

4. The time I tried using a toothbrush (mine) to masturbate.

5. The time James's housemate walked in on me masturbating (not using a toothbrush).

6. The time I came on to my maths teacher.

7. The thought that I will never have sex with anyone else except for James.

8. The thought that I will never have sex with George Clooney.

9. The thought that George will never leave Amal because she's so damn smart and successful and worthy and beautiful.

10. The time in the middle of the night when I could hear that Eddie Vedder had brought in an animal of some kind and I needed a wee, but I knew if I got up to go for a wee, I would have to deal with aforementioned dead animal, so instead, I peed in a vase and left James to deal with the dead animal in the morning because I knew he'd be up first.

11. The time I pissed myself walking home and had to run upstairs so the babysitter didn't see me, but he didn't hear me calling that I was home so came to check what the noise was and walked in on me naked from the waist down.

12. The time I had the runs and shat my tights.

13. Working out the cost of all the tweakments and treatments and maybe plastic surgery I would need to look good.

14. The time, egged on by Tanya Tits, I flashed my tits at my boss on a night out.

15. The time I squeezed my maths teacher's arse because I had no concept of boundaries and thought we were buddies or something (different maths teacher).

16. The time I told Felix just to piss in the pool on holiday in France thinking that no one could understand me and the French lady next to me went mad.

17. The time I sent Jack in with what was clearly chickenpox, but because it was on his stomach, I could hide it, and then the whole nursery came down with chickenpox.

18. The thought of my children dying before me.

19. The thought that James might die before me and how horrible that would feel, and also I really must get him to write down all the passwords, especially for Netflix.

20. The thought that people might read my old diaries if I die, so maybe I should get rid of them, also because I can't even read them without cringing but then, maybe in ten years' time, I will still want to look back and remember who fingered who at what party.

21. The thought of my children reading about who fingered me when I was fifteen.

22. The memory of walking in on my dad going down on my mum.

23. The thought that I will never be able to erase that memory from my mind.

24. The memory of Chloe walking in on me masturbating.

25. The thought that she will never be able to erase that from her mind.

26. The thought that I never wash cucumbers and have therefore, probably, irreversibly damaged my children. Ditto strawberries, grapes, tomatoes – all fruit and veg, actually.

27. The thought that Jack and Felix will grow up and just never bother to come home and Chloe will still hate me and I will be alone or left with James, who will either still be working all the time or doing an Ironman somewhere and still not drinking.

28. The time I pretended to sprain my ankle so I wouldn't have to go on a bike ride with James.

29. The time I got off with Emily's boyfriend that I have still not told her about.

30. The time I stopped talking to Emily for three weeks because I decided she wasn't cool enough.

31. The time I got so drunk at one of James's posh colleague's houses that I insisted we play a drinking game even though the colleague was an ex-alcoholic and didn't drink.

32. Which was the same time I then went on to call the ex-alcoholic posh colleague a boring prick.

33. The time a work experience runner at Lowdown got so drunk she pissed herself while sitting on an exec's lap and passed out on the pavement outside the pub and had to have an ambulance called and I can't remember her name now, but I wonder if she lies awake at night like me and remembers that and cringes, but really she shouldn't worry because it's just a funny anecdote now and no one can actually remember her.

34. The fact that we're all going to die.

35. And when we're all dead, what will be the point of all these sleepless nights spent cringing about past events and worrying about future ones?

36. My open-mic night.

37. The fact I have screwed up my first big live show before it's even started.

23

WHEN FELIX was going up to secondary school, I forgot to get the form in on time. The form through which you select which school you want them to go to. The form that everyone talks about, obsessively, for three months beforehand. The form I myself was obsessed with when I had to fill it in for Chloe. Somehow – general life chaos that it was over a half term, or that I was ignoring the parent WhatsApp groups, because holy crap, who needs to message that much? – somehow, I missed the deadline.

The solid, heavy ball of dread that sat in my stomach then sits in my stomach now as I make my way to the *After Hours* production office. Made even more solid and heavy by the fact I am running late, because after my grand total of approximately two hours sleep last night, I fell asleep on the Central Line and woke up at West Ruislip. Luckily, I had intended to get to work early today to try and fix some of my mess, so I'm only late by half an hour, but it's still not a good look for someone well and truly in the dog house.

Betty didn't tell me all the details in the voicemail, just that the equipment hadn't turned up and she couldn't get hold of the scientist. And something about me not doing the release forms properly for the pre-recorded segment I shot. And something about the call sheet being wrong. My mind is spinning, has been

spinning all night, going back over everything, working out what exactly went wrong, all the ways in which I dropped the ball.

The tension in the air hits me as soon as I walk through the slightly knackered doors (the studio office is the opposite of the sleek main office). Gavin Cortado and Betty are in a heated discussion, Gavin in his 'stressed man' pose – knees spread apart, elbows on knees, head partially in hands. I swallow hard, the acidic taste of no sleep and failure sticking to my mouth.

Dorit stayed with me once I got the messages – made me coffee, helped me brainstorm solutions – but we realised there was nothing really to be done at that time in the night, so I formulated a game plan to offer up this morning, like some kind of sacrificial lamb to the slaughter. Except this lamb has messed up. Big time.

Gavin sees me come in, lifts his head and does a Cruella level scowl. The ball gets heavier.

"Hi, guys," I say.

I adjust myself to look professional and in command. To look like a person with solutions, rather than one who is absolutely crapping herself. I reminded myself last night, constantly, that I have worked in live TV before. That things are always going wrong. That this kind of stuff happens all the time. We adapt, we hustle, we improvise, we get it done somehow. This is a slightly racy and very silly late-night TV show. This is not Chernobyl.

"Sorry I didn't return your calls last night, Betty," I say. "My son hurt his leg playing hockey and we ended up at the hospital – it's all fine, just a sprain – but my phone ran out of battery. All a bit of a nightmare."

Every ounce of me cringes at using my child in this way, knowing

that I'm doing a disservice to working mothers everywhere and worrying that I am in some way tempting fate. But needs must, and if I'm constantly being punished for being a working mother, I may as well use it to my advantage every now and again. And besides, it's only an extension of the truth, the truth being that Felix was playing hockey.

"Your participant just pulled out," Gavin says, his eyes all dark and doomy and the opposite of foxy.

My head pounds, a sudden rush of blood. "What do you mean? That was on my list for this morning, to double-check everything. I sent her the call sheet yesterday. I *spoke* to her yesterday."

Betty is looking uncomfortable.

"I asked Betty to double-check everything you'd done," he says. "She called her this morning, she's had a change of heart, decided that it would be too compromising if one of her students saw it."

"But I explained she'd be completely hidden, no one would be able to know her identity. We talked about that, extensively."

And it had been extensive – hours. I'd had to seriously woo her. I found her through Instagram – she was one of those sex accounts, Debbie.16732100, the ones with a saucy profile photo that like your story but have no proper account, only some sex emojis and a link to their website. I thought she must be a safe bet if she was basically selling porn anyway. But she still needed convincing, because, according to her, appearing on live national TV having an orgasm with your identity completely hidden was way worse than sending people videos of you masturbating.

"Can you forward Betty the contact details for your back-up, please?" Gavin said.

My stomach lurches. I don't have a back-up. Why would I have a back-up? It took me long enough to get this contributor. But of course, I *should've* had a back-up, especially for a segment this controversial. Of course I should've seen this coming, prepared for it. Stored all the loo rolls and tinned meat for it. Shit.

"You do have a back-up, don't you?" Gavin asks, the anger coming off him like rippling supersonic waves.

"I . . . it took me . . ." is all I manage. So much for professional and in command.

Gavin doesn't even grace me with a response, just shakes his head and puts it back between his hands. He stays like that for a minute.

"I'm pulling the segment," he says, eventually. "We haven't got anything in place for it now – we can't even show the VTs because the releases haven't been signed properly. Betty, can you get on to Joss and have him work out what we can use instead – I'll speak to Nish and have him rewrite. We'll just have to script more for Kaya and Rafe, maybe do an extra segment with Kiki and . . . who else have we got on?"

"Frank, from Celebrity Dentist," I say, trying to gain back some integrity.

"We need to issue amendments as soon as possible, we've got a tech run at two and I honestly don't have the energy to deal with Kaya giving me grief today."

He grabs his stack of papers and coffee and stands up.

I feel like I should ask him what he wants me to do, but I'm slightly worried that his answer would be to piss off out of his face so I keep quiet, nod and look serious. And repentant. Like a cat

who's proudly brought a mouse to its master. Actually, cats are never repentant. Like a dog who's shat on the carpet. That's how I look. And how I feel.

As soon as he's gone, I sit down next to Betty. "I'm so sorry," I say. "I honestly don't know how all that happened. I mean, there was nothing I could do about—"

"I've got to go and see Joss," she says, not even making eye contact with me.

"What do you want me to do?" I ask.

"A coffee run," she says. "And maybe write down the orders."

* * *

Somehow, I get through the rest of the day. I skirt around on the outside of the action, the dog that shat on the carpet now desperate for attention and to prove its worth. I get coffees and lunches and props and pass messages on, and am just about trusted to distribute amendments to the talent. I welcome the contributors with a smile I don't feel, pretending like I'm a valued member of staff and not a total dickhead who everyone is side-eyeing. When I can escape, I cry silently in the toilet and drink gallons of Red Bull – I know it won't do my sleep any favours tonight, but it will at least get me through the day. I get messages from every member of my family communicating a problem to me – Felix wants me to come and pick him up from detention because he doesn't want to walk home that late (4.30 p.m.), Jack can't find his football boots, Chloe wants me to transfer twenty pounds to her current account. James is running late so won't be home in time for the boys, can

Chloe cover until he gets home? Chloe cannot cover because Chloe is at a netball tournament somewhere near Staines. But I don't tell him this. He can work it out for himself. He knows I'm working and he knows this is a big day for me. Whether he's remembered and whether he cares are different questions. I don't reply to any of them. I boil over. And freeze. All at the same time. And I cry in the toilet more.

By the time the show is about to go live, I have a new burst of energy. I remember this – the adrenaline keeps you going, pushes you on. And the thing with live TV is that when you're in it, when it's happening, you're all in it together. Even if you've mightily messed up beforehand. I ride the adrenaline wave like a pro surfer, never stopping, never giving myself a chance to think about anything other than what's happening in front of me and what I need to do.

I have to run to get one of the celebs a different pair of shoes from their dressing room because they decide the green stilettos they're wearing make them look like a giant, I have to grab a cushion for Kaya because she got a dolphin tattoo on her arse yesterday and it's hurting, I have to run to find a corner shop that's open and sells baked beans because we don't have enough for the 'celebrity in a bath of baked beans' segment. I run all show. Run and smile, run and smile. And it all goes well.

No one watching would even know that fifteen minutes of the show had to be re-scripted, that we had to put in a pre-recorded segment that was shot for next week's show, that one of our presenters arrived two hours late, that the other one had a total meltdown two minutes before we went live. All that work and pain

and carrying around that solid heavy stone for basically nothing.

The show finishes, mutual pats on the back are administered, people make a move to the hotel bar round the corner which is the usual post-show piss up venue. No one invites me. Maybe no one invites anyone, maybe it's just an unspoken thing. And maybe I would be welcome, but I've had a boat load of the side-eyes and tiptoeing around and the not feeling good enough, and brown-nosing D-list celebrities whose only discernible talent is looking good while parading around in swimwear on national TV.

So, I head home, through the streets of a late-night Friday in London, drunken groups of lads lads lads spilling out from pubs and identikit orange women in tiny clothes. Big, cackly laughs ring out – people having fun. I want to be having fun. The longing for it curls inside me, squeezing my insides. When did things stop being fun? Working in TV used to be fun. It doesn't feel fun now though. Is it me or TV or both? Am I too old to be working in TV? Is dowsing minor celebrities in baked beans for entertainment a young person's game? It's not that I've matured – willy gags and fart jokes are still my favourite.

Who the hell knows? All I do know for sure is that I am blindingly, lost-all-mental-function exhausted, and the suburbs-not-suburbs suddenly feel half a globe away. I drag myself on to the Central Line, with the lads and the orange women, find a seat, have another silent cry and promptly fall asleep.

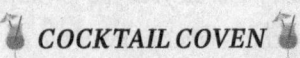

COCKTAIL COVEN

Me: *OMG had a nightmare day yesterday. My contributor*

for the segment fell through, and some other bad stuff.

Me: *Not good.*

Emily: *Oh no. That sounds stressful.*

Me: *SO stressful. And Gavin Cortado is actually a dick and I don't want to have sex with him any more. Besides which, one of the runners told me he's a sleazebag and is constantly having affairs even though he has a lovely wife and two small kids, so lucky escape, I guess.*

Emily: *You were thinking of sleeping with him?!?*

Me: *Well, no, not exactly. Maybe more, I was imagining sleeping with him?*

Cath: *That's quite a difference.*

Me: *Yeah, well, neither now.*

Me: *The universe is messing with me and ruining my job. Can't believe my contributor just pulled out like that.*

Cath: *Maybe you need to just focus on your job for now and doing that really well. If that's what you want to do. Put the list and the mad nights out to one side for a bit.*

Me: *That's not what this was. It was out of my control.*

Me: *And the list is not causing me any problems with my work!*

Cath: *OK*

24

MOUNTAINS ARE not my friend. Mountains have never been my friend. I'm more a hill kinda gal. Or a small mound. And yet.

Dr Deb said we should work on compromise and empathy. She made us do an exercise where we drew round our shoes on a piece of sugar paper, took off our shoes and stood in each other's footsteps. We had to close our eyes and imagine we were the other person. A primary school activity that's great in theory, but in practice made us both resentful of the other's luxuries – me, that he can leave the house whenever he wants, for as long as he wants, and focus on his work, his career, without having to spare a single thought for his children, their play dates, their homework, their laundry, the status of their PE kit (always missing) and birthday parties that require responses and presents. Or what everyone's having for dinner. Every day. For eternity. Him, that I don't have the pressure of paying the mortgage and putting food on the table, that I get to spend as much time as I want with the children and with the exception of cooking and some light cleaning, I can sit in front of the TV all day if I so wish. We'd ended up moving swiftly on to the next exercise.

One of Dr Deb's directives that I was more keen on was leaning into each other's interests. I ruled out taking part in an Ironman – I'm not mad – that would be the quickest way to head straight

to divorce. And local politics, or politics of any kind, again, not my thing. But walking is one I was willing to experiment with, especially if it was up a mountain so I could tick it off my list. I was safe in the knowledge that even remotely thinking, talking or partaking in it in any way gives me the upper hand and immediately makes James more amenable. And happy. I haven't seen him as happy as he is halfway up this mountain since we went to a Paul Weller gig circa 2001. Back in the days when he liked going to gigs.

"Do you remember that Paul Weller gig at Brixton Academy?" I ask, panting with the exertion of walking up the very slight incline. "We'd gone to that seedy pub on Coldharbour Lane beforehand where that drunk woman was trying to get you to go back to her place."

"Oh god, yeah," he says. "And you were convinced she was a prostitute."

"She totally was!"

"Because you didn't believe anyone would legitimately want to have sex with me."

"Uh, it was more because she kept nodding to this big burly dude in the corner who was staring at her the whole time who I'm certain was her pimp."

"Yeah, yeah. Excuses. You just didn't think anyone wanted to shag me."

He holds his hand out to help me navigate over a big squelchy mud bit.

"Everyone wanted to shag you. I knew that."

"You even wanted to shag me." He says it with a laugh, going for a joke, though recently jokes have become prickly balls that you

have to deliver, and handle, in just the right way to avoid nuclear fallout.

I'm not sure how to handle this one, but I know I don't want a nuclear fallout when we're two hours into an eight hour hike up a mountain in miserable, grey fog that I could very easily get lost in if James decides he's had enough. Jesus, I would be one of those people you read about on a news app: 'Body recovered of (stupid) woman, forty-four, who decided to walk up a mountain completely unprepared, not knowing how to read a map and with only a Kinder Bueno for sustenance.'

An image flashes before me – me sat cowering under a rocky overpass, broken leg sticking out at a vomit-inducing angle, rationing my Kinder Bueno and wishing I'd just laughed at his joke – and brought a more substantial chocolate bar choice.

I laugh at his joke. Give him a playful tap on the shoulder as some sort of confirmation. Of what, I don't know, but it feels appropriate.

James pauses and studies the map, angling himself away from the howling wind that is slapping my cheeks so hard they feel numb already. He glances up at an extremely steep and unwelcoming path to the left of us, puts the map away and gives me a bit of Kendal Mint Cake from his pocket. "You OK?" he asks. "Do you want any water? Need a pee break?"

"Fine for now."

He tucks a strand of my hair back into my buff and gives me a little kiss. Since me going back to work and comedygate and counselling, it's the most love and attention I've felt from him in a long time. I soak it in.

"You're doing really well," he says. He's proud of me. "And just

think of the massive gin and tonic you'll have earnt when we've finished."

"Margarita. I will need a margarita," I say, the thought of it sparking some hope. "Or a negroni. Or an old fashioned. You promised cocktails."

James laughs, like I was making a joke. I wasn't, but I realise I need to laugh along or risk coming across as the pernickety, too-fancy princess he sometimes accuses me of being.

We start walking again, my feet already throbbing in my hardly-ever-used boots, a blister beginning to form on my ankle. I look up to see we are heading straight for the extremely steep and unwelcoming uphill path. My feet want to cry.

"Tell me we're not actually going up there?" I say.

"It looks worse than it is," James says. "And we can take it super slowly and have lots of breaks. There is another way but it's longer – I thought short and sharp is better than long and never-ending. Think of it like childbirth – you'd rather have a quick burst of intense pain than a thirty-six-hour marathon of labour with quite bad pain, right? And the end result is all worth the pain."

"Are you talking about the view or the kids now?" I ask. "I'd rather have none of the pain, thanks." And then, worried for the prickles, immediately feel I have to clarify that I do love our children and I am happy we (I) went through the pain to have them. "I'm joking, of course. It's all worth it. No pain, no gain, hey?"

"Exactly!" He looks back at me and grins, like I've finally understood his ethos. "Ahhh, do you remember your labour with Chloe? When you were delirious on gas and air and kept screaming at me to push the baby back up and that actually you'd decided you

didn't want it after all? And you accidentally kicked the midwife in the face."

This is our schtick. One of our many histories that we have honed and perfected over many years of retelling. We have a whole back-catalogue, but the birth stories are some of our favourites. They feel comfortable and safe and epic all at the same time – they tell of a time when we were perfectly whole.

"Well, she deserved it," I play along. "She was telling me I needed to stop messing about and push."

We spend the rest of the steep incline bringing the stories out (me, through the desperate panting and generally not being able to breathe) – we go through all three births: the madness and the kick of Chloe's; James stripping off and trying to get into the birthing pool for Felix's until he realised a) I'd shat in it and b) the midwife was just telling him to lean over and catch the baby; and the fact that he nearly missed Jack's as he came four weeks early and James was on a work trip in Paris. We reminisce about the trip to Croatia where Chloe took her first steps, the flight to Malaysia during which Jack threw up over everything and everyone and we were all covered in vomit for approximately twenty hours, the trip to Italy where they upgraded our room and we got a private pool which we all skinny dipped in, Jack's second birthday when I'd painstakingly made an Iggle Piggle cake and Chloe pushed it off the counter, the time we were supposed to go to Connie and Joe's wedding but all got food poisoning and had to watch *Finding Nemo* on repeat for forty-eight hours, the New Year's Eve we got drunk on margaritas and James sprained his ankle dancing . . .

The list goes on. Memories preserved in amber. They're

snapshots of our story, the story of James and I and, more specifically, the story of our family – the family we made, our little unit. We like them because they belong to us, are of our making, but also because they remind us of how far we've come, of what we share, what is ours.

What we don't mention are the other stories – the fact that Chloe didn't sleep for longer than forty-five minutes for the first nine months, that James was working away so much and I was so alone and exhausted I nearly left the baby on the change mat and walked out of the house, and if it hadn't been for Emily moving in for a few days to give me a chance to breathe, I probably would've done. The fact that, although he did just about make it back for Jack's birth, he then had to leave again and missed most of the first month of Jack. The fact that the cake Chloe pushed off the counter was around the time she was deeply unhappy at nursery and would scream and cry for hours every morning when it was time to leave. The fact that, apart from the skinny dipping in Italy, James and I were barely on speaking terms for most of that holiday. The list goes on. Which is to say, every cloud has a silver lining, but also the reverse.

Now – with the heavy rain lashing against my cheap waterproof trousers that seem to no longer be waterproof – is not the time to bring up the reverse silver linings. Besides which, I'm not sure I ever want to bring them up for fear of our family myths becoming tainted. I wonder what will happen to Emily and Rick's family stories – will she hold on to them tightly and lovingly or will they all become painful reminders of When They Were Happy? What will happen to their photo albums? The thought causes my already

freezing cold skin to goosebump. Jesus, what would happen to ours if we split up? And, more importantly, all the photos that now just live on James's computer? Would they just be lost to me? Maybe I should start printing some out.

I spend the next bit of the walk making mental notes of things I should do to be in a better position if we do ever break up. These include:

1. Get all passwords – Netflix, Disney, all streaming apps, also bank, mortgage etc.

2. Check the mortgage is in my name too.

3. Find out what bank our mortgage is with.

4. Print out photos from James's computer.

5. Make a silent inventory of any pieces of art/furniture that def belong to me.

6. Make a silent inventory of any pieces of art/furniture that def belong to James – e.g. ugly wardrobe passed down from his parents, weird Buddha sculpture, smelly knackered armchair, ugly pouffe, massive Smiths poster, horrible old quilt thing made by one of his dead relatives.

7. Make a record of good parenting examples in case he

tries to take the kids from me.

8. Be nicer to some of his friends (John and Marcus esp) so they don't bitch about me too much.

9. Start taking small amounts of cash out of joint account and hiding in a drawer?

10. Find out if he wants to be buried or cremated and what songs he wants played at his funeral.

I accidentally veer into him dying territory, rather than just us splitting up territory, which makes me overwhelmingly sad. By the time we finally, finally make it to the summit, the thought of him dying when I love him so desperately much, along with the hideous pain from my now multiple blisters, makes me burst into tears and grab hold of him like he's on his death bed.

"You did it!" James says.

He takes off his gloves and puts his hands on my cheeks, staring right at me, his face a ruddy-cheeked vision of happiness and pride and love – like he's my long-suffering coach and I've just landed gold at the Olympics. I revel in it, pushing the searing pain and the rising panic about him dying one day to the side.

"Isn't it gorgeous!" he glides his arm through the air, like a fine purveyor of the view. Except, as far as I can see, there isn't much view, only fog-covered hills and lots of grey and ant-like people making their way up paths.

"Lovely," I say, pleased I'm one step closer to getting some kind

of warmth and alcohol. And actually, pleased for the moment. Maybe it's one we'll add to our amber-preserved bank – the time we left the kids with his mum and dad and walked up a mountain together and James was happy and he treated me like a queen and someone he actually wanted to spend time with.

I nestle into him, milking the moment. We used to have more of these. I liked them.

"Let's get you that drink, then," he says, kissing me on the forehead.

"You mean, in like another four hours, let's get me that drink?"

"Yeah. But once we're there, that's it. I'll bring you gin on tap, massage your feet, even carry you up to the room."

"But I have to walk four hours to get there first?"

He hands me another piece of Kendal Mint Cake, pulls my zip up higher, tucks my hair back into my buff again. "Afraid so."

25

THE NEXT morning, I am delicate in all the ways it is possible to be delicate; my head is pounding upon pounding upon big-steel-drum pounding, my legs seem to have given up their ability to hold me upright, to the point where I am having to lean against the wall to lower myself onto the toilet in some kind of deranged-old-lady, Spiderman fashion, and my feet are so sore and swollen I can't bear to try and wrestle them into any of the shoes I brought with me.

James is still surfing the happy wave – and the Doting Husband wave – so doesn't even get mildly frustrated at my inability to move or do any more walking. He brings me up some cheap supermarket individually wrapped pastries from the continental breakfast the B&B put on and even goes on a mission to find me a decent coffee. I am hashtag "blessed' and it makes me wonder if I should do this big-exercise-for-attention thing more regularly. Though my feet tell me to sod right off with that idea.

I spend the day mostly in the room. I watch bad reality TV on my phone, then the first *Bridget Jones*, which happens to be on TV, I read the magazines James brings up for me, I doze and I eat and I text friends.

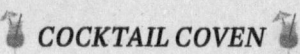

COCKTAIL COVEN

Me: *I climbed the mountain! I can't walk or piss without using a zimmer frame, or feel my feet, but I made it! Another one ticked off the list.*

Me: *And now James is treating me like a queen because I managed it and it's actually really nice.*

Me: *And god, it's just nice to not have the kids around sometimes, isn't it?*

Emily: *I wouldn't know! I'm in summer holiday hell. Kian was supposed to be at forest school but has broken out in a rash that may or may not be contagious so is having to be at home and I'm having to do really important meetings on Zoom with bloody CBeebies on in the background. FFS.*

Me: *Oh no! That's rubbish! I'll leave you to it. Just wanted to share the mountain news.*

Emily: *It's great, well done.*

Me: *Quick question – what are you going to do with all your photo albums if you and Rick end up getting divorced?*

Emily: *Where did that come from?!*
Me: *It just occurred to me. And has he got loads of photos*

on his computer? James has loads of our photos on his computer and I just think, if we ever separate, I'll probably never see those photos again.

Emily: *I literally have no headspace for thinking about that kind of stuff right now.*

Me: *Sorry! As you were. Good luck with the rash.*

To Cath:

> *Hey Cath. You've been really quiet on the group WhatsApp lately. Wanted to check everything's OK. We're good now, right? Did you see I climbed a mountain?! Go me!*

To Dorit:

> Me: *I climbed the mountain! I can't walk or piss without using a zimmer frame, or feel my feet, but I made it! Another one ticked off the list.*
>
> Dorit: *YAAASSSSSSS QUEEN!!! That's my girl! Moving and grooving and DOING THE THINGS!*
>
> Me: *Ah thanks! Think I'm going to do some more of my book now too – James is out on a walk and I brought my laptop with me just in case. And I figure, if I can climb a mountain, I can definitely write a book.*

Dorit: *YOU KNOW IT!!*

Me: *Cocktails and a debrief once I'm back?*

Dorit: *For sure.*

The warm glow of Dorit's congratulations fires me up to retrieve my laptop from my bag and open my document. Ever since Jodie made a vague and passing comment about how my scripts 'had promise', I've made it my mission to finish my book. Sometimes when I'm stuck in my 3 a.m. to 5 a.m. not sleeping window, I go downstairs and write. I listen to writing podcasts on my commute, I got *The Artist's Way* and religiously do my morning pages – except for this morning when I was far too shattered, or yesterday morning I suppose as we were up early, or the few mornings before when James's parents were with us. And the week before that when work was mental. Some days, I do my morning pages. I got Stephen King's *On Writing*, and Ann Lamott's *Bird by Bird*. I'm doing all the writerly things.

Except for writing. I haven't done a lot more of that, but that's partly because I need to plan what is going to happen and partly because I'm exhausted from doing all the other writerly things, which don't actually leave me with that much time to write. But I feel inspired now. And, as one of the authors on one of the podcasts said, you have to write the thing. And as another one said, you can't edit an empty page. And as another one said, just write the damn thing.

I'm currently eight thousand words in. I've done my research

and, although there isn't a standard number, an average word count for an adult novel is around seventy to one-hundred-and-twenty thousand words. So I'm aiming for seventy, clearly (why would I choose to write one-hundred-and-twenty?!). Children's books can be much less, and I did consider that for a minute, but I decided there are no stories worth telling that don't include swearing and sex. So here we are, with sixty-two thousand words left to write.

My main character, Chantelle, is about to embark on a trip to Thailand with her two best friends, Cate and Emma, where they are going to have huge amounts of sex and fun. And adventures. And I might include them seeing the lady who blows ping-pong balls out of her vagina. Although blows is probably the wrong word – expels? That sounds too dictionary. Ejects? That sounds like they're fighter pilots. I'll cross that bridge when I come to it.

Apart from getting to Thailand and the sex and fun and adventures, I have very little idea what the actual plot is, but I'm fine with that because apparently it has a name, when you don't know what you're writing – it's called being a pantser – and loads of bestselling mega-rich authors write that way, including some who write whodunnits and don't even know whodunnit when they start writing. Because apparently your characters just speak to you and make their own decisions, so I'm going for that.

For now, though, I am telling Chantelle she needs to get fired from her job at a top law firm for speaking the truth in a court of law, which, I figure, shows her being essentially a good person and someone who the reader will root for (I also bought *Save the Cat!*). Because lord knows readers do not like a flawed woman!

Once I start, I can't stop.

I write the Chantelle being fired scene, adding a touch of *Jerry Maguire* to it, I write her getting together with her friends. I make one of them a bit Cath and one of them a bit Emily and I get to put the words into their mouths and it is FUN. I don't know if it's any good, and at this point, I don't care – I'm enjoying it and it's taking me places outside of this stuffy B&B room littered with Monster Munch packets and before I know it, the evening is setting in and James comes back red-cheeked and worried he's been gone too long and I'd be cross and he's bought me some sliders so I can actually come out for dinner.

* * *

"It's so fun!" I say, slathering my bread with a whole little butter packet.

Just down the road from the B&B we found a restaurant that was somewhere between a tourist tea shop and a brasserie – beef bourguignon and steak frites served on wipe-clean orange pine tables with a lone candle and sauce sachets. And a depressed dessert fridge with half-eaten cakes wallowing under fluorescent lights watching over us.

"I just really got into it and it's like everything else just fell away. I really want to get it finished."

James pauses his buttering. "That's great. But you're still going to concentrate on your work placement for now, right? That's what we're paying out all this childcare for?"

"Of course," I say, the seed of disappointment sown so early into dinner.

He never just all-out supports me any more, never finds the unconditional enthusiasm – there's always ifs and buts and how it will impact him taken into the equation.

"I've been doing it in the night when I can't sleep, and sometimes getting up early. I might try writing on my phone on my commute – a lot of writers do it."

"Why don't you just focus on your running job for now? The thing we've upended our life to accommodate. One thing at a time. The list feels like it was a fun thing to do for a while, but should probably be put to one side now, hey?"

I deny the sigh that's desperate to escape, because I don't want us to fall out now when we've been having such a nice time and because maybe he's a bit right. Since my *After Hours* disaster – which, a part of me still thinks, was not that huge a disaster – I've been trying my best to be the perfect runner and to chisel my way back into everyone's good graces, but I just seem to keep messing up, no matter how hard I try. They moved me off *After Hours* and on to a dating show (*Show Me Yours*), which felt safer and seemed all good for a while – I was doing everything fine except for the odd coffee and food order, until a couple of weeks in, I managed to accidentally send the wrong call sheet to a contestant, which essentially gave the whole game away, and the researcher had to frantically find some last-minute contestants who were nowhere near as good on screen as the others had been.

I'm hanging on by my fingernails and those fingernails are beginning to break. So maybe James is right, for once, even though it was delivered with a patronising tone that's about as heavy as this disgusting peppercorn sauce on my steak. I change the subject

and ask him about his walk, which sets him off on a twenty-minute TED Talk about the greatest walks, which gets us on to the Scottish Highlands and how wonderful it is and how one day, when he's retired, he'd like to buy a house there.

"Really?" I'm surprised, but not as surprised as you'd think, given that I've not been consulted on this retirement dream. "But it's so far away. *So* far away. And always raining."

"It's stunning there," he says, his eyes all glittery and swoony. "I mean look, how stunning was it today? And even further north, up there, I don't know what it is, but the light there is just different. The colours, the landscape – there's something special about it. It's my happy place. You've loved it when we've been together."

I did quite like (not love) Skye, the one time we went, though I definitely did not enjoy the million-hour journey.

"Could you not have your happy place somewhere near the south coast and a big city for culture?" I ask. Only half joking. "Somewhere I would enjoy too."

"You wouldn't have to come."

"Woah there, tiger. I thought when you retire, we'd actually get to see each other for more than twenty minutes a day?"

"We will! Up here in Scotland – going for lovely walks."

He reaches across the table and strokes my hand, giving me one of his prize-winning cheeky grins and a wink, the blue in his eyes brighter than it's been for a long time, despite the lone candle flame.

"Anyway," he says, leaning back in his chair, "it's not for ages so we don't have to think about that yet."

My overcooked, over-sauced steak gets cleared away. I make

the mistake, two wines in, of ordering a pudding from the cabinet which looks and tastes exceedingly sorry for itself. We go back to family stories and talking about the kids, because I can't ask him about his work for fear it will send him down a stress hole and he never asks me about my work and the only common ground we seem to have at the moment is the kids. But the retirement stuff is still swirling around my head and refusing to be ignored, a woodpecker on my temple. I feel like we're on a precipice, that having survived the young kids who need you for everything stage, we're about to free jump into the next stage of life – and I'd like to know if there's a safety net at the bottom of the cliff. Or a parachute. Though then it wouldn't be free jumping.

Maybe it doesn't feel like that for James, because he's been existing in the same kind of life anyway, just with more to do at the weekends and no lie-ins. Maybe his next stage really is retirement. But my next stage, whatever it's going to look like, is definitely beginning to kick in – the tectonic plates are shifting underneath me; all three of the kids will be at secondary school next month and that's a whole different mothering ball game. No more school runs, or relentless parents' WhatsApp groups, no more costumes for historical civilisations on random days, or quiz nights, no more birthday assemblies and sponsored bounces. And it won't be too long before they're all gone.

I've never understood women who talk about empty nest syndrome, always wishing for my nest to be even a tiny bit more empty than the can't-breathe, full-to-bursting it's always felt. But already with Chloe and Felix that bit older and more independent, I'm noticing a difference – they go round to friends' houses after

school, hang out with friends at the weekend, go to Nando's for dinner, get themselves to and from sports clubs. Before I went back to work, I had two whole hours to myself after school some days. Which was lovely to begin with, but then actually quite lonely. And I'm beginning to see it. My nest is starting to feel like it's emptying.

"What else do you want to do when you retire?" I ask, stirring the Irish coffee I ordered to try and take the taste of the stale carrot cake out of my mouth. The Irish coffee which appears to be instant Nescafé with a double shot of whisky.

"Ooh," James says, rubbing his hands together. "Now you're talking. I think about this a lot. Some more Ironmans, definitely, the one in Hawaii is supposed to be the toughest. Maybe another marathon. A massive bike ride around the world. Or something like that – a really long bike ride, like, months long, while I still can."

I nod, taking in the fact these are all things that do not include me. Though, I suppose I could handle going to Hawaii – not that that was even remotely a consideration in James wanting to do it.

"I mean, you could come too, to any of those," he adds, reading my reaction. "I'm just assuming you wouldn't want to."

"That assumption is correct," I say. "What about travel? Other than your round the world bike ride, and the Ironman in Hawaii, where do you want to visit? Unless you're going to cover it all in your solo bike ride, of course. Outside of the British Isles," I stipulate.

"Um, I don't know, actually. I'm perfectly happy exploring more of the British Isles, thanks. I'm not into the long haul so much. Apart from for the Ironmans and all that."

"Thailand?" Thailand has been on my list for years. It was once on his list too.

"I kind of feel like I've done Southeast Asia." He sips his chamomile tea.

"We've been to Malaysia," I say.

"Yeah, so that box is kind of ticked."

I shake my head at him, trying to still feel the good humour, though the doubt is beginning to creep in.

"I want adventure and physical challenges," he says, eyes gleaming again.

I stir my disgusting coffee, wishing I'd just gone for gin. Wishing I had a vat of it. I sigh, a million thoughts swirling round my mind.

"Do you think we'll stay together after the kids have gone?" I ask. It comes out before I've really thought it through, but the moment feels right. Or OK, at least.

"Do you think we won't?" he says.

I shrug. "We're so different. We want such different things. I feel like I've been trapped in a dark cave for fifteen years and now I'm free – or a bit freer – I want to have fun. I want to travel, go to new restaurants, try new things, meet new people, go dancing, sit on exotic beaches and not do anything that's physically challenging or involves a bicycle."

He rolls his eyes at the mention of the dark cave. I have used my dark cave analogy before and he doesn't like it. Takes it personally almost, like I'm suggesting he's kept me a prisoner in a dark cave.

"We used to have more things in common," I continue. "We used to like more of the same things."

"We've changed, Charlie." He runs his fingers through his

hair, a silver curl springing straight back where it was in defiance. "We've been together over twenty-five years – people change. We were totally different people then – babies, practically. It would be more worrying if we hadn't changed."

The teenage waitress comes over and clears our table, her awkwardness mirroring the tension sitting heavy on us.

"I don't want to end up like my parents," I say.

He straightens up in his chair, his jaw tensing. He knows where this is going, it's another conversation we've had before. Like we have our carousel of fond family stories, we also have a carousel of difficult conversations and this is one of them.

"They're always bickering," I say. "Not even bickering, more like constant passive aggressive comments – who got the most sleep, how my dad set the table wrong, how my mum didn't get the right food in. It's relentless. And like they're not a team at all – they're on totally different sides, in a silent war against each other. Which I'm sure is why they go on so many cruises with friends – because they don't actually like spending time with each other. I think we're heading that way and I don't want that. I want us to be a team again. And I guess I thought the sniping and the being against each other was because of the kids and just logistics and you being busy and stressed and the built-up resentment and stuff, and that when the kids left, and especially when you retired, that would fade away and we'd be back on the same team. But seeing my parents – they don't have any of that, the kids and the stress and the logistics, so I'm worried that maybe it isn't that and maybe when that all goes, we'll still be left on different teams. Against each other."

I take a breath. Maybe the terrible Irish coffee was stronger than I thought. My cheeks are hot, a nip of a cry is in my throat.

"So what are you saying?" James asks.

I think.

I stare at the tea-stained plasticated table cloth and think. "I'm not saying anything in particular. Or maybe, I'm saying I'm worried. And all these retirement plans you have that don't seem to feature me – that's fine, but I need to know if I'm going to feature at all in some way. If we're going to feature at all, together. Just something to think about."

"Which is what we're doing with Dr Deb at the moment," James says, weary.

"Sure."

The awkward waitress hovers near us with the bill. James pays, his face now devoid of any mountain happiness. That's the effect I have on him, I think; I drain him of his happiness. I'm like one of those soul suckers in *Harry Potter*. Maybe that's what we do to each other.

"Maybe you should get into cycling," he says as he opens the cafe door for me, trying for a thin smile. "You'd look good in Lycra."

We both know this is a lie.

September

26

JODIE HAS asked to see me.

So I have ditched the high-waisted jeans and donned my best smart-casual black trousers, complete with trendy red band down the side. I've paired it with a black shirt and big hoops, but rather than feeling the boss-bitch vibes I was going for, I'm definitely giving off more try-hard drama teacher. Or 1920s fascist.

I absolutely one hundred per cent made sure I got to the office early and absolutely one hundred per cent had an early night. Though I was still awake for approximately half of it and as such, my eyes feel like little red pinholes and my brain feels like a swamp.

I'm not assigned to any production at the moment, so I make myself busy around the office – clean the kitchen, set the pastries out, ask if the few who are in want a tea or coffee. People arrive in dribs and drabs, the daze of Monday morning evident in their movements, their expressions. There are chats about weekend excitements – Zac went to a bar in a disused toilet, Lulu did a crochet course in Hackney, Betty got high at a festival in Brockwell Park and ended up hooking up with a famous drag queen. I am not told this information, I overhear it. And no one asks what I got up to over the weekend, though for reference: I went to the garden centre and bought loads of plants, including tomato plants that we buy every year and that die every year, did the laundry, did

more laundry and yet more laundry, went for dinner at the local overpriced Italian with James's work friend and his wife where they talked about advertising for approximately three hours and we ate under-cooked pasta, I nagged the boys to do their homework, and to stop wrestling, and to stop calling each other idiots, read *The Sunday Times* and spent approximately three hours worrying that I seem to be developing a moustache and researching how to deal with that. Probably just as well no one asked, it would've sunk my stock even further, and it's already bottom feeder level.

"Hey," I say to Zac.

I've settled myself in the runners' corner and am trying to look busy.

"Hey," he says, not making eye contact.

"Did you have a nice weekend?"

"Yeah, good thanks. Bit tiring, but good."

There's an awkward pause. I shuffle some papers, open and shut a drawer.

"How was yours?" he asks, eventually.

"Yeah good, thanks." I decide not to launch into my garden centre antics, for both our sakes.

This is painful. Over the weeks, we have used up all our mutual ground, which was minimal to begin with, and now we are at the point where we have nothing to talk about, besides work, that would be of interest to the other person. There is a gulf between me and this twenty-something. Between me and all these twenty-somethings. They give absolutely no shits about my new anti-ageing skincare regime, or my concern over secondary school curriculums or my possible but probably-not-because-my-mum-went-through-

it-so-late-and-it's-genetic perimenopause symptoms. And I can't even begin to find a way into whatever it is that might concern them – I'm guessing which pronouns to use or the fact that my generation has screwed them over on the environment or that they will never be able to get on the housing ladder? Though Zac does wear a lot of 'vintage' nineties fashion, so I guess that's something we kind of have in common, except I wore it the first time round.

"You're looking . . . smart," he says.

"I've got a meeting with Jodie."

"Ah." He looks away, makes himself busy, just as Jodie walks through the office and beckons to me to follow her into her office.

I feel the eyes of everyone in the room on my back as I walk through.

"Have a seat," Jodie says.

She's the epitome of professional yet cool elegance – cropped, tailored trousers, a red, bold, patterned silk-like vest top and gold heels.

She turns on her computer, fills up glasses of water for both of us and taps a message on her phone before turning it to silent and putting it face down on the desk. I try to sit in a way that looks comfortable yet confident but my arms can't find any position that doesn't feel stupid or schoolgirl.

"So," she says, taking a sip of water and leaning back in her chair. "How do you think it's all been going?"

"Uh, well . . ." My mouth is suddenly dry. I don't know how to play this. Should I go for honest, with full on accountability and a promise to do better, or a more 'shit happens, it was all OK in the end, we all make mistakes' vibe? "It's been a challenge. But I'm

really enjoying it and I feel like I've learnt so much over the time I've been here already. Learning every day, to be honest."

She looks at me, scrutinises me. I want to hide under the desk.

"I've asked all the producers for their feedback – as is routine for the scheme. And I have heard quite a few things that are . . . worrying."

I nod. But raise my eyebrows ever so slightly, going for somewhere between accepting and enquiring.

"I completely understand that coming back into the industry after so long will be difficult and an adjustment. And I'm absolutely prepared for there to be mistakes along the way and teething problems. But some of what has happened, particularly on *After Hours*, seems to be a total oversight – and, dare I say it, stupid, needless mistakes. Mistakes that ended up costing us a lot of time and money."

"I know," I say, feeling like a child. "And I'm so sorry. But it really was just that I was learning the ropes and—"

"Having a back-up contributor, especially for a sensitive segment, is common sense. Getting release forms signed properly is basic running. Sending out call sheets – again, basic. I've also been hearing reports of repeated lateness and turning up to work very hungover. And look, we work in entertainment TV, I'm not stupid and I've been there myself, but when it's regular and it's impacting your ability to work, it's not OK."

Heat rises to my cheeks, my stomach roils. I haven't felt this ashamed since the sixth form when Mrs King hauled me into her office and let rip on me for smoking at break time. Or actually, I guess since Chloe walked in on me masturbating. I don't know

what to say, how to stick up for myself. So I bite back the tears and focus on the zigzag pattern on the rug.

"I got a bit overexcited at being back in the industry," I manage. "I was acting like I was in my twenties again – and maybe took my eye off the ball a bit. But I promise I can do better – I'm going to focus on work and double check everything."

"Are you sure you really want to be back in the industry? And have to work your way up again?" She sighs. "It's pretty relentless – and, like I said before, you have to be passionate about it. I'm just not sure you have that passion."

"I do," I say, nodding emphatically. She looks at me, searching, intense. "I *really* do."

"Look, this is your last week on the scheme and I'm sorry, but I don't think we will have a position for you here after that. I admire what you're doing, but I need people I can rely on, and it seems that just isn't you."

🍹 *COCKTAIL COVEN* 🍹

Me: *Just got fired.*

Me: *From my internship.*

Me: *Is there anything more depressing than that?*

Me: *Turns out making porn is not my calling.*

Emily: *Oh mate! Sorry. That's rubbish.*

Me: *Jodie called me into her office and told me I'm too old to work in TV.*

Emily: *OMFG!*

Me: *I mean, not exactly those words. She said it's relentless and you have to be passionate about it and maybe I didn't have that passion for it any more.*

Emily: *Is she right?*

Me: *I'm still deciding.*

Me: *But maybe she's right. Maybe celeb food fights and debate segments on the topics 'women should never wear jeans' and 'which is better: beauty or brains?' and dating shows that involve genitals aren't what gives me life.*

Emily: *And the in-studio live porn.*

Me: *Yup. And that.*

Me: *Which I still think would've been a good segment.*

Emily: *Really?*

Me: *Maybe not.*

Me: *Who knows?*

Me: *Who knows anything? What's the point anyway? We all get old and die. Maybe it would've been a fun legacy to have – the woman who was responsible for the woman orgasming on live TV.*

Me: *God, maybe I should've been the woman. I could've put it on my list! 'Have an orgasm on live TV.'*

Emily: *Dude.*

27

"**I CAN'T LOOK** directly at it," I whisper to Dorit. "It feels wrong."

"It's just a penis," she whispers back. "An old, wrinkly one, but still just a penis. It's not like you can leave a blank space there."

We're in a room above a pub in the middle of Vauxhall at a life drawing class – ticking another thing off my list. Which is basically what I'm living for at the moment.

I enjoyed the first few weeks of not having a job, once I'd licked my wounds about getting fired and reminded myself it was a piece of crap job making piece of crap shows for drunk or stoned people and one that I was paying out to be able to do. And is clearly a job for young and dumb twenty-somethings – which I'm allowed to say because I have had that job as a very young and very dumb twenty-something and also as a very old and somewhat wiser forty-something. Jodie was right though – I'm not passionate about TV any more – or not that kind of TV, at least. Who knows if I would've still been passionate about it if I'd stayed in the industry the first time round. I'm thinking maybe not.

So now I'm back to working on my list and my book and having no external validation from anyone other than Dorit. She came round with a bottle of tequila when I told her I'd been fired and we worked on my CV before deciding my career history is actually too abysmal to put into written form and then we danced and

played truth or dare. I dared her to streak and shriek in our garden for one whole minute, which she did, and which I'm one hundred per cent certain the annoying old couple two doors down saw from their wanky loft conversion with the big window. She dared me to kiss her, which I did, and which was actually great because that's another thing I can cross off my list. I think she may have got a bit handsy, but I had had a lot of tequila by then so I may be wrong.

I've hardly heard from Cath or Emily. I know they have a lot going on but I feel like they're deserting me in my hour of need. Which sucks, because they're normally the people I turn to in times like this. In all times, actually. Thank god for Dorit, who has been an absolute rock and who is not only a marvellous cheerleader, but also a great partner in crime and very good at finding list-worthy activities. Like this – drawing an old, bearded man in all his resplendent, naked, flaccid willy glory.

Everyone in the room is standing at their easels and looking very serious. Some are even holding their pencils out and doing that one-eyed measuring thing which I vaguely remember from art lessons is something to do with perspective. Maybe that would make it easier to draw the willy. I have a go – extending my arm and closing one eye. It does not help.

Dorit starts giggling, which draws the attention of Lorraine, the kaftaned, bangled-up class facilitator.

"I am rubbish at this," I say. "Why did I let you talk me into it?"

"Anything for the list, babe," Dorit says. "I'm sure you're not as bad as you think. You look like you know what you're doing."

"I'm pretending."

I peer round Dorit's easel and look at her drawing, shocked and dismayed to see it's actually remarkably good. "Dorit! You didn't say you're a full-on artist."

She peers round to look at mine and dissolves into giggles. "Oh, babe. Turns out you *are* as bad as you think."

I make it through the rest of the class, fuelled by wine and embarrassment, and we decamp to the pub downstairs.

"I thought that was fun," Dorit says. She brings two old fashioneds back from the bar.

I'm already feeling a bit more buzzed than I should – the sleeping tablets I'm taking in an attempt to remedy my 3 a.m. to 5 a.m. anxiety fest do not sit well with alcohol. Or life in general, really. I mostly feel like some kind of walking dead creature – so exhausted and brain foggy I can't deal with even the small things. Simple things. Things like online grocery shops or working out what the hell everyone is going to eat all week.

"You failed to mention that you're some kind of Vincent van Gogh when we signed up for this."

"Hardly," she says. "Mine just looked impressive next to your epic failure."

I look outraged. She laughs. A big belly laugh.

"Honestly," she says, through the snorts. "It was like you'd never held a pencil before."

"Dorit! You can't say that!"

"Well, at least we can rule out any jobs in the visual arts from the job hunt. How's that going, by the way?"

"It's kind of not," I say, sipping my old fashioned and relishing the hard liquor. "I've registered back on the website and put some

feelers out with some people I used to work with, so we'll see. I'm not holding my breath though."

"Those are some proactive moves though, all good. And as I keep telling you – you need to finish that book of yours. That's how you'll make your fortune. Become the next *Fifty Shades of Grey* lady."

"I mean, I was hoping for more the next Margaret Atwood."

"*Fifty Shades* lady is rolling in it – millionaire, if not billionaire. And I've read those books – they're not even that good. You wouldn't have to learn fancy vocabulary or even how to write that well."

"Um, thanks?" I laugh, not sure whether to take that as an insult or as genuinely helpful advice.

"The book and the list," Dorit says. "That's all you need to focus on for now. Remember we have pottery class on Tuesday and the drag bottomless brunch followed by the football match on Saturday and the opera the following Saturday. And the protest about the potholes. I think that's next Thursday? I'll check."

"We're protesting potholes?" I ask.

She waves her bangled hands. "I know you said you wanted a women-centred issue, but this one fits into the schedule well. Turns out potholes are a very inflammatory issue."

I shrug. "I guess a protest is a protest. I do actually need to find time to write, too."

I have been focusing on the list a lot – maybe in an effort to distract myself from the shame of my firing, and maybe also in an effort to distract myself from the loneliness of my marriage. Since the fleeting lovely moments on our mountain getaway, James and I have gone back to how things were, or even a bit worse. We've

hardly seen each other, and when we do it's usually for about half an hour at the end of the night when he's knackered and doesn't have the energy for a conversation, so we flick through the streamers for twenty minutes before watching five minutes of the news and then heading to bed. Often to separate beds as he's up so early to get some work in before work and I'm not really sleeping.

I told him I felt lonely. He asked me how that's possible when I'm always complaining about not getting enough time to myself. I explained that's not the kind of lonely I meant. He said he didn't understand then and is it all right if he goes for a big training session on Sunday. I went to a boxercise class and bloody loved boxing the bejesus out of a punch bag imagining it was James.

"And we have to get Cornwall booked in," Dorit says. "Have you asked Cath and Emily for dates?"

"I have," I say. "But they need a bit of persuading. Cath is worried about being too far away from her mum – even though it's only one weekend and she does have a brother she could ask to be there. And Emily is just really busy. But I'll keep chasing them. I think it's what we all need."

I definitely need it – to escape my house, to have a break, to try and sleep and to reconnect with the girls.

"It'll be fun!" Dorit beams. "My friend's house is amazing and it's super close to the sea – we can kick back and party and get some wholesome sea air. It'll be perfect. And I've been looking into lining up some good list-ticking activities too." She winks at me. Cheeky grin, big wink.

"Oh, now you've piqued my interest," I say.

"Well, let's get it booked in and then I might tell you more."

"As long it doesn't involve drawing or flaccid penises, I'm in."

"Definitely no drawing!" She laughs. "Though I can't promise on the flaccid penises."

"Dorit!"

Updated on 20th September.

1. Have sex with George Clooney.

2. Take up parkour. ✓

3. Swim with dolphins.

4. Climb ~~Mount Everest~~ a mountain. ✓

5. ~~Have a threesome.~~ Go to a pottery class.

6. Go to a bottomless brunch. ✓

7. Eat caviar.

8. Eat an oyster. ✓

9. Eat snails.

10. Have a martini. ✓

11. Make a sex tape.

12. Kiss a girl. ✓

13. Go to a strip club/sex party.

14. Use a sex toy. ✓ ✓ ✓

15. Eat an insect.

16. Go scuba diving.

17. Do a spin class. ✓

18. Learn to street dance. ✓

19. Read War and Peace. ✓

20. Get a tattoo.

21. Volunteer. ✓

22. *Try boxing.* ✓
23. *See a woman shoot a ping-pong ball from her vagina.*
24. *Have a Hollywood wax.* ✓
25. *Do anal.* ✓
26. *Stand-up comedy.* ✓
27. *Surf.*
28. *Take ecstasy.*
29. *Learn how to do make-up.*
30. *Go to Thailand.*
31. *Have sex on a plane.*
32. *Write a book.*
33. *Skinny dip.*
34. *Attend a protest.* ✓
35. *Go to a drag show.* ✓
36. *Rock climbing.* ✓
37. *Puppy yoga.* ✓
38. *Go to a football match.* ✓
39. *Immersive theatre.* ✓
40. *Go to an opera.* ✓
41. *Go to a life drawing class.* ✓
42. *Go to pop choir.* ✓
43. *Go to Soho House.* ✓
44. *Learn how to manifest.*
45. *Have a tarot reading.*

October

28

IT'S *OCEAN'S ELEVEN* George.

The suit and the wide collar and the slick, salt and pepper hair.

I'm at a desk in the *After Hours* office. Gavin Cortado's desk, actually – the big one in the corner. George struts in, takes off his sunglasses and smoulders at me with those beautiful eyes of his. He kisses me. Just one, lush, lingering kiss. Then he disappears under the desk with a cheeky grin and starts to slowly, sexily, remove my shoes (high heels) and tights (sheer). I feel the heat instantly, delicious butterflies forming in my fanny. He removes my knickers (lacy thong) with his tongue. I glance down under the desk, searching for that cheeky grin, but the salt and pepper hair looks different. It's longer and not slicked back. Gavin Cortado hair. He looks up at me, angry.

"Why didn't you get a back-up?" he screams, partly to my face, partly to my vagina. "Now you have to do it! Live on TV! You have to have an orgasm!"

I start to protest, to say I can't, it's not happening, and where is George, but then Betty walks in and she's shouting at me too.

"The call sheets are wrong!" Her face is all scrunched and red and blotchy and bits of spit come out with every word.

I close my eyes, try to bring back George. I picture his grin,

his chiselled jaw. I look back down between my legs, hoping the manifesting worked. But it isn't George's head there, or Gavin's. It's deep brown and curly. Wildly curly. I start shaking my head, scrunch my eyes closed and hope it's gone away but when I open them again it's still there. Dorit's head. She looks up at me, smiling, from between my legs.

"Yes, girl! You got this! We'll get this orgasm. Go, Charlie! Go, Charlie!"

* * *

"Charlie!"

The back of my throat is tight with tears.

"Dude, wake up!"

My body starts bouncing, light filters through my eyelids, the *After Hours* office disappearing.

"What time did you get to bed?"

It's a different voice; Emily's. I creak my eyes open to see her sitting on my bed, cup of tea in hand, fresh-faced and dressed. It takes me a minute to get my bearings, but the dazzling white walls and bold seascape artwork remind me we're in Cornwall. In the cottage.

"Finally!" Emily says. "Here, I have tea. Cath and I are going to go for a walk on the coastal path, check out the village. Do you want to come?"

I go to sit up, but my head has other ideas, the room suddenly spinning. I slump back down.

"What time is it?" I mutter.

"It's half ten," Emily says. "I let you lie in for ages but it's a beautiful day and we're desperate to explore. What time did you guys go to bed?"

I flash back to last night – to the eight-hour car journey down here, the pitch black, can-see-the-stars dark, and the tiny, winding roads. Finally getting here and opening the champagne straight away. Cath and Emily sitting on the sofa in deep conversation while Dorit and I danced in the kitchen and cooked. Fajitas, I think. I remember trying to grab the girls up to dance and them being boring. I remember a shot of tequila. Maybe two. I remember Dorit telling me about how she walked out on Phil and the kids three years ago and I remember being shocked and asking questions and Dorit just deflecting and changing the subject. And throwing up. I remember throwing up. And I remember lying in bed completely exhausted but not being able to sleep, despite the sleeping tablets I took. I remember looking at the clock on the wall at regular intervals – 3 a.m., 4 a.m., 4.30 a.m., 5 a.m.

"No idea," I say.

"Well, we came up at about one and I heard you guys singing when I went for a wee around two, so it must've been a late one."

"Makes the not sleeping between 3 a.m. and 5 a.m. more fun if you're awake partying," I mutter, trying for funny.

I cringe at my stupidity. This was supposed to be a bonding, getting-the-friendship-back-on-course weekend. That's how I'd sold it to Cath – and boy, had it taken a lot of selling. And apologising. Grovelling, really. She didn't want to be too far away from her mum, even though Dan was going to be with her, and had suggested somewhere closer to Margate, but I pushed for the

plush cottage and a road trip. She also wasn't keen on Dorit being here, but I explained that Dorit is super fun and has been really supportive and, perhaps more importantly, has a friend who owns a gorgeous cottage we can stay in. So here we are, and I ballsed up already on the first night. I really should go for a walk with them. That would definitely be good bonding time. But I just can't seem to move.

"Come and get some fresh air," Emily says. "Fresh air and life chats. We can come up with a plan for what you're going to do now."

I notice dark circles under her eyes. Which is unusual for Emily.

"I'm going to stay in bed and feel sorry for myself. That's what I'm going to do now."

She sighs. "I meant for the future."

"So did I."

"Come on, Charls," she persists. "It would be good for you. And we haven't seen you for ages. There's a lot to catch up on."

I try to think of an excuse that is more worthy and less like I'm a terrible friend than just feeling woolly-headed and exhausted, but come up with nothing. "I don't think I can get out of bed."

I see the disappointment settle in her jaw and make a mental note to be an amazing friend for the rest of the trip – to have one-on-one, deep and meaningfuls, to be positive and upbeat but also a good listener and to give amazing life advice. Not that anyone should be taking life advice from me.

"I'll sleep this off, then be ready and raring to go!" I say. "You know what I'm like, I always get overexcited on the first night away."

"That is true," Emily says. And a part of me pinches remembering that we all used to get overexcited on first nights away. "Fine, we'll

see you later. Why don't we say to meet in the pub for a late lunch – maybe two?"

"Perfect!" I manage enthusiastically. Pub for lunch is a plan I can stick to.

"Happy hangover," she says, closing the door behind her.

"I don't think it's a hangover—" I go to explain, but she's already gone.

I do a calculation of all I had to drink last night, which really wasn't excessive – definitely not by Past Me standards – and conclude that it can't possibly be a hangover. And then feel cross about how little I seem to be able to drink these days and resolve to do better with that: as in, train myself to be able to drink like I used to.

I down the paracetamol I thoughtfully left out for myself on the bedside table and grab my phone. I ignore the messages from the kids asking for various things and ignore the three from James asking if he needs to take the spaghetti bolognese out of the freezer, what time Felix's hockey match is and if Jack has to do all three of the science worksheets that were set. I ignore these because before I left, I spent two days cooking, sorting, arranging and writing out a full list of instructions. The price I pay for any amount of time away. If he can't be bothered to fully read what I painstakingly wrote out or to work it out for himself, then as I say to Chloe when she begs me to extend her curfew because all her friends are staying out later – tough titties.

I open Google and search: 'Why did I have a lesbian dream about my friend when I'm straight?'

A long list of answers appear. A few at the top from forums

suggest it's calling a spade a spade and lesbian dreams mean you're a lesbian, but as I get further down and open the more legit ones with dream psychologists, relief floods over me. It seems it can be basically anything, but particularly – to do with being open to new ideologies, or career aspirations (that might explain the presence of Gavin Cortado and Betty too), or wanting more intimacy or, my personal favourite, it could indicate that an exciting new opportunity is coming your way.

I plug my phone back in and set my alarm, satisfied that I'm not lusting after Dorit, and fall asleep to the sound of the crashing waves.

29

THE WALK down to the pub is not long, but I want to use it to prise more information out of Dorit after last night's revelations. It's a gorgeous day. My favourite kind of day – bright sunshine, but cold. Jumpers and scarves and big coats and sunglasses. The sea sparkles far below us, looking more inviting than it would feel.

Dorit is perky, as always. Beautiful, immaculately turned out, and stylish in her huge Prada sunglasses and bright red scarf. I only did the smallest blush when I saw her this morning and have now managed to fully put the whole lesbian dream debacle to one side.

"Last night was fun," I say, as we make our way down the hill.

"Sure was. I do love that I've found someone who is into kitchen discos as much as I am."

"Is Phil not into them?" I ask, probing.

She pauses, turns to look at me. "If you want to ask me about Phil, ask me about Phil. Don't insult me with your shit interrogation skills."

I fish-mouth for a second, trying to work out if she's angry, if I've crossed a line. She grins; I'm in the clear.

"Sorry, it's just . . . my head is like cotton wool at the moment, but I think we had a chat about it last night and I can't remember

everything and I feel like it's the first time we've really spoken about that stuff. About you and Phil at all really. Which is weird, but—"

"We've been focusing on your drama," she says. "Which has been the more pressing one. Mine's done and dusted. And I've been enjoying your list – it's a good distraction."

"So, what was your drama?" I ask.

"I'll give you the edited version for now, because it's boring, and I'm bored of talking about it and thinking about it. Basically, Phil and I were wild childs – wild children? Whatever – we were both wild. We met as the sun was coming up at Glastonbury, completely off our tits, and it was love at first sight. We were always up for fun and new experiences and pushing boundaries, we were spontaneous and free-spirited – travel, clubs, drugs, sex festivals – I'll tell you all about that one another time." She laughs, her eyes all wistful and nostalgic. "So, anyway – we were loved-up, I never wanted kids, he did, he pressured me for them, I succumbed, thinking that's what you do when you're in love, and then, sure enough, when they came, I didn't enjoy them, and Phil assumed the full 1950s husband role – out to work early, home late, expecting dinner on the table, barely interacting with the children – or me, for that matter. I struggled on. I was depressed. I drank a lot. I wasn't myself. I tried to talk to Phil about it, but he got defensive, wouldn't listen to what I was saying – which was that I was deeply unhappy. I spiralled and wrestled with it all and then, eventually, I decided I had to save myself, for everybody's sake, and I left. And I know, that makes me a terrible person, because what kind of mother leaves her children? But you see, I didn't want those

children and that's not to say I don't love them – I love them with all of my heart and I actually love them more now that I see them less and don't feel like I'm shackled to them. And now they're older and are fully formed people who are actually very cool and smart and fun."

"But," I start to say, then falter, not knowing how to finish. I've never met a woman who's left her children. It's . . . brave.

"I know, shocking, right," she says. "Though it's actually not. Men leave their families all the time and people don't bat an eyelid." She sighs. "We had a couple of really tricky, nasty years with horrible legal fights and lies being thrown around, but now we're on the other side of it, we're just a regular divorced couple, except I'm the man. Phil's the one who's stayed in the family house where the kids are based, I'm the one who ended up with the bachelor pad and free evenings, dipping in now and then for some sports club drop-offs and lifts to the station. I do pickups a couple of times a week and the kids come to mine every other weekend, though we're quite flexible. They prefer it at Phil's because that's where they're used to and where's closer to school and their friends."

"I mean, it sounds . . . pretty amazing," I say, trying to fathom a life like that.

"It is, in a way. But it's taken a lot of heartbreak and bad decisions and burnt bridges to get here. There's something really sad about not being a family unit like we were, but then I remind myself that that family unit didn't work for me – was never going to work for me. And it was pretty horrible for everyone for a while."

"I can't believe I'm only just finding this out now, after all this time we've been spending together." We're side by side on the road.

I turn to glance at her, seeing a new note in her posture.

"Well, you've been going through your own stuff, I didn't want to impact on you working that out. Plus, it's not something I go around telling every Tom, Dick and Harry about," she says. "Society still views women, and mothers, in a certain way, doesn't it? And I can't be bothered with all the looks and judgement and feeling like I need to explain myself. I choose my friends carefully."

"Does that mean I've officially broken out of the Tom, Dick and, indeed, Harry category?"

"I guess so."

"Good!" I link arms with her, the waft of Chanel No. 5 hitting me through the salty breeze.

"FYI, on the subject of Harrys, I'd totally shag Prince Harry," she deadpans. "I bet he's a dirty little sod in bed."

* * *

The pub is small and dark, flagstone floors, deep windows and sea memorabilia on every available wall. It's a Cornish pub from a Richard Curtis movie, complete with ruddy-faced locals propping up the bar. The girls are already there, tucked away on a corner table, deep in conversation. I feel a pang of longing at all the deep conversations they're having without me.

We order drinks at the bar, served by Brae, a lively-eyed and handsome bartender who Dorit flirts with, and take them over.

"You're alive," Cath says, in a tone I can't be sure is pleased that that's the case.

Her eyes look red. I see a scrap of tissue in her hand. Emily

looks like she's been crying too. My stomach knots – this was not the plan. The plan was to have a wonderful, joyful, bonding weekend, away from all our big, tough, scary life stuff, to be silly and carefree and back to us again. The weight of it all is like a boulder on my back, or a really huge, towering travelling backpack that's so enormous and heavy that one tiny push will tip me over face down in the mud, unable to get back on my feet. I hate seeing them like this, and I know I need to be a better friend, but death and divorce are so huge and real and grown-up, I don't even know where to start. I feel like I'm unqualified.

I make a mental note to woman up and have proper chats with them later, but I feel like the best thing I can do for now, maybe the only thing I can do, is to raise everyone's spirits and create some fun. They need a break. We all need a break. A chance to forget our problems – which will still be there on Monday – and to lean into distraction. So I swerve. Avoid. Pretend I haven't noticed. Force the cheer.

"Certainly am." I disrobe, peeling my many layers off, and take a seat. "Sorry for not joining you on the walk. I got a bit—"

"Overexcited," Cath finishes. "Emily said."

The judgement slaps.

"But I'm here now and ready to go!" I raise my pint to cheers.

"Good, because we've got a surf lesson booked later," Dorit says, the only one joining in my cheers. "And we've got caviar and snails to eat and I've got a beauty Instagrammer coming over from Newquay to give us a make-up lesson after that. And a few other tricks up my sleeve."

"What?!" I grin. "You didn't tell me you'd booked all of that!

Amazing, thanks Dorit!" I turn the enthusiasm up to eleven in an attempt to raise the mood. "Apart from the caviar and snails, obviously. That's scary. But, y'know, why not, hey?"

"Anything for the list, amirite?" Dorit says, giving me a not-very-well-executed high five.

I see Emily and Cath look at each other and anger prickles through me. I push it down and carry on with my cheer offensive.

"Right then, we should probably order some food," I say.

We eat Cornish-pub-from-a-Richard-Curtis-film-worthy food – steaming plates of beer-battered cod on a mountain of thick chips, piles of fresh prawns with long tendrils and beady black eyes, a creamy fish pie. We make the kind of small talk that I have never made with these girls and which hurts my heart. Small talk like we don't really know each other, like we haven't been in each other's lives for twenty-plus years and heard every intimate detail of every sexcapade throughout that time. Small talk like we haven't been there to hold back hair and rub backs at the end of a night out and drink wine and spout shit and provide tissues and pep talks and stupid text chats.

I put some of it down to the fact Dorit being there is disturbing our usual equilibrium. But what worries me is the feeling that it might be more than that. That something else, something deeper and harder, is at play. I drink through the unease, notching my cheer and positivity up a level, determined to bring the party.

We survive lunch and make it to our surf lesson. The sexy Cornish Richard-Curtis-movie surf instructor doesn't seem impressed with me and Dorit. Even when Dorit brings out her best flirting. We assure him that we only had half a pint and are perfectly safe to go

in the water. It takes some persuading and some behaving, but he lets us in. Cath goes back to the cottage, frustrated that she can't get a signal and wanting to check on her mum. Emily, Dorit and I brave the waves. I discover that wetsuits are incredibly hard to get into it and not at all flattering, that I have no core strength and therefore no balance, that I do not enjoy getting mouthfuls of freezing cold saltwater and that the sea can very easily kill you. Especially if you had three pints at lunchtime. For one horrible moment, as I'm tossed around under the waves and completely disoriented, I think I might actually die. Which seems extra sad as I haven't finished my list yet and would die trying to complete it. I'm not sure if that would be poignant or just pathetic. Or ironic, even. Probably the latter. But Alanis Morissette ironic.

The whole thing is deeply unpleasant and I'm pleased when it's over and we're back at the cottage for drinks and the much more mundane make-up lesson. The make-up lady teaches me to contour like a Kardashian, lectures me on the importance of bronzer and tuts at my hooded eyes which are apparently a nightmare to make nice. I end up looking like a cross between an oompa-loompa and an angry potato, but I kind of dig it, and Dorit and I find the whole thing hysterical in that trying-not-to-laugh-in-the-middle-of-a-lesson kind of way.

Dorit howls with laughter as I attempt the tiniest mouthfuls of caviar and snails that I can get away with, both of which are as rank as I anticipated. Once they're ticked off, we tuck into a selection of M&S's finest nibbles and picky bits, washed down with champagne and pre-mixed negronis, which I even manage to persuade Cath to partake in. Just the one though. And just the one

for Emily. Because they have suddenly become people who don't really drink. Which makes me sadder than it should.

Dorit heard from Brae that there's live music at the pub tonight and the band aren't totally rubbish so, with difficulty, we manage to persuade Cath and Emily back there. And we're here again, on the corner table, except now the pub is rammed and hot and the music is loud and I'm trying so hard to have fun but Cath's expression is so sour and angry it's killing my buzz.

"You missed out on some good make-up tips," I say. "You could've learnt how to look like a Kardashian."

"Pretty sure I'd need thousands of dollars and a ton of plastic for that," Cath says, sipping her non-alcoholic beer.

"Well, yeah. Closer to a Kardashian then, I guess."

She looks me up and down and I swear I detect a sneer forming on her mouth.

"What's the plan for tomorrow?" Emily asks, moving the subject on. "It would be nice to do a big walk somewhere."

"Maybe an earlier night?" Cath says.

Another prickle of anger sets in.

"Or maybe a late night and some fun." I don't mean it to come out as mean as it does.

"We've still got skinny-dipping to tick off," Dorit says. "And I've got some party favours too, another one on your list, I believe."

She digs around in her pocket and produces a small cellophane bag with a selection of multi-coloured tablets in. It takes me a minute, but then I realise what she's talking about. Taking ecstasy. Is she serious? Did she actually manage to get some for me? She's such a great friend!

Cath rolls her eyes, glances at Emily, a shared look, again. The kind me and Cath used to share about Rick. I don't like being the other side of it.

"What's wrong with that?" I ask.

"Nothing at all," Cath says.

It's the kind of tone a parent uses with a toddler, or a spouse in an argument. It's a gaslighting tone, the words belie the meaning.

I take a breath, remind myself that Cath is going through a hard time and this is supposed to be time for us to reconnect.

"No one has to join in with anything they don't want to do," I say, easy breezy. "It's just a bit of fun. I mean, it's more than a bit of fun, it's me turning my life around, but fun too. And skinny-dipping is bonding, right?"

"Especially skinny-dipping in October." Dorit laughs.

"Exactly. And we can totally do a walk too. I'd love that," I say.

Cath seems to ease off a bit, removing her tightly clenched fist from her beer bottle, leaning back into her chair. This is good, we've navigated the stormy waters. I've captained our ship away from the iceberg.

My phone beeps, a small and fleeting pocket of reception. More messages – James asking for the babysitter's number because he needs to go into the office for a few hours tomorrow and Chloe will be at Rupert's, Felix begging me to come home because Dad burns everything, Chloe asking if I got any more tampons in like she asked.

"Jesus Christ," I mutter. "I can't shake them off, even for a weekend. You'd think James has never looked after his own kids before and the kids – well, they're so bloody needy. I military

planned their whole weekend for them. And I'll pay for it when I get back, you know, the house will be a tip and James will be in a mood for at least five days. Boils my blood."

I sense Cath stiffen. What the bloody hell did I say wrong this time?

"Anyway," I say, "they'll work it out. How's your mum doing, Cath?"

I've asked the question. I didn't want to ask the question because I wanted to keep the mood light, but I've done it. Maybe she needs time to talk about it, maybe ignoring it isn't the way forwards.

"Not great last time I checked," she says. "Though the reception here is appalling so who knows."

"Charlie was telling me about your mum not being well," Dorit says. "That's so tough for you, I'm sorry. I've been there, it's hard."

Cath relents and gives Dorit a small smile. It's like sitting on a bloody seesaw wondering if she's going up or down, but this seems like an up and I'll take it.

"It's so awful how everyone's getting old," I say, leaning into it. "I mean, us, for a start, all this bloody menopause talk – I am still so not there yet, by the way, holding out," I hold my hands up. "But the parents especially. Last time I saw my mum, when she could fit me in between their many holidays, she was looking so much older, and she found it hard to do anything – even just cook and do stuff around the house. We walked into town and she went so slowly because her hip was giving her grief. And I really need to make the most of her having the kids because I can tell that window will close up soon too. It's really depressing."

I'm expecting a round of recognition, or maybe one of our

rounds of jokes about ageing or Janice, but I'm met with silence. One that cuts through the really loud music. Cath is glaring at me. Even Emily is glaring at me. I sip my gin and tonic, wait for someone to say something.

"Fuck this," Cath says. She grabs her coat and heads out of the pub, the locals at the bar watching her with bemused expressions.

"What?" I ask, looking to Emily and Dorit for support.

Emily grabs her coat and bag and edges herself out from the corner. "You need to think a bit more about what you're saying. I'm going to check she's OK."

"OK, what was that about?" I turn to Dorit, my compadre. "I was trying to sympathise with her."

Dorit frowns. "What she's going through is pretty horrendous. You're talking about your parents ageing, but her mum is dying. And from what you told me, she's having to deal with nearly all of that on her own. I think just have a bit more tact?"

When it's put so frankly, I see it. I see that my words could have been misconstrued. Or come out wrong. Balls.

"I'd better go and explain," I say.

The girls are huddled together on one of the outside tables, Emily with her arm around Cath, comforting, calming, like the million times we've comforted each other, though never about each other before. Cath is crying and muttering, rage-filled sobs.

"I'm so sorry, Cath." I walk over, pulling my coat tighter against the cold sea wind. "I totally didn't mean . . . I was just trying to sympathise. To explain that I kind of get what you're going through." Her head snaps up at me. "Though obviously totally not what you're going through. I just mean . . . I was trying—"

"You have no fucking idea," she snaps. Her venom catches me off guard. "My mother isn't just walking a bit slowly and not able to look after my kids as much. My mother is dying. Slowly, excruciatingly, dying. In front of my eyes. Some days, she doesn't remember who I am, some days she won't eat and won't sleep, some days she's in so much pain I want to just end it all for her. And I'm the person looking after her, because guess what – my dad's already dead. And those children she's not able to look after any more – they don't exist, because I never found someone to love who loves me back and I never had those kids I wanted and now it's too bloody late. And I know we always laugh at you and your main character syndrome, but seriously, LOOK AROUND YOU! Pay some attention and have some fucking consideration for once in your life."

"Cath, I'm—"

"I had a miscarriage the day after your birthday – did you know that? Did you notice? No! Did you bother to ask me anything about my life other than wanting my hideous dating stories for your own amusement and to make you feel better about your life? No. You are so far up your own arse you can't even—"

She doesn't finish the sentence. She bursts into more tears instead.

"Cath," I say, taking a step towards her, my insides twisting like a helter-skelter.

"Oh, I'm not done." She stands up, takes a step towards me, bats Emily away when she tries to calm her down. "You are blessed, Charlie. Blessed up to the bloody tits – a wonderful husband who loves you, three healthy, beautiful, smart children, a gorgeous

house with a bloody driveway, financial security. Blessed and blessed and then blessed some more and all you do is bitch and whine about it. Do you not understand how hard it is for me to sit and listen to you go on and on about how much your life sucks and how you can't stand your kids, while I'm over here with nothing, struggling to breathe – and Emily's over there dealing with the break-up of her marriage?"

Emily is stricken. She's never been one for confrontation at the best of times, this must be ripping her apart.

"You're bored. You live a sheltered, suburban, selfish life and you're bored. And I know you think that stupid list is going to alleviate that boredom, but I've got news for you – drinking martinis and eating caviar and making finger pots and getting a job and then throwing the opportunity away, because you're too busy out drinking and doing pointless shit to tick off your list, is not going to sort your life out. So yeah, you're right – I don't support you on that, because I think you're being a selfish bitch and I've had enough of it. You don't deserve the life you have if you're just going to take it for granted."

I gasp. Her words hit me like a slew of arrows. Sharp. Searing. Arrows. With poisoned tips. I want to double over with the pain, I want to look away from the acidic face of a Cath I don't recognise.

"Cath," Emily says, pulling her away again, more firmly this time. "Come on, let's go back."

"I can't believe I wasted valuable time with my mother to be here for this bullshit," Cath says, her tone more muted now, distorted by tears. "Fuck you, Charlie."

I watch them walk away, arms linked. A million words swirl

around my head – half-formed thoughts, apologies, rebuttals, recriminations. They dance and buzz and crash against each other before lodging in my throat, raw, unripe and unsaid. I wait for a feeling to come through, and when it does, it's anger. Or something like anger.

"Fuck you too," I shout into the wind, because the girls have long gone.

And then I walk back into the pub where Dorit is now sandwiched between Brae and a friend of his. She asks me if everything's OK, I shrug, still stunned, shaking, and she slides a drink over to me and I decide that yes, that is the best way forwards.

So I drink, and I dance to the not-totally-rubbish band with Dorit and Brae and Brae's friend and I drink some more and dance some more until I'm swaying on my feet and my buzz is starting to die off, which is when Dorit slips me a pill and I decide that yes, that is the way forwards. And then we're skinny-dipping, but only for two seconds because my god, that water is freezing and it almost sobers me up before Dorit hands me the other half of the pill.

And then we're dancing again, but this time in a house, Brae's maybe, and I've done that man thing of taking over the playlist and I'm lining up nineties bangers, and Brae and Dorit are grinding up against each other like they're rampant teenagers and me and Brae's friend pretend we don't notice and I teach him how to do the Macarena as some kind of distraction technique, and then Dorit and Brae aren't there any more and Brae's friend sits a bit too close and the thought, for a split second, crosses my mind that maybe I could have sex with this person and maybe I should have

sex with this person, and I start thinking about how it would feel to have sex with someone other than James and if I'd have to up my sex game, which I decide I most definitely would, and I'm really not sure I can be bothered with that, but then he says something really stupid about the reason fish don't have opposable thumbs, and I suddenly feel sick that the thought of having sex with this twenty-something year old with acne and a The 1975 T-shirt even crossed my mind, and I want to immediately text the girls because they would find this funny, in a Charlie's-a-stupid-twat type way, except tonight they wouldn't find it funny because I have used up all my good-natured Charlie's-a-stupid-twat points and am now in the bad-natured stupid twat category and I suddenly want to go back to the cottage and see them and tell them I love them and I'm sorry because I do love them, so much and I am sorry, so sorry, but Dorit had said I should give them space and maybe she's right and maybe in the morning, when we've all had some rest, it would be a better time. Except, I realise, it is nearly morning and I don't know where this house is but I think it's miles away from our cottage, so I text them to say I love them and I'm sorry but they don't reply, and then Brae's spotty friend has got his hand on my thigh and I accidentally laugh out loud at him, kind of in his face, which he doesn't like, and he turns nasty and tells me I'm an old hag anyway and my vagina probably smells of fish and I desperately want to make a joke about opposable thumbs but my brain can't quite get there.

30

WHEN WE finally made it back to the cottage, the girls weren't there. Emily had left me a note saying Cath's mum had been admitted to hospital with an infection and they'd left to get Cath back up to her. I'd messaged them – on the group WhatsApp and separately, but got no response. I presume I'm being hazed. Or ghosted. Can friends of twenty years-plus ghost you? Is that a thing?

The car journey home is long and painful and I veer between bone-deep sadness at what a total, unreserved failure this trip has been and bum-clenching fear that Dorit is driving after a boatload of pinot grigio, some ecstasy and roughly two hours sleep. My head is a dense forest of spiky, unfriendly trees, with a quagmire of squelchy mud and an incessant, pounding drum thrown in for good measure. There's a deeply unpleasant chemical slick in my mouth, like I've licked a Bunsen burner. I tuck my feet up on the seat, hug my legs and rot in my cloak of shame. And regret. And twatishness of the worst degree.

I catch a glimpse of myself in the wing mirror and am drawn in by how utterly terrible I look; my skin is pale and waxy, my hair even limper and flatter than usual and my eyes . . . they're so dark and haunted I barely make the connection they belong to me. I look away and focus on the outside view. The never-ending

motorway that whizzes past me, the glimpses of dull green barely visible through the rain. I let the events of the weekend carousel through my mind – the bits of it I can remember, and try to assess my behaviour, my choices, but I can't make sense of everything. It's like scenes are playing out, but they're behind a wall of clingfilm, vague and hazy and indeterminable.

"How you doing?" Dorit asks.

She sips her giant coke from the McDonald's drive-thru, her chunky-ringed fingers curling round the cup. The quarter pounder with cheese I wolfed down is sitting heavy in my stomach, another regret.

"I'm OK," I try.

She glances across at me, eyebrows raised. The car veers into the next lane along briefly.

"Maybe not super OK," I say. "I just ... I'm confused. And hurt. And I feel bad, like I've been a bad friend. I feel all over the place, to be honest. My head is fried, I'm exhausted, I haven't slept properly for months, my best friends hate me and feel like totally different people, I'm worried my marriage is falling apart and that my life has petered out into nothing of any value and I'm going to be stuck watching *Housewives* and eating a tube of Pringles for dinner for the rest of my life. Until I die of sodium and E-number poisoning. Die alone, probably, based on how things are currently going." I sigh, hug my knees in tighter. "It's a lot. It all feels a lot."

"Oh, hun." Dorit gives me a shoulder rub, veering slightly into the next lane again. "It is a lot. You're not being a bad friend, you just have a lot to deal with yourself. Everyone has their own problems and you can't make it your mission to solve everyone

else's at the cost of working out your own. You've got to look after yourself. I always remind myself that we're born alone and we die alone."

This was not as comforting as I assume she was going for.

"You think people are there for you," she carries on. "And they are, in some ways, but ultimately the only person responsible for you is you. Friends, lovers, husbands – they come and go, you're the only one who stays the distance and the only one you can rely on. I can't tell you how you should be feeling or whether your marriage is going to last – or if you should want it to, but I will say this – you need to put your own oxygen mask on first."

"Huh?"

"You know, like on an aeroplane. You have to put your own oxygen mask on first before helping others. Help yourself so that you're able to help others. I feel like you need to find your oxygen."

I untangle my legs and sit up straight. "You're so right! I need to find my oxygen! But at the moment, I can't reach it. Like, it hasn't even popped out for me to grab. I've got the faulty oxygen mask."

"You'll get there," she says, giving me another shoulder rub. "You'll reach it. And FYI, you won't die alone – if no one else, I'll be there, sat right next to you, passing you the Pringles."

* * *

"Hi, honeys, I'm home!" I shout with an energy I am not feeling.

I'm surprisingly happy to walk through the front door and don't even let the pile of coats and bags dumped in the hallway bother me. Or not as much as they usually would, anyway. Some muffled voices from the living room greet me in response. I make my way

through, patting down my hair and fixing my smile, wanting to look like someone who's had a restorative, healthy weekend away with good friends.

"Hey, guys." They're all on the sofa watching a film, James in between the boys, Chloe cuddled up in the corner. The fire is lit, it's every bit the picture of familial Sunday bliss. Just without me.

Jack shushes me, James waves without looking up.

I stand in the doorway for a moment, wondering if they'll pause the TV to acknowledge me properly. They do not.

"There are leftovers in the kitchen if you want any," James says, still without looking at me.

"Thanks."

The kitchen is strewn with half-empty takeaway containers and dirty plates, curry covered spoons thoughtlessly discarded on the white worktops, crusty cereal bowls where they were the morning I left. I'm not hungry, in fact I'm pretty sure I can still feel the quarter pounder in my gullet, so I set about tidying the kitchen, aware that this is part of my penance for daring to go away. I put my headphones on, press play on a Pearl Jam album and lose myself in deep nostalgia as I scrape lamb bhuna into the bin.

* * *

"Ah, Felix said he missed me," I say, walking into the living room after doing bedtime, another part of the penance. "How were they?"

James is on the sofa, the light from his phone illuminating his face, a nature documentary he's not watching on in the background.

Besides the takeaway heads-up, he hasn't actually spoken to me properly since I got home. I went to give him a quick kiss when he came through to the kitchen after the film and he ever so slightly swerved and stiffened as I approached, like I was about to wedgie him. It made me paranoid that the smell of wine and ecstasy was seeping through my skin, despite the excessive amount of Dorit's Chanel No. 5 I doused myself in.

I slump down next to him. He stiffens again, edging away.

I consider asking him what's wrong, or telling him about my weekend – an edited version – but I can't summon the energy. I suddenly, intensely, have a need for my bed.

"I might go up," I say. "It was a long drive. And a busy weekend. You coming?"

He turns the TV off, shifts his body so he's facing me. "Can we talk a minute?"

Crap.

"Sure." Light and breezy. Nothing to see here.

"Charlie," he rubs his face, runs his hand through his hair.

He never calls me Charlie. It's normally Charls, Charlsberg, Charlie Warlie, Chugs – never Charlie, not even in company.

He speaks slowly, intentionally. "I did a bit of thinking over the weekend. And don't take this the wrong way..." *Of course I'm going to take this the wrong way*, I think. "But it was actually quite good having a bit of space to think, not having you here."

I open my mouth in outrage but he bulldozes on.

"Not like that, I just mean ... it felt easier and lighter and it made me realise how tense things have got, how everything, even the little things – cereal bowls, the laundry, how things are put in

the dishwasher – everything between us just feels so loaded at the moment and I don't know about you but I spend so much time when we're around each other feeling . . . heavy. And depressed. Kind of. Sorry, I'm not explaining it very well." He twiddles his wedding ring, jiggles his leg – his tension tells. "Do you not think that? That things feel pretty bad?"

I manage a shrug, which comes out a whole lot more carefree than I feel. I literally have no idea what I think at this point, I just about know my name. I consider asking him for a match postponement because I'm medically incapable of having this conversation due to my first proper drug comedown and barely any sleep, but I figure that wouldn't go down well.

"I love you, and I know you love me," he says. "At least, I hope you still do. But things aren't good and something's going on with you and it's something I can't really help you with."

Oh well *that* pisses me off. Detached comedown mode is suddenly deactivated.

"So, it's my fault?"

"That's not what I said."

"I mean, it basically is," I say, my eyes fixed on him, not prepared to let him get away with this. "You literally just said something's wrong with me and you can't help so you're out."

"You're being dramatic."

"I'm being dramatic?! Sorry, my husband of twenty years just told me – actually what *are* you telling me? Other than you had a nice time when I wasn't here because I didn't ask you to put your dirty cereal bowl away. Your dirty cereal bowl, which, by the way, I tidied away earlier."

He stops the nervous jiggling and glares at me, his eyes turning stony and cold. I'm taken aback, again, by how my feelings towards that face can veer so violently between love and hate.

He takes a breath, adjusts his tone like he's speaking to a petulant child. "I'm saying that I think we could both benefit from having some space and some time to think."

"And how do we go about that?" I ask. "We barely see each other as it is – how much space do you want?"

He glances to the floor, his temple twitching. "I was talking to Henry and he said he's going away to Japan for work and will be gone for a few months. He said I could stay at his place if I wanted."

I rub circles on my palm, try to calm myself down, ground myself, because at the moment I'm having an out-of-body experience in which my husband is telling me he's about to move out and I'm not quite sure how we got here. How everyday gripes and the usual domestic drudgery has suddenly become A Proper Big Horrible Thing.

"It's only ten minutes up the road, I'd still be around for the kids and they can come and stay, though they'll probably want to be here most of the time, especially in the week but—"

"Except you won't be around for the kids, will you?" The venom in my voice takes me by surprise. "You're barely here for the kids as it is and just about manage to see them as they go up to bed, how are you going to be there for them when you live ten minutes up the road?"

"Oh, here we go. Punishing me for working." His body relaxes into the argument, it's one we know well. "I tell you what – how about I quit my job so I can be here for the kids and we live off your

work experience salary – what was it again – two-hundred pounds a week?"

I go to reply, to explain that the reason why I have no job and no decent salary and probably no chance of getting one now is that I gave up my career to bring up our children, because one of us had to and how the hell was it ever going to be him with the hours he works and the amount he's away? I go to explain that I would LOVE for him to stay at home and do everything connected with the kids and their schooling and the running of the house and for me to go out to work and to not have to think about it. But the exhaustion hits me like a sledgehammer – from the lack of sleep, but also from having the same conversations over and over again. I cannot make myself say the words. Words I know will just float into the ether and pop like pointless bubbles anyway, words that chip away at my soul every time I have to speak them out loud, again.

Maybe he's right, maybe a break would be good, because, apart from anything else right now, I can't bear looking at his face with its smug, self-important expression and I can't bear the jiggly, manspreading legs and the way his chin juts out when he's making a point and that mole on his cheek and that one stupid curl that is poking up aggressively. If he's not here, that's one less toilet seat to wipe the piss off of, one less set of skids to clean from the bowl, one less set of laundry, one less dirty cereal bowl left on the side to go solid and impenetrable.

A flicker of excitement joins in with the random mixed party bag of emotions that are already kicking off.

"Fine." I push myself up off the sofa, my legs stiff, my everything sore. "Can you go tonight?"

He looks surprised. Which I enjoy.

"Uh, I was going to go tomorrow, get my things together and—"

"Just go tonight," I say, wanting, more than anything, for him to leave. "You can come by tomorrow and collect your things properly – and you'll need to tell the kids, obviously."

He looks surprised again. And I know responsible parenting is telling the kids together and making it sound like it's no one's fault, which I'm sure is what we'll do, but for a second, I want him to take some accountability for this, to sit with the horror of having to explain himself to the kids.

I leave the room, too exhausted to think of a zinger to end the conversation with. As I pass his pristine Adidas Gazelles in the hallway, I give them a quick kick. I've always hated the bloody things – they make him look twelve. Maybe it'll be nice not to see them in the hallway every day. Fuck him and his childish trainers.

Messages I would send to the girls if I could message them, and what I imagine they would message me back, Part 1:

Me: *So, James just dropped a bombshell on my coming-down arse – he wants a trial separation!*

Me: *At least I think that's what he said. I was very tired.*

Cath: *SHIT!*

Emily: *OMG. Are you OK? Do you need us to come over?*

Me: *I need to sleep first, I think.*

Emily: *Why does he want one?*

Me: *I'm not sure exactly? I think because I tell him to put the cutlery in the dishwasher facing up (OTHERWISE IT DOESN'T GET CLEANED PROPERLY).*

Cath: *FFS everyone knows that!*

Me: *I know, right!*

Me: *So yeah, he's leaving me because I nag him about cutlery.*

Emily: *Are you still going to go to counselling?*

Me: *I think so? I don't know. All very unclear atm. All I know is I'm v tired, he doesn't seem to love me any more and he's left. And it's nice not to have his teenage trainers in the hall.*

Cath: *Man, I hated those trainers.*

Me: *ME TOO.*

November

31

JAMES HAS been gone two weeks and I don't know, I'm kind of enjoying it – apart from heartbreak Tuesday where I sobbed nearly all day and thought my life was over. But then Dorit told me that Low Tuesday is a post-drugs thing so maybe it was the ecstasy more than my husband walking out on me? Or maybe it was the menopause? Perimenopause. Or maybe it was that my friends hate me? Or maybe it was that I got sacked from work experience? Who the hell knows at this point.

It was probably my husband walking out on me. Though he assures me it isn't that he's walking out on me. Though it feels like that. But it also feels strangely normal because I'm used to not seeing him much in the week and actually it's just the missing Adidas Gazelles and the absence of his dirty cereal bowl and most of the time, I don't notice those, so I'm going about my day and it all feels fine and I start wondering what we'll have for dinner and then I remember he won't be here for dinner and that does send me spiralling a bit, but then I remember I can just have hummus and picky bits for dinner if I want, or a tube of Pringles, because I don't have to think about what he's going to eat and there's something kind of liberating about that. Although, when I did decide I should cook a proper meal and made a chilli, it didn't feel very liberating eating it on my own and having tons left over.

The kids seem completely fine about it all. No different. No compassion. Still constantly asking me for things, still needy. I've decided if James wants this separation thing, he can start having them more, so I'm making him have them every other weekend and at least two nights in the week. This week he bought them a takeaway and played computer games with them. Of course he bloody did. Apparently there's some nesting bollocks about how he's allowed to come and be here with them on the days he has them which seems all kinds of messed up to me, but I suppose it's not like I'm bringing a hot lover back for hot sex. Yet. We haven't talked about if that's allowed. God, what if he's already doing that? What if he's been having an affair? I mean, I think he's too busy for an affair, unless all those client meetings have been with a lover. OH MY GOD, MAYBE THEY HAVE.

Maybe I should've shagged spotty The 1975 Cornish dude after all. Jesus, am I going to need to get another Hollywood? I want to ask the girls, but I can't. The last message I got from Emily was that they're both dealing with a lot and maybe we should just have a bit of breathing space. My friends *and* my husband want a separation from me. I'm that bad a person. Shit.

I don't care. I'm throwing myself into my book and my list. I got up at 3 a.m. this morning because I couldn't sleep. Wrote five thousand words. They just flew out of me. I need to check some specifics about Thailand but I'd read about full-moon parties so I had my character go to one of those and she met the handsome bartender, George, and had some hot sex on an exotic beach bordered by palm trees and fairy lights and now I need to decide if they end up together or if I need her to have more sex with other

people first because really, the book is about finding herself.

My list is looking pretty good – I've got a manifesting ritual to do and need to go to a tarot-card reader and get a tattoo, then the other stuff is harder – swimming with dolphins, sex on a plane, sex club, sex with George Clooney. I realise now there are quite a few that are sex based. Maybe Cath was right, maybe I do need to get laid. I think that's what she said, or did she say I was missing something in my sex life? It was something disparaging. But possibly true. Go to Thailand is on my list too. Maybe I should just book a solo trip, or see if Dorit wants to come. Except I have no money apart from what James puts in the joint account and I can't see him transferring three grand for me to swan off to Thailand and have sex with a random on a plane and go and watch the ping-pong vagina lady. And I feel like Dorit would be a liability in Thailand.

I wish I had my own money. How have I managed to not have my money? I wish someone had told me to always have my own money. My mother should've told me that. Instead, she told me it was a good idea for me to give up work to ease the strain on me and the family. What kind of a mother tells you that?

I will make a point of telling Chloe she should never rely on a man for anything. That sounds harsh, I don't want her to hate men and never find love – maybe more like, make sure you're independent, can always afford to leave if you're not happy, can pay for yourself to go on a trip to Thailand and see ping-pong vagina lady if you so wish without having to ask your separated husband if he could please transfer you the money. That's what I'll tell her.

I have to go and write. The kids are in bed, my brain is on fire,

my book is calling. If I get this finished and I sell it for a six-figure deal all over the world and become a *Sunday Times* bestseller then I will be able to afford to take myself to Thailand. Have to keep writing. And finishing the list. My book and the list. My book and the list. That's what matters. And my kids.

* * *

Messages I would send to the girls if I could message them and what I imagine they would message me back, Part 2:

> Me: *I got a tattoo (it was on the list).*
>
> Me: *I kind of got a tattoo. I started getting one – a Celtic symbol for strength I found on the internet, but holy crap, it hurt SO much I passed out and then the guy refused to do any more. So now I'm walking round with a little curve on my wrist that looks surprisingly like a bellend.*
>
> Cath: *HAHAHAHAHAHAHA!!!!*
>
> Cath: *Well, maybe a good reminder that you are indeed, a bellend!*
>
> Emily: *Oh NO! I'm sure you can get it fixed later? I'll come with you and hold your hand.*
>
> Me: *I'm such a failure, I can't even get a tattoo right.*

Emily: *Don't be silly, it's fine, it can be fixed.*

Me: *Do you think I need to get another Hollywood if I'm ever going to have sex with someone who isn't James and therefore as accepting of my bush?*

Cath: *Amazonian bush.*

Me: *Yes, that.*

Cath: *Have you started wiping front to back yet? I'd maybe work on that before you have sex with anyone else.*

December

32

MESSAGES I would send to the girls if I could message them and what I imagine they would message me back, Part 3:

Me: *MERRY CHRISTMAS DUDES!!! How's everyone's day been?*

Emily: *Difficult. Tried to do the fake family get together thing.*

Me: *Me too!! Such hard work. I had to make an effort to be super cheerful all day and tidy up after myself in the kitchen and to not drink too much and to not get aggressive during board games. I'm exhausted.*

Me: *And James was weird.*

Emily: *Weird how?*

Me: *Well, for a start, he helped with the cooking.*

Emily: *Wow.*

Me: *Yup. Weird.*

Me: *Did Rick get you a present?*

Emily: *He told me to get myself something and wrap it up and put the tag from him so the kids think he got me something.*

Me: *WTF? Jesus, makes the Molton Brown gift set (which James's assistant one hundred per cent ordered) I got seem amazing.*

Cath: *Christmas sucks. I hate this Christmas.*

Me: *What is happening to us?*

Cath: *Life. Life is happening to us.*

Me: *Well, it sucks.*

Emily: *I've just been drinking mistletoe margaritas and watching rubbish Christmas TV.*

Me: *Good plan.*

Me: *Love you guys. Maybe let's have next Christmas together?*

January

33

ANOTHER YEAR. One that's looking very different from this time last year when I was so hungover I could barely get out of bed and James went on a New Year's Day bike ride. James doesn't like New Year's Eve, he says it's a drinking man's night. Though even when he was drinking, he didn't like it, so that's bollocks. I think he just doesn't like socialising and fun and people. So last year we'd gone to Mark and Vanessa's, who James likes because Mark doesn't drink, and we'd had a board games night with the kids and I made up for all the people not drinking by drinking three times as much as I normally would.

This year, I'm spending it with Eddie Vedder as James has the kids – he's taking them to the cinema and doing a 'party at home', whatever the hell that is. Dorit tried to persuade me to go with her to some swanky party in town, but I don't feel like celebrating, or pretending to be happy, or ringing in the new – god knows what's happening to my life – year. I thought about trying the girls again, but I can't bring myself to. I'm still hurt. And don't want to beg for friendship.

So, I'm drinking a bottle of champagne on my own, and a bottle of wine on my own, and trying to coax Eddie Vedder onto my lap briefly (she's enjoying the quiet) and I'm going to write some of my book, with Jools on in the background.

And I'm writing New Year's resolutions, of course. I write them every year, but this year they feel important, like the stone thing Moses wrote or whoever the dude from the Bible was who wrote things on stone. I need to carve these into my forehead.

1. To finish my list.
2. To finish my book.
3. To drink less (kind of – out drinking is fine though, I still want to have fun).
4. To make some new friends.
5. To get a job (or to get my book published, which would then mean my job is being An Author).
6. To be a better mum (this includes: playing board games on a school day, reading to them at bedtime, checking what homework they have even when they say they have nothing, not screaming at them for the state of the toilet, teaching them how to clean a toilet, cooking non-freezer food at least three days of the week – (though freezer food is fine while I'm finishing my book. Needs must).
7. To exercise for twenty minutes at least once a week, not including walking in the park.
8. To go back to volunteering.
9. To wear non-lounge pant clothes for at least two days a week (though lounge pant clothes are fine for while I'm finishing my book).
10. To become hot.

It's a mixed bag. And I know you're supposed to make them a SMART target type thing – specific and attainable and all that, but some are hard to quantify. My main ones though are still my list and my book. Once I get those done, I'll feel like a new woman and the others will fall into place. I'll for sure look at least ten per cent hotter once I'm a published author, because I'll have money for botox and fabulous new clothes and fabulous places to wear them to and I'll want to exercise and I'll make loads of new glamorous author friends and I'll be happier and feel validated which will lead me to be a better mum, somehow, and I'll just naturally become hotter because I'll be oozing with all the confidence and self-esteem that comes with having achieved something.

So I have to keep writing. I'm at eighty thousand words. Which is amazing. Though I'm still not quite halfway through the actual story, or what I think needs to happen in the actual story. But I'm taking myself to cafes to write, like Carrie Bradshaw, and writing in the pub, like Charles Dickens (I don't know if this is actually true but he wrote about pubs a lot) and I've written until three in the morning drinking wine, like Ernest Hemingway (again, TBC) and then got up to write again at six, like Stephen King (though I'm pretty sure he does it without the wine session preceding the 6 a.m. wake-up – which makes more sense, because that morning the words were HARD to find).

I feel like I'm in a trance with it, like I can't live without it, like it's going to be the making of me, like it might be a masterpiece, like I just need to get it finished and if I just keep going, keep going like this, in this trance, and just keep writing, keep writing, I'll get there. I can catch up on sleep and hygiene and life when it's done.

I refuse to let this year be as totally rubbish as it has the potential to be. Go me.

34

THE HOUSE is blissfully quiet. The boys are staying over with James, and Chloe is out with friends and I am on my seventh hour of writing. The screen is turning a bit blurred and I'm pretty sure I just hallucinated a penguin on my desk, but I figure that's all part and parcel of a big writing session. I'm at the bit where Chantelle has to choose between George, her Thai bartender love interest, who she recently found out is also a millionaire but has opted to live a quiet life with simple pleasures, and Jamie, the hot Irish actor with the sexy accent who is incredible in bed and values her mind as well as her body.

I've just had to write a sex scene where, against my better judgement, I used the terms: 'throbbing member', 'thrust his seed into me', 'penis as shiny and erect as the shard', 'wet as a waterfall', 'rode me like a rodeo bull' and 'tit wank'. Which reminded me of one of the last times James and I had sex and I suggested we record it on my phone (for the list, of course), and I was a bit drunk and I always fancy myself as some kind of athletic porn star when I'm drunk, so I decided a nostalgic tit wank would look good on film but actually, watching it back, I looked like I was having a fit of some kind with his penis trapped between my tits. My tits looked pretty good though – less saggy when you're holding them and thrusting them together, so that was a win.

I hear Chloe come in the front door and I call out a hello, though I don't know why I bother because she'll likely have her AirPods in and/or go straight up to her room.

She bangs up the stairs, then there's a light tap on the spare room door.

"Mum." Her voice is creaky and not at all Chloe-like.

I turn round and see her red, blotchy, tear-stained face and my heart leaps.

"Darling, what's the matter?"

She collapses into my arms. She's taller than me now, but she shrinks herself to fit, her head on my shoulder, where it used to be back when she still hugged me properly. She smells of apple shampoo and Marc Jacobs's Daisy. She smells like Chloe.

"He . . . dumped . . . me . . ." she manages to get out through the sobs.

I rub her back and mum 'shhh' her, calm her down. We stay like that for a while, until I manage to get her to the living room and onto the sofa, draping the cosiest blanket I can find over her. She nestles on my chest, still as I rhythmically stroke her hair, my heart breaking for her, whilst also slightly enjoying the moment – the closeness, the way she needs me.

"What happened?" I ask, once I think she's able to talk.

"He's been acting weird for a while," she cry-hiccups. "I knew something was wrong."

"In what way was he acting weird?" I'm careful to keep my tone friendly and supportive and not at all interrogation like.

"He kept only wanting to see me round at his house, and loads of times he'd just cancel last minute or give me a reason that sounded

like an excuse. Like, one time he said he had to do a history project with his friend Dan, but then I saw Dan in town and when I asked if he was seeing Rupert, he said he hadn't planned to."

I nod. Aware of the dodginess.

"And when we were together, he was being way less affectionate and I had to keep asking for him to kiss me or hold my hand which made me feel really needy, which I'm not, but it was that he used to do that stuff all the time and then stopped, and that felt weird."

I roll my eyes, as hard and as big as I possibly can, though really, I need some kind of exaggerated cartoon eye roll to convey the level of eye roll needed for this standard teenage boy behaviour. Actually, not just teenage boy – male behaviour. Cath and Emily both went out with plenty of guys in their twenties who did almost exactly the same.

"And then – don't freak out, Mum." She stays with her head on my chest, presumably so she can't see my I'm-quite-likely-to-freak-out expression. "We'd been . . . doing some stuff. More than kissing." I clench my jaw. "And he wanted to . . . do more. But I didn't. And yes, I know, don't worry – you've drummed it into me enough – don't feel pressure to do something you're not comfortable doing – all of that. So I said no, which he said was fine. And that was three days ago and today he dumped me. And he said it was nothing to do with that, and that he just isn't ready for a serious relationship, but then Daisy messaged me and said there's rumours he's getting with Alicia, who everyone knows has sex with boyfriends. And not boyfriends."

"Oh, for god's sake!" I can't help myself. I know I should be calm and diplomatic and all that good parenting stuff, but this boy

has crossed a line. "What an absolute dick."

Chloe pushes herself up, a zip mark from my hoodie imprinted on one side of her face.

"I'm sorry, love," I say. "But that is prime dickhead behaviour and I know you won't believe me when I say this, but you're better off without him. A thousand per cent."

"I loved him, Mum." She looks so sincere, and crushed. She blinks away the tears. "He was amazing in the beginning. He's so confident and fun and was always so nice to me – he made me feel really special. And he's exciting."

"He's rich, Chloe. And he goes to a private school. He's got the kind of confidence and charm that wins people over, but not the morals to see it through. Clearly, he thinks he's entitled to whatever he wants, at whatever cost to other people. He's going to be the kind of man who works in finance and wears loafers and gads about Chelsea and the private members' clubs hooking up with three girls at the same time. Not in a threesome type way – foursome, I guess. I mean, he'll be seeing lots of women and not treating any of them well. Definitely not someone who deserves a girl as smart and gorgeous and brilliant and funny as you." I stroke a tear-wet strand of hair off her face. "Darling, I hope you know that you can do so much better than him and you *will* do so much better than him. I'm so sorry you're hurting, and I know it feels like the end of the world, but it will get better and one day, you'll look back and wonder what you ever saw in him – besides the big house with the gaming basement. And one day, you might even bump into him and you'll look at his god-awful shiny loafers and thank the universe for a lucky escape!"

She sniffs, and half smiles. For the first time tonight. It lights me up.

I grip her tighter, pull her into me. I want to click my fingers and make her pain go away, time travel with her to some time in the future when this pubescent dirtbag will be a speck in her past and she'll be with someone deserving and wonderful. I kiss her on the head instead, give her one last squeeze.

"Do you know what I do when I'm sad?" I ask.

"I hope you don't mean the thing I walked in on you doing." She laughs.

"Chloe!" I say, outraged, but also pleased we seem to be at the laughing about it stage. That's a good development. "I watch *Housewives*."

"Don't you just watch *Housewives* all the time? Sad, happy, bored . . ."

"Cheeky!" I nudge her, relishing this new, extremely fragile bond we seem to have going on. "Trust me, it'll sort you right out. And there are way bigger arseholes than Rupert that these women have survived. And thrived after."

We settle down to watch *The Real Housewives of Beverley Hills* (classic) from the beginning. I make popcorn and we sit close enough that I occasionally reach out my hand to pat her leg and Eddie Vedder even ventures into the room, though not as far as the sofa.

* * *

I manage to persuade Chloe to try and get some sleep, tuck her in like I used to five years ago, and head back to my work, with a

bottle of sauvignon. I write for an hour, or something like an hour, until I know my sentences aren't making sense any more and the words are floating on the screen, little sailboats bobbing about on the water. I can't be tired. I have to keep going. I have to finish this. For me, but also for Chloe. I have to set an example for her – be a role model of a hard-working, independent, successful woman who doesn't need to rely on a man. Or something like that.

I stare at my vision board – printed out pictures of champagne (to signify celebrating good news), of *The Sunday Times* bestseller list (self-explanatory), of Soho House rooftops and New York skyscapes (where I will be flown first class to meet my incredible publisher), a photo of a stack of money, and photos from an author's Instagram feed of their incredibly luxe launch. I let my mind wander into its mega fabulous bestselling author daydream, the one I fantasise about at least twice a day. Some days, I even write my acknowledgements in my head, always wondering whether I'll include Cath and Emily, leaning towards, 'yes I will' because all will be forgiven by then and we'll look back on this blip when we weren't speaking to each other as 'that weird time we all went a bit mad'. These daydreams keep me going. And my manifesting. Which reminds me – my new manifesting set arrived the other day and I haven't got round to doing it yet!

I decide I need food before manifesting though, figuring it will help the drowsiness brought on by only having popcorn and wine as sustenance this evening. I head to the kitchen and put some pasta on, turn all the lights on and up to full brightness to avoid the creepiness of a dark kitchen at two o'clock in the morning. I find the manifesting kit in the pile of post. It's beautifully packaged –

layers of tissue paper that smell of magic and moondust and Black Orchid, the kooky shop we used to get our skull rings from in sixth form. There's a perfectly round and smooth crystal in a hessian pouch (I can't remember the name of it, but I remember choosing one that was good for self-care and loving yourself), a candle, tiny candle holder and elegantly calligraphed manifestation cards that look like something out of *Harry Potter*. Just holding it all in my hands feels magical and powerful; the hope that this could be the key to transforming my life rings through me, bright and burning – maybe the magic is working already.

I go up to the spare room, thinking maybe the magic will work better if it's done in my working space. I read the instructions twice, the words dancing in front of me. As instructed, I shuffle the manifestation cards, light the candle and pull a card:

I am open to new experiences and opportunities and welcome abundance into my life.

The instructions say to repeat this over and over again while looking at the flame of the candle and holding the crystal. I stare, I repeat, I stare, I repeat, I stare, I repeat, I have a sip of wine, I stare, I repeat, I stare, I have a sip of wine, I stare, I repeat ...

* * *

It's *Three Kings* George, which is weird because *Three Kings* George is the lesser of the Georges – military uniforms and guns do not normally do it for me. But I can't deny he looks hot.

He's kissing my hand. Asking me if I'm OK, his dark brown eyes searching and sincere. I go to tell him I'm fine, I'm happy, but when I open my mouth, I start crying. He swoops down and puts his arms around me, starts kissing my neck. He smells of musk and the forest, but in a clean way. He rubs my back and tells me he loves me, that he never loved Amal, was just tempted by her extreme intelligence and philanthropic work, that he loves me and actually I remind him of Amal in that I'm gorgeous and smart and have great hair. I go to touch my hair, because that doesn't seem right, but my fingers don't find hair, they find a perfectly soft and shiny bald head. I scream and George pulls away and looks up, except it's not George, it's James – and he's angry. Furious. He says he knows I've been seeing George all this time and it's all my fault. Everything is all my fault. Then Cath and her mother and Emily are all circling round me shouting at me and I can't find George anywhere and I touch my head and I'm still bald and I start sniffing, because I think I smell musk and the forest, but actually it smells like a camping fire and suddenly Chloe is there and is shouting at me and that makes me cry again because I love her so much and she's still shouting and she doesn't stop...

"MUM! MUM! WAKE UP! THERE'S A FIRE! MUUUUM!"

My eyes spring open. Chloe is shaking me, her face all anguish and tears. And fear.

"There's a fire in the kitchen. I don't know what to do. We have to leave. I don't know how to put it out."

I'm instantly switched on, my heart thumping in my chest, white fear shooting through me. I run down the stairs, Chloe following behind me. The smoke hits my throat as I'm halfway

down the stairs, catching, choking. I glance into the kitchen and see a plume of wild, furious flames licking all the way up and over the oven hood, spreading along the bottoms of the upper kitchen cabinets. For a split second I consider trying to close the door to the kitchen, the fire door that we were required to put in when we had the extension built, the fire door we never keep closed because Eddie Vedder just meows to be let out. But we're closer to the front door and I don't want to risk going towards the fire. And shit, where is Eddie Vedder?

"Have you got your phone?" I shout to Chloe, the smoke catching at the back of my throat. I bring my jumper up to cover my mouth, motioning for her to do the same.

"Yes," she says, crying.

I pick up some random shoes by the door, thankful for once that we're not a neat and tidy family. I grab Chloe's arm and open the front door, the air from outside whooshing past us, a new bang and crackle, the sound of crashing, coming from the kitchen. I slam the door, run down the driveway and grab Chloe's phone. It's locked. I panic, pounding random numbers on the screen. She takes it from my hand, uses her thumb, unlocks it, hands it back. I dial 999.

* * *

Messages I would send to the girls if I could message them and what I imagine they would message me back, Part 4:

> Me: *HOLY SHIT. I nearly burnt the house down. It was so bad. Horrible. Horrible.*

Emily: *OMG! Are you OK? How did it happen?*

Me: *I put some pasta on and forgot about it because I went to manifest and I fell asleep because it turns out manifesting is surprisingly soporific.*

Cath: *You were what now?*

Me: *I was manifesting a better life.*

Cath: *A life in which you don't have a functioning kitchen?*

Me: *It was really scary. I could've died. I could've killed Chloe.*

Me: *The fire brigade were called. And James came and was screaming at me. Once the fire brigade were gone.*

Emily: *How's Chloe?*

Cath: *Were there any fit firemen?*

Me: *I think you'll find it's fire people.*

Me: *James said the kids are going to live with him for a while, until I've 'sorted myself out', whatever that means. He thinks I'm a drunk who can't be trusted with her own children.*

Me: *Plus, I guess it makes sense for them to be somewhere that has a working kitchen.*

Cath: *Are you? A drunk who can't be trusted with her own children?*

35

"**SHE WAS** drunk," James says, with a cruelty I've never heard from him before.

"I wasn't drunk," I clarify. "I had been drinking. There's a difference. I was tired. Exhausted. I'd been . . ."

I'm not going to finish the sentence. I'm not going to explain that I'd been averaging two hours sleep a night because I can't sleep, because I have so much anxiety roiling in me, because I keep thinking over every single questionable thing I've done in my life, because even though I can barely keep my eyes open, sometimes it's worse when they're shut, because I'm desperately trying to finish my book, because I need it to make my life better. I don't say any of that because he doesn't understand. He doesn't understand my book, he doesn't understand my list, he doesn't understand me. Not any more. Did he ever? But he finishes it for me anyway.

"Working on your list?" he scoffs, shaking his head. "Is that what you were doing? Drinking and working on that stupid bloody list of yours?"

"James," Dr Deb says, her warning voice. "Watch your tone, please. We're aiming for a constructive conversation, in which we show respect. Please remember that."

He turns a beetroot red, the vein on his neck bulging. His rage is like a third person in the room today. I know he wants to shout

at Dr Deb, part of me is willing him to, happy to watch him blow himself up.

"We've discussed the list in the sessions before," she says. "We've talked about how it's something that feels important to Charlie."

I nod.

"And that was fine," he says. "Before it became an obsession and something that puts our children directly at risk. I put up with the endlessly going out, with the bizarre sporting attempts, I even agreed to some of the ridiculous sex ones."

"What was so ridiculous about them?" Dr Deb asks, in her soft therapist voice.

He mutters something under his breath, goes to open his mouth then closes it again. I watch as his eyes flit around the room, taking in the posters of motivational quotes written on a floral background hanging on the wall:

Success is not final
Failure is not fatal
It is the courage to continue
That counts

Kindness is one thing you can't give away
It always comes back

"I can't do this any more," James says. "We're going round in circles. Staring into each other's eyes and standing in felt-tip shoe prints is not going to fix us. I'm tired. I've been missing out on

work for this – and before you say it, yes, I'm happy to miss out on work for this, but only if it's fucking working, having an impact. And it clearly isn't."

He stands up, turns his body towards me. The circles under his eyes are dark, his posture slumped. He looks tired. And old. When did he get this old?

"Charlie, I love you. I'll always love you. I've said that before. But I can't do this. I don't know what we do now, but we need time. And you need . . ." He runs his hand through his hair, his eyebrows twist in frustration. "I don't know what you need. But I don't think it's me right now."

He walks to the door, looks at Dr Deb, then leaves, the door slamming shut behind him.

Dr Deb and I sit in silence for a minute. I'm not sure whether I should leave too, whether she'll banish me because this is couples counselling and I am no longer in a couple. I glance at the demure and elegant clock above her desk. We have half an hour left.

"How does James leaving make you feel, Charlie?" she asks.

I shift my bodyweight, rearrange my legs, not enjoying the new dynamic, the attention all being on me. I start to cry. It takes me by surprise, I thought I was more angry than upset. But that keeps happening to me – the crying. All the time, over everything.

Things I have cried about recently:

1. *The Lloyds bank advert with the horse running along the beach.*
2. *Not being able to get the printer to work.*
3. *Not being able to open my wine because I couldn't find*

the bottle opener and I didn't have the foresight to get a screw top.

4. Imagining my children dying before me.

5. Imagining me dying and my children having to live life without a mother and with only a father who burns everything he cooks for them.

6. Imagining Eddie Vedder dying.

7. Remembering when James and I first got Eddie Vedder and Jeff Buckley as kittens and they'd sit on our laps and we'd stroke them and look at each other lovingly and imagine having babies.

8. The Cancer Research advert where the woman gets told she's cancer free and cries.

9. A disappointing jacket potato.

10. James leaving me in the middle of our counselling session.

February

36

I KEEP MYSELF up in my bedroom and the spare room, occasionally venturing down to the front room where I've put an electric two-ring hob I bought from eBay and the only slightly melted microwave. I exist mainly on Pot Noodles and Super Noodles. I was going to include pasta but I seem to have developed PTSD around pasta since The Incident so have ruled that out for now. Which is probably just as well because making pasta requires at least ten per cent more effort and time than either of the noodle options.

I've spent so much of my adult life agonising about what to cook every day and experimenting with new recipes and trying to keep people healthy that I'm finding the noodles development revolutionary. Food is fuel. You need it to keep going, to power you through your day, to power me through my writing. Nothing more. And Pot Noodles and Super Noodles do that just fine. I simplified it even more by doing a massive supermarket shop – based on some not very accurate maths – to work out how much I need to survive a month of writing my book and potentially not leaving the house. I now have ninety packets of Super Noodles and ninety Pot Noodles stacked rather pleasingly on the bookshelf in the corner that I cleared of books. I also bought cat food for Eddie Vedder, the good stuff, now that it's just the two of us, and paper plates and

wooden cutlery so I don't have to do any washing up. And wine: sixty bottles of wine and two bottles of celebratory champagne – one for when I finish the book and one for when I finish the list.

There's something about the set-up I like – the not having to cater for anyone else, the simplicity of cooking what I want, when I want it. Sometimes for breakfast, sometimes for dinner, sometimes at two in the morning, sometimes not at all if the mood doesn't strike me. It's freeing.

I don't go into the burnt kitchen. I stand in the hallway and stare at it sometimes. But I never go in there. I find a strange comfort in it being there; a constant black hole, a reminder of how close you can come to danger and death, how we're going about our daily lives on a tightrope, worrying about laundry and groceries and dinner parties and parents' evenings and if you're having an acceptable amount of sex and if skinny jeans are still in and if you should lose weight, or wax your pubes off or have an affair or get a divorce or a pension or both, and the million other things we spend our time and energy thinking about. There's something grounding about the burnt kitchen being there. It reminds me there are More Important Things.

Everything smells of smoke still. The house, my clothes, my hair. It's deep and ingrained and has a putrid edge to it. The insurers will put the claim through soon, they say, but until they do, I'll stand and stare and sniff the smoke and be grateful.

I write. And write. And eat my noodles. And write. And drink wine.

James said he doesn't want me seeing the kids for a while until I've 'sorted myself out'. I don't know what that means, and I don't

really have the time to think about it just yet because I have to get my list finished and I have to get my book finished.

I write. And write. And eat my noodles. And aggressively manifest.

The book says to imagine the *feeling* of what you want to bring into your life. How these things will make you *feel*. How you want to *feel*. So, I stare at my vision board, squeeze my eyes shut and imagine *feeling* successful and competent and in demand and wanted and valued and validated until I'm squeezing so much, I get eye cramp and worry my eyes will explode.

I write. And write. And eat my noodles. And ignore calls from Dorit, because I can't think of anything else but finishing my book and finishing my list and I can't remember when the last time I had an actual conversation was, but that's fine because I really do just need to focus.

I write. And write. And eat my noodles. And manage to persuade Eddie Vedder onto the bed. And watch *Sex and the City* and cry because it makes me think of when we first left uni and all moved to London and the girls and I decided we were going to do brunch every weekend, just like Carrie and Samantha and Miranda and Charlotte. We managed it about three times before the reality of us all being skint and busy kicked in.

* * *

Messages I would send to the girls if I could message them and what I imagine they would message me back, Part 5:

Me: *I'm watching Sex and the City. From the beginning.*

Me: *Can you believe the first season was so weird – Carrie spoke to the camera all the time and her and Big is just as weird and nonsensical on forty-third viewing as it was on first viewing.*

Cath: *Big is a toxic arsehole manbaby. I still stand by that.*

Emily: *Aiden all the way.*

Me: *We've discussed this – Aiden and Carrie would never have lasted – he didn't understand the real Carrie.*

Cath: *A prissy, self-important city girl who's desperate for attention?*

Cath: *Intense jazz musician all the way.*

Me: *Berger. Swoon.*

Emily: *And you say I have bad taste in men!*

Me: *Do you remember when we tried to do brunch every weekend?*

Cath: *And you took us to that twenty-four-hour dive in Vauxhall because you said you thought it had 'New York*

diner vibes' and the food looked like it had been sat there for three days and Emily got food poisoning and we said leaning over a toilet vomming was not very SATC.

Me: *I don't remember that!*

Emily: *Yup. It was gross. Put me off brunch for life.*

Me: *Probably because you are very Charlotte.*

Cath: *Charlotte on the outside, Samantha once she's had two cocktails.*

Emily: *You are not Carrie, Charlie. We have discussed this before too.*

Me: *I'm SO Carrie now that I'm a writer (all the books say you have to call yourself a writer even if you haven't published anything, FYI).*

Me: *Please can I be Carrie now?*

Me: *Please?*

Cath: *Your vibrator wank fests have earnt you Samantha.*

* * *

I write. And write. And drink wine. And write.

And I watch *Sex and the City* and *Friends*. Which makes me cry because I remember the time I was really down and had really bad period pains and James came home to the Vauxhall flat with the new *Friends* box set and a bottle of wine and cooked me dinner. He made me stay on the sofa and he used my eyeliner to draw on a fake moustache and pretended to be a French waiter, draping a tea towel over his arm and coming in asking 'if ze lady would like sum fancy fwench vino?'

* * *

Messages I would send to James if I could message him and what I imagine he would message me back, Part 1:

> Me: *Do you remember how you used to do little skits and put on accents and do mimes? How you would tell me what was for dinner through the medium of dance and then do some weird modern dance that looked like you were having a fit? You'd do it when I was down or in the middle of one our silent stand-offs after an argument. And you used to bring me home treats – one time the* Friends *box set, sometimes wine, sometimes flowers, one time a piece of toast that you swore had an image of Madonna in it, one time a Caramac because I'd said it was my favourite chocolate bar when I was younger and I could never find them any more.*

James: *I remember that.*

Me: *I miss it. I miss you.*

James: *I miss you too. I'm sorry. I'm sorry I changed. I love you. I'll treat you like that again.*

* * *

I write. And write. And drink wine. And write.

And I look through all our photo albums and all the photos and videos on my phone and all the photos and videos on the computer. Many times over. Jack and Felix in their dinosaur onesies and tiny welly boots, with chubby cheeks and baby-toothed smiles, their hair blonder then, their curls untamed. Wrestling, but in a cute way, Chloe watching on from the sidelines laughing. All three of them asleep in Chloe's bed, pyjamaed limbs stretched out over each other, nights when they would insist on being together. Family photos of us on holidays, birthdays, special occasions, smiling faces, a happy unit. I stare at the photos, but I don't recognise what I'm seeing. I don't remember when they were like that.

* * *

I write. And write. And drink wine. And write. And I try to sleep, but I can't, so I take a sleeping tablet but still don't sleep and just feel like I'm walking through treacle and I can't form any proper thoughts.

And I clean up Eddie Vedder's shit – which seems to be everywhere now. And write. And I listen to the music I used to listen to before James, when I was young and passionate and full of emotions and intensity and a searing ambition and drive and hope. I listen to Pearl Jam and Nirvana and Soundgarden and Smashing Pumpkins and Stone Temple Pilots, to Alanis Morissette and Garbage and Elastica and Belly and Weezer and Oasis when they were good. I listen to them loud and I shout-sing along and I dance round the front room while I wait for my noodles. I remember each song, like it's etched somewhere just below my skin. I remember listening to them on my yellow Walkman, I remember where I listened to them, I remember the crushes and loves and break-ups and friendship fall-outs they soundtracked. It feels good, like I've cracked myself open and am digging for my soul, like I'm the big Russian doll getting closer to the original Russian doll me with each song. The small one. The core one.

* * *

Messages I would send to the girls if I could message them and what I imagine they would message me back, Part 6:

> Me: *Do you think nineties music was the best music or do you think we think it was the best music because we were the right age when it came out? I mean, noughties music was rubbish, right? No one's going to look back lovingly on how they felt when they listened to Gnarls Barkley.*

Emily: *You are so random.*

Cath: *I have never said nineties music was the best music. For the record.*

Me: *Do you ever want to go back to the nineties – when the music was amazing, and there were no smartphones and you had to just turn up somewhere when you said you were going to and all you had to worry about was getting off with boys and where you were going to buy 20/20 and losing your virginity?*

Cath: *That's just nostalgia. Of course you want to be that age again, you had no responsibilities other than homework.*

Me: *Sometimes I miss it so much it's like someone has ripped my heart out.*

Cath: *You're such a bloody drama queen! No one should miss bucket hats and cargo pants and Britpop that much.*

* * *

At some point, I decide to Blu-Tack all the Super Noodle wrappers to the wall in the hallway. I think it will look dramatic, like an art installation, and will serve as some kind of account of my writing process.

At some point, I take a bath and when I get out, the water is cold.

At some point, I notice Eddie Vedder's cat food is sitting there untouched and that she is being remarkably more tolerant with me cuddling her.

At some point, I watch our wedding video. And then watch it again. And again. And again. And I remember how madly in love we were. And I watch it again. And again.

At some point, I order tarot cards online and look up how to do a reading and pull the Three of Swords which, it turns out, represents heartbreak, loss, sorrow, sadness and all the other bleak words you can think of and is about the worst tarot card you can get and then I spin out and try and find out if there's a way to undo a tarot reading (there is not).

At some point, I go into Chloe's room and sit on her bed and am suddenly filled with a rage that is hot and heavy and desperate. How dare that stupid, entitled, ignorant boy treat her like that. How dare he hurt my smart, funny, beautiful daughter. Boys like that, men like that, they never learn. They swan through life in their loafers and expensive chinos expecting everyone to bend to their needs, their wants, without the slightest regard for anyone other than themselves. The rage scorches me, pulls at me, eats me up, until I find myself walking the hour it takes to get to Rupert's house and I find myself at his gates at one in the morning and of course there are gates and I don't know what I was hoping to do anyway, but I go back down the road I walked up and find one of the many dog shits that so enraged me and I scoop it up using a scrap of tissue in my pocket and I smear it on his gate and some of it gets on my fingers but I don't seem to care.

At some point, I come downstairs and Eddie Vedder is lying in

the doorway to the kitchen, where she never lies, and she doesn't move or meow at me when I go to stroke her and I think she's dead, but she's just about still alive so I put on some Crocs and take her to the vet in my pyjamas and he puts a thermometer up her arse and tells me she's so cold she's basically shutting down and I need to have her euthanised now to save her any more pain and asks me if there's anyone else I want to be there and I want James to be there, so badly, but I can't bring myself to call him so I hold her paw and let him do it and in my mind I apologise for all the times I called her a moaning bitch or shouted at her because she wouldn't stop meowing, and then the vet's receptionist asks me all kinds of questions about if I want her cremated and if I would like her ashes returned to me and if so, in what kind of container and I feel too bad to say the cheapest one but I do anyway, and I think the cheapest one is actually a plastic bag but it's too late to change it now and I don't know how to tell the kids because it will give them another reason to hate me and I don't know how to tell James because Eddie Vedder dying feels like a really bad sign.

At some point, I finish my book. And I drink one of the champagnes.

* * *

Messages I would send to the girls if I could message them and what I imagine they would message me back, Part 7:

Me: *I finished my book! Finally! I AM Carrie!*

Emily: *That's amazing! What an achievement! Well done you! Let's celebrate!*

Cath: *You will always be Vibrator Samantha now.*

37

DORIT HAS brought me to a sex club. That is the fact of the matter. Though I did not know that fact before we arrived here.

She came round a few days after I finished my book, said she'd been texting me and had tried to call and was worried about me. I stood at the doorstep, trying to keep the door as closed as possible without fully slamming it in her face, aware, suddenly, that the house is a disaster zone and that maybe not everyone would appreciate my Super Noodles art installation. She said I looked terrible and asked if I'd been eating. I explained I had. I didn't go into detail about the Great Noodle Epiphany though. She asked if I'd left the house recently. I explained I had not. She made me get my coat and took me to the cafe in the park for a coffee. The posh cafe with the Stepford Wives.

Dorit asked me how I was doing. I told her about the burnt kitchen. She was shocked. She bought me coffee and a piece of carrot cake. The coffee burnt my mouth. The carrot cake stuck to my teeth. I've never really liked carrot cake, even though I always seem to order it. Maybe that's some kind of metaphor for my life.

She asked me how the book was going. I told her it was finished. She said that's amazing. She asked me how the list was going. I said I hadn't looked at it recently. Which made me realise I hadn't. I said there were some left to do. I said there were some

I couldn't do. She asked me which ones. I explained about the exotic ones (sex on a plane, swimming with dolphins, scuba diving, go to Thailand, sex with George Clooney). I said there were some I wasn't sure I wanted to do. She asked me which ones. I explained about the sex ones (have sex on a plane, go to a sex club). She said there was nothing stopping me doing the sex ones, or the exotic ones, and that I'd come so far it would be a shame not to finish it. Then later, she called me and told me to keep Friday free because she had a surprise for me and I was to shower and put on a nice dress and she would pick me up at 10 p.m., which seemed a very late time to go out, but I agreed and that is how I have come to be in a private members' sex club somewhere in Cobham called Soixante-Neuf.

"Just enjoy," Dorit says as she flashes a card at the door of the disused bank and is welcomed by a man in a uniform that looks like it belongs on a hotel doorman. "There are always lots of newbies here and you're not required to get involved. It's supposed to be fun and creative and exploratory. No pressure at all, OK?"

I nod. I'm nervous.

We hand over our phones and Dorit takes off her coat to reveal an extremely sexy, skimpy and revealing lacy black dress that shows off all of her amazing, curvy figure and leaves very little to the imagination. My floral Mint Velvet maxi dress in all its Puritanical Villager glory doesn't quite have the same impact. I run my palm over it, flattening out a wrinkle, as if that will fix the problem.

"Sorry." I shrug. "You said a nice dress."

The hotel concierge doorman doesn't look impressed.

"I thought I said sexy?" Dorit says.

"I don't think ... I ... I'm sure you said nice."

"It looks lovely." She puts her hand on my arm, a comforting mum gesture which feels strangely out of place. "It's just the dress code is 'nothing you could wear in public'. I'll go in my underwear, you can have my dress, come on, let's go to the toilets."

* * *

"Sorted. You look great," Dorit says, unconvincingly. She is wearing a lace thong and the sexiest bra I have ever seen that I know for a fact would give me nipple rash. Needless to say, I do not look as good in the dress as Dorit did, though I'm at least pleased my enormous M&S shapewear is providing some level of cover-up underneath the lace.

I swallow, try to calm myself down. This is quite a big step in our friendship that I'm not entirely sure I'm prepared for. I'm finding it hard to look at her and make sure I very firmly keep my eyes on her face, fixing my sights on a particularly elegant mole.

"Are you sure you're all right in ... just that?" I ask.

"Darling, it's what I would've been walking around in after about seven minutes anyway, it's fine. Keep your bag with you, condoms etcetera." She winks, I panic, she smiles and I can't tell if she's joking or not, but I keep my bag anyway, thankful that at the last minute I chose to swap out my tea-stained Books Are My Bag tote. "Right, let me give you a tour. Drink first, though."

We make our way through a dimly-lit corridor. The carpet is thick and spongy and black, the walls a deep red. It has Pete

Doherty's hotel in Margate vibes. Dorit opens a door and we emerge into a bar, which is basically an extension of the corridor – dark and sumptuous – sex chic. The room is busy – couples huddled on the sofa, people playing pool, groups stood chatting – there is a definite buzz. I'm surprised to find that none of them seem in any way scary or intimidating or sex-dungeon masterly; they all appear to be averagely attractive and normal, to the point that you could almost be in a Pizza Express if it weren't for the lack of children and the overwhelming amount of latex on display. I've definitely felt more threat from a small-town club full of lads in Paul Smith shirts and clubbing shoes. I take the cocktail Dorit gives me gratefully.

"Cheers," Dorit says. "Here's to finishing your book. That's an incredible achievement."

I raise my glass, take a sip, the strong liquor coating my throat in the most welcome of ways.

"And here's to ticking another one off the list," she says.

Goosebumps of excitement and fear and something else I can't quite identify domino up my spine.

"Have you been here a lot?" I ask, taking another big gulp of the cocktail. The buzz is there already. It's good.

"Phil and I used to come together, actually. That's how I found out about it. We wanted to spice things up a bit, try something new. We've both always been quite adventurous in that department."

I blush. I can talk with the girls about sex until the cows come home – embarrassing sex, gross sex, disappointing sex – but it jars hearing Dorit talk about it.

"But once we had the kids, he wasn't so into it. Said he didn't

like seeing the mother of his kids in that kind of 'situation'. It was one of the things we fought about – him expecting me to change even though he knew exactly what I was like, who I was, when we got together."

"That doesn't seem fair," I say.

"Yup. People change, I get that. But you can't expect someone to change and you definitely can't expect people to change in the way you want them to, that suits you."

I rub my thumb over my wedding ring and think of James. People do change. Especially after twenty years of marriage. But James has changed in a way that makes him almost unrecognisable to me, like I can't access the James I married any more. That doesn't feel fair either.

"You all right?" Dorit asks.

"Yep. Away with the fairies." I sip my cocktail, push thoughts of James and change and marriage-not-marriage away. "So how does it . . . work?" I blush again.

"The first thing to know is, like I said before, you don't have to get involved – but obviously, feel free to if you do want to. It's all really safe and accepting. There are play areas and a dungeon and a couple of rooms with beds. There are toys. People just do what they feel like doing with each other – and if they want to involve you, they'll probably hold a hand or give you a sign and you can join in if you want or just watch or walk away. No one gets offended. It's all really free flowing. And fun! That's the main objective, right? To have fun."

I nod. My fanny started fluttering as she was talking. There's an exciting tension in the room. I'm proud that I've made it this

far. I down the rest of my cocktail and Dorit gets us both a glass of champagne.

"Ready for the tour?" she asks.

I nod, the courage the cocktail gave me buoying me on.

Dorit walks along the bar and pushes through a big black double door. We walk along another sex-chic corridor, dimly lit by giant chandeliers, and then down some sex-chic stairs where she pushes another door open and all of a sudden, I'm stood in front of some kind of *Fifty Shades* scene. It takes my eyes a minute to work out what I'm looking at exactly, and when I do, part of me wishes I hadn't. There are two prison cells, one of which houses a swing on which a couple are having sex while three other couples around them watch, some of them playing with each other as they do. There's a woman strapped to a bench while a couple take turns spanking her and she gives her partner (I presume?) a blow job. There's a man lying on the floor with what looks like a doormat strapped to his back while two women in incredibly high heels walk over him.

It takes all of my restraint not to gasp or lift my hands to my eyes in a watching-a-horror-movie type way. I feel Dorit's eyes on me and sense I should smile or something, not wanting to disappoint her. I manage a weak one. The lady in the prison cell starts groaning, in a surprisingly gentle and un-porn way.

"This is the dungeon," Dorit whispers. "This is for the more S&M inclined. Or anyone wanting to experiment. The Dungeon Master is always happy to teach people new tricks if you ask."

The man spanking the woman on the bench offers the whipping implement to Dorit, she shakes her head politely, he shrugs and

gets back to it. Each crack of it making contact startles me.

"Come on," Dorit says. We leave the dungeon and go past another door. "That's a glory hole room."

I must look confused because she continues, "for anonymous penis play."

I nod, not wanting any more detail on that.

We go up the sex-chic stairs to the corridor we were on before, then up some more sex-chic stairs. We pass a room with a king-size bed, a giant TV showing porn and a woman giving her partner a blow job while masturbating with what, from the low-level buzz, I assume is a vibrator.

"That's a couples room," Dorit says. "Though everyone's welcome to watch, obviously. Lots of toys to use too."

"Do people ... share?" I ask. I try to make the words sound casual and non-judgemental, though the thought of sharing vibrators makes my stomach churn. Suddenly my vibrator adventures seem very insignificant and childish.

"People share," Dorit says. "There's plenty of cleaning equipment in every room – and you're expected to clean up after yourselves, whatever you do."

It makes it sound clinical. And liquidy. And gross.

"There's another couples room over there." I follow to where she's pointing, see almost exactly the same room, but the couple on this bed are having such gentle, intimate sex, it feels wrong to look, like I've broken into their house or something. I look away.

We walk further along the corridor. There are bold prints on the walls, all, I realise as we pass them, of people having sex. Big brush-stroked breasts and penises being stuck in very questionable

places. Twosomes, threesomes, orgies. Bodies and bodies and tangled limbs and ecstatic faces that feel like they're watching me. I think of my Super Noodle installation, use the memory of it to ground me. Suddenly desperate for the comfort of home.

"And this is one of the play rooms," Dorit says, pushing open a heavy double door.

This room feels more sedate. There are still tangled bodies and genitals on show and piles of people writhing but there are lots of clothed people standing round the perimeter just watching and drinking. People in various states of undress saunter around the room. I see one lingeried woman carrying a feather, walking from writhing group to writhing group running her feather along various body parts, giggling and then moving on. She's older than me, mid-fifties maybe, and I wonder what her name is, what her day job is, if she has kids. I imagine she's called something like Joan or Linda and works in a building society. I imagine bumping into her. Then I suddenly panic – if Dorit is here, it could be likely other school mums or other people I know are too. I scroll through my Tollingford acquaintances, seeing their faces flash up on my mental Rolladex – Jim, the plumber who came to fix our radiators, Liz, the pensioner who lives opposite us and always posts on the street WhatsApp group about bin collection days. It would more likely be Rob, Handsy Dad, so named for all the times he 'accidentally' touched women's arses at class drinks. What if they were here?

"That's pretty much it," Dorit says. "I won't show you the other sections, I don't think they'd be your thing."

God only knows what 'the other sections' might be. I'm partly grateful and partly offended she isn't showing them to me.

We keep to the outskirts of the room, make our way round to the table in the corner where there is a giant ice bucket with bottles of champagne wedged into it. Pol Roger, I notice, wondering how much Dorit has paid for this evening, making a mental note to pay her back.

Dorit leans in, her voice low and quiet. "What do you think?"

What do I think? I think there is too much bodily fluid being shared between strangers, I think having sex on a swing is extremely impractical, I think I've seen more exposed genitals in thirty minutes than I've seen in my whole life, I think people are strange, I think I know I'm trying to allow more fun and adventure into my life but this seems excessive and not necessarily fun, and I think I'm scared by all the sex – the mountains and mountains of open, untamed, raw, in-your-face sex.

"It's certainly different isn't it?"

Dorit laughs – a short, sharp guffaw. A couple of people turn to look at her.

"It depends on what you're used to, I guess, but yes, it probably is different from what most people experience. Relax into it, try and let go of all the inhibitions we're all so conditioned to have."

"Well, clearly not all of us," I say, raising my eyebrows at some of the writhing couples.

I notice that Feather Joan has made her way over to a throne-like chair where another lady's head is between her legs, going at it through Joan's crotchless panties while Joan runs the feather over the back of her neck.

I look away. It seems to be the theme of my night. I'm not sure I'm quite cut out for voyeurism.

I drink my champagne, aware that getting as drunk as humanly possible is probably the best way to go. I notice a man on the sofa, getting a blow job from a blonde-haired woman, is looking our way. For a terrifying moment, I think his gaze is aimed at me, before I follow his eyes and see Dorit grinning back at him. He gently pushes the woman's head away, pulls her up and leads her over to Dorit, his penis so shiny and erect and glistening it's like it's a magic wand with gravitational pull. I take a step away as he approaches. Up close he's so average it surprises me. He has a dad bod, slightly acne-scarred skin and a receding hairline. How he thinks Dorit is in his league, I do not know. He holds his hand out to Dorit, no words. The blonde woman behind him smiles enticingly, her lips still wet from blow-jobbing.

Dorit looks at me. Please god, don't be inviting me too.

"Are you OK if I . . . ?" she says.

I nod, because a) I'm relieved she wasn't wanting me to join in and b) what else am I supposed to say?

"I won't be long," she says, and they head off down the stairs hand in hand, like one of the school trip trains you see where five-year-olds are instructed to hold their partner's hand tightly.

And then I'm suddenly on my own. In this crazy, squirmy, dark room that smells of bodies and sweat and sex and disinfectant. My chest tightens. I feel alone and out of place and exposed, even though I'm by far the most dressed person here.

* * *

Messages I would send to the girls if I could message them and what I imagine they would message me back, Part 8:

Me: *Guys, I am at a sex club. In Cobham. There is a lady with a feather. And a dungeon. And a swing. And I honestly don't know where to look.*

Cath: *Nobham. LOL.*

Emily: *OMG. You're mad! What's it like? Does it smell gross?*

Me: *It smells of disinfectant.*

Cath: *And jizz?*

Emily: *Cath!*

Cath: *I don't understand what you're doing in a sex club. The most adventurous you've been is the time you had sex in Brockwell Park and the two minutes of anal you had recently. I feel it's not your vibe.*

Me: *Definitely not my vibe.*

Emily: *Missionary and lights out. That's more your vibe, Charlotte.*

Cath: *But she's Samantha now, since the vibrator epiphany.*

Me: *I'm Carrie! I've told you!*

Emily: *Carrie would never go to a sex club. She's way more prim and proper than she likes to think she is.*

Cath: *She keeps her bra on for sex, FFS – of course she's prim and proper.*

Me: *Oh god, a couple has just started having sex up against the wall next to me. Help me.*

I take a step to the side, politely getting out of their way. The man turns his head to look at me, smiles, then slinks down, pushing the woman's legs apart and starting to slowly lick up her leg. I go to take another step but bump into another couple the other side of me. The woman is facing the wall, her hands up either side of her face, the man thrusting at her from behind. I am sandwiched. I am a giant piece of useless spam wedged between two pieces of fucking bread – *literally* fucking.

I look around the room, searching for a slice of space, desperately hoping that Dorit might be back from her travels. There are bodies everywhere. I feel like I'm in the middle of a painting of a Greek orgy. It's hot in here. So hot. I-can't-breathe type hot. The room is spinning. I need air. I need escape.

What the fuck was I thinking? In what world did I think this would be fun? I don't even like porn, there's never enough story or emotional engagement. This is not fun. This is not for me. Would coming here with James feel any different? Would that have been fun? The thought of him walking round naked with his magic wand out and proud, or of people watching us having sex, or of

watching another woman do anything with him makes me retch. Then the realisation that, although it won't be happening in a sex club or anywhere I have to witness it, it is going to happen. He is going to be having sex with another woman, at some point.

It hits me like a blow to my chest, winding me. I miss him. But more than that, I miss my life, my normal, my people. I don't know who this new me is, but it's not me. Not the real me. I don't know who the real me is any more. I haven't known for a while. I'm spinning, I can't breathe. My mouth fills with saliva, a rush of vomit rising up to my throat, the other-worldliness that comes just before you pass out.

I manage to remove myself from the sex sandwich, run down the stairs and out of the door. I throw up on the pavement, acidic, stinging, champagne and shame vomit.

* * *

Messages I would send to the girls if I could message them and what I imagine they would message me back, Part 9:

Me: *I need you.*

Cath: *We're here for you.*

Emily: *We've got you.*

38

I RING THE doorbell.

It's raining.

I'm wet.

And cold.

Shivering.

I ring the doorbell again.

After what seems like an eternity, I hear footsteps, see lights going on. The door opens and I burst into tears at the sight of a familiar face.

"Charlie?" Emily looks surprised. Crumpled and roused from sleep, and surprised. "My god, what's the matter? Come in."

She opens the door fully and I tumble in, dripping onto her parquet floor, onto Mattie's *Frozen* slippers.

"I'm so sorry." The words are small, through my clattering teeth. "I didn't think about the kids. I just—"

"You're freezing." She takes me in.

Me and Dorit's short, skimpy, way-too-tight, meant-for-sex dress. God only knows what my face must look like. I have the sudden urge to completely cover myself. To stand in a scalding hot shower for days, to let the heat soak away my sins and my shame and my misery.

"Go through to the kitchen," she says. "I'll go get you something warm."

She rushes upstairs while I stumble through to the kitchen and turn on lights, glance at the clock that says 2 a.m., wonder what has happened to time, what alternate universe I have been in tonight, and these last few months. Emily's kitchen looks different, though I can't place why. She's changed something since I was last here. When was I even last here? I don't like it. I don't like that something has changed and I have not been privy to it.

She comes back down, a towel, a big dressing gown and some pyjamas piled in her hands. I take them gratefully, relish the warmth and the freshly-washed smell of the towel I know she's got straight from her airing cupboard. I peel off Dorit's dress, dry myself with the towel, bury my face in it, wrap my hair in it, put on the pyjamas and the robe, the comfort and warmth enveloping me.

Emily boils the kettle, gets two mugs out from the cupboard, pours us both a chamomile. I sit on a stool at the kitchen island, where I've sat a hundred times before, muscle memory taking over. The simplicity of it, the familiarity of it, the comfort. The tears come again. I have no control over them.

Emily hands me my tea, her face drawn with worry. "Has something happened tonight? Have you been hurt? Do I need to call the police?"

I shake my head.

"I'm sorry," I manage. "I'm sorry for tonight. And for before. I'm sorry."

"It's OK." She takes my hand and leads me to the living room, settles me on the sofa, draping a blanket over us, her arm around me. "It's OK," she says again.

* * *

It's *Gravity* George. Short hair, space suit.

I go to wave and say hello but I realise I'm strapped to a bondage bench in the dungeon. The loud thwack of a whip, a bolt of sharp pain rails through me. I don't want to be here. I want to leave, but I can't. Then all of a sudden, I'm in our kitchen. With James, 2005 James. He's cooking his famous Vauxhall pasta, which basically consisted of whatever they had in the local Costcutter mixed with cream and pasta. It's 2005 James, but it's our Tollingford kitchen. He's dancing along to The Pussycat Dolls, putting the tip of his finger on his tongue and pretending to sizzle every time it says the word hot. I'm laughing. Then I'm hot. Burning hot. And coughing. And my nostrils are stinging and I look to James but he's surrounded by fire and now the kids are next to him, crying, and the fire gets bigger and bigger and hotter and hotter, and I try to walk towards them, to reach them, to save them, but I can't get to them and I'm screaming and screaming.

I wake with a jolt, my heart pounding, my back drenched in sweat, my mouth dry and acidic.

Relief floods through me when I see the blue and white stripes of Emily's spare room curtains. Images of last night flit through my head, Dorit in her underwear, the lady on the bondage bench, Feather Joan, the sex sandwich up against the wall, Emily standing at her doorway. I can't remember getting to Emily's, though I must've got a cab. Shit. I left my phone and my coat and my Mint Velvet dress at the sex club. And double shit. Dorit must be worried out of her mind. I don't have her number, it's only on my phone,

which is still, presumably, at the club. How will I let her know I'm all right?

I take a breath. The main thing is I'm OK.

Though another main thing would be to check Dorit hasn't set a police manhunt on me.

My stomach growls. I can't actually remember the last time I ate. It was noodles, obviously, but I can't remember when. The carpet feels comforting against my sore feet as I stumble out of the bed, my legs wobbly. I've crashed in this room many times, but never the night after a sex club.

I put the fluffy robe on and make my way downstairs, family noises floating up from the kitchen – Kian's loud giggles, Mattie getting cross about something, Emily's soothing voice trying to calm the situation. It occurs to me I may well see Rick, and the thought is almost enough to make me run back upstairs. My stomach won't let me though.

"Auntie Charlie!" Mattie says, running towards me with sticky hands and an enormous grin. I can feel the tears again, but I swallow them down.

"Well, hello," I say, wrapping both kids in hugs.

"Why are you still in your pyjamas?" Kian asks.

"I've just woken up," I say.

"But it's nearly time for football," he says, looking horrified.

I look at the clock. Midday. Balls.

"I guess I slept in then," I say.

"Morning," Emily says, handing me a coffee in the Little Miss Sunshine mug I got her forever ago and two pieces of Marmite toast, my favourite. "You sleep OK?"

"I did," I say, surprised. "Like a log. Which is – amazing, actually."

"Dad will be here in a minute, Kian," she says. "Make sure you've got your football boots."

"Is Rick . . . ?"

"He's in his flat." She nods. "But he's taking Kian to football—"

"And me for a milkshake!" Mattie says, twirling in excitement.

"Yes, and you for a milkshake."

"And a sleepover!"

"Yes, and a sleepover. So go and make sure you've got everything – he's running a bit late."

The kids scramble to get ready, Emily deals with lost toothbrushes and teddies, Rick comes and gives me a suspicious glare, then the door is shut and the house is quiet and it's just me and Emily.

"Let's go and sit down," she says, and I can't work out if she's angry with me or disappointed in me or just outright hates me and I wouldn't blame her for any of those reactions.

We sit on the sofa, I drape the same blanket over me, tuck my feet up.

"I texted Dorit, by the way," Emily says. "I didn't get much sense out of you last night, but I gathered you'd been with Dorit. She was worried about you. Said she's going to drop your stuff off later."

A small trill of relief. "Thank you!"

"What happened last night, Charls?" she says. "I'm worried about you. You were mumbling something about Dorit and someone called Joan and Nobham. You weren't making sense but it seemed like something more than just being drunk. Were you on drugs?"

I laugh. Or rather, I mean to laugh, but it comes out with a side

order of sob. I cannot cry again. I don't even know how I have tears left. I could've filled a dam by now, a deep bath at least.

I don't quite know where to start so I just dive straight in. "I went to a sex club in Cobham with Dorit."

Emily's jaw drops, her eyes cartoon wide. "You what? Dorit didn't mention that!"

"Yep, like the giant twat that I am. Although, to be fair to me, Dorit didn't tell me where we were going – which is why I went in a Mint Velvet dress."

"The one with the flowers and the pilgrim collar?"

"The very same."

Emily laughs. "Sorry, it's not funny, it's just, I can kind of imagine you doing that."

"You can laugh. I'm sure I will, one day. In the very distant future."

"So, what happened at the club?" she asks, serious now. "You were really upset when you got here. Did you—"

"God, nothing awful, no," I say, because I know she must be imagining something hideous. "I basically was stood in a room which was full of people in all kinds of sexual . . . situations . . . and then Dorit left to . . . go and do something with some people, and I panicked and spiralled and felt sad, and then I ended up in a sex sandwich with a couple either side of me having sex and I had a 'come to Jesus' moment and my whole life flashed before my eyes and I thought I was going to pass out so I ran out and vomited and didn't want to go home because, well, I'll get to that, so I came here, because I really, really needed to see you."

I cry again. Bloody tears. Endless bloody tears.

"Oh mate." Emily scooches next to me, puts her arm around me. "That's a lot. What's been going on?"

I tell her everything that has happened since Cornwall. The ecstasy night, James wanting a trial separation, my book, my list, the not sleeping, the crying, the aggressive manifesting, the fire, the noodles, my art installation, the dog-shit incident, Eddie Vedder dying. I show her my bellend tattoo, she says it looks more like a singular bum cheek.

She makes chilli, we eat, it gets dark outside, we light a fire, she tells me everything going on in her life – how it turns out Rick was having an affair, is now in a new relationship with the woman and has moved into a flat with her.

How she nearly lost her job because she was finding it all so hard, how she wasn't sleeping either, but is on HRT and doing a bit better now, how she wonders if that's it now and she'll be on her own for the rest of her life and how maybe that's OK because she'd rather be on her own than be with Rick, and my god why didn't we tell her what a total dick he was, and I said we did try and she says we should've tried harder.

"How are you feeling now?" she asks.

Saturday night TV is on in the background, my legs on her lap, and we both have more chamomile tea.

"Wrung out," I say. "I feel like I've run a marathon across forty countries, through deserts and mountains and mud and rain, all while carrying an incredibly heavy rucksack."

"Wow, that was some sex club." She laughs.

"I honestly feel exhausted. And kind of shell-shocked. Like I don't know what happened the last few months – Jesus, the last

few years. I don't know who I am any more. And I was trying to find myself again, except the me I was trying to find doesn't exist any more because that was a twenty-five-year-old, no responsibilities, no experience or wisdom me who could drink like a fish and still do her job well." I take a breath, push the tears away. "I thought I was fed up of the boredom of my life, of my kids and my husband and my house. I thought that bloody list would somehow fix that – make me feel like I'd achieved something, at the very least give me some temporary distraction, but holy crap, it's cracked me open. In a way I'm not entirely sure I like."

I think about that. "Actually, in a way I'm entirely sure I *don't* like. I haven't achieved anything, and I wasn't even temporarily distracted – I was obsessed to the point of madness. And look at me now – I've blown my whole life up for nothing. I don't know what I want," I say. "For now, but also, I don't know what I want my future to look like. It scares me. I don't know what will fix me."

I wipe away a snot trail. Swallow hard.

"I totally understand," she says. "But, can I make a suggestion?"

I nod.

"I think the first thing you should do is go to a doctor. And sleep. But doctor first. You need some help, Charlie. Beyond any help that friends can give you. Proper help. Maybe HRT, maybe antidepressants, maybe both, I don't know, but you need some help."

I nod. Dr Deb had told me to go to the doctor after the James exit session. And I had meant to, but it felt too much to even make the call, to be on hold, to know what to say. So I didn't.

"And if it's any consolation," Emily says, "and it should be – I think we're all going through it to some extent. It's our age.

And our hormones. We spend all that time growing up and in our twenties striving for the things we think we should want – and I'm not saying we don't want them. A career, partner, marriage, kids, a decent house. Then we survive the sleep deprivation and the madness of little kids, either still trying to cling on to a career or having given up or adjusted a career, and then everything shifts again. Our bodies mess with us all over again, our relationships change beyond recognition, our hormones kick in. Our parents start ageing and dying."

"Oh my god, how's Cath?" I say, sitting myself up.

Emily's face drops. "Has she not been in touch? She said she was going to."

I shake my head, my stomach flipping because I have a horrible feeling I know what she's about to say.

"Her mum died," she says.

"Oh god!" My whole body drops with the weight of it. The fact I didn't know, the fact I wasn't there for her, the fact she's lost her mother. "Shit."

"It was a couple of weeks ago. It happened quite fast after she got another infection. Cath was with her. I'm sure she was going to let you know, but she's been frantically trying to deal with everything."

"I should've been there for her," I say, the tears coming again.

Emily sighs. "Yeah, you probably should've. But you've had a lot going on too. You can be there for her now."

We sip our tea, fix our gaze on Ant and Dec. Tears silently fall down my face. I think about the time I went to the pub with them and how that feels like a lifetime ago because it kind of was.

"I'm scared to go back to my house," I say.

Emily pats my leg. "I'll come with you. Rick's got the kids until tomorrow night."

"You'd do that?" I feel so much love for her I think I might burst. "After I've been such an awful friend and such an awful twat?"

"Dude, I've cleaned up your vomit countless times, witnessed you being varying levels of twat even more countless times and had to help you do the end-of-tenancy-clean on your uni house. I'm equipped."

"And there was that time you helped me find my tampon string."

"Jesus, I think I'd blocked that from my mind."

39

DORIT'S FLAT is everything you would expect it to be – light and open and airy and stunningly decorated. One thing you can definitely say about Dorit is that her taste is impeccable. Her design taste that is, maybe not so much her taste in extra-curricular activities.

"It's gorgeous, Dorit!" We've just finished the tour, during which I just said 'wow' a lot and gaped at things with my mouth open.

"Aw, thanks babe." She ushers me onto one of the two outdoor swinging egg chairs that are on her balcony. She turns a heater on and hands me a blanket. "It's taken me a while, but I think I've got it just how I want it. It's my sanctuary now."

I do feel a bit like I'm in a very fancy spa. The kind with pale wood and luxurious soft furnishings.

"I'm going to make tea," she says. "Be right back."

I take a deep breath and gaze out at the beautiful view of the river. A few months ago, weeks ago even, I would have thought I'd love to live in a place like this, mostly on my own, without the constant skid marks and mess of my children. But now I know I would not. I'd like a small relaxing holiday here, don't get me wrong, but nothing more, nothing longer. And besides which, I'd be too scared to mess up any of the flawless interior. Which is

why my house is, and will always be, a bit messy and a bit chaotic. Maybe I'll ask Dorit about flat-sitting if she ever goes away.

"Here we go." She comes back out, placing two steaming mugs on the small rattan table between the chairs. She pulls the lush cashmere blanket over her shoulders and sits on the other chair. "So, lovely lady, how are you doing? Actually, before you answer that – I know I've said this over text, but I just want to say in person how completely and utterly sorry I am for dragging you to Soixante-Neuf."

I go to speak, but she waves her hand at me to stop.

"It was completely well-intentioned and I did genuinely think it would be a helpful thing to do – not just for ticking it off the list, but also for giving you a bit of fun, getting you out of your shell. I shouldn't have sprung it on you, and I totally *should've* taken the time to read the situation better. And for that, I'm so, so sorry."

She takes a breath, sips her tea. "Have I traumatised you for life?"

"Maybe not for life," I say. "I'd say a good six months, though."

She looks wide-eyed and horrified, until I smile.

"Oh, thank god." She laughs. "I thought you were being serious! It was seeing me in my underwear, wasn't it?"

"Uh, that was the least of it – it was more the two couples having sex right next to me. And Feather Joan. Which is an image I will never be able to erase from my poor broken mind."

"Feather Joan?"

"The lady who was walking round with a sexy glint in her eye, stroking random fornicating people with a feather."

"Ahhh, Margaret!" Dorit says. And to be honest, I feel like Joan was in the right ballpark.

"I'm so sorry," Dorit says. "So, so sorry. I thought you'd find it fun."

"To be honest, *I* thought I'd find it fun – clearly, otherwise I wouldn't have put it on the list. Who knew I was such a prude?" I blow my tea, wisps of steam escaping towards the river. "I mean, Cath and Emily knew I was such a prude. And I guess I should've known. If I'd thought about the reality of it all for more than ten seconds."

"It sounds like you were in a really bad headspace," Dorit says. "And I had no idea it was that bad. I wish you'd returned my calls."

"I couldn't," I say. "I was barely managing to keep myself conscious and fed."

She looks at me, her gorgeous eyes so intense and worried. "I was right here," she says. "I could've helped."

"If it's any consolation, you kind of did help by taking me to that sex club and forcing me to have a breakdown."

I don't mean it to come out as flippantly as it does. Me going to that club really was a breakthrough. A breakthrough in my breakdown. But one that was much needed. Without that, who knows how long I would've stayed in my burnt-out house eating Super Noodles? Probably as long as it would've taken the additives to kill me.

"But anyway," I carry on. "It's done now. In the past. It's been a journey. I'm still travelling – or some shit like that. And the main thing is, I'm feeling much better and much more like myself."

"That's the most important thing," Dorit says. "I'm very much of the only looking forwards, leaving things in the past outlook. Apart from when it comes to therapy, though even then . . ."

We sit and gently swing in amiable silence for a minute, the

winter sun making a fleeting appearance and lighting up the surface of the river.

"It took me a long time to get back to myself," Dorit says, eventually. "After all the stuff with Phil. I drank way too much – which, as you're probably aware, is saying a lot! I slept with some horrible people and put myself in bad situations. It was like I was self-harming. Or self-sabotaging. It was bad. And I wasn't the person I wanted to be – or the person I knew I was deep down. I think we get to this point and it's all been such a slog and we feel so weighed down by it all and think that we want our old lives back – our twenties – but actually, we just want a better, more enjoyable, less draining version of our current life. We want to breathe again. And for what it's worth, I think the list was a great idea for that. I know you're feeling bad about it all now, but the intention of it was good. It gave you the chance to reset a bit. Which is what we all need." She takes a breath.

"And hormones," I say. "We all need decent hormones."

"And those, too." She laughs. "My biggest piece of advice, as someone who's been there and done that, or a version of that, and come out the other side better for it, is to take baby steps. And to be kind to yourself. Don't expect to turn everything around overnight – make small, meaningful changes that build up over time."

I nod, still looking out to the river, watching a pair of geese waddling and shitting – living their best, easy, simple waddling-and-shitting goose lives.

"Do you want to go to spin class this week?" I ask. "One of my baby steps is doing some exercise, and I actually quite enjoyed that last class – even though I couldn't walk for days after."

She grins. "I told you you'd be a convert!"

"Let's not go too far."

"But no pub afterwards," she says. "I am a good influence now. Walks and exercise and herbal teas all the way."

"No pub afterwards," I agree.

March

40

WE DECIDE to meet in the park. I have no finished kitchen, though work has started, and I thought it would be weird to see James's flat. Plus, Dr Deb always suggested neutral spaces for important conversations. Not that we are seeing Dr Deb together any more.

It's one of those days where it's cold and sharp, but there's a sniff of spring in the air. The light is different, the edge has gone, and early bursts of blossoms are out. A few enthusiastic crocuses have pushed on through, out at the front of the house. I smile at them in recognition – today I have crocus vibes about me – I have survived the long, cold, miserable, debilitating winter, I have pushed on through, and better times are ahead. I am crocus!

I have slept, which I think is probably the biggest difference. The doctor I saw wouldn't prescribe me sleeping pills and actually wouldn't prescribe me HRT to begin with either. He saw that I was forty-four and still having periods and said it 'wasn't time for all that yet' and that it sounded like I needed antidepressants, which part of me can understand as I did totally break down in his office and sob uncontrollably, with snot strings and all. I took the prescription, but before I started on them, Emily said I should ask to see another doctor and that all surgeries should have a menopause specialist. She also insisted I watch and read Davina, which I did.

And she was right, it was eye-opening. After that, things kind of fell into place like a cruel jigsaw. The female doctor I saw was amazing. She asked me all kinds of things, showed real compassion, didn't even raise her eyebrows when I told her about my noodles era and prescribed me HRT – with follow-up appointments booked in and a list of useful websites.

So yeah, I've slept. And I'm realising that sleep makes a REALLY big difference to everything. As does eating decent food. Emily spent the day after sexclubgate batch cooking for me – chilli, veggie chilli, bean stew and soup – all things that can be heated in one pan on a two-ring electric hob. We transported them to my freezer, and even though they've run out now, I felt so much better for having eaten something other than freeze-dried noodles with a ton of additives. It inspired me to bulk buy some of those super posh, super expensive, healthy frozen ready meals.

Dorit brought round an extremely extravagant fruit basket, herbal teabags, a pillow spray and a natural supplement she swears by that costs around one-hundred-and-fifty pounds a pop. I don't know if it's working, but something is, because I am starting to feel better. More myself, in some form.

Nerves pinch at me as I walk towards the designated meeting bench. It seems ridiculous being nervous to meet up with your husband, but I guess that's where I'm at now. He's already there. Towering, even when sitting, his curls looking particularly out of control. In another life, a few months ago, I would've told him he needs to get a haircut. I won't do that today.

"Hey," I say, walking up behind him.

He turns round, his expression unreadable, but maybe even a

smile that is veering towards pleased to see me. He's tired, his eyes are hollowed out, his skin pale.

"Hey," he says. "Shall we ... uh ... get a coffee?"

"Sure."

He stands up and we start walking, side by side, and for a moment, I'm winded by how much I've missed his physical presence, by how safe and familiar it is to be next to him like this.

"How are the kids?" I ask.

I spoke to them last night, and have been speaking to them regularly, but I feel like if I don't ask this as my first question, I'll be deemed a bad mother.

"Jack's still really upset about Eddie Vedder," he says. "Though I think having the little ceremony helped a bit."

I had broken the news to the family, to varying degrees of sadness (Felix had forgotten we had a pet) and it was decided we should scatter her ashes under the tree by the trampoline. I decanted them out of the plastic bag into a wooden box to show Eddie Vedder some respect. It was a nice send off.

"Apart from that, they're good," he says. "Still wrestling."

"Always."

"Chloe seems to be taking her revision a bit more seriously since the boyfriend has gone."

The mention of Rupert makes me equal parts ashamed and furious still, even though he has since apologised and tried to win her back. Thankfully, she decided she was better off without him.

"That's great," I say. "She mentioned she was going to the revision camps at school – that's a big step."

"Felix did well in his hockey tournament."

"Yeah, that sounded great too. Did you go and watch?"

"I had to work on Sunday. We're launching a big campaign next week and..."

He stops himself, presumably so we don't end up in usual argument territory, or so that I don't think he's a bad parent for not going to watch the hockey.

The small talk is painful, I'd rather just rip the Band-Aid off.

"What are we doing here, James?" I make a gesture that I realise may seem like I'm referring to the park. "I mean, what are we doing with our marriage, with our family? Where are you at with it all? Actually, before you answer that, let me tell you where I'm at – I had a really rough patch, as you know." He makes some kind of scoffing noise at that. "I think it was a lot of things – lack of sleep, perimenopause stuff, as it turns out. But I can't just blame it on that. I was obviously really unhappy too."

"You were," he says.

"I still am, to some extent," I say. "I think I lost myself somewhere in the process of having and raising a family and I have to work on that. I still feel like I need to do something else with my life, I still feel fed up with doing the lion's share of all the housework and kids' stuff." He goes to interrupt, but I stop him. "I don't want to argue about it – I know, you have a big job, I understand all of that. So what I need to work out now is how we navigate that, as a family, whether we're together or not, and what I want to do with my life going forwards. I've got some ideas, but for now, I'm just working on getting back on my feet a bit."

"Right." He doesn't sound convinced.

"But I guess the question is, what are we going to do about us?

I think we've had problems for a while, maybe even since having the kids. It's understandable – family life and small kids, it's hard. I always thought we'd get through this stage, then once they were older, we'd go back to being us again, Charlie and James. But now I'm not sure. I think we've both changed so much – I don't know who Charlie and James are any more."

I take a breath. That was a lot. And I just referred to us in the third person, which was weird. We pass a couple pushing a pram loaded with a scooter and snacks and plastic water bottles, a red-faced toddler stomping along behind. The mum is clutching a coffee so tightly I worry it's going to pop, the dad snaps at the toddler, the mum mutters something clipped to the dad. It instantly transports me to when Chloe was that toddler, Felix that baby and I was that completely exhausted, bored, CBeebies-zombified mum. I want to go and wrap her in a hug, tell her it gets better, in some ways, worse in others, but she'll survive. And to tell her she should keep her career.

"How are you feeling about everything?" I ask, seeing as James is staying silent.

"Exhausted," he says, "to be honest."

"Okaaaay." What am I supposed to do with that, I wonder.

"It's been impossible working in the way I need to work and looking after the kids," he says. He's drawn up to his full height now, his earlier slump stretched out. "I've had to get my mum over from Spain to help out a couple of times, and that's not ideal as she's getting too old for that. And trying to get my head around everything has been . . . I've started working two days a week from home, because there's just no way—"

We've made it to the queue for the coffee window, a silver-haired lady with an ugly bulgy-eyed dog turns round to stare at us, James's tone making it obvious we're having An Important Chat. He picks up on the glance, stops talking.

We stand in the queue in silence. I don't know where to look and suddenly my arms seem extremely awkward and unfortunately placed, perhaps because I'd usually link them through James's or pick off that bit of fluff that's clung to his stubble. A part of me is pleased that he's feeling the pressure of the kids, of holding down a household, though I know he'd say I was only doing that and not trying to hold down a job as well, to which I would say, yes, exactly, because having a job and doing everything for the house and kids with no help from anyone is too much. But I won't say that. Not today.

Eventually, we get our coffees and start walking again.

"Honestly, Charlie," he says. I flinch at this new use of my proper name again. "I don't know how I feel about anything because I barely get the chance to piss at the moment. All I can think about is work and what I need to do for the kids. And yes, I get it, this is what you've been saying to me all along, but also . . . " He sips his latte and I try to remember when his coffee order changed from a cappuccino to a latte.

"Also, what?" I ask, not sure if I want to know the answer.

"This is going to sound harsh, and I don't mean it to be, but I am quite enjoying not having to think about you too – in terms of what you're going to be pissed off with me for, when you're going to ask me about dates for a holiday, that kind of stuff. There's something, kind of . . . simpler about us being apart. I dunno."

That stings. Like a slap in the face. But a part of me gets it. Wasn't that the whole pull of the Super Noodle era – the simplicity? I don't point out that we still need to have conversations about holiday dates and actually, they'll be more in advance and more set in stone, because if we're going to stay separated, you can bet your ass I'm going to expect him to have the kids more over the school breaks, and you can bet your ass I am going to be away on an exotic beach somewhere sunning myself and not around for any last-minute changes in the schedule.

"This might help then – when the kitchen's done, I'd really like the kids to move back in," I say. "We can work out weekends or what nights in the week they come to you, but I'd like to have them based back with me in the house."

He turns to look at me. "Will you cope with that?"

His tone seems to be one of genuine concern.

"Absolutely," I say, with full confidence. "I'm OK now. I'm hardly drinking – more because I don't bloody sleep when I do – and I'm not manifesting, you'll be pleased to hear." I expect a small laugh, at least, but get nothing. Too soon, perhaps. "I'm good. Really."

The push and pull of concern mixed with relief at him not having to do it all any more plays out on his face. I know which one will win.

"Well, if you're totally sure, I'd probably be OK with that."

He says it like he's deigning to do me a favour. I take it.

"But, you know, I'd like to have them for a bit too. And I'm going to keep those two days working from home, so maybe I can do a bit more . . ." He pauses. "A bit more just general stuff. In case you wanted to look for a job and have two clear days."

This sounds like nothing, to an outsider, but to me, he's almost offering me the world, and I know that wouldn't have been easy.

"Thanks," I say. "I appreciate that."

We walk on a bit. I resist the temptation to reach out for his hand, or to rest my head on his shoulder.

"And where are you at on the counselling?" I ask. I make my voice gentle and meek, like I'm coaxing a bear, which I assume one does with a gentle and meek voice.

He huffs and puffs, panics. "I just can't . . . I just . . . I've got so much on at the moment with work and I—"

"That's fine," I say, another chunk chipped away by the fact that even now, in this crisis point in our marriage, in our family's life, he can't prioritise us. "But do you think you'd be up for another go, at some point? With someone new. No more felt-tip feet outlines and staring into each other's eyes. Though I must say, I'm still seeing Dr Deb and I'm fully on board with the hippy shit – she had me talking to my inner child the other day and I am so here for it."

He laughs.

"Maybe," he says.

A cold breeze winds through the trees, a squirrel crosses the path right in front of us, its acorn bounty in its mouth. I'm trying to notice these things now. Emily tells me it's called mindfulness and that it's better for your brain than scrolling through hundreds of Instagram posts full of young, gorgeous, successful people doing yoga poses and brands trying to sell you products to fix your eyebags that can never be fixed.

"Yeah," he says. "Sorry, yes, I would like to go to counselling. Definitely. But also yes, definitely with a new person. I do just have

to get through this patch at work. We've got a big new client and it's so full on at the moment."

I just nod, don't say anything, because this is what he's been saying for about fifteen years. I don't know if he tells himself it will calm down, because the reality of it being never-ending would make him give up, or whether he truly believes it, but my experience has been it's always full on. Relentlessly so. I realise, with a breath, that I don't think I want that any more. I want a partner to spend time with, one who wants to spend time with me, rather than feeling obliged to, one who is excited to go on holidays and to travel to new places, one who wants to go to new restaurants and gigs and doesn't confine themselves to our postcode. One who calls me silly names and makes up dances for me, who brings me home gifts to cheer me up when I'm low, one who makes me feel valued and special and loved.

Maybe, hopefully, that will be James, if we make it through this. But if it's not, I feel like maybe I'm OK with that too.

My phone pings. A text from Dorit:

Hope it's going OK. Coffee and debrief at mine afterwards?

"I've actually got to head," I say, throwing my coffee cup in the bin with something that feels like peace of mind.

"Oh, OK, I thought we could—"

I look at him, questioningly.

"Never mind. Another time. It was nice to see you. I'm glad you're doing better, genuinely. And . . ." He runs his fingers through his hair in need of a haircut. "I'm sorry I wasn't there for

you more, or more helpful. I was out of my depth with it all."

"Me too," I say.

It's hard to know exactly how to end an interaction with your partner of twenty-five years who you may or may not be breaking up with, but I go in for an awkward peck on the cheek, sadness rolling over me that that's all I'm entitled to now.

I go to walk away, swallowing down tears.

"Charls," he calls out. "I meant to say – I got you tickets for Paul Weller for your birthday. You're always saying that you want to go and see more live music again and I thought . . . it was ages ago and I totally forgot, but . . . would you like them? I got them for both of us, but I mean, I don't have to come . . . I just thought . . ."

His expression is sweet, and humble, and hopeful.

"Do you want to come?" I ask, readying myself for his usual blanket no.

"I would actually, if that's OK – and not too weird."

"That would be great. I'm sure a bit weird, but also great."

41

LEEDS IS gold and grey, just as I remember it. Though the university itself, apart from the grandeur of the outside, was not at all how I remember it.

"What did you think?" I ask Chloe, projecting my voice over the onslaught of wind.

"It seems good," she says, with a shrug.

"It's probably hard to tell as we just did the self-tour. Maybe it's worth coming back for one of the in-person open days in the autumn."

"I'm hoping to be in some far-flung exotic location like Thailand by then, Mum."

I smile, happy in the knowledge that even if I never make it to Thailand, my daughter will.

"Oh my god!" I stop on the pavement, caught by a familiar sight. Delighted that I finally recognise something. "We used to go to that club. You see that building, over the cobbles and up those stairs?"

"Jesus, Mum. You worried me!"

"Sorry, just excitement." I squint to read the sign: 'Frosty's'. That doesn't ring a bell. The cobbles do though, and the treacherous stairs. Both the cause of many a humiliating fall – though that could also have been the many one-pound pints consumed beforehand.

Chloe pulls her coat tighter. "I don't want to interrupt your

nostalgia trip, but I think it's going to rain. Let's go and get dinner."

"As long as you can direct us there – I'm telling you, this looks nothing like it did when I was here. I have completely lost my bearings."

"OK, dinosaur," she says, loading up the map on her phone. "Did they have buses when you were here?"

Chloe navigates us through the streets of a Leeds I barely recognise. In the twenty-two years since leaving university, I have only, I realise, been back twice. At the best of times, I have no sense of direction, but this officially messes with my head – I have vague recollections of areas, mostly based on clubs or bars that were there, but just as I think I've got my head round where we are, I discover we are somewhere entirely different.

Eventually, we make it to the restaurant – a kind of rum-bar-cum-street-food fusion place with loud music, beanbag seating and dim lights. It is *very* studenty and I feel *very* old. Chloe elegantly sits herself on a beanbag and I try to copy, though my attempt comes off more beached whale.

"This place is nice," I say.

Chloe rolls her eyes at me. Which, to be fair, is only the second time today – the first one being when I brought out the tinfoil wrapped pre-prepared snacks on the train.

"Oh, come on," I protest. "What's wrong with saying somewhere is nice?"

"Because I know you don't mean it," she says.

"I am very much enjoying the relaxed seating and the loud reggae beats and the general ambience," I say. Just as my beanbag gives way slightly and I sink into it more.

Chloe laughs.

"This area was never really a thing when I was here. Although I think I got my belly button pierced just over the road there."

"Sorry, WHAT?" Chloe is shocked. "You?"

"Yep," I nod. "I went with Cath and we got a bit drunk beforehand and then we went to the pub afterwards and it was rammed because it was St Patrick's Day and it was all fine until I looked at the dressing and saw some blood had come through and then I just passed out, right on to the table. Got a proper big egg on my head too."

"What happened to the piercing?"

"It went all infected and manky and ended up stinking, so I had to let it close up."

"Glamorous, as always."

I laugh.

It's decided that Chloe needs to order the food and drinks as I am only getting myself out of this beanbag once and even then, it may take me a bit of time. And a lot of embarrassment. I wish I'd brought a TENA Lady with me.

I observe the scene while she's gone. It's a mixed bag of young professionals in their version of power suits and scraggly-haired students, a few obvious out-of-towners and at least two sets of parents taking their underfed, poor children out for dinner. It gives me flashbacks to when my parents would come up – the excitement of having a proper meal and the knowledge that you could order freely from the menu. My dad would always slip me a twenty-pound note from his wallet when they said goodbye and I would carry it back to Cath, and often Emily if she was over from

Liverpool, like it was the Holy Grail. Twenty pounds equalled twenty pints in those days and that's not nothing.

"One virgin mojito," Chloe says, putting a very umbrellaed cocktail down in front of me. "And one not so virgin mojito."

She delicately slumps herself back into the beanbag. It's a wonder.

"So how does it feel being back here?" she asks.

"Like a total spinout," I say.

"Why?"

"I don't really know. I thought I'd love being back after so long, but it's changed so much and I can't get my bearings and it's making me feel old and sad."

"Oh, Mum," she says. "That's because you are old and sad."

"Oi." I give her a scowl. "More importantly, how are you finding it?"

"Grey." She shrugs.

"Yep, it's very grey. A lot." I stir my mojito, getting a gorgeous waft of the mint. "But it is a great city. I did love it here."

"Though you told me you went to London a lot to see Dad. And didn't make that many friends apart from Cath."

This is all true. I was pining. Full on lovelorn, mooning-Victorian pining. I had told her this in a moment when she was vaguely considering getting back together with Rupert, who had come back to her, tail between his legs, and apologised, begging for her to give him another chance.

"Which is why I said it's a good idea not be in a relationship with someone when you come to university. It's good to fully give yourself to the experience. Like I didn't."

"Do you wish you hadn't stayed with Dad when you came to uni?" She asks this quietly. So quietly that it's drowned out by the loud reggae music and I have to attempt to lean forwards and ask her to repeat it.

I have thought about this a lot, over time. This and other crossroads in my life – should I have split up with James before I came to university? Should I have fought more to keep my career in television? Should I have waited to have kids? Should I have retrained to do a job that was meaningful and rewarding? Should I have not started the list? Should I have not gone to that sex club? (Though that one's pretty obvious.) The conclusion I've reached, maybe partly down to all the philosophy books of James's I've read (the irony), is that things happen for a reason and it's like the butterfly effect in that every tiny little decision has led me here, and here is where I need to be.

"Not at all," I say. "I'm glad I stayed with him and yes, I made things harder for myself and yes, I maybe should've made more effort meeting new people and doing new things and just, you know, being here a bit more, but I also had some really great times with your dad over that period."

"Here we go," a rainbow-haired waitress says. "One Clucking Hot, and one Moosic To My Ears."

She places enormous plates of food in front of us as I try to navigate my way to being more upright. We tuck in, relishing the explosion of flavours.

"Do you think you and Dad will get back together?" Chloe asks.

I'm grateful that the enormous forkful I just shoved in my mouth gives me the opportunity to think.

"I really don't know," I say, eventually, deciding on going full honest. "I love him. And he loves me—"

"I know, you've said that."

"Well, yes. But it's true." I sip my mojito, part of me wishing it wasn't virgin. "We've been together a really long time. And people change. What we need to work out now is whether we can change together."

Chloe looks at me, intently, and part of me wants to tell her that yes we'll get back together and yes it will all be OK. But I just can't.

"But either way, we love each other and we adore you lot and that will never change and we'll always be a family – in whatever form that takes."

"Can you at least teach him to cook, please? If this does end up being long term."

"Sure," I say.

"And for the record," she says. "I'm fine with whatever."

"Thanks, that means a lot."

The rainbow-haired waitress comes back. "How is everything over here? Can I get you anything else?"

"We're good, thanks," I say. "It's very nice round here – I used to go to the university, a long time ago. This was never here. We've actually been looking round because my daughter might come here."

"Mum!" Chloe rolls her eyes at me. And smiles, ever so slightly.

42

CATH IS beginning to look more like herself again – bit by bit. She still wears the residual pain and trauma, a heavy chain round her neck, but her shoulders have eased slightly and there are flecks of light back in her eyes every now and again. It's taken me a while and lots of profuse and sincere apologies to get her to let me back in, to move towards forgiveness. We're not totally back to where we were yet, but we're getting there, bit by bit.

Knowing I wasn't there for her when she was going through the hardest time of her life will stay with me forever. But I've realised, with the help of Dr Deb, that there's nothing I can do about things that have happened in the past. All I can control is my behaviour now – so I've been controlling the shit out of that and doing everything I can to show her I love her and am here for her. Which includes, but is not limited to, texting her every day to say exactly that. She replies with an eye roll emoji, but I think deep down, she appreciates it.

"This one is amazing," I say, holding up a bright red power suit. "Holy crap, these are proper vintage gems, aren't they?"

Cath looks at the suit, from across the room where she's working through a different pile of bold patterned fabrics. "I wish I inherited her eye for fashion. I never saw her in that one, I've only seen it in photos. She wore it when she was first elected as a councillor."

"She definitely had good taste," Emily says. She's in charge of the boxes and the labelling and the general overseeing, in the way that only Emily could be.

"Yeah, you didn't inherit that either," I say.

Cath gives me a vague laugh, and a comedy scowl. I'll take it. I'll take anything at the moment, I'm mainly just pleased she's letting me be in the same room as her. And honoured she's letting me help her through this hideous task of sorting through her mum's possessions.

Cath's mum was a legend. Fierce and passionate and wildly funny. She was a miner's daughter and was outraged at all the injustice she witnessed growing up, deciding to make a career out of doing something about it. She campaigned fervently, her whole life, was always fighting for the cause, whatever that cause was, always saying it like it was, but with compassion. She'd been mayor, a councillor, even an MP briefly. And she liked a good party too. She had some wild stories about the Houses of Parliament and the shenanigans that had gone on there. I only met her a few times, but each time left an impression and each time, I could totally see where Cath got her Cath-ness from.

There's something so incredibly wrong about someone whose personality and life was so big being reduced to just their belongings – the suits and the correspondences, the books and the jewellery and, more recently, the tablets and medical equipment.

Cath wanted to get rid of that stuff first, so Emily and I threw away all the prescriptions and moved the equipment through to the garage ready for the hospital to pick it up. There are still traces of the illness though – a freezer full of ice lollies, bowls full of fruit pastilles on every surface.

"What do you want me to do with the suit?" I ask. "You can't sell it, surely?"

Cath shrugs, pinches between her eyes. "I don't know. I don't bloody know. What am I supposed to do with it all? I have a one-bedroom flat in Leyton with sod-all storage. I'm painfully aware that I don't have any kids to pass this stuff down to, that no one in the family is going to get to wear that beautiful suit. Dan is telling me to give it all to charity, even though he's the one with the big arse house and storage, but that doesn't feel right either. These are her things." She pauses, takes a breath. "I'm not ready to let go of them yet. And there's so many things, and they're all precious, but I can't keep them all and I don't even have time to go through them all. And I just don't know."

She runs out of steam, the tears coming, a dam broken. Emily and I go and sandwich-hug her.

"You can keep some stuff stored at mine for a while," Emily says. "Now that Rick has taken his home gym and two wardrobes full of designer suits, I have more space."

"And mine," I say, pleased to feel helpful. "I don't know what's going to happen to the house or whatever, but for now I have a bit of space with James's stuff gone. It will give you a bit of extra time to go through things, work out what you want to do. You don't want to have to make decisions this soon. And my house doesn't smell of smoke any more. Or cat piss."

That gets a half-smile out of Cath. "Thanks, guys. And thanks for today. I really can't do this on my own."

"Of course," Emily says.

"Right, can I get anyone anything?" I ask, feeling the need to

reset the room. "Tea, coffee, hot chocolate. I think I spied some Bourbons in the cupboard."

"Dude, we've accepted your apology. Apologies, plural," Cath says. "You're off probation, you can be normal now."

"Are you saying it's not normal for me to be nice and offer to make my friends tea?"

"That's exactly what I'm saying."

"Well, maybe my noodle era has changed me. Maybe I'm nice now, have you considered that?"

Emily laughs. "It's your birthday, Charlie. Traditionally, you expect everyone to pander to you on your birthday. That's like your birthday schtick."

"Exactly – and have I done that today? No ma'am, I have not. I'm a changed woman."

"I actually could do with getting out of here for a bit," Cath says. "Let's get a blast of sea air and then maybe fish and chips and wine back here?"

"Sounds good," I say.

* * *

The sea air is good. Fresh and salty and sharp and very much needed. The sun is fading from behind the patchwork of grey clouds, the streets of Margate already settling into their Saturday night fervour.

"How are you doing?" I ask, linking arms with Cath.

"Shit. Really totally shit," she says. "I need some distraction, tell me again about your sexcapades in Cobham."

"Feather Joan!" Emily says. "I wonder what she's doing now?"

I look at my watch. "Probably sitting on a throne getting head from a random woman in latex," I say.

"Or just finishing up her shift at the building society," Emily says.

We laugh.

"I still can't believe you actually went there, Charlie," Cath says. "Like, you're the person who would always take a coat clubbing, who makes sure they're home an hour earlier than the online shop is coming in case it arrives early, who looks up parking before you go anywhere so you don't get caught out. You're safe."

"Exactly! That's why I needed to push out of my comfort zone."

"And the noodles?" Cath asks. "That's hardly out of your comfort zone?"

"Oh, that was sleep deprivation and menopause madness I think."

"Or maybe it was grounding you, in that comfort zone kind of way, you know?" Emily says. "Nothing dangerous to catch you off guard with Super Noodles. You know where you stand with Super Noodles. Maybe you needed the security of them because everything else around you was imploding."

"That's pretty obvious, Freud."

"Or maybe it was literally just all the E numbers and additives in the Super Noodles that were doing something to your brain and making you go actually mad," Cath says.

"It was Pot Noodles too, for the record."

"You should write an article about it," Cath says, pushing a wind-blown, errant hair out of her face. "My Noodle Insanity: How a diet of just artificial noodles drove me to sex-club madness."

"In Cobham." Emily laughs – a big guffaw. "Don't get her started on the writing again, she'll go down the rabbit hole."

"How many words was your masterpiece in the end?" Cath asks.

"Three-hundred-and-twenty-six-thousand." I grimace.

"Holy crap, dude. You were supposed to read *War and Peace*, not write it!" Cath and Emily high five. I let them have it, knowing it's part of my penance, and also that I am ridiculous.

"Did I tell you about the agent?" I ask.

"Uh, no!" Emily stops walking. The people behind us tut as they're forced to detour around us.

"Don't get excited, it's nothing exciting," I say. "I don't entirely remember this, but looking back over my emails, it seems I submitted my work to quite a few agents. You just send the first few chapters, or ten thousand words or whatever, not the whole tome. Thank god. Anyway, most of them either didn't reply or just sent back rejections, but one agent replied saying something like she didn't quite connect emotionally with my main character, and a book that long is not commercially viable, but she saw potential in my writing and to send her anything I write in the future. Which I'm kind of taking as a win."

"That *is* exciting!" Emily says. "Really exciting."

"Thanks, I was chuffed. So my plan now is to have a look at writing courses that start in September once Chloe's exams are out of the way. Maybe just an online one or something, I dunno." A bubble of excitement builds in my stomach as I think of it. "But I did really enjoy the actual writing, in the beginning."

"Before the madness set in," Cath adds.

"Yup, before the madness."

"Are we ever going to get to read any of this book?" Emily asks.

"Oh, hell no! I told you about the shiny erect Shard penises and vaginas as wet as waterfalls, didn't I?"

Emily honks again. "No, you did not!"

"Oh, I have to read this now!" Cath says. "Please send me an edited version to cheer me up!"

We turn a corner onto the main drag, pubs overspilling with smokers, groups of teens vaping, flashing lights on shop fronts.

"Oh my god! An arcade!" Emily does an excited hop. "Remember the one we went to on the Isle of Wight that time? Charlie got obsessed with the dance game and refused to get off until she'd beaten me. Come onnnnn! Let's have a go – we have to!"

It's so nice to see the old Emily emerging again – the fun, enthusiastic, spontaneous Emily. The one who was always smiling and laughing and being silly. For so long, it was like her shine had been rubbed off, and now she's beginning to sparkle again. It's hard to resist her when she's like this.

"I mean, I'll totally beat you now I'm back into my boxing," I say. "And now you've got a dodgy knee."

"Guess we'll see," she says, her eyes gleaming with the challenge.

"I think I'll sit this one out," Cath says. "You go ahead, though – I'll cheer from the sidelines."

We go into the arcade, fighting our way through teenagers wearing bucket hats and crop tops and cargo pants of the nineties, past raucous groups of hens and intertwined loved-up couples. We find the dance game, a more sophisticated version of the one we're used to, and we dance and we laugh and we dance and Emily falls over and we dance and I wet myself a little bit laughing so hard and

we dance and Emily pulls a muscle and Cath reluctantly has a go because we're 'being total muppets' and she's rubbish, which feels like the funniest thing we've ever seen and people watch us from the sidelines and laugh and I don't care in the slightest, because this feels like the most fun I've had in years and eventually, we feel the pressure to leave because a queue is forming and also because we're so out of breath, I'm worried at least one of us will have a heart attack.

* * *

Back at the house we settle down with sweaty, vinegary fish and chips on our laps and mugs filled with wine. I don't question Cath as to why she didn't use the wine glasses, she must have a reason.

"Cheers, birthday girl," Emily says. "Another year, hey?"

"Seems that way," I say, sipping the lukewarm wine.

"Go on then," Cath says. "Get it over with."

"What?"

"The birthday moan."

"What do you mean?" I ask, my mouth full of chips.

"Every year you have a birthday moan about being old and how even though you moaned about it last year, this year you *really* feel it and what is your life and what's happened to your hopes and dreams and we sit and listen and come up with a few pleasantries that you dismiss. So, let's go."

"And don't forget last year's fabulous rooftop friends," Emily says.

"Of course, how could I forget?" Cath grins.

They stare at me expectantly.

"Well, I'm not where I thought I'd be at forty-five, for sure."

"Hear, hear!" Emily says, waving her fork in the air.

"Totally." Cath's face darkens.

"But I'm actually feeling OK about that. So, no moaning today."

Cath and Emily look at each other, exaggerated expressions of shock. Emily puts her plate on the coffee table and slides off the sofa pretending to faint.

"Very funny, guys." I sigh. "What can I say? A lot has changed in a year."

"Damn right," Cath says, an edge of sadness.

"Like I said, I'm feeling OK about it, maybe even hashtag blessed."

Cath still looks shocked. "Is this for my benefit – are you actually moaning internally but you've learnt enough to realise you can't really moan to me, of all people, because I am alone and childless and my mother just died?"

"Not at all," I say. "I mean, yes, I've learnt that, thank you. But also, I genuinely feel OK. I'm looking forward to getting into doing some writing, I'm enjoying the boxing and getting stronger, I'm enjoying my children more and I've made peace with my eyebags – there's nothing you can do for eyebags, have I told you that?"

"Many times," Emily says.

"And you know, I'm beginning to be OK about whatever's going to happen with me and James – one way or another, something needed to change, and it has. So yeah, no moaning this year."

There's a moment of silence. No one knowing how to take my revelation. I continue to shove heaped forkfuls of fish and chips into my mouth.

"Holy shit!" Cath shouts. "Are you saying the list worked?"

I chuckle, but then think about. "It definitely does not feel like the list worked. It feels like the list blew up my life."

"Maybe that's what you needed?" Emily says.

"Jesus, maybe it was." The revelation hits me like a frying pan in the face. "That's . . . ironic?"

"And not in the Alanis way!" Emily says.

"You didn't finish the list though, dude? Are you going to carry it on?"

"Hell no."

"What was left?" Emily asks.

I do not want to re-engage with the list.

"Go on, have a look," Cath pushes. "You did loads of them. Come on, it was a year ago, pretty much. You're safe, the madness has passed – let's have a look, for shits and giggles."

Reluctantly, I wipe my greasy hands and open my phone where I have a saved version of the list. I have not looked at the list in a while. It does strange things to me seeing it typed out like this. Covers me in a blanket of shame. I read them all out loud.

1. *Have sex with George Clooney.*
2. *Take up parkour.* ✓
3. *Swim with dolphins.*
4. *Climb* ~~*Mount Everest*~~ *a mountain.* ✓
5. ~~*Have a threesome.*~~ *Go to a pottery class.* ✓
6. *Go to a bottomless brunch.* ✓
7. *Eat caviar.* ✓
8. *Eat an oyster.* ✓

9. *Eat snails.* ✓
10. *Have a martini.* ✓
11. *Make a sex tape.* ✓
12. *Kiss a girl.* ✓
13. *Go to a strip club/sex party.* ✓
14. *Use a sex toy.* ✓ ✓ ✓
15. *Eat an insect.*
16. *Go scuba diving.*
17. *Do a spin class.* ✓
18. *Learn to street dance.* ✓
19. *Read War and Peace.* ✓
20. *Get a tattoo.* ✓
21. *Volunteer.* ✓
22. *Try boxing.* ✓
23. *See a woman shoot a ping-pong ball from her vagina.*
24. *Have a Hollywood wax.* ✓
25. *Do anal.* ✓
26. *Stand-up comedy.* ✓
27. *Surf.* ✓
28. *Take ecstasy.* ✓
29. *Learn how to do make-up.* ✓
30. *Go to Thailand.*
31. *Have sex on a plane.*
32. *Write a book.* ✓
33. *Skinny dip.* ✓
34. *Attend a protest.* ✓
35. *Go to a drag show.* ✓
36. *Rock climbing.* ✓

37. Puppy yoga. ✓
38. Go to a football match. ✓
39. Immersive theatre. ✓
40. Go to an opera. ✓
41. Go to a life drawing class. ✓
42. Go to pop choir. ✓
43. Go to Soho House. ✓
44. Learn how to manifest. ✓
45. Have a tarot reading. ✓

"You did really well," Emily says. "Nearly all of them."

"It doesn't feel like I've done anything 'really well' recently." I push away the thought spirals and the flashbacks. "God, I was such a twat."

"A giant twat, some would say," Cath adds, unhelpfully.

"Cath!" Emily reprimands. "She was having an out-of-body twat experience."

"There were certainly lots of twats in Cobham."

They find this so funny they nearly choke on their food. I can't help but join in.

"OK, OK," I say. "I'm an awful person and an idiot and you're very funny. Am I ever going to live this down?"

"Nope." Cath shakes her head, tears in her eyes, but this time, tears of laughter. "And you've got a bellend tattoo to constantly remind you!"

"You don't need to feel bad about the list," Emily says. "It was a process. And you clearly needed to do it – or do something. And look, while some of it may feel pretty grim to look back on—"

"Feather Joan," Cath coughs.

"Some of it was fun, right? Pushing yourself like that?"

I think back – most of it was not fun – the Hollywood wax, the stand-up comedy fail, the sex club, but I guess some things were maybe OK, if not exactly fun – the parkour and the spin class and the street dance and the drinking a martini.

"Come on, the sex toy was fun," Cath says.

Oh yeah, and that.

"This is how I think about these things." Emily leans forwards on the sofa, ready to deliver her speech. "You can't look back and regret things – things you did do or things you didn't. We've ended up where we've ended up, and we have to make the most of it. Everything that's happened in your life has got you to here, and you'll eat yourself up if you spend precious time and energy raking back over it all. You have to be grateful for what you have and work with it."

"And there endeth your TED Talk," Cath says, clapping.

"That is the most Emily thing you've ever said." I smile. A smile that reaches all the way through me. Because god, I love her, I love them both – and because she's right.

"Oh my god!" Cath sits up straight. "We should totally go to Thailand! Girls trip! I SO need a break and something to look forward to and you could tick off the last things on your list. It would be amazing – you've wanted to go forever and my god, we could all do with it after the year we've had."

Emily's face lights up. "I am so in! Yes, yes, yes!"

Excitement courses through me. This. This is exactly what I need. Time away with my girls – somewhere exotic, somewhere

new, somewhere I've always wanted to go, but more than that, just with my girls. "That is a genius idea! But NOT for the list though. I'm done with the list. For good."

"Probably just as well, I was worried you'd try to have sex with one of us on the plane," Cath says.

"Ew!" I throw a cushion at her.

"Oh, I forgot to mention," Emily says, "you know Jen Holden?"

I nod, remembering Jen Holden very well – the four bestsellers, the TV adaptation, the perfect kids and Maldives holidays and the untimely death that was part of what led me to the list.

"Well, through work, I've got tickets to the London premiere of her show – the book adaptation." She pauses for recognition. "The one *George* is in! AND . . ." She pauses for dramatic effect. "He's over for it! But I guess, if you're not doing the list any more . . ."

* * *

It's *Nespresso* George. Silver beard, dressing gown over fancy pyjamas, holding a coffee seductively. Strange choice, but still hot.

"Charlie," he says, all gravel and sophistication. "How are you?"

He raises those thick, suggestive eyebrows at me.

"I'm good," I say.

I feel warm and happy. I'm sat on a beach, sipping a cocktail from a coconut. George walks over, holds his arms wide for a hug. Those big, strong arms. I relax into the hug, feeling safe. And warm and happy. Safe and warm and happy.

He goes to kiss my neck, flashing me that saucy, crooked smile he has before he gets down to business.

"Not today, George," I say. "I'm bonding with my friends."

He nods, gives me a kiss on the cheek and a little salute and walks back down the beach. I sit down on my sun lounger, noticing my super-hot body and that Cath is one side of me and Emily the other.

"Holy fuck, I see it now – he *is* hot," Cath says.

"Love you guys," I say.

"Love you too," Emily says.

"Love you too," Cath choruses. "Even though you're a giant twat."

Acknowledgements

I FEEL LIKE I should start this with a disclaimer – because we have a tendency to think that everything women write is based entirely on their own lives and because my friend Rachael insists that every single one of my characters is based on someone we know. This book is not about me. I am not Charlie, my husband is not James. There are definitely similarities (I used to work in TV, my children wrestle, I am a BIG *Housewives* fan, my husband is partial to a bike ride and works a lot), but that is roughly where it ends. I will not disclose how many things on the list I have personally ticked off – but I will say, the only time I have been to Cobham (thus far) was to drop my son off at a paintballing party . . .

At the heart of this book, there is an emotional truth, though. And that is very much based on my experience. Perimenopause hit me like a monster truck and *45 Things* was conceived in the midst of a perimenopausal shitstorm, before I realised that's what it was. It came from a place of boredom, frustration, restlessness, fear and confusion; why do I suddenly hate all my family? Why am I awake between the hours of 2–5 a.m. running through a list of all the possible things I should be worried about? Why can I no longer drink wine without feeling like total dogshit the next day? Why can I no longer get my head around a food shop? Why can I not remember . . . words? Why am I crying at the Lloyds bank advert?

And the McDonald's advert? And the Pampers advert? Why do I not feel like myself? Why do I suddenly hate all my family? Have I already said that? Am I losing my mind?

The more I started noticing these things and talking about them, the more I realised how many of my friends were having exactly the same experiences and then, bit by bit, a whisper at first, the mention of the perimenopause found its way into our conversations.

I was forty-four when I wrote *45 Things*, and while I didn't have a list, writing the book was my way of exploring the thoughts and feelings and the enormous, seismic shift that I noticed happening to me, my friends and so many women around me. It's a tough and tricky time (understatement), but, as with everything, it's also funny, and I really felt the need to highlight the humour and the absurdity of this time. Our shared experiences, our gynaecological horror stories (coil fitting, anyone?!), our rage and tears and frustrations – it's the stuff that bonds us and the stuff that makes us laugh, together. It's a book about losing yourself and finding yourself again, starting new chapters in life, and female friendships that get you through anything.

And on that note, I have soooo many incredible friends to thank: Danielle, my best friend since we set eyes on each other on that first day at secondary school – no one gets me quite like you do and no one has had to put up with me for as long as you have. Thank you for the ridiculous text chats, the Thailand trips, the food fights, the fully-clothed baths and everything in between. You are a superstar, even though we don't see each other nearly as much as I would like.

My girl trippers – Rach, Vicky, Liz, Carmel, Jill, Amber, Marisa – thanks for all the perimenopause chat as it happened, even though some were more reluctant than others to discuss!

Georgia Bowers, without whom this book would never have been finished. Both in 'sub-optimal' places in our writing careers, we made a pact at a friend's book launch that the only way through it was to get what we were working on finished – which we did, tiny bit by tiny bit, checking in with each other every day – and now we both have book deals. (Georgia's writing is hilarious – definitely check it out.) Thank you for the motivation and the laughs and the pineapple-themed merch and the very strange coaster.

Amy Beashel – eternal thanks for all the reading and re-reading of early drafts you did and for never complaining about my moaning and anxiety-ridden texts. Let's be honest – that's never going to change! You're a rock and I'm so pleased we found each other.

Holly, Andreina, Ava and Amy – thank you for the 6 a.m. sessions, the Screenwriting for Novelists crew, the Goodship Crew, Kate Weston, my local writing crew, Sue Wallman and Lucy Hope, my 66% published crew, Alice Ross and Becca Langton (come on, Becca, get that amazing book finished – I know you have three small children and a full-time job, but get on with it . . .).

Huge, huge, never-ending thanks to my superstar agent, Clare Wallace. Your belief in me, and this book, at a time when I needed some belief in me, has been joyous. And on a similar note, massive thanks to Hazel Holmes at Fox & Ink Books for your enthusiasm for this book when I hadn't even finished writing it. Thanks to everyone at Fox & Ink who has worked on getting this out into the world.

Thank you to the women who have brought such much-needed attention to the perimenopause – there are many, but the ones whose work particularly resonated with me are: Louise Newson, Mariella Frostrup, Naomi Watts, Sam Baker and, of course, Davina McCall – whose books were a total game-changer for me and I know have been genuinely life-saving for others.

Last, but in no ways least, thank you, thank you, thank you to my husband, Will – for your unwavering support in me and this book, both emotionally and financially, for being understanding (eventually) when I walked out of our family holiday, for your patience while I worked out my hormones and for trusting me enough that you didn't take me up on the offer of reading through the final draft, despite me pointing out lots of people will assume you're James. You're the best, and I'm very excited for all the adventures we have yet to come – we may or may not include mountains and bicycles.

About the author

AFTER A brief (but fun) stint working in television and as a primary school teacher, Julia decided to take her writing dreams more seriously. She lives in South-West London with her family and ragdoll cats (Billy and Nora) and spends her time writing, reading, dreaming of holidays and watching too much reality TV. She aims to write the kinds of books that will have people laughing out loud – and crying – on their commute. Her young adult novel, *Hexed*, was nominated for the Laugh Out Loud Awards, and its sequel, *Twice Hexed*, won the children's category at the Isle Of Wight Book Awards. *45 Things To Do Before You're 45* is her debut book for adults.

If you liked this, you'll love ...

Harriett de Mesquita
The Magickal Summer of Evie Edelman

A small fortune. A countryside cottage.
A witch in search of her coven.

IT'S ALL GREEK TO ME

Andrea Christodoulou

Is life really better with a little feta?

young love

suzanne ewart